THIS LIGHT
BETWEEN US

A NOVEL OF WORLD WAR II

THIS LIGHT
BETWEEN US

A NOVEL OF WORLD WAR II

ANDREW FUKUDA

TOR
TEEN

A TOM DOHERTY ASSOCIATES BOOK
NEW YORK

THIS LIGHT BETWEEN US: A NOVEL OF WORLD WAR II

Copyright © 2019 by Andrew Fukuda

Illustrations copyright © 2019 by Euan Cook

All rights reserved.

A Tor Teen Book
Published by Tom Doherty Associates
120 Broadway
New York, NY 10271

www.tor-forge.com

Tor® is a registered trademark of Macmillan Publishing Group, LLC.

Library of Congress Cataloging-in-Publication Data

Names: Fukuda, Andrew Xia, author.
Title: This light between us / Andrew Fukuda.
Description: First edition. | New York : Tor Teen, 2020. | "A Tom Doherty Associates book."
Identifiers: LCCN 2019041410 (print) | LCCN 2019041411 (ebook) | ISBN 9781250192387 (hardcover) | ISBN 9781250192370 (ebook) | ISBN 9781250762573 (international)
Subjects: United States. Army. Regimental Combat Team, 442nd—Fiction. Pen pals—Fiction. Friendship—Fiction. Prejudices—Fiction. Japanese Americans—Evacuation and relocation, 1942–1945—Fiction. Jews—France—Paris—Fiction. World War, 1939–1945—Fiction.
Classification: LCC PZ7.F9515375 (print) | PZ7.F9515375 (ebook)
LC record available at https://lccn.loc.gov/2019041410
LC ebook record available at https://lccn.loc.gov/2019041411

Our books may be purchased in bulk for promotional, educational, or business use. Please contact your local bookseller or the Macmillan Corporate and Premium Sales Department at 1-800-221-7945, extension 5442, or by email at MacmillanSpecialMarkets@macmillan.com.

First Edition: January 2020

Printed in the United States of America

0 9 8 7 6 5 4 3 2 1

For John

THIS LIGHT
BETWEEN US

A NOVEL OF WORLD WAR II

PRELUDE

He was seventeen the first time he saw her. A February dusk in 1943 on the cold plains of Manzanar. The snowcapped Sierra Nevada mountains loomed in the distance, stoic and stark. She appeared for but a few seconds; an ashy smear of light on the other side of the barbed fence. Her clothes seemed too large and flapped in the wind. Her hair swirled madly, too, but slowly, even luxuriously, as if underwater. Dust swept across the plains and blew into his eyes. He blinked once, twice. She was gone.

An optical illusion, he thought. A dusk-lit reverie of dancing dust playing tricks in the windswept plains. Nothing more than a figment of his overripe, yearning, lonely imagination.

He stared at that empty space where she was and then was not.

Still he whispered her name:

"Charlie."

1

Dear Alex Maki,

Hello! My name is Charlie Lévy. I am your new "pen pal" in France. Nice to meet you!

You are in America! Ouah, so far away! Last week Mme Dubois say to my English class avancé, "Who want to do a letter exchange program with American school?" And everyone is so happy. Me the most! Because I am wanting an American pen pal for a very long time. Now I am very excited—can you see my shaking words? Sorry! And sorry for my poor English. Even though I am studying English for many years and have English nanny at home, I think I have a lot of grammar and spelling mistakes.

Anyway, Mme Dubois say I must introduce myself in this first letter.

My name is Charlie Lévy. I am ten years old. My Papa owns a big shoe factory. My Maman is busy at home with me. Our English nanny, Katherine, is from London. We live in Paris, a beautiful city. Do you know the Tower of Eiffel? It is famous! I can see it from my bedroom window. Maybe if you have a big world map you can find Paris.

What about you? Do you have brother and sister? Do you play sport or music? What are your hobbys? I like to study English, play cello, paint eggs, eat <u>anything</u> with Dundee marmalade, and *swimming (but I hate swimsuits. I wish I was a boy—it is so easy for them, no?) And now I have a new favorite hobby—writing to my American pen pal!*

Do you like reading? I love to read! My English nanny say the best book in history is <u>Jane Eyre,</u> and one day I will read it. But only when my English is good enough. (I will not read the French edition—that is cheating, no?) My dream is one day I am studying English Literature at Sorbonne University. Do you know Sorbonne University? It is the best university in the Earth!

I tell you something funny now. I make a new friend last week. She is from Helsinki, Finland, and her name is Aleksandra Mäki. We call her "Alex" so her nickname is Alex Mäki! Like you, no? Maybe you are relatives? Maybe you are twins? (I am laughing now.)

Please write back. I am excited!

Yours sincerely,
Charlie Lévy

April 9, 1935

Charlie,
    Wait . . . you're a girl?

Alex

April 13, 1935

Charlie,
    My teacher Mrs. Graff wasn't happy when she learned I wasted a stamp on a letter that was only one sentence long. So she's making me write a "real" letter now. It has to be at least one page, she said.
    I actually complained to her about you being a girl. She said it was a simple mix-up—she thought you were a boy. Anyway, it's too late to change pen pals because everyone is already paired up. She

told me that I'm just going to have to make do. So I guess I'm stuck with you. The worst part is the whole class knows now.

Mrs. Graff is making me introduce myself, too. There's not much to say. My dad's a strawberry farmer, my mom's a strawberry farmer's wife, my brother's a strawberry farmer's son.

I looked up France on a world map. I'm not impressed. It's really puny compared to AMERICA, isn't it? And Paris is just a tiny black dot on the map. No offense, but that's your capital? What's that like, living in such a small city? Do you feel trapped all the time? Is it hard to breathe?

So you can see the Eiffel Tower from your bedroom, can you now? Tell me, will they ever finish building it? Because I've seen pictures of the Eiffel Tower, and it looks like they started building it, then realized how ugly it was going to turn out. So they just up and left. Nothing but the ugly metal scaffolding left behind.

I also read that you French people don't like to shower, and that you're all really smelly. I think that's true. When I sniffed your letter, I smelled something really foul. Like underarm odor combined with a fart. Maybe your farts are especially nasty because you eat too much Dundee marmalade. And just what the heck is <u>Dundee marmalade</u>?

I don't have any hobbies. I don't play any musical instruments. I don't like to fish or hunt or play sports. I especially don't like writing letters. The only thing I like to do is read and draw comics. The <u>Famous Funnies</u>. #3 and #5 are cool. #8 ain't too bad.

And now I've finished filling up this one page so I can stop.

Alex

P.S. If you ever want to stop this stupid pen-pal thing, I won't be offended. In your next letter, just write two words, I QUIT, and I'll show it to Mrs. Graff. You don't even have to write it in English, you can just write <u>Je quit</u> if that's easier for you.

Dear Alex Maki,

  You are funny American boy! Let us keep writing!

Yours sincerely,

Charlie Lévy

THREE YEARS LATER

18 March 1938

Dear Alex,

  Hello! This letter is celebrating our three-year anniversary as pen pals! Can you believe it? I can't. I never think we will be pen pals for so long. All my classmates stopped after only one year, but we are still writing. Thank you for putting up with all my poor English! Pouah, will I ever improve? You keep telling me yes, but I wonder!

  Oh, and thank you for listening (reading?) to everything in my life: my fights with my parents, my different hobbies (now I like tap dancing!), and the new boy I like at school (as you say, my new "flavor of the month"!!).

  Your letters and funny drawings always make me forget the horrible things that are happening here in Europe. They make me forget Hitler and his stupid moustache and his oily hair and his crazy eyes, and how he comes closer and closer to France.

  Haha! You keep asking me what I look like! You are always asking me! Okay, I will tell you now: I think I am a little pretty but not _very_ pretty. Maybe pretty but in a different way. I think I have a certain fire in my eyes, like a purpose? A sharp focus that boys find pretty? Sometimes when I am reading a book in English class, I see them staring at me. And when I look up, they quickly move their eyes away, blushing.

Okay, now that we are writing for three years, I have a confession. I lied to you two years ago. You ask if I like strawberries and I said yes. But now I tell you the truth: I do not like strawberries. They are pretty to look at, but when I eat one, J'ai envie de vomir. Sorry. I lie before because you are a strawberry farmer son. I do not want to offend you.

Sorry for this small lie. Even small lies can destroy a big relationship. So inside this envelope I put a French flower. This is how I say sorry to you. I do not know the English name of this flower but in France, we call it œillet rose. It has a nice smell and pretty pink color, no? But maybe when you get it, it is dead. Maybe it is black and has bad smell in envelope (I am laughing!).

Au revoir!
Charlie

April 15, 1938

Dear Charlie,

Your œillet rose arrived œillet dead. But it wasn't black or smelly so you can stop laughing now. By the way, how the heck do you pronounce œillet? Because what is œ? Why are the o and e mashed together like Siamese twins?

Anyway, you don't need to apologize about not liking strawberries. I'm not too keen on them myself. All my life I've planted them, sown them, picked them, harvested them, smelled them, sold them, eaten them. My <u>whole</u> life. I'd be fine never seeing another one again. Which is why I can't wait to go off to college and do something else with my life. Like become a cartoonist. Actually, not <u>like</u> a cartoonist, but to become <u>exactly</u> a cartoonist. That's my dream job. (Note: this is a carefully guarded secret. My parents would have a <u>fit</u> if they found out. Because they've got designs on their youngest child becoming a dentist or something.)

Speaking of secrets . . .

Since you made a confession, I feel it only right that I confess something, too. Sit down because this is kind of a big confession. Okay, here goes.

I'm not really who you think I am. Do you remember how you once asked me to describe myself? And I may have told you that I have blond hair and blue eyes. Well, that's not quite true. In fact, it's not true at all. I actually have black hair and brown eyes. And my surname Maki is not Scandinavian in origin (in fairness, I never claimed that, you simply assumed it was. Yes, you did, I can show it to you in your very first letter). My family name Maki is actually Japanese. My parents are from Japan. My father was born in a city called Hiroshima. My mother is from Osaka. But my brother and I, we were born in America.

The reason I never corrected you is because you kept saying how excited you were to have an American pen pal. I guess I just didn't want to disappoint you that I'm not actually a "real" American.

Sorry,
Alex

---

11 May 1938

Dear Alex,

You are an <u>idiot</u>. That's how we French call someone very very very stupid.

You should never tell me such stupid lie about you. No, it is worse than stupid lie, it is UGLY lie. I am so mad at you I can't remember my English and spelling is bad and grammer is bad and everything are bad because I am so angry, you are an idiot.

Maybe you are disappointed in me, yes? Because I am not a "real" French pen pal? Because I do not have yellow hair? Because I do not have blue eyes or green eyes? Because I have ordinary brown hair and brown eyes? Because I have a Jewish name, and Jewish face? Because I do not have French last name like Dubois or Beaumont or Lefebvre?

I am so angry I think I will not write to you for two ~~weeks months~~ years.

Charlie

P.S. You are an IDIOT!!

---

12 May 1938

Dear Alex,

Okay. I am calmer now. But you are still an idiot.

Charlie

June 1, 1938

Dear Charlie,

Yes, I'm an idiot. Sorry. I should never have misled you.

To apologize, I'm sending you a pink hair band. And no, I didn't steal it from my mother, I actually had to go into the city to buy it. Just so you know, it took me hours—first the ferry to Seattle, then hours walking the hot downtown streets. Then finally Tilton's department store where I had to fight through the crowds and fork over my hard-earned cash.

Since I'm sending you an expensive pink hair band, can you send me something in return?

Like a picture of yourself?

I'm only asking because Frank doesn't think you're real. He keeps saying you're nothing but a figment of my lonely imagination. Even though I've shown him all your letters, dozens stored in milk crates over the years, he still doesn't believe me. He says he doesn't see how any girl—especially a <u>Paris</u> girl—could find a loner like me interesting, all I do is read and daydream at home all day, my head in the clouds.

So if you could just send me one picture, I think it would convince him you're real. (Especially if you're pretty. And I think you are. Sometimes you can tell, just from a person's handwriting.)

Would you, Charlie? Send me a photo?

Let me ask in my high school French. Maybe that'll sway you. *Voulez-vous envoyer à moi une photo de vous s'il vous plait?* That's two years of French, baby!

Thanks!

Alex

---

29 June 1938

Alex,

No, I will not send you my picture. Why should I when you never sent me <u>your</u> picture? Of course, now I understand why—until a few months ago, you were pretending to be a <u>white</u> person.

Also: in your letter you wrote that my picture will "make a difference" but only if I am pretty. What does that mean? If I am not a pretty girl (and I am not saying if I am or am not)—do I now suddenly not matter?

And don't call me "baby." <u>Never, never, never!</u>

I think I will not send you my picture. Ever. Even if you send me your picture now, I will not send you mine. So don't bother!

Actually, I change my mind. Send me your picture. I need a new dartboard.

Charlie

11 August 1938

Dear Alex,

I got your letter this morning. Your apology is <u>not</u> accepted. Being shy and an "introvert" is no excuse for saying stupid, careless things.

And now I want to tell you something serious.

Alex, I think you need friends. I think you need even <u>one</u> friend on Bainbridge Island. It is not healthy to be all alone! And I don't care how okay you think you are!

Your brother Frank is right. You cannot hide yourself away all the time. You cannot be like a turtle retreating deep into his shell, away from everyone, away from the world. Otherwise you will become like Bertha Mason, the crazy woman locked away in the attic in <u>Jane Eyre</u>.

Charlie

P.S. Where's your photograph? I need a dartboard!

September 9, 1938

Dear Charlie,

So you want my picture? Sure, no problem. But it'll take a while because I'm not rich like you, I don't have photos lying around that I can just pull out of albums. But in the meantime, I've enclosed something else. Something even better. Tada!

An original self-portrait drawn by yours truly.

One day I'll be famous and my drawings will sell for a million bucks. So yes, <u>You're welcome</u> for this million-dollar gift: a self-portrait, based on how you see me: a turtle with his head in the clouds.

The convenient thing about this new body of mine: when I visit Paris one day, I won't have to climb the Eiffel Tower. My long neck will put me at eye level with you on the observation deck.

Alex

Bonjour, Mme. Charlie Levy. Je suis ton ami Américain, Monsier Alex Maki.

---

2 October 1938

Dear Alex,

Wow, you are so strange. But talented! Your drawings are getting even better!

Here is your drawing back! I added my words to it! Maybe you are mad at me for ruining your $1 million pièce de résistance? I am laughing!

Hey, I have an idea! Let's keep sending this picture back and forth!
Your friend (no matter how bizarre you are!),
Charlie

PART ONE

BAINBRIDGE ISLAND, WASHINGTON
AMERICA

2

Alex Maki is in church when his world shatters.

It's a typical Sunday. The pews are filled with people in their Sunday best, the men in suits and hats but still smelling of wet soil, the women with faces powdered and hands gloved to hide wrinkles and calluses on dark, leathery skin. And though the teens skulk and shift restlessly, they too have groomed themselves for church: the boys with front licks curled and dangling, sides gelled back, the girls with hair fashioned into finger waves and pinned curls and updos. Sunday is the one day of the week when both the Issei (first-generation) and Nisei (second-generation, American-born) members get to dress up.

A typical Sunday. Nothing unusual at all, nothing to suggest that Alex's life—all their lives, in fact—are about to fracture.

If anything, things are looking brighter than usual. Certainly more crowded. Quite a few white families have joined the Japanese service.

This happens sometimes. The Bainbridge Methodist Church building is actually shared by two congregations: the Japanese congregation that meets on Sunday mornings, and the "regular" white congregation who have their service later in the day. Sometimes a community or school event—like this afternoon's high-school football practice—will conflict with the later service.

On those Sundays, many from the white congregation will instead attend the earlier Japanese service. When that happens, Pastor Ken Momose makes sure to conduct the service in English.

A few more families arrive. Including the Tanner family. They slide into the pew in front of Alex.

His back straightens. The Tanner family is well-to-do and highly respected. Their daughter, Jessica Tanner, is popular at school, and now sits down directly in front of Alex. Although they've known each other for years, and share the same homeroom at school, they've rarely spoken.

The congregation is called to worship, and rise. As they begin to sing, the scent of mint and a vanilla extract floats into Alex's nostrils. From Jessica Tanner. He's sure his own breath is foul and egg-soured and wafting down her back. He lifts the hymnal to block his breath.

Next to him, his parents are singing with religious fervor and abandon. The Japanese hymns have been replaced, and the archaic King James English with its *thee*s and *thou*s is throwing them off, making their thick accents even more garish. That doesn't stop Father, though. An elder and leader of the Japanese congregation, he's known for his demonstrative singing. But this morning Alex wishes Father would stop singing because the Tanners—especially Jessica Tanner—can hear each and every butchered syllable.

After the song ends, Pastor Ken smiles at the congregation and exhorts them to greet one another.

"Henry," Mr. Tanner says, turning around to Alex's father. Nobody ever calls Father "Henry" except white people who stumble over "Fusanosuke." He extends his hand out to Father. "How are you this morning?"

"Good. Real good." Father takes his hand with a wide smile,

baring his crooked yellow teeth. His sun-darkened farmer's skin is an embarrassing contrast to the white complexion of the Tanners.

Next to him, Alex's older brother, Frank, is play-punching Josh Tanner. They're teammates on the Bainbridge High football team, Josh a wide receiver, Frank the star quarterback, and they're talking about that afternoon's practice, and how they're going to destroy Vashon High School on Friday—

Jessica Tanner turns side to side, looking for someone to greet. She starts whirling around. Toward Alex.

He panics. Looks down—

"Hi, Alex," Jessica Tanner says brightly. She holds out her hand.

Hesitantly, he takes it. Her skin is so soft and porcelain smooth. His own calloused hand, which only an hour ago was cleaning out the chicken coop, is a monster wrapping itself around a swan.

"Looking forward to the game on Friday?" She's looking at him with a friendly, focused gaze.

"Y-yeah." His throat is thick and clogged. She seems even more beautiful up close. Her eyes are a blue that even the purest sky would envy. There's a faint splatter of cute freckles over the bridge of her nose he's never noticed before. "You?"

"We're gonna crush 'em," she says, winking before turning around.

Everyone sits. He's still holding the hymnal in his left hand, and as he reaches forward to place it into the holder, Jessica Tanner flips back the long sweep of her hair so it doesn't get caught behind her. Her hair waterfalls over the back of the pew, and pools softly on the back of his hand still on the hymnal. A few strands of her hair slip through the small spaces between his fingers.

He freezes. Can't breathe. Jessica Tanner's hair is on his hand, between his fingers. Strands of gold, the softness of lips.

And then it happens. The doors of the church slam open.

Everyone jolts and spins around. Jessica Tanner's hair flies off Alex's hand.

Backlit by the outside light and framed by the doorway, Bruce Fukuhara—a senior in high school who defiantly stopped coming to church a year ago—pauses. He looks around, panting, sweat beading his acne-ravaged forehead, unsure of what to do. Then he rushes up the center aisle to Pastor Ken in the pulpit:

Everyone leans forward. They're all curious; they're all guessing.

Somebody has passed away.

Somebody's fishing boat has been vandalized, or worse, pillaged.

The price of strawberries or celery collapsed overnight.

But it's none of these. It's far worse.

Pastor Ken frowns as he listens to Bruce. His face goes white; his left hand trembles as he leans on the pulpit.

"I'm sorry," Pastor Ken says, and Alex will always remember those first words of apology, how they might have set the tone for what is to come. That maybe if Pastor Ken hadn't apologized as if he were somehow responsible, as if they were all responsible, perhaps things would have turned out differently?

"But I have just learned . . ." He swallows, stares down at his Bible. "This morning, a few hours ago, Japan attacked Hawaii." His voice cracks. "We are at war."

Someone gasps. Most sit in shock, hands covering mouths. Mrs. Tanner clutches her son's arm, her fingertips going white. Josh Tanner is old enough—or will be, in a few short months—to enlist.

Pastor Ken murmurs something about the need to pray in this time of—

A white man stands. This single action so decisive, it shuts up Pastor Ken as effectively as if he were slapped. The man looks around, almost frantically. He finds what he's looking for two pews away. Another white man. He stands, too. And soon it seems all the white men and white women and white children are gathering together, their voices getting louder. With stern expressions as they look around. This is what they must see:

Not Henry and Joe and Bruce and Tim and Cindy and Janet and Susan. But now Fusanosuke and Hideo and Kaito and Hidejiro and Hitomi and Kayo and Megumi. The exotic, the yellow, the inscrutable. The enemy.

One thing is clear: church service is over.

"Come on," Father whispers to Alex, leading his family out of the pew. The other Japanese families follow suit, quietly leaving the sanctuary. The church isn't theirs; it never was.

Alex and Frank hop into the cargo bed of the pickup while Mother sits in the front cab. Father speaks curbside to a group of Japanese men: each is to drive his own family back home, then head over to Father's place. He's the only one with a radio.

One by one the cars leave the church parking lot. Orderly as a funeral procession.

The town center is strangely quiet. The few people strolling about seem oblivious to what is happening, to how history has just veered off course.

Father drives just below the speed limit. At the last intersection before leaving the town center, the traffic light turns red. Father stops. Across the street, outside a tavern, a group of men in denim overalls are huddled around a transistor radio.

One of them peers up at the line of pickup trucks, then back down to the radio. A second later, his head snaps up like a man who can't quite believe his eyes. His gaze sweeps across the three vehicles behind, at the drivers and passengers. He mutters something, and the other four men stand up.

They come as one, their anger raw. Elbows crooked, eyes red-rimmed, cheeks scruffy. Frank leaps forward in the cargo bed, pounds the cab window. "Go, Father, just go!"

Father slams the pedal right as the five men close in. Alex feels something moist strike his cheek. Spit. Then a cussword, swallowed up by the squeal of tires. They take off, all four trucks, in a cloud of swirling dust.

No one speaks as Father speeds home. Alex stares at the passing farmlands, his thoughts like flies buzzing over roadkill, flighty and restless. The football Frank normally cradles is left forgotten on the floor of the cargo bed. It rolls around, side to side, back and forth. Nothing seems anchored anymore, everything is dislodged.

Back at the farm, they hurry into the house. Hero comes bounding toward them, wanting to romp. But he stops, head cocked, sensing something wrong. Whimpers. Mother and Father speak in hushed tones even though there's no one around for miles.

Alex doesn't change out of his Sunday clothes. No one does. Father is at the kitchen table, turning on the radio usually used to receive sumo news from Japan. Mother starts boiling water. Frank leans against the counter, his fingers tapping, tapping. Static hisses from the radio. Father works the dial. A voice blares out, angry and declarative.

". . . the Japanese have attacked Pearl Harbor, Hawaii, by air, President Roosevelt has just announced. The attack also was made on all naval and military activities on the principal island of Oahu . . ."

The report dies out to a wave of static. Father turns the dial, finds another live report from Honolulu, Hawaii.

". . . we have witnessed this morning a distant feud from Pearl

Harbor, a severe bombing of great intensity with considerable damage done. This battle has been going on for nearly three hours—" The report suddenly cuts off.

The water boils. Mother brings tea to the table. But neither she nor Father drinks. They sit rock-still, their faces stoic and unreadable, heads bowed toward the radio as if in apology. Father turns the dial, finds another report that Japan has begun to attack Manila. A minute later and the radio channels have resumed their regular programming.

Alex leaves the kitchen. He shuts the door to the bedroom he shares with Frank, sits at his desk. He thinks about the regular programming that has resumed on the radio. As if the attack on Pearl Harbor isn't actually such a big deal. A minor skirmish, a boys-will-be-boys scrape. Dust off, shake hands, move on. Perhaps life will go on as usual? He stares outside. The day is bright, the sky blue, the sun blazing and glorious. As before. As usual.

But then he thinks about the group of men back in town. The way they approached the truck, elbows crooked, hands bunched into fists. The hatred in their eyes.

Nothing is the same, he thinks. Everything has changed.

From outside his window, a sound: *whack*. Coming from the barn. *Whack*.

Alex knows the sound. Years ago, Father hung an old tire on the cypress tree by the barn. The two brothers spent endless hours swinging on the tire until they outgrew it. A year ago Frank turned the tire into a football target, throwing the pigskin through it from varying distances, often on the run, sprinting right, breaking left, the tire swaying like a pendulum, the football sometimes striking rubber, usually sailing right through.

Alex goes to the window. He sees Frank at the tire. Hero standing at a distance, ears pinched back. Frank is holding a baseball bat. He raises it above his head, then swings it down on the tire furiously like he's splitting firewood. *Whack. Whack.* Even from the window, he can see his brother's chest heaving, his Sunday clothes twisted and disheveled. The bat rises again. Falls. *Whack. Whack. Whack.*

3

On Monday morning, less than twenty-four hours after the Pearl Harbor attack, Alex steps off the school bus. He has never in all his life ever felt his Japaneseness more keenly.

He tugs down his woolen hat, wishes he had a pair of sunglasses. As he walks to the front entrance, every eyeball at Bainbridge High School seems to turn to him. Or maybe not, maybe no one is paying him any mind. Maybe he's as invisible as always. The Nisei students tend as a rule to be unseen in this community, anyway, but even among them Alex usually goes about unnoticed.

Not that he especially minds. So long as he has his ABCs— Art, Books, Charlie—he's fine.

Mr. Johnson, the gym teacher, stands on a landing at the top of the stairs before the entrance. This is unusual; Alex has never seen Mr. Johnson out here. He's greeting the arriving students with an enthusiastic "Good morning, God bless America," thumping the shoulders of some of the bigger boys. An American flag is pinned on his jacket. When Alex walks past, Mr. Johnson clams up.

In the hallway, Alex keeps his eyes on the floor. He stops by his locker to throw in his jacket, then slams the door shut. His homeroom is only three steps away, and he takes a deep breath before entering the classroom.

Surprisingly, it's business as usual. Craig Webster and Jack Wells are goofing around. Josh Hunter is carving into the wooden desktop with a penknife. Leo Dalton and Jimmy Myers are arm wrestling, grunting red-faced. Mary Billings is copying homework. Charlotte Coplin is brushing her hair, pretending to ignore the gawking boys.

Only Billy Hosokawa, probably the funniest kid in class with his Daffy Duck impersonations, seems out of sorts. He's sitting alone, hunched over and perfectly still. Like a tiny mouse caught out in the open field as eagles circle overhead.

Mr. Hartford tromps in. The class rises as one, chairs scraping against the wood floor. Mr. Hartford's face often has a reddish hue to it, and there are rumors of a drinking problem. But this morning there's a harder tinge to the redness. The red of anger.

"Good morning, everyone." His eyes shine with an uncharacteristic clarity.

"Good morning, Mr. Hartford," everyone chimes back in unison.

He pauses a moment, taking in the class. When he sees Billy Hosokawa, his salt-and-pepper moustache twitches with annoyance. He unfolds a sheet of paper.

"I have an announcement to make. From Principal Roy Dennis." A look of mild disgust crosses his face as he reads aloud.

"'Yesterday, Imperial Japan attacked Pearl Harbor. We are right to be angry about this. But we must not let our patriotic anger boil over into an unrighteous rage. I want to remind everyone that the Japanese American students here at Bainbridge High School are not only our fellow students but our fellow Americans. We will have no part of race hatred at our school today or any day. God bless America.'"

Mr. Hartford stares at the paper. In a blur of movement, he suddenly scrunches it up into a ball. The sound is impossibly loud, almost violent. He tosses it into the wastepaper basket across the room. Then squares his broad shoulders to the classroom, and stares at the American flag on the wall.

"Let me," he says, "translate what Principal Dennis just said. Yesterday the Japs attacked us. A sneak attack I can only describe as cowardly and gutless." His face twists into a scowl. "But they picked the wrong country, didn't they? Because when we get punched, we punch back, don't we, fellas? And no country punches back harder than the United States of God Bless America. So you just watch, we're going to punch every rat-faced, squinty-eyed, bandy-legged Jap, every last one of them I'm telling you, all the way back to Tokyo."

Some of the boys clap and *booyah!* Alex stays very quiet. Anthony Donner raises his hand and asks Mr. Hartford how long it'll take President Roosevelt to officially declare war on Japan. "Before this day is done, and I'll bet my britches on it," Mr. Hartford answers, jutting out his meaty chin. "On that note, it's time for the Pledge of Allegiance."

The class recites the pledge louder that morning than any other time. Mr. Hartford, hand over heart, gets misty-eyed. Alex makes sure that his voice is neither too quiet nor too loud. And when the class sits down, he is similarly careful that he isn't the first or the last to sit, that he stays right in the middle of the pack.

When he walks out into the hallway ten minutes later, it's as if he's grown a second head and become covered in leprosy. Every eyeball turns toward him. Whispers, whispers. And stares, glares. He keeps his eyes down. He has never felt so conspicuous.

A tall senior bumps into him, almost knocking his books to the floor. An accident, probably. But by the end of the day, he's bumped two more times. When he goes to his locker to retrieve his jacket, he notices something scrawled on the front. Three words.

Go home Jap.

The three words are short, blunt, and cut deep. Alex has only wanted to be left alone. But now someone has thought of him. Someone has taken the effort to write these words on his locker.

He reaches forward to wipe the words away. But the ink holds, smudging only a little.

A group of girls, walking past behind him, start to giggle. Probably at something unrelated, probably they haven't even noticed the words.

A few lockers down to his left, a boy laughs.

He should walk away. But he is frozen, unable to pick up his feet.

Someone approaches him from behind. Puts a warm hand on his shoulder.

"Alex." It's Frank. "I already spoke to the janitor. He's gonna take care of it." Frank squeezes his shoulder. "C'mon, let's go."

Alex nods. He tucks his head down and together they head down the hallway. Frank walks right next to him, and Alex is glad for it. He wonders if Frank has any idea how much he worships the ground he walks on, how his heart swells with pride every time he walks past the trophy case at school and sees Frank's beaming face on the team photograph, front and center. How, at home, Alex secretly watches him practice for hours on end, throwing the pigskin through the swinging tire or into open trash cans placed at specific distance markers. Because it's super popular Frank, with his ungodly athletic prowess and aw-shucks grin and happy-go-lucky personality, who is the sole reason why skinny, introverted, and more-than-slightly strange Alex Maki hasn't been bullied mercilessly at school. Nobody touches the star quarterback's little brother.

When they get on the bus, Frank, for the first time in years, sits next to him. Without speaking a word, they ride home together.

4

Dear Charlie,

Can't believe it's been only three days since the Pearl Harbor attack. This has been the longest week of my life.

There're all these dumb rules for the Japanese American community. No traveling more than five miles from home. No radios. Our bank accounts frozen. Yesterday we had to register ourselves at the police station and turn over contraband. I even had to give up my pocketknife and flashlight. Just in case, I—yes, me, scrawny Alex Maki, the skinniest bookworm from sea to shining sea—decide to lead a revolt at night armed with nothing more than my puny pocketknife.

At school no one speaks to me. There are a few other Japanese American students but we avoid each other. I guess we don't want to come across looking like the enemy, plotting an attack on America or something ridiculous like that.

My homeroom teacher, Mr. Hartford, has been sober for the whole week. Yes, Mr. Drunk himself. On Tuesday he flat out told Billy Hosokawa and me that he didn't want us reciting the Pledge of Allegiance anymore. He told us we should stand out of respect, but he didn't want "no Jap" defiling the flag. If I was blond with blue eyes and had a surname like McCarthy, I'd have told him to go to hell, no one is stopping me from pledging my allegiance to my home country. But all I did was stare down and wish I could disappear through the floorboards.

But I get the last laugh. Because I'm still saying the pledge every morning. I whisper it secretly like a ventriloquist. Mr. Drunk doesn't have a clue. Betty Baldwin sits in front of me, and she hears. She always gives me a quick sideways wink as she sits down.

I'm sorry that this letter is all doom and gloom. They say writing helps clarify your thoughts and emotions. Well, it has. And my thoughts and emotions are clearly just the darkest of clouds pouring down the bitterest of rain.

Alex

Alex leans back in his chair, rubbing his hand. Night presses against the window. In the darkened glass, he sees the reflection of the small guttering candle on his desk. He sees his own reflection, too, his thin arms poking out of the blanket thrown over his hunched shoulders.

He folds the letter and inserts it into a stamped envelope. Later today, he'll drop it into the mailbox where it'll begin a five-thousand-mile journey to Paris: first from Bainbridge Island to Seattle to New York City, then a long flight to Lisbon, Portugal. Then by rail across Spain and into the *zone non-occupeé* to a town called Perpignan where it'll hopefully slip past the prying eyes of censors, and arrive at long last in Marseille.

There a man named Monsieur Wolfgang Schäfer, to whom the letter is addressed on the envelope, will pick it up. Monsieur Schäfer, a close friend and business partner of Charlie's father, is an exceedingly well-connected and influential industrialist in possession of great wealth and, importantly, the necessary travel documents. He makes biweekly business trips to and from Paris, and his briefcase, which is always stuffed with documents and contracts—and on occasion a letter from or addressed to Bainbridge Island, USA—is never searched.

"Alex," a voice says from across the room.

Alex almost cries out. "Frank? You scared the hell out of me."

Frank laughs quietly. "What time is it?"

"Almost three."

"Dang. The dead zone." He rubs his eyes with the balls of his hands. Ever since Pearl Harbor, he's been waking up at all hours, very unusual for him especially during football season.

"Can I ask you something, Frankie?" Alex hasn't called his brother "Frankie" in years.

But Frank doesn't seem to notice, much less mind. "Go ahead."

"What's going to happen to us?"

Frank stops rubbing his eyes. "What do you mean?"

"I mean, are we okay?"

Frank stifles a yawn. "I'm too sleepy to read your mind. Just spit it out. What's buggin' you?"

Alex lifts the pen nib off the page so it doesn't blot. "Are we going to be, I don't know, expelled from school or something?"

"Expelled from school?" He snorts. "Whatever the hell for? Don't be ridiculous. Nothing's going to change, okay? We're Americans, born and raised."

"How about Mother and Father? Will they be sent back to Japan?"

"Nah, don't be stupid." Frank pulls himself into a sitting position, his knee bent, an elbow resting on top. His eyes tired but wide, the flames of the candle flickering softly over his face. A handsome face, breaking into full manhood, gazing at Alex. "Everything's going to be fine, kid."

"Will they let you stay on the team? And still be quarterback?"

Frank gives a cocksure grin. "Now I know you're nuts." He rubs his thick forearm. "Without me, there is no team. And just today, Coach was telling us we're going to be busier than ever. Maybe play some charity games after the season, raise money for the military." He leans toward Alex. "Nothing's going to change, Alex. Everything will be fine, you worrywart."

Alex stares out the window, then back at Frank. "I hope you're right. Because I heard rumors about roundups and other stuff."

"Hey, when have I ever been wrong? Don't worry." He flicks his chin at Alex's desk. "Whatcha drawing?"

"Not drawing." Alex pauses. "Writing a letter."

"To Charlie again?"

"Yeah." Alex turns his eyes away, a little embarrassed.

"It's good to have a friend," Frank says softly after a moment. "Especially now."

"Really?"

"Yeah."

Alex hesitates, puts the pen down. "Frankie, can I ask you a question?"

"Shoot."

He pauses. Then whispers, "Do you think I'm weird?"

"Of course you are, you little goober." He leans forward, rests his chin on his kneecap. "But what do you mean?"

"Never mind."

"No, seriously, Alex." His face curious but also tender and protective.

Alex stares down at the page, swallows. "Is it normal to . . . feel this way for someone I've never met?"

"And what is *this way*?"

Alex shrugs. "I don't know. Just like, real close. Like we're best friends. But maybe even closer than that."

"Closer than best friends? Yeah, that's called a *girlfriend*." He clucks his teeth in amusement.

Alex shakes his head. "Never mind."

Frank's voice turns earnest. "Hey, I'm just joshin'. Look, I think it's fine, kiddo. Not everything has to have a clear label. You can be somewhere between *best friend* and *girlfriend,* and that's a perfectly okay place to be." He rubs his bicep. "She feel the same way?"

"I don't know."

"You've never told her how you feel?"

Alex pauses before answering. Soon after he turned fourteen, he'd confessed his feelings to her in a feverish, blathering nine-page letter. Two seconds after he dropped the envelope into the mailbox he wanted to reach into the slot and retrieve it. But it was too late.

She didn't reply for six weeks. The longest period he'd gone without hearing from her. He thought maybe this was her way of ending things, ending the awkwardness. He wished he'd never sent that letter.

He returned home one day to find a letter from her. He ripped open the envelope. In reply, she told him he was—

"Well?" Frank says. "You ever tell her how you feel?"

"Once I might've confessed my feelings."

"Yeah? How'd she respond?"

Alex pauses. "She basically called me an idiot."

Frank laughs, not unkindly. "Too funny. And true." He grabs his pillow, throws it at Alex, hitting him on the head. A perfect strike. Of course. "Because you are an idiot, kid."

Alex picks up the pillow and throws it right back. It thuds against the side of the bed, missing badly, and flops to the floor. Of course.

"You guys ever talk about it again?" Frank asks.

"Nah. We just let it drop."

"And how were things after? Weird?"

Alex stares down at his hands. "We . . . actually got closer. I don't know, maybe it showed we could be completely honest with each other?" He shrugs. "Something like that."

Alex is half expecting Frank to rib him again. But when he looks up, Frank is gazing at him with a strange expression. "In some ways I really envy you," Frank says.

"*You* envy . . . *me?*"

"Yeah. To have a friend that close."

"You've got friends all around! You're Mr. Popular!"

He looks down to the floor. "Yeah. But no one really that . . ." He shakes his head. "Nah, never mind." He picks up his pillow, plumps it into shape. "But do me a favor, okay, Alex? Maybe you should, like, go out on a date once in a while. Take a gal out to the Bowlmoor. Or the drive-in some Saturday night. Take *someone.* Just so, you know . . ."

"Just so what?"

"Nothing." He lies down, settling under the blanket. He looks at Alex, head on pillow. "Just so you stay grounded. So you stay real. So you don't get too lost in fantasyland." He turns to the wall, and a minute later is asleep.

Alex stays at his desk a while longer. Not to finish writing his letter. Instead, after Frank starts snoring, he opens up the drawer and slips out a letter he's reread countless times. He unfolds its page with all the care of a museum archivist over an artifact. The pages were once lightly perfumed, and Alex likes to imagine he can even now detect a lingering whiff. He turns to the paragraph where Charlie had called him an idiot. He's read this paragraph countless times; not because he particularly enjoys being called an idiot, but because of what follows.

. . . you're an idiot, Alex. Because you don't say these kinds of affections now. Not at 14 years old, not when we don't have a chance of seeing each other for many years. No: you say it when you are 18 or 19, when you are old enough to travel to Paris and see me. When

you are old enough to—maybe as a university student!—live here.
That is when you say, "I love you." You are an idiot!

She never brought the topic up again, thankfully. But even now her words—every curlicue and loop of each character indelibly etched into his mind—bring a small smile to his face, and make his heart, even after almost three years, beat a little faster.

5

Alex wakes before the crack of dawn. Picks his head off folded arms, his neck creaking. A pool of drool splotches his letter, next to a blot of ink where his pen bled. It's his morning to do chores, and with a groan he pushes off the desk.

He walks down to the kitchen, fills a glass with water. A voice suddenly whispers in Japanese, "Your turn for chores?"

"Father?" He almost drops the glass. "I didn't see you." He walks over to the kitchen table, pulls out a chair. Sleep lines crease Father's face. He's been down here all night. Nobody is sleeping well these days.

An almost-empty bottle of sake sits on the table. Beneath the faint aroma of alcohol, Alex smells damp soil and strawberry wafting from Father's clothes, from the pores of his leathery, prematurely withered skin. Spread out before him, letters and postcards and aerograms from Japan lie scattered around the bottle. When Father drinks—which isn't often—he becomes sentimental. He'll bring out old letters and talk everyone's ears off. This is how Alex has learned of Father's past: through the vapor of sake, beer, whisky, the spillage of slurred words.

It's in those moments, looking into Father's drunken eyes (the only time he can gaze directly into them), that Alex sees the restlessness rooted deep into the bones of every immigrant. That spirit of adventure that made Father gaze across the seas and wonder about a land called *A-me-ri-ka*. When the economy in Japan and especially his prefecture collapsed, he left his parents and two older brothers, and set sail. And never once looked back.

When Father speaks of his first years in America he speaks of the adventure lived. He never mentions the hardships endured, or the racism faced. He speaks only nostalgically and even gloriously of his days working at the Port Blakely Mill—a sawmill on Bainbridge Island that had taken to hiring immigrant Japanese after its usual supply of Chinese laborers was cut off by the Chinese Exclusion Act. The work was hard but the pay at least steady. And the community of Issei was tight-knit, living together in a segregated settlement of barracks built along a steep hill. *Yama,* they called it. "Mountain."

When the Port Blakely Mill folded, the Issei looked elsewhere for work, and they didn't have to look far. For years, they'd noted the soil of Bainbridge Island, how it seemed suitable for fruit agriculture. And there was ample land on this sparsely populated island that was occupied only seasonally by wealthy Seattle families in summer homes. The Issei community spread themselves across the island, and with no-nonsense grit, cleared land, removed tree stumps using horses, and blasted the ground with dynamite to clear it of glacially deposited rocks.

In that way they went from millworkers to strawberry farmers; in that way they went from immigrants to settlers and then neighbors. Their roots dug deeper into this American land with each new strawberry harvest, and deeper yet with each new birth of what never stopped being miraculous to them, their *American* child.

"Before your grandma died," Father says now, "she would write twice a year. On my birthday and on the date I left Japan." He runs his fingertips over yellowing envelopes. "I wish she could have met you and Daisuke. She'd have been so proud."

So unexpected, this tenderness. Father could be like that, spring on you a sudden softness. He was usually an uncomplicated man of authority, and this authority was absolute and total. Over his wife. His boys. Over the chickens whose necks he wrung and slashed, over the land he tilled and browbeat into submission. Even seemingly over the weather itself by sheer force of his indomitable immigrant will.

But one day when Alex was seven, perhaps eight, something happened after which he never saw Father quite the same way. They'd gone downtown, the two of them, to buy supplies. They were in a hardware store, just leaving, when Alex went to the restroom. When he came out, he saw through the storefront windows Father waiting outside on the street, hands clasped behind his back.

Then.

A school bus—yellow, massive—screeched to a halt. Its appearance was like a large background stage prop sliding behind Father. The bus was packed with a visiting junior-high-school baseball team.

Father turned his back to the bus, faced the storefront window. For a second his eyes seemed to meet Alex's; but then they slid away. The storefront glass was a mirror in the bright sunlight.

The students in the bus were staring outside, bored and hot. Damp hair stuck to their sweaty faces.

The traffic light was still red.

One of the players spotted Father. His lips twisted into a sneer. He mouthed something, thumped the bus window.

Don't, Father, don't turn around—

Father turned around. Like a stupid, obedient dog. His neck twisted awkwardly as he gazed upward. He seemed so impossibly small and tiny. So ridiculously out of place.

The teenage boy had a rash of angry zits, and he shouted something. He was excited now. Another boy joined him at the window. They were all angles and bones, these boys. They pointed at Father, the tips of their fingers turning white against the glass.

At the next window, another boy, then another, gawked at Father.

Father gazed back at them, his neck contorted.

Turn around, Father, stop staring back—

The traffic light was still red.

One of the boys pulled the corners of his eyes down into a slant. Puckered his lips, buckteething the upper row. Alex couldn't hear the boy's laughter, but the sight of those white teeth and deliriously happy faces seemed to possess its own horrific sound.

Father finally turned around.

They pounded the windows louder, rattling them. A boy pulled down a window. Now the gales of laughter rolled out of the bus like a hot tongue. From even inside the store, Alex could hear the meanness in them.

And all the while, Father did nothing. Stared expressionlessly down the street, his back to the yelling kids, the pulled eyes, the intoned accents.

For the first time in his life, what Alex felt toward Father wasn't fear. It was shame.

A police officer came walking around the corner, drawn by the hooligan sounds. He was about to yell at the kids when he saw Father. His stance changed. Now he turned to Father. With a flap of his hand, he waved Father along. Like Father was the offending one.

And he did. He moved along. With a nod, a nervous smile.

Everything changed that day. With that courteous nod, that accommodating smile, a bubble burst in Alex's mind. He never saw Father the same way again. Father went from being a leader in the Japanese community, a towering being of complete authority—almost a deity—to what he was. An immigrant. A foreigner. A mocked, clueless, misplaced immigrant, put in his place by white boys, kowtowing to all.

When Alex exited the store, the bus was already gone. Father was standing halfway down the other street. Alex went to him, not knowing what to say, if anything at all. Father's expression was the same as usual. Stoic and unreadable. Without saying a word, they walked to the truck parked a few blocks away. Got in. Drove down the street, out of town.

They didn't talk on the ride home, not about the bus incident, not about anything at all. It was like it never happened. It was a rock cast into a flat lake; and when the ripples faded it was as if nothing had ever disturbed the water. But the rock was still there, buried deep and hidden, like a lump in the throat.

So strange, Alex had thought, that you could love someone so much, yet also be so ashamed of that same person.

He looks at Father now sitting at the table. At home, away from the outside world where he is regarded a dithering fool, he is the accepted anchor of this family, giving stability and protection. He fills his sake cup one last time, tosses it down, his eyes watery.

"Well, since I'm up anyway," he says, "might as well get an early start." He places the envelopes and aerograms and postcards carefully back into the shoebox. "Maybe you should get an early start on your chores, too."

Alex nods. Outside, a gout of purple-pink is breaking the horizon; in a few minutes, the dawn sun will poke shyly but decisively through.

Father rubs his face with his coarse palms. "I know it's hard work. I know it's no fun. So study hard, Koji-kun. Get into a good college, then dental school, right? You've got the brains, certainly. Then you won't ever have to clean out chicken poop. You can leave this farm and live in the big city. A nice house in the suburbs of Seattle. Come by on weekends to visit us." He nods at Alex. "Right, Koji-kun?"

"Yes, Father. " He lowers his eyes quickly. Truth is, he doesn't want to be a dentist. But what he really wants to do—what he dreams about, spends endless hours fantasizing about—that'll break Father's heart.

"Good, good." Father throws on his jacket, opens the door. For a moment he's silhouetted by the dawn sky, his breath fogging up before him. And then he casually steps out like it's any other day, and the door closes behind him.

In the afternoon when Alex and Frank return home from school they spot Mother in the field. Something is wrong; even from a distance her distress is obvious. They drop their bags on the dirt path and sprint.

"Mother?" shouts Frank, panting hard. She's on one of the raised beds, bent over a row of strawberries. "What are you doing?"

She doesn't answer.

Alex gets there seconds later. "Are you okay, Mother?"

Slowly she straightens, turns to them. "Father is gone. And the fields, they need to be prepared—"

"What do you mean he's gone?" Frank says. "Where's Father?"

"They took him."

"What?" The boys look at each other. "Who took him?"

She shakes her head. "Men in suits." She scrunches her forehead, trying to remember. "F-B-I."

"The FBI?" Frank says. "Where did they take him?"

"I don't know." Her voice is as unsteady as the legs she stands on. The boys lead her back into the house, one on either side of her. They sit her down at the kitchen table. Alex boils water, makes tea for her.

She tells them what happened, her voice quivering at first, then steadier as she draws strength from the concern of her boys. She speaks of how the agents came. How they forced him to leave right there and then. Didn't even give him time to pack a small bag. Or say goodbye to her. They just led him to the car. And then the car left, taking him away. Will she ever see him again, are they shipping him back to Japan?

Frank gets up from the table. Starts making phone calls.

He hangs up a few minutes later. He's called five of his Nisei friends. Two have a similar story: FBI agents took their fathers earlier that day. "No one knows where they were taken." He sits down, his energy sapped.

"How can they just take Father?" Alex says, incredulous. He looks at Father's chair at the dining table. Father, gone. His presence ripped away, leaving a gaping black hole in the universe. "Frank? How can they do that? Just snatch him away like a common criminal."

"I don't know." His face is pale with shock, flushed at the cheeks with anger.

"How can they just—"

"I don't know!"

"But where—"

"I said *I don't know!*" He suddenly stands up, sending the chair flying backward and into the cabinet. He walks over to the window, presses his forehead against the glass. As if searching for Father somewhere far off in the distance.

Alex has never seen Frank so unsettled. And it's at this moment that he realizes things aren't going to be fine, that things are only just beginning to unravel. Because Frank—his lips trembling, his eyes squeezed shut—isn't reassuring them with his aw-shucks grin, isn't waving off their worries with a joke.

After a minute, Frank leans down to pick up the fallen chair from the floor. "Kyle and Pete," he says to Mother in a somber voice that seems too old. "They both said their homes were searched. The FBI took away anything that looked Japanese. Anything that might suggest they're Japanese spies."

"Spies?" Alex says. "Sato-san and Muramoto-san, spies? That's crazy."

Frank runs a hand through his crew cut. "Did they search our home, Mother?"

She shakes her head.

"They might come back later." Frank looks around. "We need to destroy everything Japanese. Any books, clothes, anything with kanji."

"Are you sure?" Mother glances worriedly around the kitchen.

Frank nods grimly. "If they come and find Japanese stuff here, it'll only hurt Father. We need to throw it all away."

For the next few hours, they throw into a pile outside anything remotely Japanese: ceramic rice bowls, chopsticks, novels, kimonos, Hinamatsuri and Tango no Sekku dolls, phonographs by Noriko Awaya, old photo albums, Mother's favorite *kintsugi* ceramic cups and bowls, calendars with prints of Utagawa Hiroshige's work.

Finally, they pour gasoline over the pile. Frank strikes a match, flicks it into the pile. At first, only black smoke curls out in thin wisps, and a crackling sound—not unlike the static of a phonograph—scratches out. Then the bonfire suddenly roars to life. Dancing flames lick higher and higher until after a few minutes the boys are forced to retreat a few steps.

Mother walks back into the house. Alex figures she's seen enough; she has no desire to see her past burned into ashes. But she returns less than a minute later. She is carrying a shoebox. The one containing all of Grandma's old letters.

"Maybe we can just hide that," Alex says. "Bury it somewhere. When Father comes home—"

Mother throws it in. The box flips over, upending its contents.

Letters and envelopes and postcards and aerograms spill out. The fire comes after them quickly, possessively, lapping them all up. The letters curl in the heat, their edges glowing and fire-lit, then taken whole, devoured. Two minutes later, and there's nothing left. Decades of thoughts and hopes and feelings turned to ashes, forever disappeared.

6

Dear Alex,

I began this letter three times, but ended up tossing each away. It is so hard to find the right words.

Alex, I am so sorry about your father. I cannot imagine the pain you are in. Even though your words were few, I sensed you are hurting very deeply. I wish I can be there with you. This is one of the times when I feel so much the 8,000 kilometers that separate us.

I worry that you have no friends to talk to. I have been telling you for years now to make friends! But you haven't listened, have you? MAKE FRIENDS, ALEX!!! And no, I don't count even though we are really good friends, maybe even best friends. You need friends who are there with you on Bainbridge Island! And do not give me such nonsense about how books-are-my-friends and my-drawings-are-my-friends. They don't count! They're not human! And this is coming from someone who loves books, who wants to be an author when she grows up! You need actual living, breathing people around you! And no, your dog doesn't count, either!

Oh, I should stop now before I work myself into more anger, and say something I will later regret.

Charlie

Dear Alex,

I feel bad. I should not have yelled at you in my last letter. You are going through so much, and your only friend in the world is screaming at you. I remember all those times when my world was falling apart. When my cat died, or my English nanny returned to London, or my boyfriend Pierre decided to stop seeing me (how silly that seems now!). You were such a good friend, writing lots of letters, sending me a new Jane Eyre book, and drawing lots of funny cartoons. You were so thoughtful and kind. You did not yell at me.

I will not make excuses but recently I have been angry. I am not angry about the lack of food or coal or dairy things like milk, eggs— everyone has to deal with rations (except the Nazi doryphores, of course, they still get everything).

But I am angry at the unfair things. All the nonsense I face because of who I am. Because I am Jewish. Our radios and bicycles taken away. Our phone lines turned off. We can't use public street phones, can't enter parks or theaters or swimming pools or music halls or cafés, can't borrow books from libraries. Can't even cross the Champs-Élysées.

All these stupid rules simply because we are Jewish.

When I think about it too long I get so angry! And sometimes the anger spills over and hurts the people closest to me. Like you. I should hit instead at the Nazis walking around like peacocks on our streets, I should spit in their proud faces. Instead I say angry things to my best friend halfway across the earth who is going through a similar nightmare.

Sorry.

Yelling at you is especially stupid because you are my only friend now. I am serious! Even more of my Jewish friends have left Paris, to secret places in the south, or maybe to another country. So I can not even write to them. Only Hélène and Ruth are still here but they're leaving soon too.

They tell me I must leave. But I will not ever leave Paris. This is my beautiful home, my La Ville Lumière. I think everyone is over-reacting. When the Germans invaded France last year, everyone fled Paris in a panic. Then they returned a few weeks later, red-faced, needing to take down the shutters from their apartment windows. And now they are doing it again: overreacting. Just watch. Eventually, after the dust has settled, my Jewish friends will return.

But for now I am alone. And I think maybe this is why recently I feel so close to you (despite how I scream at you!). Even though we are so different—you are a shy American strawberry farmer, and I am an extroverted, (sometimes) bratty Paris girl—we somehow understand each other so well.

Oh Alex, sometimes I wish for a magic door. A door that connects my room in Paris to your room on Bainbridge Island. We could see each other so easily. Just open the door, and voilà, hello there! (Oh! Maybe this is not such a good idea! Promise you must knock first!) But with such a door, we do not have to wait weeks for a reply letter.

But this makes me wonder about something. Do you ever worry if we did meet in person, we might find that we do not like each other? Maybe we only like—how to say in English—idéals of each other? Maybe in real life we are quite different?

Oh, my thoughts get so deep and negative when I am all alone! Does this happen a lot to you, my lonely turtle boy? Do you find yourself thinking strange, depressing thoughts?

Your fellow lonely turtle,
Charlie

January 16, 1942

Dear Charlie,

Still no word from my father. My mother waits for the mailman every day, and every day she's disappointed. Without my father, *it's like she's lost substance. I'd never have guessed she needed him so much. The house is so empty and quiet now. At mealtimes my father's empty chair seems to loom over us.*

You're right: I don't have anyone to talk to. Not even Frank, anymore. Ever since our father was taken away, he's changed. It really bothers him that someone could just be snatched away. He's careful at school to hide it, and he's the same old upbeat varsity captain, popular as heck. But at home, wow, complete turnaround, he turns really gloomy. Total Jekyll and Hyde.

Doesn't help that he's got even more chores to do with our father gone. So he's tired all the time. I know he feels the pressure to be the man of the house now.

But I'm fine. Even without Frank, I'm doing okay. Because I honestly don't need people. Give me a comic book, and I'm perfectly content. Or better yet, a sketchbook and an HB (or Eberhard Faber!) pencil. But put me in front of an actual person, and I tend to shrivel up. I never quite know what to say.

I've actually been thinking about the 5,000 miles that separate us. As much as we both hate the distance, it might ironically be the reason why we've become so close. It's allowed me to be completely open and honest with you, something I can't be when face-to-face with people.

Don't worry about me, Charlie. As long as I got you, I'm fine.

Alex

P.S. Put to rest your silly notion that in real life we might not get along. That's crazy, Charlie, that's a really negative and weird and depressing thought! As you always tell me: MAKE SOME FRIENDS!!!!

7

They return weeks later. Four FBI agents. They don't bother flashing their badges or asking for permission to enter. They tromp in with their boots, kicking aside the shoes and sandals neatly lined up in the *genkan*. Within minutes, they've tracked in more sand and dust and dirt than has ever been brought into the house.

"Someone shut that damn dog up," one of them says.

"His name's Hero, by the way," Frank says, arms folded. He's standing against the kitchen wall, still in his football uniform.

"What did you say?"

"I said the dog has a name. Hero."

The agent cocks his head. "As in *Hiro*hito? Figures. Got anything else from the Jap emperor in this house?"

The agent wants to provoke. Frank presses his lips together, looks away. The agent sniffs, moves to the bookshelf by the faded chintz couch. His fingers hook into book spines; he pulls them out, flips through them one by one, letting them drop to the floor when he's done.

From the coffee table, he picks up a thick book, its leather cover worn and distressed, its thin pages crinkled and well thumbed. "Well, well, what do we have here?" He holds the book out to them, upside down, the opened pages printed with kanji. "What's this?"

Frank looks at him with a sneer. "It's called the Bible. Know it?"

"That so?"

"Yeah, you should read it sometime. Might learn a thing or two."

The agent returns Frank's stare, then turns to Mother. "You got any more books written in Japanese?"

"No." She shakes her head vigorously. "No more Japanese book."

"'No more Japanese book,'" the agent intones, mimicking her accent.

Alex can hear the other three agents moving about the house. Sounds of drawers being opened, clothes thrown to the floor, bed mattresses lifted and dropped.

"Do you recognize any of these agents?" he asks Mother. "From when Father was taken away?"

She shakes her head. "These white men," she whispers, "they all look the same."

"No talking in Japanese," the agent barks at them.

"We're talking, is all," Frank says, pushing off the wall. "What's it to you?"

"Okay," Mother says, putting a hand on Frank. "Okay. No Japanese."

The agent snorts. His eyes settle on something on the other side of the kitchen, and he moves eagerly to it. He pulls out a sack of rice from beneath the sink.

"That's a lot of lice. Sorry, I mean rice." He sticks his hands into the sack, running his hand through the grains. He draws out two fistfuls, lets the rice sift through his fingers. "We've found all kinds of contraband in your *lice* in other homes." He suddenly grabs the sack, upending it. The grains of rice go scattering across the floor.

"Come on, now!" Frank takes a step toward the agent.

"Don't!" the agent warns, straightening.

"Why'd you do that? It's just rice."

"I said back off!"

"Yeah, you go to hell—"

Mother stands. "Daisuke!"

The agent spins around. "I said don't speak in Japanese!" His pointed finger almost jabs her nose.

Frank steps forward, his hands balled into fists.

Do it, Frank, Alex thinks. *Swing a haymaker. Give that idiot a shiner.*

"Daisuke!" Mother shouts at Frank, clapping her hands sharply. Frank pauses, breathing hard.

Another agent enters into the kitchen, his eyes swinging between Frank and the other agent. "What's going on here?"

"Nothing," the agent answers, shrugging.

Mother sits down, her fingers trembling.

The other agents return from the other rooms. They're carrying a Japanese vase, a camera, a pair of binoculars, even a wire clothes hanger. "Contraband," one of them mumbles. They walk out, stepping over the scattered rice.

"Hey, wait!" Alex says after them. This is his chance to find out about Father. "When's my father coming back?"

They ignore him, walk out the front door.

Frank follows them outside. "Hey! Didn't you hear my brother? He asked when you're releasing our father!"

They ignore him as they saunter toward their car.

"Don't even think about leaving until you answer me!" Frank shouts, and now he is stomping across the porch, now he is leaping off the stairs, his bare feet striking the frozen ground. The agents pile into the car. Mother cries out after him, telling him not to do anything stupid, to just let them go. But Frank doesn't stop.

Alex pushes open the screen door. "Frank! It's okay, just forget it!"

But Frank ignores him. He runs right up to the government car, and stands directly before it as the engine roars awake. He stares through the windshield at the four agents inside; they stare back, one of them grinning, the others glaring. The driver, his lips twisted in a sneer, leans on the horn. Frank doesn't budge. The car suddenly lunges forward—Mother screams—and although Frank flinches, he holds his ground.

"When's my father coming back?" he shouts, his voice almost a screech. "*Tell me!*"

"Frank!" shouts Alex, running toward him.

The car lurches forward again, stopping mere inches from Frank.

Still he stands his ground. "Get out the car and tell me! When's he coming home?" He raises his hands, and slams them down onto the hood of the car.

"Daisuke!" Mother screams from the porch.

The driver's door opens. "Listen, kid, get the hell out of the way before I arrest your ass."

Frank raises his fists, about to strike the hood again.

Alex grabs hold of Frank's shirt from behind. "Frank," he says urgently, trying to tug him backward. "Please stop!"

But Frank is unmovable. Alex can feels his hard muscles bunching under his clothing, readying to unleash.

Mother hurries over. Doesn't try to physically pull him away, knowing better. "Daisuke," she says. "You can get us into trouble. And then they'll send Father off. Far away. Maybe back to Japan. Stop this."

Frank stares at her, his chest rising and falling. His jawline jutting out. He closes his eyes, shakes his head.

"That's right, punk," the agent says. "Listen to your mommy.

Whatever she said." He gets back into the car. Guns the engine, the tires spinning and kicking dirt into their faces.

Frank stares at the car disappearing into the distance. His shoulders taut, his fists still balled, his body trembling. Quaking, like a volcano about to erupt.

8

January 19, 1942

Dear Charlie,

I just wrote a letter to my father. It was full of lies. I painted a too-rosy picture of home, told him Mother is doing great even though she's not. She's exhausted. At night she screams out in her sleep. It's scary.

And I told him I'm doing great. That I'm doing well at school (not a lie), and that yes, as he'd asked, I'll happily consider dentistry as a career (A COMPLETE LIE!). Truth is, I don't want to be a dentist, I'm not cut out to be one. Teeth, lips, gums, all that saliva, blood, bad breath. So gross. Last month in Biology we had to dissect a frog and I almost passed out. Over a stupid frog. How am I supposed to pry out black diseased human teeth from rotting gums that stink of halitosis?

Of course, I didn't tell Father what I really want to do with my life. That would crush him. Because he didn't immigrate all the way from Japan to raise a . . . cartoonist.

Maybe I'll just, I don't know. Force myself to love dentistry over comics? Is that even possible? I don't know. What I do know is I can't let him worry over us, not while he's in prison.

Wow. What a gloomy letter. Okay, enough with the self-pity. Let me tell you about some new comics I've been reading. These days, that's the only way I can forget all the crazy stuff happening around me.

So yesterday I was at the five-and-dime store and I came across this new comic called Sensation Comics. Splashed across the front cover was a brand new superhero who is—you'll never guess—a woman! Yes, a woman! She's wearing these cool red boots with high heels, and dressed in what looks like the American flag. Must've been a small flag because her outfit is a bit . . . revealing? Like a sexy bathing suit, to tell you the truth. The cover announces her name: The Sensational New Adventure Strip Character: Wonder Woman!

Wonder Woman! What a name! I cracked open the magazine but that's when Mr. Thompson threatened to kick me out unless I shelled out a dime. Best dime I ever spent. This Wonder Woman, she's pretty cool. Way better than Namor the Sub-Mariner or Bozo the Iron Man. She's got these awesome wrist cuffs that deflect bullets. She can't fly like Superman but get this: she flies in an invisible plane.

And best of all: she kills Nazis. Do I have your attention now?

Wonder Woman reminds me of you. I mean, I don't know what you look like (because, ahem, someone <u>still</u> hasn't sent me a picture of herself!). But look at that strip where she's knocking out the Nazi soldier with a righteous haymaker. With that feisty spirit, she could be you! Anyway, I ripped out a few pages and enclosed it (along with a few sketches I drew yesterday). Enjoy!

Alex

---

14 February 1942

Dear Alex,

Thank you for Wonder Woman! What a wonderful gift! You will be happy to know I taped Wonder Woman on my bedroom wall right next to Charlotte Brontë.

You seem quite fascinated by Wonder Woman. And by her clothes. Or the lack of it. Me, I am not so impressed. Because invisible plane? Pssh! Because even if the plane is invisible you can still see her sitting in it, no? Especially if she's in a bathing suit—all the men's eyes will snap up to her like helpless magnets.

But this is what I do like about her: she has dark hair! And brown eyes! Like me! I like that her hair is not blond and her eyes are not blue. Nothing wrong with this, of course, I have lots of friends with blue eyes and blond hair. But all around me on posters, in movies, is the "pretty woman"—and she always has blond hair and blue eyes. So it is nice to see a superhero who looks like me.

Oh, in case you are wondering, that is where our similarity ends! Because if you put me in a bathing suit, I look nothing like Wonder Woman! She has much longer legs (like a space alien!) and a chest that is much bigger . . . Oh! this is embarrassing! How did we end up talking about my body? I am laughing!

Actually, I am more like Jane Eyre: "obscure, plain, and little." Because no one looks at me. Not anymore. Or if they do, it is with scorn. As if I am ugly. Because now they only see a Jewish girl. And all Jews are ugly. That is what they are told. That is what they see in stupid films like Le Juif Süss, and in stupid exhibitions like Le Juif et la France at the Palais Berlitz. There were many images of le Juif at that horrible exhibition. We have dirty hair and big, bent noses. We are ugly. We are scary. We are big hairy spiders drinking the blood of France. We are sewage polluting this land.

And now the French boys believe all these lies. I used to be Charlie the fiery girl, Charlie the funny girl, Charlie the girl full of joie de vivre, Charlie the girl with fire in her eyes. Now I am just Charlie, le Juif girl. Now I am just an ugly hairy spider.

Of course I know these are all lies. But sometimes you hear a lie so often, you come to believe it. You get treated ugly for too long, and one day suddenly you are ugly.

Oh, this is so depressing. Especially on la fête de Saint-Valentin (you Americans call it Valentine's Day).

Back to a brighter topic. Your sketches! They are so wonderful. Promise me one thing, okay, Alex? Promise you'll never give up this

*special talent. Promise you'll never become just another dentist.
Because there'll always be enough dentists in the world. But there'll
never be enough true artists. And it is Art that touches souls and
moves hearts, that makes the world a deeper, warmer place. I wish
I could say more but Maman is banging on my door, saying we must
depart for synagogue. Bye!*

*Your friend,
Charlie*

P.S. Happy la fête de Saint-Valentin!!

---

15 February 1942

Dear Alex,

*Synagogue yesterday was even emptier than last week. Papa
and Maman argued all the way home. Maman says we must leave
Paris. She says it is too dangerous here, and that we must flee like
our friends. She says, we have money, we have Monsieur Schäfer,
we have opportunity. But Papa does not want to leave. He says Maman
and I should go to Nice, but he must stay behind to look after
the factory and apartment. Maman says she will not leave without
him. But he says he will never leave. Maman calls him a fool. Papa
calls her stubborn. And then she says he's the stubborn one.*

And back and forth they go.

*I agree with Papa. Because this is my city and I love it like it is
my family. I love the obvious things like the Eiffel Tower, the Grands
Travaux of Mitterrand, the beautiful walls of the Sacré-Coeur at
sunset, eating foie gras at the Café de la Paix. But also smaller
thing, too: reading books at Gibert Jeune, looking into a bakery in
Marais at the macarons on display, haggling with the bouquinistes
at the Seine bookstalls. Worship service at my synagogue, the smell
of wet cobblestones after a hot summer rain. I do not ever want to
leave Paris.*

But this afternoon as I walked around, I realized something. Paris feels different. Not only because of so many swastika flags flying everywhere, or the German bottes doing their stupid exercises on the Champ-de-Mars parade ground. But as I walked in the cold rain I realized that Paris has changed in a deeper way: she's lost her vitalité. She's somehow become a stranger to me. She was once the Ville des Lumières but now she's only the Ville Éteinte.

Last night I heard a song on the BBC radio (shh! don't tell anyone). Oscar Hammerstein's "The Last Time I Saw Paris." This line, Alex: "Her streets are where they were, but there's no sign of her."

I do not cry often. I think it is a weakness. In my <u>Jane Eyre</u> book I have underlined a sentence maybe a hundred times: "Even for me, life has its gleams of sunshine."

I like this sentence. It reminds me to always find beauty even in ugly places. To not cry sad tears but to smile with brave, happy lips. And the truth is there are many gleams of sunshine in my life: my big apartment, my records, Walter de la Mare's poetry; soap and coal to avoid the chilblains; meat we can still buy in the black market at Aubergenville, milk, even if it is tinned, lemonade and orangeade at the Luxembourg Gardens.

But last night after the song my eyes became very wet. Paris is gone. Everything has changed, everything has gone dark.

Maybe we should leave.

Alone,
Charlie

February 18, 1942

Dear Charlie,

Did you get the Wonder Woman cartoon I sent you yet? Isn't she awesome?

So this strange thing's been happening. Bainbridge Island is the only home I've ever known but recently it's changed. It doesn't feel the same.

When I walk into the town library or hardware store, it feels weird. It's not that people stare at me. It's more like I can feel them trying not to stare. The air becomes thick and tense. And if I stay too long, or take my time sipping my ice-cream float at the soda fountain, I can sense them all willing me to leave. So they can finally exhale.

At school, everyone is just awkward around me. In Biology, we had to pair off to work on a frog experiment. There's an odd number of students in my class, and I ended up the only one without a partner. Mr. Webb gave me a choice to either join a pair and make a team of three, or work alone. I chose alone.

Honestly, I'm fine with that. Tomorrow I'll go out alone to the rocky shores on the west side of the island and look for a frog. For the experiment. Did you know that if you drop a frog in boiling water, it will instantly leap out? But if you put it into room-temperature water, and then slowly heat the water to a boil, the frog will stupidly remain in there until it overheats and dies. Sounds pretty interesting—I'll let you know what happens. If I can stomach killing a frog, that is.

Alex

February 19, 1942

Dear Charlie,

It took me almost an hour to find a frog. Eventually I came upon an Oregon spotted frog squeezed between two rocks. It was so wet and slimy and squirmy in my palm.

I tried. I really did. But when it came time to boil it, I couldn't. I stood there in front of the stove for a good five minutes, trying to will myself to turn on the flame. But I froze.

Anyway, there's more to this story. At dinner Frank was ranting about some political cartoon in the newspaper, how it put Japanese Americans in a really unfair light. He tossed the newspaper away in disgust and went to the stove for seconds. "Why is there a frog in here?" he said, pointing to the other pot. So I had to tell him about the frog experiment.

He sat back down. Chewed his food slowly. "We're just like frogs then," he said after a while. Mother and I stared at him quizzically. And then he snapped. Went off on us.

"All this crap happens to us," he railed, "and we do absolutely nothing. We just sit here like a stupid frog boiling to death. The government comes and takes away our belongings? We do nothing. Our bank account gets frozen? We just sit there! Father gets yanked away by the FBI when he's done nothing wrong? We do nothing but suffer in silence like good model citizens. We're nothing but stupid frogs." He slammed his fists down on the table, rattling all the dishes. "We should do something. Protest. Make our voices heard."

He tossed the newspaper at me, jabbed his finger at the political cartoon: a crowd of bucktoothed Japanese Americans, cruelly caricatured, carrying TNT dynamite. Frank pointed at me with his fork. "Why don't you put your drawing skills to use for once? Send in a cartoon in response to this nonsense about us being fifth columnists. Something that'll put—" He turns the paper around, reads the signed cartoonist's name. "—this idiot Dr. Seuss in his place."

Mother shushed him, saying, 出る釘は打たれる. It's the nail sticking up that gets hammered down.

Frank said, "Well, I don't care. Maybe we should be that nail. At least we'd be sticking up for something." His face turned really determined like I've seen in football games right before he throws a winning touchdown pass.

"This is what I'm going to do," he said. "I'm going to write a release petition on Father's behalf. Tell them they've got the wrong man, that Father is completely innocent. I suck at writing, sure. But

I'm tired of sitting on my hands doing nothing. I'm not going to be that frog."

Mother's lips pinched together. *"But that might just stir up trouble for Father."*

Frank shoved a drumstick into his mouth, reenergized. *"The FBI, the gov, whatever, they're so obviously wrong. This petition will wake them up. Because America doesn't do this kind of thing. You just watch and see."* He reached for another helping of mashed potatoes.

Mother shook her head. *"We must be patient. Don't do anything rash."* She looked at me. *"Don't you think so, Koji-kun?"*

But I wasn't interested in getting dragged into this. I got up, put my plate in the sink, then picked up the pot. I opened the door and tossed out the frog. It hopped away into the darkness.

It's hours later and I'm sitting here at my desk. My eyes are heavy but I can't fall asleep. Outside my window the world is so empty and dark.

In your letter, you wrote that it wasn't good to be alone, that I should make more friends. Maybe you're right. But there's only one friend I want with me here, and that's you, Charlie.

Alex

9

In the middle of the night Alex thinks Father has returned home.

When he was young and often sick, it was Father who'd sit with him through the night. He remembers those endless hours: shivering under a mountain of blankets, the ladderback chair creaking by his bed, Father removing the damp warm washcloth from his feverish forehead. The *wish-swish* of the towel submerged into water, then the soft trickle of the cloth wrung out. A strangely melodic sound, soothing. Then Father would lay the cool washcloth back on his boiling forehead, and it would sizzle on his hot skin. A soft cloud against a scorching sun.

When the fever would finally break hours later, the shiver-chills subsiding, Alex's clothes would be soaked through. Father would gently lift Alex into a sitting position, his sweaty head flopping forward, and lean him against his wiry, tensile farmer's body. Alex, slumped and exhausted, would barely be aware of Father lifting his soaked pajama top through uplifted arms, and sliding on a fresh, dry shirt.

And even then, even after Alex had been changed, Father would stay with him. Not reading, not sleeping, not even, it seemed, thinking much about anything. He seemed content to simply sit all those hours. Not a single utterance. Strangely, it was the rare time when Father seemed untroubled. And when dawn arrived and Mother took over, Father, without having slept a wink, would go out to the fields and work a full day, none the worse for wear.

Alex will never admit this but sometimes, terrible as they were, he misses those nights.

And now, on this night, he thinks Father has come home. *Already?* he thinks drowsily. *Frank's release petition for Father was processed so quickly?* He senses a warm hum of a presence beside him, believes he even hears the creak of the ladderback chair. He half expects to hear the trickle of water. When he opens his eyes, there *is* someone sitting in the chair by his bed.

"Father?" he croaks.

The person doesn't answer. Then he sees her now, Mother. Her head is fallen to the side, her mouth opened. Softly snoring. He sits up.

In her hands, held loosely, is a small picture frame. Alex pries it gently from her, turns it around. It's his parents' wedding photograph, the one Alex keeps on his bedroom bureau, the only photograph ever taken of just the two of them. A black-and-white, taken at a downtown Seattle studio. She's dressed in a kimono rented just for the shot, and Father has put on a suit, similarly rented. Their faces are stern, reluctant.

The photo was taken the day after they first met. She has described that first meeting to Alex and Frank many times. How she'd come walking down the gangplank onto the dock in Seattle, one of dozens of Japanese mail-order brides arriving in America that day. She was struggling with her suitcase when he came to her. He was wearing a threadbare black coat and grunted her name. His breath was hideous. She'd stared in disbelief at this man old enough to be her father, who bore no resemblance to the young man in the photo. A photo she used to fawn over while lying on her tatami mat back home in Osaka, which made her smile shyly with schoolgirl fantasies.

There on the dock, he'd reached for her suitcase and tried to tug it from her grip. But she wouldn't let go, no matter how hard he yanked; so in that manner they had walked, both carrying the suitcase. On the outside, they had the appearance of togetherness; but it was, in fact, a stubborn tug-of-war. An apt image of their initial years of marriage. Together, but not really.

She'd once told Alex—drunkenly one night when he was nine, and (or so she mistakenly thought) too young to remember, much less understand, anything—how over time she had come to, if not love, then at least respect Father. It was the way he threw himself into the work, season after season, year after year. His skin darkening, his body hardening. His chapped, tireless hands sifting through enough soil to fill Fuji-san; the way he gripped shovels and axes, dug trenches to handle excess rainfall, mixed fertilizer, planted strawberry seeds one by one, weeded grass, pulled out sickly strawberry plants, pruned fruit trees, cut leaves after harvest, removed large tree stumps, propagated rhododendron plants, fixed broken machinery and flat tires and plumbing in their home. Held her boys, cut their umbilical cords, their hair, soothed their colicky screams.

And at night—she'd mumbled this while tossing down one last cup of sake before collapsing into a drunken stupor—when those same rough, sun-blackened hands reached for her in the dark, their hangnails and calluses grating across her skin, she would let them: because of everything they had touched and healed and nurtured into submission, because of how they had so ruthlessly, doggedly, miraculously fashioned into being in a harsh and alien land, this farm, this home, this family.

Alex looks down on her now. Asleep, cradling that photograph of her husband. Her body racked with pain, her bones heavy with fatigue. Yet in the middle of the night she had awakened and come here to gaze at her husband.

Alex pulls out the velvet kickstand of the frame and places it back on the bureau. Stares for a long time at the image of Father. Then he takes his blanket and, as gently as he can, lays it over Mother's sleeping form.

10

Dear Alex,

   I woke up this morning to the sound of Maman and Papa arguing again. I dressed quickly and left the apartment.

   I walked to the Maison des Lettres on rue Soufflot, and listened to some records. Schumann's concerto and then Mozart's requiem mass. Afterward, I walked along boulevard Saint-Michel, hoping to maybe see someone. But there was no one. All my friends have left Paris.

   Under dark clouds, I walked to Sorbonne. It's my favorite place in all of Paris. I walked past their magnificent buildings, the library, the observatory, the English Literature department. Soon, I told myself, after the war is over and the Nazis have left, after all my friends have returned and everything is back to normal, I will be a student here walking this courtyard, my arms full with Kipling and Wordsworth, chatting with friends. The words of John Keats came to me: "the excellence of every Art is its intensity."

   At noon, my feet were aching from the shoe's wooden soles (rubber soles are hard to find now). So I stopped for lunch at one of my usual cafés. The maître d' recognized me—Hélène, Nicole, Ruth, and I ate there often—but if he was surprised to see me alone, he said nothing. All my Jewish friends have fled Paris, I thought to explain to him, but didn't. He showed me to our favorite glass table in the shady part of the outside terrace even though I'm not allowed to sit there anymore. Later, a group of Nazi soldiers arrived and sat at the table next to me. They were loud and drunk and kept ordering more beer and Camembert. One of them started leering at me, blowing cigarette smoke in my direction, suspicion entering his glassy eyes. The skies darkened again. When I felt a few drops, I used that as an excuse to end my lunch and quickly leave.

Paris hasn't just lost her joie de vivre. She's become scary. Even the familiar places—the cul-de-sacs, boulevards, buildings—they somehow feel threatening.

Charlie

---

24 February 1942

Dear Alex,

Yesterday, I went to Aubergenville to buy some meat. On the way back, the Métro was crowded and stuffy and smelly. An inspector was staring at me, his small eyes sharp. I turned away but a moment later felt two hard taps on my shoulder.

The inspector told me les Juifs are not permitted to ride in that carriage. He informed me that I had to step out at the next station and walk down to the carriage for les Juifs. His eyes were going all over me. He stood so close to me I could smell his cologne. I could feel his breath on my forehead.

I turned red with shame and anger. I kept waiting for my fellow Parisians to yell back at the inspector. But no one did. Everyone was looking away. Some at books, some behind closed eyelids, some to the far side of the carriage.

I remember back in 1941 a man on the BBC radio said Parisians must fight back against the German invaders. We must resist. He told people to paint resistance graffiti on the streets of Paris. To paint a red V.

And soon, there were Vs everywhere. On city walls, under bridges, on schools, all over Paris. I remember how proud I was of my fellow Parisians. They stood up to evil, to all the stuck-up Hauptsturm-führers and Sturmhauptführers. But no more.

My Parisians are not evil. Or even cowards. They are only people—good people—who are now too busy and tired and distracted, trying to survive in these difficult times. But this is how evil grows, no? When good people are too tired.

At the next station when the train came to a stop, I stepped out. No one said a word.

Charlie

March 17, 1942

Dear Charlie,

I wish I could've been there. I wish I could've grabbed that racist sonofabitch conductor's neck and squeezed, my fingers sinking like talons into his flesh. I wish I could have thrown a haymaker right into his pudgy nose and boxed in his jug ears. I wish I could've delivered a vicious kick at his head, snapping it back, breaking it off.

So much anger in me, Charlie. If you could see me now writing this letter, hunched over my desk, you'd see how hard I'm clenching this pen, how white my fingertips are gripping it, the splotches of angry red on my hand. Do you see how the words on this page carve into the paper, like a rake into soil, a blade into flesh?

Alex

11

For the first time in months, Alex wakes up to the sound of laughter. Coming from the kitchen.

He throws on his clothes, rushes downstairs.

"You overslept," Mother chides, but she's smiling about something. "Hurry up and eat or you'll miss the bus."

"What's going on?"

Frank is grinning at the breakfast table. "I should get extra credit for this. Mrs. Pope in English class will be impressed with my writing chops."

"Will someone please tell me what's happening?"

Frank scarfs down his eggs and bacon, washes it down with milk, enjoying the moment.

"Frank! Just tell me."

"Fine. You remember that release petition I wrote on Father's behalf?"

"Yeah," Alex says cautiously. "Wait. No way."

Frank grins.

Mother comes around and scoops a boiled egg onto Alex's plate, and a generous serving of bacon before Frank. She's still smiling. "I wasn't sure what Father was saying in his letter," she says. "It's so complicated. But Frank just explained it to me."

Alex glances at her, then back to Frank. "And?"

"Father said the release petition might be working. He heard back from some committee at the prison. Said they were going to make a decision soon."

Alex sits down. "That's it?"

"What do you mean, *that's it*?"

Alex shrugs. "I guess . . . I was hoping for more. I mean, you were so upbeat just now. I thought Father was already released."

"Oh, who invited this killjoy to breakfast?" Frank says. He rams bacon into his mouth, chews with his mouth open. "Things are looking up, Alex. No need to be such a sourpuss."

Alex stares down at his food. "Sorry, I just . . . I don't know."

Frank waves it off. He stuffs more food into his mouth. His eyes suddenly light up. "Okay, this one you can't be phooey about." He gets up, grabs a newspaper from the counter. "Check it out," he says, grinning as he taps the *Bainbridge Review* newspaper.

"What is it?"

Frank starts reading aloud from the front page. "'This Friday's special charity football game against West Seattle High . . . okay, blah blah blah . . . blah blah blah." His eyes scan down. "Here it is. 'Led by the All-American quarterback and charismatic leader, Captain Frank Maki, our boys are poised to deliver a resounding victory!'"

Grinning, Frank points to a picture beside the article. "No one told me I was *this* photogenic!"

"They called you a 'charismatic leader'?" Alex says, taking the newspaper.

"They called me 'Captain Maki.' That's how you should address me from now on."

Mother pours milk into their glasses. "You boys finish up now. Or you're going to miss your bus."

"You too, Mother. 'Captain Maki,' okay?" He rams toast into his mouth, washing it down with milk.

She playfully smacks him on his shoulder. "You're too chatty this morning."

"Hey, did you read this editorial?" Alex asks a moment later, pointing to the next page.

Frank snorts. "And here I thought you were staring at my picture, admiring my handsome mug."

"No, seriously. Did you read it?"

"The editorial? Nah. You know me, sports and comics only."

"Well, check it out. It says here that people on Bainbridge Island should be treating its Japanese friends and neighbors better. That Bainbridge Island needs to stand up for us, and make sure that our Bill of Rights don't get violated any more."

"Yeah?" Frank says. "No kidding. Who wrote that?"

"Walter Woodward. The owner of the paper. Says everyone should be appalled by what's happening to us."

Frank leans back in his chair, beaming. "See? What I've been saying all along. America will come to her senses. America will do right by us. Soon Father will be back home and everything will be back the way it was. You watch and see. And then all your fears about roundups will seem stupid. Never doubt the good U.S. of A."

"Go now!" Mother chides. "The bus will be here in a minute."

The boys hurry out, Frank grabbing Alex's uneaten boiled egg. "Remember I'll be home late tonight, Mother," he says, pushing through the screen door. "It's Dan's birthday so a bunch of us are grabbing floats after practice."

Frank's cheerful mood continues as they wait for the bus at the end of the long driveway. He makes Alex run routes on the dirt road, throwing the football to him.

"You keep dropping them, kid!" he shouts, grinning good-naturedly at Alex.

"Then stop whipping them so hard!" Alex jogs back, tosses the football back to Frank.

"I'm baby-throwing them. Soft as marshmallows." He spins

the football, puts seams to fingertips. "Okay, let's do a slant route at fifteen."

"Frank, I'm pooped."

"You only ran three, four times!"

"Frank!"

"Never mind," he says, picking up his bag. "Bus is here."

They get on. Alex takes his usual seat near the front, and Frank moves past to the very back row, greeting his friends boisterously. Morning sunlight pours into the interior, flaring through the windows into a soft, rainbow-hued haze. The banter about him is light and cheerful. Alex brings out his comics and for the next twenty minutes gets lost in them. It feels like the best morning he's had in months.

He's so focused on the latest issue of *Captain America* that he doesn't notice the posters in town until the bus stops at a traffic light.

Someone two rows ahead says, "Look at that."

And before Alex can look up and see for himself, he hears words he will never forget. "They're kicking out the Japs!"

Alex's head snaps up. Looks out the window. Sees the poster nailed to a telephone pole right outside:

INSTRUCTIONS TO ALL JAPANESE LIVING ON BAINBRIDGE ISLAND

All Japanese persons, both alien and nonalien, will be evacuated from this area by twelve noon, Monday, March 30, 1942.

From where he sits, Alex can't read the smaller print that follows. But he doesn't need to. He shifts his eyes away, stung, his breath snatched away. The comic book is somehow on the floor now. He does not remember dropping it.

He fights the urge to turn around and look at Frank. Instead he closes his eyes, presses his forehead against the cold sting of the window.

It's happening. After holding out hope, yet fearing the worst, after all the weeks and months of anxiety and uncertainty, it's finally happening. They're being kicked out. In only six days. *Evacuated from this area.* Like a pest. A *nonalien.*

The traffic light turns green. The bus pushes forward with a loud groan. In the row behind him, Sarah Dunston wonders aloud if Doug Chesterfield will ask her out to the game on Friday night. The idle chatter in the bus resumes.

Alex finally turns around to look at Frank. He's sitting in the middle of the back row, the empty center aisle directly in front of him. He's stunned, his face pale, oblivious to the banter and laughter around him. He has the look of someone who's been set up, then horribly betrayed. Slapped in the face, then kicked in the gut for good measure. For one awful raw moment their eyes meet. Then Frank flicks his eyes away, stares out the window.

Alex turns back around, looks down the street. The poster is everywhere. Dozens, stapled onto every telephone pole, in storefront windows of obliging owners, barbershops, pharmacies. Along the pillars of the town hall, the sides of mailboxes. Like skin lesions suddenly, inevitably breaking out, the cancer that never did go away. He sees two men next to the library in military garb wearing MP armbands and green berets, hammering more notices into a billboard.

The bus gusts past. The posters come suddenly to life, like the wings of pinned moths and butterflies resurrecting, flapping and fluttering, maniacally, as if desperate to take flight.

When Alex returns home after school, he finds Mother packing boxes in the kitchen. She stands up when he comes in, her hands on her waist. She looks like she's been crying.

"You heard, then," he says.

"Mrs. Tanazawa dropped by and told me." She puts a hand to her cheek. "Six days. *Six.*"

Alex hangs his head. The thought alone of what they need to do exhausts him. Put their farm in order, hand it over to someone responsible and honest. Store their things away. Find a place for Hero. Buy suitcases because they've never been on a trip before. All in only six days—

"Do you know where they're taking us?" Mother asks.

"No idea."

"Or for how long?"

"I haven't heard a thing. No one knows anything."

She moves over to the glass-door cabinet, touches lightly the glass that she cleans every day. "What about Father? He's getting released soon. What if we're not here when he returns?"

A long pause. Then, reluctantly, he whispers, "I don't think he's coming back, Mother."

In the cabinet glass he sees her reflection. Her face falling, her body concaving onto itself. She can withstand whatever lies ahead. Just not without Father.

"What are we going to do?" she asks.

"We should wait for Frank. He'll know what to do."

"But he won't be back until late. He's out with friends tonight, remember?"

But as it turns out, he returns home hours early. He stomps in, his face dark and tense.

"I thought you were going to be late—"

"They've imposed curfew," he says.

"What?"

"Curfew. Just for the Japanese community on Bainbridge."

"How do you know this?"

Frank smirks caustically. "Only because everyone's talking about it in town. Public Proclamation Number Three, or something. No Jap"—he spits this word out loathsomely—"may be out after eight P.M."

"That's ridiculous."

"Yeah? Well because of that ridiculous law, the soda fountain wouldn't serve me. The law was *just* announced, but they still booted me out. Like they couldn't wait to get started."

Mother goes to the stove. "I can heat up the leftovers."

"Don't bother," he says, heading for the bedroom. "I'm not hungry."

Alex sits down at the table. The whole room is tilting and swaying, everything is spinning out of control.

The next morning, another poster is put up. This one, with its bright colors and cheerful design, seems even crueler.

Alex sees it as soon as he steps into the school foyer. A crowd of students have gathered before it, huddling and squealing with excitement. It's an announcement for the tenth-grade dance.

Lindy Hop through the Night! the poster declares. *The date: Sunday, March 29th, 1942. The hours: 7:30 P.M.–10:00 P.M.*

The news is not unexpected. Everyone has known for months there'll be a dance this Sunday. But the exact time of the dance has taken weeks to finalize, on account of the war and last-minute security protocols. Alex just assumed the dance would be in the afternoon, especially since the new curfew law would prevent the Nisei students from attending.

But there it is in black-and-white (actually pink and lavender): *The hours: 7:30 P.M.–10:00 P.M.*

Alex peels away from the crowd. At his homeroom desk, he slumps down, all energy vaporized from his legs. He can barely keep from sliding off his chair.

They could have moved the dance to the afternoon. It'd have been so easy to do that on a Sunday. But they didn't.

He knows why. Because he doesn't matter. Not anymore. None of the Nisei students matter. It's as if they're already gone. Already discarded, flushed out, purged. All these *nonaliens,* as the poster had put it, *evacuated from this area.*

Students enter the classroom, talking excitedly. Already, everyone is chatting about what they'll wear, who they might ask to dance. No one looks at him. Jessica Tanner is speaking breathlessly to Shirley Deckham. The two girls are whispering intently, excitement sparking off their shoulders like static electricity, their giggles bubbly. When the class rises for the Pledge of Allegiance, he finds, for the first time in his life, he can barely utter the words. The phrase *liberty and justice for all* caught in his throat.

The whole day he sits in classrooms and walks the hallways with eyes averted to the floor. He is afraid of meeting the inadvertent gaze of another Nisei, and finding in their eyes the same burning shame. He finds himself licking his lips a lot. Cutting short the swings of his arms as he walks off to the side of the hallway, his sleeve catching on the metal grill of lockers. When he almost bumps into someone rushing out of a classroom, the apology leaps out like a reflex. *Sorry, sorry.* The apology of an intruder. Of a coward. Of a *nonalien.* Alex bites down on his lip. He had no idea how much he loathed himself.

12

Every day that passes is another day closer to evacuation.

But no one at school seems to care. All anyone wants to talk about is the dance. And about Friday's football game, of course, an exhibition charity game against archrival West Seattle High to raise money for war bonds. The perfect community event for a town where football fever and patriotic fervor are one and the same.

Except there is one inconvenient fact. The new curfew law will keep Frank Maki, their star quarterback, at home, away from the stadium.

But that fact is never brought up. A day goes by, and another. Alex waits with trepidation for the unwanted news that Ernest Schwinn, the second-string quarterback—a nervous, twitchy sophomore—has replaced Frank Maki as quarterback. On that day, Frank will stomp home disconsolate and moody, and refuse to speak or eat.

But that day never arrives. Frank comes home on Wednesday and Thursday in a freshly muddied uniform, carrying his helmet, his hair damp and disheveled. He's regained a ravenous appetite, and is constantly reaching for another helping, taking chicken drumsticks off Alex's plate.

On the morning of the game, Alex wakes to find Frank

already up, sitting on his bed cradling a football. His eyes are alert but lost in the *X*s and *O*s of offensive schemes.

"Are you playing tonight?" Alex asks.

Frank blinks with surprise. "Huh?"

Alex raises himself on one elbow. "Are you playing tonight?"

"Of course I am." He tosses the football from one hand to the other, back and forth, pendulum-like. "Why wouldn't I?"

"What about the curfew?"

"What *about* the curfew?" He gets up and walks to the bathroom.

Later at breakfast, Mother asks Frank the same question.

He skirts the question, a little more practiced this time. "Coach said don't worry about it. It's a special night, the team gets a charity exemption." He speaks quickly, using English occasionally, knowing Mother won't understand. He rams a piece of toast into his mouth, chews loudly. Crumbs go spraying out of his mouth across the table, and Mother scolds him, tells him his manners are atrocious, and just like that, he's successfully evaded the question.

But when Mother is noisily washing dishes at the sink, Frank looks at Alex. "You're staying home tonight. You hear me, Alex?"

"But the game—"

He glowers at Alex. "Can it. Don't even think about going."

"But if they're letting you—"

"Stay home, Alex! I'm not kidding around." He's using his football-huddle voice now, his natural authority humming off him like bands of heat from a sun-baked freeway. Alex thinks of all those times he's admired his brother from afar, those broad shoulders slightly stooped in the center of a huddle of white boys, commanding their respect, directing their next move, their blue and green eyes fastened on him, their ears tuned to his voice. His brother like a Greek god.

"You hear me, Alex?"

Alex drops his eyes to the table. He gives a small reluctant nod.

But of course he doesn't stay home that night. He's never missed any of Frank's games.

Alex waits for Mother's closed bedroom to go dark. She's exhausted from all that needs to be done before the evacuation in only three days, and Alex knows she'll fall asleep quickly. To be safe, he waits another ten minutes before creeping out of his bedroom. It's already seven forty-five. The football game begins in fifteen minutes. He shuts the front screen door slowly, steps carefully over the two creaky planks of the front porch, then sprint-tiptoes across the cold grass.

Hero comes bounding toward him from behind the house. Somehow he knows not to bark. Alex reaches down to scratch the underside of his chin. "Stay, Hero."

Hero whines, paws the dirt ground.

Alex retrieves his bike from behind the shed. Quietly, he back-heels the kickstand up, guides the bike off the grass and onto the dirt road. Swaying left to right, right to left, he pumps the pedals, coaxing speed into the bike. The surrounding fields become spinning plates of earth lined with neat cultivated rows. Nearby trees rush past, while those farther away, gray silhouettes against the darkening skies, glide slower or hardly at all. A tractor left out in the middle of the fields is an iceberg in a black sea. Wind flows past him, rustling his jacket.

He cuts across the neighbor's fields—a shortcut his parents have forbidden. Not that the Marshalls would mind. They're good, hardworking people, and the two families have always gotten along. When Alex was born, the Marshalls celebrated with a shivaree—a traditional serenade accompanied by clanging pots and pans and jubilant shouting that shocked his parents. Sometimes during picking season when Filipino itinerant workers are hard to find, the fathers help each other out, working well into the night.

A stir in the fields. Something darting through the rows of crops, running alongside him.

"Hero!"

Hero barks once, twice, a joyous sound. Alex throws his head back and laughs. "You silly dog, Hero!"

He rides on, Hero racing by his side now. The stars beginning to emerge out of the darkening sky.

Fifteen minutes later, Alex crests the last hill. Below on the valley floor is his high school. The football field is lit up, shimmering like a snow globe. In that miniature world, bleachers are packed with townsfolk, and cars swing headlights into the last empty spots in the adjacent parking lot. On the field, he sees dots of players lined up in formation; a second later, like a swarm of wasps quickly scattered, they break apart. A distant *ooah* sounds from the packed bleachers.

Something about this sight—his whole town, all the people of Bainbridge Island contained in that small globe—catches him. A feeling twists in his rib cage, hard to identify. Even a minute later, coasting down the slope toward the field, Hero bounding next to him, he's still unsure of the emotion. If it is a deep affection. Or its opposite, a resentment.

Something is wrong. He senses it almost as soon as he pulls into school. He dismounts his bike, slants it against the brick façade of the gym. Staying in the shadows, he studies the scene. The bleachers are teeming with people, their cheerful din lifting into the night. Nothing out of the ordinary. Children running beneath the stands, high-school couples off to the side nearer the baseball diamond holding hands, people chatting in long lines at the concession stand. A festive atmosphere. But he still can't shake the feeling that something is off.

Charlie's words from her most recent letter come to him: *Even the familiar places somehow feel threatening.*

"Stay, Hero."

This time the dog obeys. He's a rural farm dog, and all the noise and lights and people spook him. Hero sits on his haunches, ears pinned back. Tense. A whimper as Alex walks away.

Through the bleachers, past the legs of the seated spectators, Alex catches blurs of movement on the field. The gleam of light reflecting off football helmets, the mash of bodies smacking into one another, the crack of shoulder pads in violent collision. The play ends; the crowd groans. The collective sound, a gargantuan roar that transforms the crowd into a beast, unnervingly alive.

Ahead, two boys are returning from the concession stand, hands full of licorice and Zagnut bars and bags of Cracker Jacks. Off to the side, a group of men, nursing bottles of beer, are laughing good-naturedly. They're West Seattle High Indians fans, judging from their sweatshirts emblazoned with the team mascot, an Indian Chief.

Alex steps on some discarded peanut shells. The cracking sounds seem inordinately loud, shotgun blasts. The group of men turns to him, their gale of laughter suddenly cut short. Or is he just imagining this?

Behind him, a car comes to a stop, its tires crunching on gravel. A few people turn to look, curious.

He keeps walking, his legs mismatching stilts, one shorter than the other. Suddenly unsure of how to swing his arms, like they're new appendages just hung on him. Certain that everyone is watching him. He thinks, *I am not supposed to be here.* He heads between two sections of the bleachers, the field opening up before him.

Bainbridge High's offense has taken the field. He sees the

players huddle, then break into formation, the linemen crouched and ready to pounce. A running play, by the looks of it.

Alex sees Frank step back from the center, and call out a last-second change in the play. Every eye in the packed stadium is focused on him. This is Frank's sanctuary, a world in which he's always found respect and order. Where the lines don't shift, the rules don't change, no matter what's happening in the outside world. And where, hidden behind his helmet, his exotic face has never mattered, where he gets to be hero. Frank has come to lose himself in this world one last time, to breathe in its good, decent, affirming air.

He starts shouting out play calls, pointing—

It's not Frank. Too small, too short. And the voice too high-pitched, too eager to please. It's Ernest Schwinn, the second-string quarterback.

Alex frowns. Did Frank get injured? He hurries forward, is about to walk into the stadium proper when he hears the sound of a dog barking.

The play starts. The running back takes off but is quickly swallowed up by the defense in a crash of helmets and pads. The crowd groans with disapproval.

As players pick themselves up and rehuddle, the dog's barking reemerges. Only now the barking is more urgent, insistent. Alex frowns. It's Hero. Several people are turning to look.

Alex hurries back to his bike. But Hero's not there. He's at the edge of the parking lot. Barking at a car, hackles raised.

The car is a Bainbridge Island police cruiser. An officer is leaning up against the trunk, arms folded, cup of coffee in one hand.

Someone walking toward the cruiser, escorted by another officer. This person, in football uniform, still in pads, wearing his helmet. As if not wanting to be recognized.

It's Frank. He gets into the back seat of the car, sits in the middle, away from the windows. Hero barking, growling at the officers. The group of four men from earlier gaze smugly, one or two grinning, bottles of beer pressed against the Indian Chief mascot on their sweatshirts. Several onlookers, hushed in these few seconds, observing. No one asking questions, no one objecting, no one raising their voice.

The officer shuts the back door before getting into the front passenger seat. The car backs up, then starts to pull away. Alex searches for Frank's eyes. But inside the darkness of both car and helmet, his face is enshrouded, unreadable. The car takes off in a cloud of dust.

From the field, the crowd roars with delight.

Alex grabs his bike, chases after the police cruiser, Hero by his side. When it becomes obvious that the cruiser is headed not to the local precinct but to his farm, Alex carves a new shortcut through the woods. About twelve minutes later, chest exploding, he crests a hill overlooking his farm, and that's when he again catches sight of the police cruiser.

It's about a half mile from home, approaching the final turn into the dusty road that leads home. Its brake lights burn red as it pulls over, coming to a stop. A few seconds pass. Then the rear passenger door swings open, and Frank steps out. He leans over to say something to the driver before stepping away. The cruiser turns around, is about to drive off, when it stops. One of the officers steps out, cradling a football helmet, and jogs over to Frank. He hands the helmet over, lightly patting Frank on the shoulder as he does. He returns to the cruiser and drives away.

Frank stares at the disappearing car, then heads up the long dusty road to home.

"What happened?" Alex says when he catches up to Frank.

Frank turns to him. The drained look on his face—it stops Alex cold in his tracks.

"I told you to stay home," he says, his voice lifeless.

"Frank? What happened? Did you get hurt? Is it your bum ankle again?"

He doesn't answer. Starts turning back around.

"Frank?"

"I'm fine."

"Then why—"

"Someone on the other team. Or maybe one of their fans." His voice low, a groan. He looks away. "Somebody called the cops. Said there's a Jap breaking curfew."

Alex blinks. "But you're the quarterback—"

Frank snorts. "At least the cops didn't take me in. They said it was total baloney but they couldn't ignore the call. So they drove me home."

Alex dismounts the bike. "What about Coach Swenson? He just let this happen? He didn't put up a fight for you?"

Frank shakes his head.

"And your teammates, they—"

"What the hell could they have done?" he snaps.

"They could've protested! Could have threatened to walk out!"

His face hardens. "You're so stupid, Alex." He starts striding home.

Alex reels backward, stunned. "But Frank—"

"Shut up, Alex!" He stops, spins around. "And don't bring this up again. Ever again. You get me?"

"Frank—"

"I said shut the hell up!" Spittle flies out of his mouth.

Alex flinches. The football pads on Frank make his already broad shoulders even more imposing. But his face is crumbling, like scaffolding collapsing. Alex has never seen Frank look this way. On the bus three days ago, when Frank first found out about the evacuation, he'd looked like he'd been slapped in the face, kicked in the gut.

But now he looks knifed in the heart.

"Mother doesn't need to know," Frank says after a moment, his voice surprisingly quiet. He gazes down the road, to the dark outline of their home. Inside, Mother sleeping and probably dreaming, as she always says she does, of lazy summer afternoons on the tatami mat slurping on *zaru soba,* the sound of cicadas chirping outside. "She'd worry if she found out. And she's got enough on her mind."

Alex nods. He knows now why the police stopped so far from their house. Frank had asked them to. The car's arrival on the gravel road would have awakened Mother, and seeing her son in a police cruiser would have upset her.

"Okay," Alex says softly.

The boys head home in silence. Hero walks between the boys, whimpering once or twice. Sensing something is not right.

13

Dear Alex,

Something exciting happened!

All day I was in a bad mood. I was thinking I am like that frog in boiling water. I have done nothing but foolishly believe if we give up our radios, obey curfew, stop going to cafés and theaters and parks and swimming pools, stop gathering outside on the streets after synagogue service, if we did all these things, then all this will pass and everything will return to normal.

I got so angry at myself.

And then you know what? I said enough! And I decided at that moment to do something. To resist.

And so I did. I resisted.

It was only a small act. But it felt much bigger. Does this make sense?

I went to the cinema. It was packed. I was lucky to find an empty seat in the very middle. I sat down in the velvet seat. German soldiers were in the very best seats near the front, a whole row of them Boches. Laughing and shouting like they owned the place, like this was their country and we were the visitors. I hated their smart uniforms, their big smiles, their confidence.

But I didn't do anything. Not then. I waited for the right moment.

The theater lights dimmed. The audience hushed. My heart began to thump so loudly. How could no one else hear it?

The newsreel began. The usual Nazi propaganda nonsense: a loud German voice narrating about German soldiers marching through yet another foreign town; Göring at some stupid ceremony; Hitler visiting the wounded at a hospital. Blaring trumpets proclaiming victory for the Third Reich. On and on.

Two minutes in. Now. Now was the time to stop being a sitting frog. And instead become a frog that leaps out of boiling water.

I clutched the armrests, my fingers turning white. Then I pinched my lips together and . . . whistled.

It was scary. It was thrilling. It felt righteous.

No one noticed at first. I whistled again, louder this time. A few people near me sat up straighter in their seats, tensing. Heads half turned toward me. But that didn't stop me. I whistled again. And again. More bodies turned my way.

And then from somewhere else in the dark theater, a wonderful sound: another person whistling. And then a hiss, from the other side of the theater. And before I knew it, there must have been a dozen other people whistling and hissing. An amazing sound.

I sat, covered in cold sweat, with my heart beating hot blood through me. Alex, for the first time in so long, I did not feel powerless. I did not feel invisible. I had substance.

The Nazi officers were furious. They stood up, barked at the audience in German. How dare we do this during the newsreel? But there was little they could do in the darkness. One of them stormed out. When the lights came on a minute later, everyone blinked under the harsh glare. The Germans demanded to know who hissed and whistled. But nobody in the audience spoke up. No one pointed at me, not even the two men sitting on my sides who must have known.

Even now, hours later, my heart is still pounding. All of Paris is asleep but I feel alive for the first time in so long. And now I want to do more. I have heard about a resistance group made up of Jewish teenagers: *Éclaireurs Israélites de France*. I will do everything I can to find and join them. Because when I am old and look back on this time, I want no regrets. I want to know that in this brief moment of darkness and fear, I was not just a spoilt rich Parisian girl who did nothing. I want to look back and know that I lived courageously, I stood up to evil and made a difference. That I was a leaping frog.

Wonder Woman is gazing down at me now with a look of approval: "Well done, young lady," she seems to be saying. "You will go far in this world."

Hazak v'ematz!
Charlie

(Date illegible)

Dear Charlie,

I wish I could be more like you. I wish I could have the courage to fight back. To be a leaping frog. It's too late for me now. I sat at the bottom of this pot for too long, naively hoping things would improve on their own. But I know you won't make the same mistake. You're a fighter, with spunk. You're a leaping frog.

Alex

14

The last few days pass by in a blur. Six days to pack up. Six days to make arrangements for the farm. To decide what to throw away and what to store, what to pack and what to burn.

Nineteen years to build a life. Six days to make it all go away.

Still it must be done. The clothes will not fold themselves, the books will not pack themselves. When Alex and Frank return home from school this last week, they find Mother on her knees packing boxes in the attic, or in the living room scrubbing the floorboards clean, or in the bedroom dusting the shelves.

Why, Mother? they ask, exasperated. They see her drained body, hear her labored breathing. *It doesn't matter. Not anymore. Who cares if the house is dusty or the floor dirty? We're leaving.*

But still she labors.

Six days until evacuation. Then five. Four, three. And now, only two.

When Alex returns home that day, he finds Mother carrying a packed box down to the basement. A sheen of sweat covering her face even in the cold.

"Mother," he chides, taking the box from her. In the basement are dozens of stacked boxes lining the walls. He opens the nearest ones. Clothes, sweaters, jackets, all neatly folded, a few mothballs thrown in. Inside other boxes he finds books, framed pictures, old teddy bears. Their whole lives now stored and hidden away in darkness like skeletons in a coffin.

He hears voices from above. A man's voice. In the kitchen. Mumbled English.

He heads upstairs. Through the window he sees a dented pickup truck with chipped paint parked outside, one he's never seen before. In the cargo bed, a piano and oak farmhouse table secured by rope. He recognizes both items: over the years he's eaten at that very table and performed on that piano during family recitals at the Yamadas' home.

A stranger is standing in the kitchen. A beefy white man in dirty denim overalls towering over Mother. His boots still on, a trail of mud left behind. "I'll take the fridge for five bucks and the clock for one." He has the brusque air of a man in charge granting favors.

"What's going on?" Alex says.

The man turns around, hooks his meaty fingers around his suspenders. The short stub of a cigarette dangles from the corner of his mouth. Smoke curling up. "Thought I'd come by and help you guys out." The cigarette bobs up and down as he speaks. "I've made a quality offer on a few of your things. Your ma was just about to say yes."

Alex looks at Mother. Standing perfectly still in the corner of the kitchen, impossibly petite against this large imposing man. Her face starch white, her wiry frame sharp. She's upset.

Something catches the man's eye. He walks over to the glass-door cabinet, throws open the door. He pulls out a stack of Wedgwood china and brings it over to the table. These are the limited-edition plates Father splurged on years ago, after she gave birth to Alex. They use them only twice a year, on Thanksgiving and Christmas. The man slides a plate out of its protective velvet sleeve, licks his lips. "I'll take these for a buck. Total, that is." He pats down on them with his fat, grubby hands, his wedding band clinking against the ceramic.

"Too cheap," Mother says. "These plates expensive. Twenty dollars just for plates."

The man laughs. "No."

"The refrigerator thirty dollars," Mother says. "And the clock, you cannot buy. We don't sell."

The man laughs again but this time with a mocking tone, as if at her accent. He scratches his scruffy beard where peanut butter is smeared on a few bristles. "Where you're going, you won't be needing a refrigerator. Or a grandfather clock, or these plates."

"You give me forty dollars, I give you plates and the refrigerator."

Now the smile disappears completely. "Listen, lady." His eyes are cold pinpoints in his jowly face. "Case you don't realize, I'm doing you a favor. I'm offering you a fair price for these items."

"You think you're offering a fair price?" Alex cuts in. "You're insulting us, you're—"

"Quit your sermonizing, right now, son," the man snarls, snapping his fingers. "Don't think for a minute that the second you're gone other folks less honorable than me ain't gonna come up here and help themselves to what's left behind. Strip this place clean." He turns back to Mother. "So I suggest you accept my offer with an appreciative bow of the head and a really nice *ally-ga-toh*."

Mother stares at him. She only understood about a quarter of his words, but she understands him completely. She walks over to the kitchen table, picks up the plate.

"You want this?" she says. The plate trembles in her hands. "For one dollar?"

The man tut-tuts. "One dollar for all of them—"

She lifts her hand, raising the plate.

"Hey—" he starts to say.

She smashes the plate to the floor. The shatter is a thunder-clap, the pieces flying in every direction.

"And you want this?" she says, removing another plate from its velvet sleeve. Her voice, high-pitched now. "One dollar?" She picks it up, smashes it at his feet.

"Daggum it, woman." He glares at her, eyes wide. "You people have it coming for you." His elbow catches the stack of plates as he storms out, knocking them over.

"Hey!" Alex shouts.

The man brushes past him, the ripe stink of body odor thick and pungent. "When you Japs are done with your prison time," he shouts over his shoulder, "don't even think about coming back here. Ever." He smacks open the screen door, drives away.

15

And then there is only one day until evacuation.

The Japanese church service that Sunday morning is a somber affair. People are exhausted, having spent the last few days scrambling to get their affairs in order. Rushing to lease or sell their land. To pack and store what they cannot carry with them. To liquidate every asset, selling off their cars, boats, freezers, for pennies on the dollar. They mumble through "A Mighty Fortress Is Our God," their minds burdened with a thousand worries and fears and anxieties.

Alex sits in a state of disbelief. He still cannot believe they're all leaving tomorrow. That come this time next week, this sanctuary will be completely empty in the morning hour. The whole Japanese congregation absent, vanished as if Raptured away.

He thinks of the empty farmlands, the empty storefronts, the idle trucks. Will anyone notice? He thinks of Bainbridge High School, how at this time tomorrow, his desk will be empty in an otherwise full classroom. The teachers will continue to teach, bells will continue to ring throughout the day, students will continue to crowd hallways and goof off and laugh aloud. Life will go on. But Alex will be gone.

Will anyone care? Will anyone notice?

After church service, Mother, Alex, and Frank—who's been

morose and silent since the football-game incident—stop by the hardware store to pick up a few last-minute items. Like string to tie around their suitcases, and canteens for—according to rumors—a forced march through the California desert.

On the way back, Alex asks Frank to stop by church. "I left my scarf in the pew," he says. "Please, Frank."

The sanctuary is empty when Alex walks in alone. It'll be another hour before the regular congregation begins their service, and this is the dead in-between time. He walks down the center aisle, and it isn't until he reaches his pew that he realizes there's someone else in the sanctuary.

Jessica Tanner.

She's two rows in front and hasn't noticed him. She's bent over, picking something off the pew. Alex thinks to duck away before she notices him. But too late: her eyes flick up to meet his.

"Oh, hi," she says, straightening. Her face is slightly flushed from bending over. In one hand she's got a stack of worship bulletins. "My week to set up for our service," she says.

Alex nods, not sure what to say.

"Are you looking for this?" She holds up his scarf. "I found it under your pew."

He nods. "Thanks." He doesn't know what to say. The sanctuary seems too quiet and empty and airy. He hears the clock on the balcony *ticktock* louder than he's ever heard it. He gives a quick smile, turning to leave—

"Are you looking forward to it?" she asks.

"Huh?"

"Tonight's dance."

"Oh." He shuffles his feet. "Umm. I don't think I'll make it."

Her eyebrows arch with genuine concern. "You should totally come. It's gonna be real fun." She looks at him earnestly. "Seriously."

He doesn't fault her for forgetting about the curfew. It's not her world, not her problem. "I . . . the curfew." He stares down at his feet. The silence is excruciating.

She looks confused, then turns bright red. "Oh my gosh, I'm sorry, I totally forgot—"

"No, no, no," he says, holding his hands up. "It's no big deal. Besides, I have some last-minute packing to do."

"Packing?" Her blue eyes narrow with confusion; then, with an almost audible gasp, they widen with realization. Her hand flies to her mouth. "When do you leave?"

"Tomorrow."

"*Tomorrow?*" Her eyes glisten over. "So soon? Oh, Alex, I'm so sorry."

Alex is taken aback by this unexpected—but sincere—show of emotion. He's not sure what to say, only that he should say something. "Yeah, so this is my last day," he settles on saying.

"When will you be back?"

Alex doesn't know. No one does. After the Japanese church service that morning, some folks were saying the evacuation would last only a couple of months. Others suspected it would be longer, a year. Maybe two. A few thought it might be permanent.

But no one knows for sure. No one even knows where the evacuation will take them. Rumors have circulated, of course: they'll be taken across the northern border, to Canada. Or across the seas back to Japan. Or to the California desert where they'll be shot to death. Or simply left there under the baking sun to die from the harsh elements.

"I don't know," he finally says.

Her soft blue eyes shimmer in the dull light. "I'm going to miss you, Alex." She says this with the certitude and openness that only those at the very top of the social pecking order can afford.

He nervously twists the scarf in his hands. "Yeah, me too."

"We've known each other for how long? Since fifth grade?"

"First."

"First grade? Well, don't we go way back!" she says with a smile, and a flip of the hair. She glances at the clock. "Well, I gotta go clean up the Sunday-school classrooms."

The sanctuary is quiet again as she sideways her way out of the pew. The clock ticking loudly, its second hand shivering forward. He wishes he could grab it, make time stop. Or even make it go backward to when life was simpler, to before the Pearl Harbor attack, when everything was normal. When life was calm. Not this raging river full of frothy whitecaps and swirling eddies, pitching him helplessly toward the crest of an unknown, plunging waterfall.

"Jessica!" he says loudly, surprising both of them.

She blinks. "Yes?"

An air bubble is caught in his throat, making his voice high-pitched and vacuous. "I'm going to the dance tonight."

Her head cants to the side. "I thought you just said . . . What about the curfew?"

"I'm going for just a short while. Ten minutes. If I leave the dance at seven forty, I'll make it home in time."

"Oh." A tinge of confusion enters her eyes.

He wrings the scarf. "So if you're there at seven thirty, right when it begins . . ."

She stares back with wide, questioning eyes, not really following him.

He forces the next words out. "Can I dance with you . . . just once at the start of the dance tonight? Before I have to leave?" He flicks his eyes up to hers.

She seems confused, her eyebrows knit together. But then, in a blink, her expression changes and she's smiling at him. "That's so sweet, Alex. I'd love to dance with you."

"Really?" He inhales sharply. "That's great."

"Okay, then!" She spins around quickly. At the door, just before she walks out, she turns to give him a smile. "See you then!"

And suddenly the sanctuary seems brighter. The ticking of the clock slower, quieter, until he doesn't even hear it anymore.

That night, after Alex is done washing the dishes, he walks to the front door as casually as he can. "I left a book in the coop." He throws on a jacket. "Be right back." He swings the door open, pretends to take in the dusk sky. "Hmm. Looks like a beautiful sunset. Might go for a walk."

"Not too far, it's almost curfew." Mother wipes a plate dry, sets it down. "And we have to get up early tomorrow. The truck's picking us up at eight thirty. You know this."

"I won't be long."

Frank, looking up from his comics, doesn't say anything.

Alex lets the door shut behind him. He fights the urge to sprint, and strolls over to the shed where hours earlier he hid a box of clothes and placed his bike out of sight. He undresses quickly; his fingers tremble with cold, or maybe excitement. He kicks off his work boots, slips into his favorite pair of swing dancers. These are two-toned oxfords Charlie sent him a couple of years ago, a popular style from her father's factory in Paris. He'd outgrown them by at least two sizes now. But he's refused to throw them away, mostly because they're from Charlie, but also because he honestly digs the style. The fancy wing tips, the pattern swirls, the distinctive monk strap. They're worth the blisters he's sure to get.

By the time he arrives at school, twenty minutes later, it's already seven thirty. Quickly, he stows his bike against a fence, and checks his suit by the light of a distant headlight.

He stops, dismayed.

There's mud splattered all over his shoes. He can't go in like this. But the thought that Jessica Tanner might be inside waiting for him—for *him*—with her hair done up and maybe perfume spritzed lightly on her neck settles it.

Licking his palms and tamping down his hair, he makes his way through the parking lot to the front entrance and into the auditorium.

This is Alex's first dance and he has yet to learn basic truths about school dances. First truth: no one comes on time. Second truth: no one steps onto the dance floor for at least half an hour.

So when he enters the assembly hall, he at first thinks there must be a mistake. Only a few colored lights flash on the dance floor. The music hasn't even started playing yet. And other than a few volunteer staff and juniors, the place is empty. No sign of Jessica Tanner.

He finds the darkest corner and waits there.

Ten minutes pass. Fifteen. Only a handful of students have walked in. They're all chatting on the far side of the hall. Twenty minutes later, he's still in his dark corner. A few students have thrown curious looks his way, but no one has said a word to him. It's now past eight o'clock, past curfew. He should leave. He *has* to leave.

It isn't until almost eight fifteen when a flood of classmates, as if by some prearranged agreement, pour into the auditorium. For a few minutes they mingle around the edge of the dance floor, no one quite daring to dance. Only after a trio of cool kids walk onto the floor and start jiving does the dam break. Everyone surges onto the floor, and the evening begins in earnest.

Jessica Tanner still has not appeared.

I'll wait until eight thirty. But eight thirty comes and goes, and still there's no sign of her. Then he sees someone who, like him, shouldn't be here. Someone who sticks out.

Frank. Somehow he knew to find Alex here.

He is standing off to the side, scanning the hall. It takes him only a few seconds to find Alex. As if he knew better than to search the dance floor, and instead searched out the darkest corners.

"Alex," he says, not unkindly, walking up to him. "We need to go. Mom's worried."

Alex shakes his head.

"Alex."

A group of boys turn to watch. Alex shoves his hands into his pockets. "I'm staying."

Frank puts a hand on Alex's shoulder, gives it a light squeeze. In the kindest voice Alex has ever heard him speak, somehow audible even through the blaring music, he says, "Alex. She's not coming."

Alex looks up at his brother. Frank's eyes are full of understanding. "Come on, buddy. Let's go home." He turns around and walks away. After a few seconds, Alex follows him out.

They drive back in silence, the lights of the school fading in the side mirror. Before them, the darkness of the open country swallows them whole. Every time they hit a bump in the road, his bike clanks against the metal siding of the cargo bed. The bike can get nicked up for all he cares. He won't be needing it anymore. He could have just left it at school.

"She said she'd be there."

Frank turns off the radio. "Jessica Tanner?"

Alex looks at Frank in surprise. "How'd you know?"

"When we stopped by church this afternoon. Saw her coming out right before you, blushing a little. Figured it was her." He elbows Alex softly. "I know I encouraged you to take someone out, to go bowling or a movie. But *Jessica Tanner*? Jeez, Alex. You couldn't aim a little lower?"

Alex doesn't say anything. Stares out the windshield, at dark unlit lampposts flying past them. The car hits a rut in the road, bounces unsteadily.

Frank pulls out a smoke, expertly lighting it while still steering. "Don't get me wrong, Alex. I like what you did. It was gutsy. You said to hell with stupid curfew rules, and to hell with the worst odds known to mankind. You broke out of your shell and went for it no holds barred. You went for the Hail Mary."

"It's not what you think."

"No?" He looks over at Alex, and surprises him by offering him a cigarette.

Alex holds it between his fingers, not lighting it. The car hits another bump in the road. Alex stares ahead, past the farthest reach of the headlight beams, at the gaping mouth of darkness waiting there. "I didn't do it because of *her*. Not really. I did it because . . ." He pauses, trying to find the words. "It's like how you *had* to be at school this past Friday night. Because you wanted to play football."

"I'm the quarterback," Frank says defensively. "The team needed me. Why wouldn't I want to be there?"

"That's not what I mean. Not exactly."

Frank opens the window a crack, blows smoke out. "Then what *exactly* do you mean?"

Alex pauses, sorting out his thoughts. "I just wanted to feel . . . normal. Like a regular American teen. Not a *Jap*. Not a *nonalien*. Just a normal teen boy getting to dance with a pretty girl at a school dance. And tonight was my last chance. One last gasp before we go under."

He turns to look at Frank. "Because I don't know when we'll be back here, Frankie," he says, his voice cracking slightly. "I don't know if we'll ever get to be teenagers again."

Frank doesn't say anything. He keeps his eyes focused forward. After a moment, he flicks the cigarette butt away, and steps harder on the accelerator. Night flies past them, at them. Stars break out overhead, hard and sharp as tacks. Alex thinks of swirling eddies and frothing whitecaps and raging rivers and unknown waterfalls.

Back in the house, Alex expects a scolding from Mother. But she only stares briefly at his clothes, then offers him some left-over soup before retiring for the night. Frank turns in early, too.

Left alone downstairs, Alex stares out the window. He still hopes for a pair of headlights to appear in the driveway. For a car to pull up, Jessica Tanner to emerge in a pretty dress, her hair made up. *Just because it's curfew for you, doesn't mean we can't have our own little dance here,* she says with a smile.

But of course that never happens. Jessica Tanner never comes. Alex doesn't sleep a wink; he's up all night until the dawn sun rises and it is evacuation day, and now nothing will ever happen, everything is too late.

16

They wait on the front porch with their luggage neatly piled: six duffel bags fashioned out of a hardy corduroy-like material bought at Montgomery Ward. Dangling off each bag is a label inscribed with MAKI.

"So strange not to have Hero around," Frank says.

"He'll be fine with the Marshalls," Mother says, her voice a bit hollow. "Where's the truck? It's late."

Frank gets up, bored, brushes dirt off his pants. He peers into the mailbox out of habit, not expecting to find anything. "Oh, look," he says, surprised, pulling out an envelope stuck to the bottom of the mailbox. It's full of overlapping international postmarks.

Alex stands up immediately, takes the letter. It's slightly damp, with dirt caked into a corner. "How long has it been sitting in there?"

Frank shrugs. "It was caught on something. Never saw it until just now."

Usually, Alex tears open Charlie's letters immediately, devouring them in a minute. But this time he stops himself. He slides the unopened letter into the inner pocket of his jacket. He'll save it for the trip. Something to look forward to.

A large military truck, covered with a thick green canvas, finally arrives, an hour late.

Two soldiers jump out the back. They're in full military garb, wearing hard hats, cuffed trousers, and dark-green uniforms with strapped vests. The taller of the two steps forward. "Mrs. Mayumi Maki, Mr. Francis Maki, and Mr. Alex Maki?" The soldier is holding a rifle with a fixed bayonet, sunlight glinting off it.

"Call me Frank."

The other soldier, examining the piled luggage, glares at him. "Didn't you read the instructions? It's supposed to be only what you can carry."

"And it is," Frank says. "We can carry all of this."

The soldier sets down his rifle and starts loading the duffel bags. Alex helps Mother up into the covered back of the truck. She sits on a wooden-slat bench while Frank helps load up. Her eyes wander over the empty porch, the locked front door, the empty backyard.

They push off, the truck kicking up dust. They pass the coop out back, the sheds with peeling paint, the old tire hanging from the tree. This, the last Alex will see of his home for a long time, the last time he'll smell the strawberries already beginning to bloom and which the Marshalls have promised to help crop. The last time to see their farm, their home.

But it doesn't seem real, this farewell. None of it does. In the back of his mind, he still believes he'll be back later: later that day, later that week, later that month. It cannot be that they are being taken away. It cannot be that they can be wrenched away from their very own land and house *when they have done absolutely nothing wrong.* It cannot be that his motherland can be this cold-blooded, that she can be this ruthless to the bastard child he once only suspected he was but now at last knows he must be.

The army truck makes another stop along the way. The Tanaka family in a wealthier part of town. Their father—a successful businessman in the burgeoning grocery industry—was taken away months ago.

Mrs. Tanaka greets them with a tense nod, bowing as she climbs into the truck. The two Tanaka girls, twelve and ten, sit closely on either side of her. Like everyone else, the girls are wearing brown identification tags that hang off their coats like department-store price tags.

The truck heaves forward. The Tanaka girls, wearing thick overcoats, blink in synchrony. They seem bewildered. The older girl gazes out at the passing homes. She is looking for something. Or someone.

She stares at one house in particular as it slowly drifts by, a tall house with a steep, gabled roof. Scattered in the front yard are overturned bikes and crate scooters and Shirley Temple dolls and Red Ryder BB guns. Unlike the neighboring homes, all the curtains of this house are still drawn like eyelids clenched shut. As they pass, the older girl swivels her head, watching intently for any sign of movement within: a curtain drawn, a window opened, a door swung open. But nothing moves; no one comes running out. She softly bites her lower lip and when she closes her eyes, Alex sees a single tear slip out.

A few minutes before eleven, the truck slows on the south side of Eagle Harbor, stopping at the rear of a convoy of empty army trucks. A large crowd is gathered at the opposite end. More than two hundred Issei and Nisei, the young and the old, stand and sit in orderly fashion, as quiet as attendees at a funeral. Only the children make noise as they scamper around, too young to understand the enormity of the situation.

"Looks like we're one of the last to arrive," the soldier says. "Come on, let's hurry." A handful of other soldiers, identically uniformed, walk over to help out. They quickly unload the luggage.

They walk, Frank and Alex on either side of Mother.

Mrs. Tanaka, clutching the hands of her girls, stumbles forward in a daze. The sunlight is muted behind a thin veil of clouds. A southerly breeze carries the rank smell of Murden Cove that comes at low tide when the mud flats and silt-covered banks are exposed.

No one speaks. Aside from the thump of boots, it's quiet. The usually busy Eagledale Pier is otherwise deserted.

What it actually feels like—and this thought strikes Alex like a hard slap to the face—is Bainbridge Island has turned its back on them. Closed its eyes, pretending not to see. Soon this disagreeable task will be done with, and they can wash their hands of this unpleasant affair and return, humming right along, to normalcy. The island cleansed.

"Are you all right, Mother?" Frank asks. "Are we walking too fast?"

She shakes her head ambiguously, her lips thinning.

Overhead, faintly, the shriek of a heron. Or perhaps the squawk of a bald eagle.

"What did you expect?" Frank says to Alex. "A big send-off?" He stares straight ahead. "Nope. To them, we're already gone."

They reach the waiting group of evacuees and drop their luggage. Everyone is dressed in their best clothing. Fedora hats and dark suits and double-breasted peacoats, knee-length coats with fur collars, dresses with crocheted collars, cashmere sweaters, hosiery, silk stockings, bobby socks, buckskin shoes, black oxfords. As if they're heading out for a night on the town, catching a show in downtown Seattle.

It's the dangling brown ID tag attached to their clothing that gives it away. These tags, with their names and ID numbers scrawled in, are identical to the tags on their luggage. As if they are no different from cargo to be shipped.

A quick head count is made. Minutes pass. A uniformed officer walks out with a bullhorn. Speaking with the same East

Coast accent as the other soldiers, he announces that everyone has been accounted for and the time has come to board the ferry. Walk in a straight line, he instructs, two abreast and no more. Soldiers are not to aid in carrying bags. Young children may be carried. Do not stop. Do not talk. Keep walking.

They pick up their suitcases. They walk two abreast, each carrying their own suitcase. Leaving without fuss, without tears, as if they weren't being torn from this island they had sunk deep roots into, figuratively and literally; as if they weren't leaving behind three million pounds of strawberry; as if they weren't leaving empty desks and chairs in their classrooms and roster spots on varsity sports teams. They walk in silence, dutifully and without protest; with a quiet dignity, they tell themselves, but this is a lie and maybe they know it, because this silence is really nothing but the shock and shame of the dispossessed.

Be the leaping frog, Alex thinks to himself. *Do something. Say something.* But he cannot.

And then.

As they round the bend and walk toward the serpentine wall of the ferry landing, something in the air changes. The faint stink of Murden Cove is replaced by the scent of recently cut cedar. But it's more than the smell that changes.

Alex looks up. He hears a low murmur coming from around the bend. Those in the front are walking faster, their backs straightening, their strides longer and faster. Alex sees some of their arms rise, their hands waving back and forth.

Those in the back, curious now, walk faster.

"What's going on?" Mother asks, but neither Frank nor Alex answer. Laughter sounds from up ahead, squeals of delight. Some children race ahead, and it's only as Alex approaches the bend that he sees.

People. Scores of them.

They're standing on sidewalks behind a barricade. For a moment he thinks another Japanese American community—possibly from Terminal Island or Vashon—has been brought here to join the Bainbridge Island group. A collection point before shipping them all off together to who knows where.

But these people are white. With blond and brown and auburn hair, and blue and green and brown eyes. Bainbridge Island friends and neighbors standing on tired legs, having waited for hours, now smiling, now waving. They've come out in droves to bid them farewell and good luck and Godspeed.

"Yo, Frank, yo, over here!" Frank's head whips around faster than Alex has ever seen it turn. It's Preston Wilcox, a senior in high school and one of Frank's closer friends. Frank does a "no way!" face and walks over to the sidewalk, grinning ear to ear.

"What are you doing here?" Frank says, play-punching his friend in the chest. "You're supposed to be in school."

"Had to say goodbye, bro."

"Any excuse to cut class, eh?" Frank says. Two others run over. They talk, joking, smiling. When a soldier slowly ambles toward them, Frank gives them quick hugs, and breaks off.

They walk on. Every once in a while someone will call out for one of the evacuees, and there will be laughter, and hugs, and tears. Whenever Frank hears a friend yell out his name, he'll wave back and say something witty, his face beaming, his magnetic charisma rolling off his square shoulders.

Halfway down the street, Alex elbows his brother lightly. "Look. It's Principal Dennis."

Frank doesn't waste a second. He walks over to the sidewalk, taking his hat off and holding it against his chest. "Principal Dennis?"

"Frank Maki. Good to see you."

Frank pauses. "I want to thank you. For letting my friends cut school to see me—to see all of us—off. It means a lot."

Principal Roy Dennis grips Frank's shoulder. "It's the least I could do. Because this is a terrible injustice, and we'll never live it down as a community, as a nation. It'll be a blight on us. I'm so very sorry."

"You needn't be, sir," Frank says, shaking the principal's hand. The moment is broken up by a group of boys, maybe a half dozen, running over, all of them wearing varsity football jackets.

"Here's the lughead!"

"Oh, the chumps are here," Frank jokes back, smiling broadly. "How the heck did you guys blow the game? Didn't I leave you with a big enough lead? Don't say you don't need me."

"It's the lousy replacement quarterback, he's to blame," someone jokes, and Alex is surprised to see that it's Ernest Schwinn. The replacement quarterback.

There's laughter, more joking. Then someone shoves a varsity jacket in front of Frank.

"Eight, that's your number, right, Frank?"

Frank is stunned. He swallows hard, his eyes welling up. "Fellas . . ."

"Just take it, Captain."

He looks at his teammates for a long moment, then puts the jacket on. A perfect fit. He runs his fingers over the team emblem, over the embroidered lettering of the school.

"I'll wear it with pride," he says, all choked up.

"You'll wear it after you pay us back. That jacket cost us an arm and a leg, you dolt."

Frank laughs, then turns around before they can see the tears in his eyes.

They are everywhere, small groups of people breaking off to say goodbye. Smiling, squealing, dabbing at tears, lots of *You've been great friends*es and *See ya later*s and *Come back soon*s.

They reach the wooden ferry dock. Now it is just the evacuees, and the soldiers, of course. Their boots clocking on the gangplanks, hollow drumbeats. The gentle tide of the sound lapping against the wooden beams of the dock. The waters sparkling in fractals of reflected light.

By now the soldiers are doing what they were specifically instructed not to do. They are helping out. They are carrying suitcases and duffel bags and belongings wrapped in tablecloths. They are carrying in their arms small children whose mothers, their husbands long whisked away, are burdened down with luggage. Many of the soldiers, themselves far from their New Jersey homes, gaze off into the distance, eyes damp. In front of Alex, a soldier walks with a rifle slung over his back while holding the hand of a toddler. *That's America for you,* Alex thinks. *An absurd contradiction.*

By eleven twenty, all have boarded the *Kelohken*. The gangplank is raised with a loud clang, and the ferry pulls away from the pier, churning the waters. Almost all of the 227 evacuees stay on the deck. They wave and shout their last goodbyes across the waters. Soon enough, as the ferry leaves Eagle Harbor and crosses into the sound, the inland voices wane and the people grow smaller until they, and the island, are gone.

17

The ferry crosses Puget Sound and enters the dock in Seattle. The evacuees might as well have crossed an ocean. Here on Colman Dock the throng of onlookers on an overpass shake their fists and spit down on the group. Scruffy men armed with shotguns shout, "You Nips go back to Japan!"

The evacuees enter an old Pullman train, glad to be away from the leering onlookers. Seating is assigned by family, and crammed. The children, most riding a train for the first time, are excited; but even this initial wave quickly gives way to restlessness. To placate them, grandparents unwrap candy they'd meant to give on the second or third day (or the fifth or seventh, for they still haven't a clue how long the journey will be).

Teenagers swivel their heads about like submarine periscopes, looking to see where their friends are seated, and are disappointed to find themselves alone, or elated when they find the pretty girl they never worked up the nerve to speak to is sitting across the aisle and now they are thinking with stupid optimism that this train trip could be the luckiest thing to happen to them.

What will we do about food? the parents wonder as the train takes off. An unlucky few are seated in facing bays of four or six seats, and already territorial struggles over legroom and suitcase storage have, politely for now, begun. *Where will I put my dentures at night? What happens if we get sick? Will they give out blankets at night when the temperature drops? Where is the toilet? Where are we going?*

Dusk arrives. Soldiers walk down the aisle. "Close the shades." At first, no one complies. The soldiers must be joking—why pull the shades down at night? "Just do it," a soldier gruffly orders.

By eight o'clock, most evacuees have fallen asleep, exhausted by the long day. The train has traveled only a few dozen miles inland, crawling at a snail's pace. Stop and go, stop and go, the axles groaning, the couplings straining, stopping on side rails to let pass other trains carrying war materials and supplies. "The Victory Trains come first," someone intones.

Only a single portable gas lamp, hanging in the center of each train car, illuminates the interior. The faint light falls like a disease on the ghostly, slumbering occupants. Children lie sprawled over their parents, feet dangling into the aisle. Those still awake sit with heads hanging, the constant rocking motion and lack of fresh air making them nauseous. A few play cards in the weak light, the usual rummy or Goofspiel.

An old man screams out in his sleep, a garbled mix of both English and Japanese. An elderly woman coughs over and over, unable to extricate the ball of phlegm stuck in her throat. A newborn in the row behind Alex whimpers, becomes hysterical. Then the faint sound of a mother cooing, followed by the rustling of clothes. Then wet sucking sounds. A few minutes later, a small burp.

Alex, awakened by all the noise, tries to settle into a comfortable position. He can't. Too much noise, too much fear, too many people pressing in on all sides.

He sighs, then takes out Charlie's most recent letter, still unopened. He'd meant to save it for later, but he needs escape now. But with curtains drawn across the window, it's too dark to read.

He pulls the curtain up and over his head, ducking under it like a child playing hide-and-seek. Pressed up against the window and sealed off from everyone else, he blinks as bright moonlight washes over him. Outside, the grand sweep of the moonlit land-scape passes slowly by, its barrenness broken up by the occa-sional wild bush or dried riverbed. It is an alien landscape of a distant, uninhabitable planet.

He opens the envelope, pulls out the letter. Five pages, all double-sided. A long letter. Good. He reads. When he is done, he turns back to the last page and reads it again.

And so last night I did something I know was dangerous. And stupid.

I went outside after curfew. I heard that the Éclaireurs Israélites de France move at night, and I hope to find a runner. So I can join this resistance group. After my parents fell asleep, I went out.

Paris after curfew was so quiet and empty. The buildings were dark and silent. Like tombstones. Because there was no gasoline traf-fic, the night was filled with the smell of flowers, trees, shrubs. It felt like I was walking in a cemetery at night.

I saw no one on the empty streets. Not a resistance runner, not a gendarme, not a single German solider. But I did not mind. Because it felt like Paris was all mine. And each step I took felt like I was getting back my city. Mine again, mine. Down rue de l'Ecole-de-Médecine, rue Antoine-Dubois, rue de Médicis. Mine, mine.

I kept walking for many hours. It was dangerous. One time a car drove by, its headlamps covered in a blue cloth. But I hid in a dark alley.

I walked to the Jardin du Luxembourg. It was so empty and beau-tiful, I felt my heart breaking a little. Are you like that sometimes,

Alex? When something is so beautiful, you have no words, but your heart trembles, like it is cracking apart? At the Grand Basin, the pond water was so still, it was like a mirror reflecting the stars and moon above. A small toy sailing boat floated on the lake's surface. It looked so lonely and lost. I stared at it for a long time, until tears went down my face.

I found myself thinking of you. I thought of how you are the only one I can talk to these days. The only one who understands me. And suddenly, I am wishing with great feeling that you could be there with me. So I could show you this beautiful night, and show off my wonderful Paris to you. I would take your hand and walk the empty streets with you. We would walk everywhere. An American boy and a Parisian girl. We would smell the grass and look up at the stars. We would look down into the Seine, and see our reflections. And maybe we would find a secret place to draw our graffiti together, a frog jumping out of a pot. Our little drawing of resistance, no?

In Jane Eyre, Mr. Rochester says to Jane something I memorized: "I have a strange feeling with regard to you. As if I had a string somewhere under my left ribs, tightly knotted to a similar string in you."

Oh, Alex, maybe this is too much for you. Maybe I should keep all these emotions to myself. But my heart breaks with so much loneliness and anger and sadness. And I wish I could pull this string and bring you close to me tonight.

Your dearest friend,
Charlie

Alex folds the letter, holds it against his chest. He leans forward, pressing his forehead against the ice-cold window. He stares into the stark white-glazed landscape, slowly drifting past him, the alien eternity of it. "Charlie," he whispers.

* * *

Even before dawn, half the train is awake. The stink of halitosis, the moist tinge of diarrhea, the cries of the colicky newborn fill the carriage. Stomachs growl, and tongues begin to wag with complaint. Hatsue, a girl he knows from school, is sitting three rows back, and has not stopped sobbing since yesterday; Alex suspects she's left behind a secret boyfriend, a *hakujin,* if the rumors are true. Many finally take off their leather boots, bought just days ago on account of a rumor: they will be taken to a desolate desert, and forced out at gunpoint—the bayonetted rifles seem to confirm this—where they will be abandoned and forced to fend against rattlesnakes. They will wander for months, years, forgotten, their numbers dwindling to a hundred, a few dozen, until they will all perish.

"Where are we?" somebody asks.

"Are we in Washington?"

"Are we in California?"

"Are we in Canada?"

"Are we arriving today?"

"Can we open the shades now, Mommy?"

Frank, fed up with all the insecurity, all the timidity, all the confusion, stands up and moves over to the window. He pulls the shade up. Immediately, a shaft of light blazes into the interior. The effect is instant: darkness driven out, gray murkiness destroyed by bright clarity. For a moment no one speaks. Then someone lifts up another set of shades. And another. Light fills the carriage.

Frank isn't done. He slides the upper-set windows to the side. A small opening only, but fresh air glides in. Alex takes a deep lungful; already he can feel the cobwebs of his mind blown away, the stink of anxiety and desperation driven out.

Frank sits down, his jaw set. "All we needed was *one* person to speak up. To take action. One lousy person."

Everyone stares out the windows at the barren landscape. It

is unfathomably huge, this America, so full of emptiness and unconquered wilderness.

Another day passes. At dusk, the train slows to cross a wooden trestle over a dry riverbed that's nothing but rocks and stones. He sees two boys standing there. Alex is surprised. The boys have materialized out of nowhere; there is no nearby town, no road, no parent, no vehicle. Just these two boys, neither older than ten. They turn their heads to gaze at the passing train. The setting sun behind them has rendered them into mere silhouettes and Alex can't make out their expressions. He thinks perhaps they will pick up rocks to throw at the train. Or raise angry fists, or pull the corners of their eyes down, or flip their white middle fingers at this unexpected gift: a whole train of the enemy just begging to be made into targets. When one of them starts raising an arm, Alex beats him to the punch, extending his middle finger and pressing it against the glass for the boy to see.

Except the boy doesn't. Raise his middle finger, that is. Instead, his small hand waves side to side in greeting. *Hello, hello.* A second later, the other boy does the same. Two boys, standing in a dry riverbed, waving at the passing train. *Hello, hello.*

And then, before Alex can lower his middle finger and pull back his hand from the window, they are gone.

That night as the 227 Bainbridge Islanders continue their journey to an unknown destination, across the world in Poland at around the same time the first train carrying 1,112 French Jews arrives at the Auschwitz concentration camp.

PART TWO

MANZANAR WAR RELOCATION CENTER

18

On April Fools' day the train comes to a loud, rattling stop. Soldiers walk down the aisle, carrying their rifles for the first time in days, and order everyone off. On stiff legs, 227 Bainbridge Islanders stumble out. Their clothes, worn with pride the day they left Bainbridge Island, are now wrinkled. Skin sags off their bones like damp laundry on a clothesline.

They are herded into assigned buses, told where to sit. It's even more cramped than the train, but they're too tired to complain. They're ordered to pull down the shades. In the darkened interior, their eyes swell like those of a terrified horse kicking the stall in panic.

Many hours later, they are finally allowed to raise the shades. And this is what they see: nothing. Just a barren wasteland stretching as far as the eye can see to the north, east, and south. Not a single tree in the flat monotony. Only to the west do the Sierra Nevada mountains break the drudgery of the landscape, and they do this dramatically, majestically. Towering high, cragged and snowcapped, these Sierra Nevada mountains resemble in many ways the Swiss Alps.

But there are no *ooh*s and *ahh*s. No words of admiration. No fingers pointing at the splendor. Only a hushed anxiety. Everyone feels it. They are drawing near to the end of their journey.

And yet they are out in the middle of nowhere. It is no place for humans.

Are we? they wonder. *Human?*

In the distance, something emerges. A dark stain on the flat landscape, a filthy puddle. Shapes emerge within it. Dots lined up in regimented fashion. Small shacks, like matchboxes.

They draw closer. Now they see a barbed-wire fence around the square-mile perimeter. Inside, rows and columns of shacks, hundreds of them. Two watchtowers with weapons pointed inward, with six more watchtowers still under construction.

"No," someone whispers. "No way."

"It's not for us," someone says. "It's just a storage facility. Those are only warehouses."

But instead of driving past, the convoy of buses turns into the compound. No one says a word. Even the children are quiet. Wide-eyed and stunned. For Alex, as the bus pulls into the compound, this feels like a last moment. A last moment of freedom, of independence. He takes a long breath and holds it in.

The soldiers in the camp wear a different uniform from the ones who escorted them from Bainbridge Island. Fresher-looking, crisper, and because of that, more intimidating. A cordon of these soldiers is lined up along the road. Their rifles and belts of live ammunition are on full display as they bark orders to the dazed, blinking people stumbling out of the bus. They are the first of thousands to arrive at Manzanar.

"Will they separate us?" Mother asks.

"No," Frank says, taking her arm.

"But this place is so big. Maybe men and women will be housed separately. Maybe they will take you boys from me."

Frank's voice grows resolute. "I won't let them, Mother. Now stop speaking in Japanese."

The soldiers continue to yell. *Keep moving, don't dawdle. You can collect your luggage from your designated location later. Proceed to the registration tables.*

It's the wind you notice first. Then the dust. It comes sweeping across the open plains, a gathering force that catches you unawares. Too late, you shut your eyelids, turn your back to it. But it's already there, the thousand prickly grains under your eyelids, grating against the wet of your eyeballs; too late you close your mouth but the dust is already coating your tongue, dotting the wet roof of your mouth, slipping in between your teeth. Already it has sieved through the tiny sleeve openings of jackets and necklines of sweaters until you feel it crawling all over your body.

Dust, sand, everywhere. For the rest of your life you will never feel rid of it. You will slap at your clothes unconsciously, you will be forever flapping out towels and hats and scarfs. When you cough, even fifty years later, you will think you can still feel a few grains of dust rattling around in your lungs, refusing to be dislodged.

Alex glances around. Past the cordon of soldiers, past the flood of internees moving toward the registration tables. He stares at the square mile of what will eventually become thirty-six blocks of tar-paper barracks. Enough to house over ten thousand men, women, and children. But for now, the Bainbridge Islanders are the first group to arrive at this still-unfinished compound. The Issei grandparents are pioneers yet again, but this time unwillingly, in a harsh land they want no part of.

"Name." The soldier sitting before the opened registration book doesn't even glance up.

"Maki."

"Spell it."

"M-A-K-I." Frank looks down at the book. "No. I said *I* not *Y*. And there's no *E*."

"God, these Jap names. Spell it again."

"M-A-K-I."

They are handed a piece of paper, told where to go. Block 16 Barrack 4 Room F.

"Where is it?" Mother asks.

The soldier impatiently thrusts a thumb backward. An action that could mean *That way* or *Get lost.*

Frank and Alex, with Mother between them, join others trudging along the road. Everyone walks in a state of shock. The road is lined with soldiers, their bayonets pointing inward. The soldiers yell continuously at them, urging them to move faster, and the new arrivals stumble along, hurrying.

"Why are you rushing us?" Frank yells back at the soldiers. "We're in the middle of nowhere! With nothing to do and nowhere to go. So what's the damned hurry?"

Mother, waddling beside him, tries to calm him. But when the next set of soldiers yell the same instructions, Frank explodes. "Go to hell! Just shoot me, why don't you!" His neck is flushed, his face beet red. The soldiers leer back at him, some laughing, some gripping their weapons. An acne-riddled soldier tells him to be quiet. "Or what?" Frank snaps back. "Or what? You gonna throw me in prison? Look around, you lugheads, I'm already in prison!"

"Frank," Alex says. "*Frank!*"

Frank doesn't answer. He moves along, face hard as flint.

The camp isn't finished yet. They walk across planks of wood over open trenches and ditches to get to their barrack. It sits on concrete footings, the flooring raised about two feet off the ground. Crudely constructed, the rough pine paneling sided with tar paper left exposed. A shack, by any other description, identical to the hundreds of other barracks laid out in regimented formation.

Never judge a book by its cover. This is what they tell themselves.

But once inside, their worst fears are confirmed. The book is worse than the cover. The walls are just wood sheeting, splintery and thin. No paint or insulation or plaster covers them. The floor is composed of wood planks with large knotholes slapped together. No linoleum covering.

Placed around the room are seven army cots, metal skeletons. None with a mattress or a pillow. An oil furnace in the corner, standing cold as a tombstone. No desk, no chair, no running water, no toilet. Only a single bulb, unlit, hangs from a cord dangling from an overhead beam. Beneath it, coarse army blankets are thrown in a pile. Frank walks to the far side. The wall— no more than a thin partition—doesn't reach the peaked roof, leaving a three-foot triangular space.

"What the hell?" Frank says.

"At least we're together," Mother says. She gazes at the seven cots. "You think they'll make us share the room with others?"

"Probably," Frank says, dejected. "I say we take this corner."

A few minutes later, another family moves into the barrack. Not into this room, but the adjacent one. Their voices sail over the thin wall, through the three-foot space between the top of the wall and the peaked roof, their words as clear as if there were no partition at all. Privacy will be nonexistent here.

They speak of rumors about a mattress pickup location. At another block. But when Frank and Alex get there they're only handed three sacks and told to go to another building. There, a crowd is already knee-deep in a huge pile of straw and ticking, stuffing their sacks.

Alex and Frank jump right in. They ignore the jabs of pain as splinters pierce their skin. But there's no need to rush or jostle for position. There's an ocean of ticking, enough for the ten thousand or more internees expected to eventually fill this compound in the coming months.

Frank stops. "Listen. What's that?"

They all hear it, then. *Gong. Gong. Gong.*

"What should we do?" an older man asks Frank.

Frank sees everyone looking at him. "We go to it." He steps forward and starts walking, never once turning around to see the crowd following after him.

The gongs ring out from a mess hall. Outside, a line has already formed. Everyone hugs the lee side of the mess hall, still only partially built, faces turned away from the wind.

Dinner is slopped into metal containers. Canned, cold food: string beans, Vienna sausage, apricots. The rice—perhaps the only food many Issei might have otherwise eaten—is ruined by the apricot syrup poured over it. The internees, with nowhere to sit, squat against the walls. They stare glumly at the food, trying to conjure up the will to eat. A gust of wind materializes out of nowhere, catching everyone by surprise. Sand and dust coat their food. Some still gamely try to eat, their stomachs rumbling with hunger, only to have to spit it out.

Back in their barracks, there is nothing to do but sit. The single light bulb does not work. Nobody unpacks: it is too dark to see. They lie down in the same clothes they have worn for three days. Every few minutes, light from the watchtower slashes through the room, a cold invasive stark white. A scalpel.

Alex, like everyone else, finds sleep elusive. He is freezing. He is shaking. He should be safe and snug in his own bed on Bainbridge Island, an all-American sixteen-year-old living life to the hilt. Going out on dates. Hanging out in soda shops. Mastering the Lindy hop, or dancing in a zoot suit with a bobby-soxer. Doing homework, falling asleep in church pews. Discovering first love, learning to kiss, driving jalopies in the backcountry.

Thinking about prom, Yale School of Art. But instead he's lying on a cot in the middle of the desert surrounded by strangers.

The wind howls outside, whistles through gaps in the floor and walls.

He turns to the wall, mashes his face against the unsanded plank of pine. From the other side, another gust of wind thumps against the barrack.

Around him, the stifled crying begins.

19

They wake up early to find themselves blanketed in dust. Dust that during the night gusted in through knotholes and slats. Now it covers their hair, faces, floor. Most of the internees rise gamely, ready to face the day; a few sob on their cots, unable to rise, covered in dust like prophets of old in sackcloth, repenting in dust and ashes.

Some head straight to the communal restroom. It is an abhorrence. They hold their breaths as they walk in. The floor flooded. Pieces of excrement floating about the concrete slab, dark and stringy like seaweed. Twelve toilet bowls run down the center of the room: side by side and back-to-back without any partitions. Close enough to touch skin if you lean back or spread your legs too wide. Along the far wall are the urinals and across from them a row of spigots over a trough. When they flush, the pipes clank ominously. Excrement suddenly erupts from the toilet bowls, spewing out of them and splashing onto the floor.

They spend the day like shell-shocked scavengers. Following every rumor, watching other internees like hawks. Who is carrying wood? Or more blankets? Or even oil for the stoves? Their immigrant survival instincts, lying dormant for so many years, spring to life. They chase down every lead, usually just wild-goose chases. In the midafternoon, a man is seen scurrying away with planks of wood. Go to Block 3, he says. There's some discarded scrap lumber lying around.

But by the time Alex and Frank get there, it's almost all gone. Only a few ends of lath and rolled paper. Back in their room they use the lath ends to plug up the gaps between planks, and stuff the rolled paper around the doorframe.

"Good," Mother says, nodding. "That might help."

"This sucks," Frank mutters. "Livestock have it better than this."

And right on cue, five gongs sound. But this time it's not from the mess hall. It's from the infirmary. Typhoid shots next.

But they get sidetracked along the way. A convoy of buses arrive. Everyone rushes over to the main gate, curious to see who has arrived. Almost a dozen buses unload hundreds of dazed passengers.

Frank cannot help himself: his natural leadership skills spring forth. He at once drops everything and makes a beeline for them. He helps carry their things to the registration table, points them to their assigned block, or in some cases, even walks them over. He smiles, thumps teens on the back, helps the old with their luggage.

Alex tags along, glad to see some spunk in his brother again, even if it is for just a day. Of late, all he's seen of Frank is the gloom and anger eating him up inside.

For these bewildered arrivals, he's a godsend. Though he's been here less than a day, Frank gives advice with the wisdom of someone here much longer (*inflate the number in your family to get extra blankets; don't unpack your clothes until you've plugged up the knotholes, or they'll get covered in dust; when the mess hall gongs start ringing, run before the line gets too long*) and because he comes across as knowledgeable and friendly, people are asking his name, shaking his hand, remembering his face.

20

The short spring ends and summer sets in with a vengeance. The heat clamps down on you, turning every day into a slog. You wake up in the predawn stillness, and gaze up at the rafters overhead. You hope for quiet in this predawn hour, but the air is full with the wheezes and whines and coughs and murmurs of twenty-plus people in various stages of slumber. Sometimes the newlyweds will be up, and at first it's a form of entertainment (or education) to eavesdrop on them, the creaking bed, their stifled sounds. But soon enough, quickly, it leaves you feeling like a dirty louse.

But most mornings, you wake up to the sounds not of lovemaking but of phlegm and snot being cleared. Or the piss trickle of an illegal bedpan. You kick aside the scratchy army blanket and sit up, the wires of the old iron army cot creaking under you. You swing your legs and plant your bare feet on floorboards that are rutted with knotholes and again coated with dust. The air inside is stale and musty and will, by noon, become hot as an oven.

Weeks and months pass. More internees arrive, hundreds at a time from Los Angeles, from San Bernardino, from Stockton. They come aged and bent, muttering Japanese; they come clutching their mothers' hands; they come blinking away dust, in disbelief at this city of tar-papered barracks. They come, the tired, the poor, these huddled masses yearning to break free.

There is nothing to do. Later, jobs will be assigned, rudimentary classrooms built, clubs organized. But for these first few months, the day stretches long, the nights longer, and the boredom, especially for older teens, is unending. All their innate energy, along with any vestige of altruism, melts away under the harsh sun and the slow tick of time. The desert burns everything to a crisp.

Even Frank. Unbelievably, even Frank. Alex sees his brother's natural life force slowly drain away. He is slow to get up in the morning. He pouts around in the evening, sighing constantly. He curses all the time, even in front of Mother. His posture, usually ramrod straight, begins to slouch. Sometimes Alex sees him with a group of other young men. They all look the same. Bored. Restless. Angry.

21

Dear Charlie,

I still haven't heard from you. I tell myself there must be a simple explanation, and that you're fine. You are, aren't you, Charlie?

On my end nothing much has changed. People continue to pour into the camp. Thousands upon thousands. On Bainbridge Island there were about two hundred of us. But here, almost ten thousand, I heard. Everywhere I look, there are people who look like me, usually lining up. We're always lining up. For clothing. Food. Wood. Sometimes you see a long line and you don't even bother asking for what, you just get in line.

Now that it's hot, those lines can get pretty stinky. People need to take more showers but there's always a line for that too, even late at night. Some of the older men have resorted to taking baths in the laundry tubs. So disgusting.

The food remains terrible. We call it SOS—Same Old Slop. The mess halls are hot and awful: babies crying, children screaming, adults yelling, teens shouting, grandpas slurping, grandmas chewing, pans clanging, workers yelling. Families don't sit together anymore. Teens sit with other teens. The family structure is breaking apart. Not just in the dining halls, but over the whole camp. Teens roam about everywhere by themselves, and parents have lost control over them. I've seen fathers explode with rage, lashing out at their sons. And mothers crying, worried and upset. I feel bad for these parents. First they lost their homes, their jobs, their freedom. Now they're losing maybe their most precious possession. Their own children.

And Frank's no different. He's altogether disappeared at mealtimes. He used to sit on the other side of the mess hall, but recently he's been going to a whole other block. Sometimes I sit with my mother so she won't feel so lonely, but she always asks where Frank is. Even when I tell her he's probably at a different mess hall, she holds a spot at the table for him.

He's changed, Frank. A lot. In the beginning, before camp life really got to him, he had more spunk. But now all he does is hang out with a bunch of other guys. They're all bored and restless and spend their time griping about this and that. The stale food. The communal latrines that stink and offer no privacy, the boredom, the heat so intense that some people have taken to lying under the barracks in dug-up holes.

The only time I see Frank is late at night for curfew. I barely recognize him. Sometimes he even scares me.

Please write. Please?

Alex

At the post office, Alex slides his stamped envelope over the counter. As usual he asks, "Any mail for me? The Maki family, Block Sixteen Barrack Four Apartment F."

"I know who you are, Alex. You're only here every day. Give me a sec." The postal worker disappears into the back. Alex is not expecting her to return with anything. He's already half turned when she reappears. An envelope in her hand.

Alex's heart springs awake.

Fingers trembling, he reaches for the letter. Instantly, his heart drops—it's not from France. Or Europe. It's from Crystal City Internment Camp, Texas.

22

That night, as the sounds of slumber lift up into the rafters, Alex hears the door creak open. Wind gusts in, chilly even in the middle of July. Boots stomp across the floorboards. Frank's cot creaks as he lies down.

Even in the darkness, Alex knows Mother is awake. She will not allow her heavy eyelids to close, or her body to drift off to sleep, until Frank is back in the barracks and asleep. Ever since Frank first started staying away for the whole day, this is the only time she sees him.

Tonight it is Mother who falls asleep first, her snores ragged and wheezy.

Alex pads quietly over to Frank's cot. He's lying slumped on his side, facing the wall.

"Frank."

No response. Alex prods him on the shoulder. "Frank."

"What is it?" Annoyed.

"I need to tell you something."

Still facing the wall: "Go ahead."

Alex pauses. "We got a letter yesterday. From the prison facility in Texas. Crystal City."

Frank's back stiffens.

"It's about Father." He pauses, wishing Frank would turn around and face him. "His release petition was denied."

Alex waits in the darkness, willing his older brother to speak. *Please say something, please tell me what's going on inside your head, tell me what's going on inside that heart of yours that used to be as big and open as the endless blue sky, please . . .*

Alex breaks the silence himself. "How long will they keep him?"

Frank shifts, the springs of the cot complaining squeakily. "I don't know."

He stares at Frank's back. Hard and impenetrable as granite. "Will they send him back to Japan?"

No response.

"If they do, we won't ever see him again. Will we?"

"There's nothing we can do, okay? It's out of our control. Now let me sleep."

"You need to tell Mother."

"No. It'll break her."

Frank is right. Alex hears her praying every morning over her Bible. For Father's health. For his return. Her voice weaker with every passing week, her back more crooked, her very cartilage disintegrating. Without him she's crumbling like a piece of chalk.

"Still, Frank. She *should* know."

"*You* tell her then."

"You're the oldest—"

"I said *you* tell her."

Alex wants to rip the blankets off Frank, make him turn around. But he only sucks in a deep breath. "Fine, Frank. But I'm going to lie. Tell her that Father will be back soon. It'll give her hope."

Frank doesn't answer.

"And who knows? Maybe Father *will* be released. Maybe even—"

"Shut up."

The words, slaps to his face, stinging. He recoils, his cheeks smarting red. He waits for his brother to apologize or chuckle it away. But instead: "Quit being a child, Alex. Father's not coming back. That's not how the world works."

"How do you know that? Maybe he *will*—"

"You're so out of touch with reality, it's not even funny."

"You don't know—"

"Head out of the clouds, Alex. How many times do I have to tell you?" His bed creaks as he shifts in the cot.

Alex stares at him. "Can you turn around, Frank?"

"Why?"

"Please?"

Frank sighs, flips his body over. "What?"

In the faint moonlight, Frank's face seems harder than Alex has ever seen it. His eyes, which once glowed warmly, are as cold and stark as the nightly searchlight beams that sweep across the barracks.

"What do you do every day?" Alex whispers. "Where do you go?"

Frank rolls his eyes. "God," he mutters, turning around to the wall again and throwing his blanket over himself.

23

The next time Alex visits the post office, a miracle.

The clerk gives him a smile. "I think we finally got something for you, Alex. Give me a sec." She disappears into the back room.

He waits. It's probably nothing, he tells himself. A Sears, Roebuck catalog. A letter about war bonds. Another disappointing letter about Father. Something—

"Good things come to those who wait," the clerk says, returning with a smile. "A letter from France." She turns the envelope over. "With a ton of stopovers, judging from all the postmarks."

Alex takes the letter. He gulps. The crisscrossing postmarks and stamps are like the vines and branches of a dense rainforest, and through them he glimpses Charlie's handwriting.

It's like seeing her face.

He wants to scream.

She's alive. *He's* alive.

He stands, woozy, delirious, and light-headed. The world has suddenly opened up, announced its existence beyond these barbwired fences.

"Are you okay, Alex?" the clerk asks.

He nods, walks out into the blazing heat. Looks down at the envelope, afraid it won't be there, this was all his imagination . . .

It's still there. Shining brightly in the searing sunlight.

He doesn't know what to do with himself. He walks. Stops.

Stares down at the envelope, heart pounding. Charlie is seconds away. What is he doing, what is he waiting for? He rips open the envelope, his fingers quaking with excitement.

---

10 June 1942

Dearest Alex,

Alex! I received your letter! You are alive! Hourra! I didn't hear from you for such a long time, and I was worried to death! Are you okay? I wondered, Has something happened to you?

Then this afternoon when I returned home, I saw Monsieur S sitting in our living room! He looked very tired and old. And filled with sadness, very unusual for him. But when he saw me his face lighted up. He handed me a package with ten of your letters (TEN!!) and I almost exploded with joy. It was like my whole heart went whoosh on fire with life! I found my joie de vivre in that moment.

I rushed to my room and read the letters. I am so happy you are okay. But Alex, dearest Alex, I am pained to read what has happened to you. I cannot imagine what it must be like to be torn from your very home and put in some camp in the middle of nowhere.

Oh, I wish I could write more to you! I have so many things to tell you. But Monsieur S is departing now! He keeps knocking on my bedroom door and telling me he has to leave to catch his train back to Vichy. And that I must finish my letter now if he is to take it with him to mail off. So au revoir for now, dear Alex! Forgive the bad English, I have no time to write fancy sentences or to correct grammar mistakes or write better words! Maybe you think I am Charlie from three years ago! I am laughing!

I miss you,
Charlie

Oh, Monsieur S just got into a big argument with Papa so I can write more. Monsieur S says Paris has become too dangerous, and that we must all flee to the south, to Nice, to his summer apartment. Do you remember it was the place I spent one summer maybe six years ago? My best summer. I still remember the sun, the pier, the small Notre Dame church, the bowling grounds. Monsieur S says that Nice is unoccupied and free from anti-Jewish laws, we must go there at once.

But Papa is now calling him an idiot, says the Vichy zone is even worse for Jews, why would he move his family there? And now Monsieur S is yelling back, saying that Nice isn't part of the Vichy zone, it's in the free zone and that Jews are safe there. Maybe the Italians will invade, but so what? Il Duce has no desire to harm Jews.

Oh! Now they are really yelling at each other. Calling each other crude nicknames they haven't used since the French war when they fought together in the trenches. Maman is pleading with both to calm down.

Maybe Monsieur S is right. Things in Paris have become much, much worse. A few days ago, all Jews were ordered to wear a big yellow star on our clothes. Maman says we must wear this star with pride. But I don't agree. This is a badge of shame, a thing of disgrace, a bright yellow target on our chests.

Do you know what's the most embarrassing? It's when I meet others who are wearing the star. I don't know why we turn our eyes away and hurry past each other. Somebody explain this aspect of human nature to me.

And now there are rumors of roundups. And even of faraway camps.

Alex, where are the gleams of sunshine?

Oh, Monsieur S is leaving. Don't worry everything is

And just like that, the letter ends. Alex peers hopefully into the envelope. But there's nothing else.

* * *

That night, he dreams of her. She's never sent a photo of herself; but over the years he's built a mental picture, drawn from random comments she's made about her appearance.

In his dream, he is walking along a cobblestone street. It is dusk. The temperature an autumn cool. Comfortable. A row of homes flanks the street, and these houses are fluffy and comforting like warm loaves of freshly baked bread. In the air, the smell of croissants, wine, the sound of laughter. Not a speck of dust. Even as he walks he realizes this is a dream, the images nothing more than a composite of every stereotype he knows of Paris.

Rising over the rooftops to his left, he sees the distant Eiffel Tower. And to his right—

He sees her. Sitting at a table set for two in an outdoor terrace of a restaurant. The Café de la Paix. Before her, a plate of foie gras and banana flambé. She is reading a book, a frayed old hardcover of *Jane Eyre*.

Something makes her look up. Their eyes meet. She does not seem surprised.

He walks toward her grinning. She smiles back, her hair sashaying back and forth.

"Alex," she whispers, a glow in her face, a fire in her eyes.

24

A blisteringly hot Sunday. By late morning, the heat has topped a hundred degrees. The barracks are ovens; people are driven outside only to be blasted by the sun and stung by dust-filled winds.

Some head to Bairs Creek, a small stream that cuts across the southwest corner of the compound. Others find refuge under the few trees dotted around the one-square-mile camp compound. Children climb the branches, their hair plastered to sweaty foreheads as cranky parents below scold them half-heartedly, their energy sapped as they fan themselves and indulge in bootleg sake concocted out of raisins and sweet potatoes.

Alex wanders aimlessly through bands of heat that shimmer off the baked earth. Already, he is regretting his decision to wear sandals. Heat from the ground has worked its way through the thin material, singeing his calloused soles.

He stops in the shade of a barrack. His eyes lazily browse the bulletin board there. There are posted warnings (to boys) to stop peeking into the women's shower, sports schedules for the baseball league, the girls' basketball league. A help-wanted listing for the new school being set up, for volunteer teachers. No experience necessary. A writer-wanted posting from the *Manzanar Free Press,* the official camp newspaper, an unpaid position.

His curiosity piqued, he scans the bulletin for a job. International mail to France is costly, and he'll soon run out of money.

Although he hasn't heard from Charlie since receiving her letter weeks ago, he's been writing her at a fierce clip.

There are many posted jobs—a city of ten thousand doesn't run itself, after all. Listings for construction crews, farming hands, latrine cleaners. None pay well, barely a pittance for the hard, unglamorous labor. Alex is about to leave when his eye catches: WAITER WANTED. GOOD WAGES.

His first thought: *There's a restaurant here? With good pay?*

He reads the rest of the announcement. *Ahhhh,* he thinks.

"Tell me why you want this job." The flabby white man, whose name Alex has already forgotten, leans toward him from across the table, his weight supported by his meaty, hairy forearms. The staff mess hall is mostly empty this time of day.

Alex considers his options: *Because I love to wait tables. Because the staff mess hall is one of only two buildings with air-conditioning. Because nothing excites me more than the thought of serving the very white people who lord it over my people.*

Instead he simply tells the truth. "You pay well."

The man leans back. He rubs his plump jowls. "All right. You start tomorrow. Mary-Ann in the office will get the paperwork started and issue you a card for security clearance."

Fifteen minutes later Alex exits the staff cafeteria building, clutching his security card. The buildings in the staff housing zone, painted white and spread out, lend the area an airy, relaxed atmosphere. Beautifully manicured lawns sit before single-detached homes. The lush green of grass contrasts with the rock-wall patios where stand trellises interwoven by sweet peas and other climbing plants. It feels like a whole other world. Alex hurries along clean walkways lined with white-painted stones, feeling like a trespasser.

At the security gate, he shows his newly issued card to the

officer. The on-duty guard barely glances up at him, waves him out. As he reenters the main camp with its crowded tar-paper barracks and dusty roads, it feels like entering a ghetto. He tucks his head down, hopes no one notices him.

Back at his barrack, he pauses on the front steps to pat off the dust. He checks the letter box—mail is delivered now—out of habit. It's empty.

Mother is inside, lying on her cot. He takes in her crinkled, white lips, the radial lines now etched permanently into the corners of her eyes. He knows she hasn't been sleeping well. In less than a year, she's aged more than a decade and now seems less like a mother and more a grandmother.

"Mother? Are you all right?"

She sits up, her bones creaking, the cot coils squeaking wheezily. "I'm fine."

"You should quit your job before it kills you," he says. Her shift at the camouflage-net factory begins at the crack of dawn, and often doesn't end until the dinner gong.

"We need the money. And besides, it might help Father."

"Father? How?"

"We're showing our patriotism. Helping America's war cause. It'll help Father get released." She clears her throat clogged with phlegm. "We should buy war bonds, too. Maybe that'll help."

He ladles water into a cup, brings it over to her. "Drink, Mother."

She takes it with a shaking hand. "Have you heard anything back about the release petition?"

"No," he lies.

She looks up at Alex with hopeful eyes. "Soon, though. Right?"

He shakes his head. "I don't know."

"Well, I'll keep working at the camouflage-net factory. At least I'm doing something. Which is more than either of my sons are doing. My young, healthy, tall sons."

Alex feels a rush of shame. "If there were something I could do to help Father," he says defensively, "I would. But there isn't."

She pinches her lips in disagreement but says nothing more. With a sigh, she leans her head against the wall, takes a sip as she stares out the window. She's looking for Frank. Always looking for Frank.

"Oh," she says, remembering something. "You got a letter. From your French friend."

His head whips up. "What? Where?"

She points to his cot. "I left it there."

In two strides he's got the envelope in his hand.

She laughs softly, a rare sound from her these days. "I think it's good you have a friend outside." She peers out the window. "We all need something outside these fences."

He's already tearing open the envelope.

25

Dear Alex,

I am at Papa's factory. Afraid. Hiding in the back rooms. I do not know what to do, I keep pacing. So I am writing to you, maybe this will help calm me.

Just two hours ago, Monsieur S came running into the factory. He was in panic. He showed us a tract that appeared today in Jewish neighborhoods. I will translate it:

"Do not wait in your home. Take all necessary steps to hide, and hide first your children with the help of sympathetic Parisians . . . If bad people come for you, resist in any way possible. Lock the doors, cry out for help, fight the police. You have nothing to lose. You can only save your life. Be ready to flee at any moment. We must not allow ourselves to be exterminated."

Papa read the tract with a deep frown. Because there have been rumors recently. About roundups. About trains to awful camps. And I think Papa finally came to his senses. He told us we are to leave for Nice. Tomorrow.

And then Papa left for the apartment to pack suitcases with Maman. They will return to fetch me in the morning. Papa instructed me to stay here and wait for them.

Oh, Alex, I am afraid. For the first time I am truly afraid. I sensed something these past few days. A tension around the city

that is thick with danger. Like the moment before lightning strikes.
Something awful is about to happen.

Oh! Monsieur S is leaving now to catch the last train to Nice.
He will go ahead of us to make arrangements. I will end here and
give him this letter so he can send it out once he's in Nice.

Alex reads the letter a dozen times, each time *willing* its content to change. Or at least to lengthen another paragraph or page. A different ending, one more hopeful. But nothing changes.

We must not allow ourselves to be exterminated.

He rubs his thumb over that sentence. Wanting to erase it, unable to.

26

Alex ends his shift later than usual, and it's almost dark by the time he leaves the administration compound. A block away, he hears someone approaching from behind. It's Frank. Quickly, Alex zips up his jacket to hide the security pass hanging around his neck.

"Frank? Did something happen to Mother?"

"She's fine. Relax."

"What is it then?"

Frank flicks the cigarette to the ground. "Can't believe you work there, Alex. Waiting on them, serving them." He shakes his head. "Thought you were better than that, kid."

Alex keeps his eyes to the ground. "You came all this way to tell me that?"

Frank snorts. He's lost weight, his jawline more angular, his cheekbones sharper. "Come on. Let's walk home together." He turns and strides away.

Alex stares suspiciously at his brother. Something's up. But he follows anyway. A week of heavy rain has turned the ground slushy, and their pants become speckled with fresh spots of mud. They walk past the orchards, Blocks 28, 27, then 26. They reach the Catholic church, then turn left.

"Wait," Alex says. "Where are we going?"

Frank doesn't stop. "This way. Want to show you something."

When they reach Block 35 in the corner of the camp, Frank stops outside a barrack. "In here."

"What's inside?"

"Just come in."

There are five men inside. Sitting around a table, coats on, hats pushed low.

"This your brother?" one of them says to Frank. "Don't see the resemblance at all."

"You sure you have the same father?"

Before Frank can snap back, a man—the oldest of the group, in his midthirties—speaks.

"Apologies," the man says. "We're cold and irritable. There's no oil in that stove."

Alex recognizes the man. Harry Ueno. An outspoken and very popular figure in the camp. When his Block 22 was short on cooks, he signed up to be a cook's assistant even though he had zero culinary experience. He became renowned for his snacks: oil-fried and oven-dried rice snacks that became a hit, especially with the kids. And in the hottest month of the year, July, with temperatures soaring over a hundred, he built a rock pond right outside the mess hall. It gave people something to look at during the long waits outside, restored some of their dignity.

"Alex Maki," he says. "My name is Harry Ueno."

"I know who you are."

Ueno gives a small smile. "Good. We can dispense with the formalities then. Allow me to cut to the chase. We need to ask you a favor."

Curious and cautious at the same time, Alex says, "Yeah?"

"You've heard the stories? About all them babies dying these last few months."

He has. Speculation's been all over the place: germs in the hospital delivery room, or the water's gone bad. "I've heard a few things."

Harry Ueno takes out a cigarette, lights it up. "Yeah? What kind of things?"

Alex looks at Frank then back at Ueno. "Just that babies are dying for no good reason."

"Alex," Ueno says patronizingly. "Babies don't die for no good reason. There's always a reason." He lowers his voice. "Somebody's been mixing something into the milk formula."

Alex shakes his head. That didn't make any sense at all. "What kind of stuff?"

"Saccharin."

"Why would anyone do that?"

"The milk formula's supposed to have sugar in it. Except, with the price of sugar skyrocketing, somebody's been stealing our sugar to sell on the black market and replacing it with saccharin." He snorts with disgust. "And our babies are dying because of that."

Alex shakes his head in disbelief. "Who would do such a thing?"

Frank turns to Alex. "That's why we brought you here."

"Me? What can I do?"

"We have a couple of suspects. Joseph Winchester, the guy in charge of all the kitchens and warehouses. But we think it goes even higher up than him. We think the real kingpin is Ned Campbell."

Alex's head spins to Frank. "The number-two guy in command? No way. I mean, he's the Assistant Project Director."

"And it's not just sugar he's stealing. He's filching meat as well. And milk. And kitchen knives. Then selling it on the black market outside the camp. Making a pretty dime while our babies die."

Alex is stunned. "That's . . . that's a pretty big accusation. You have evidence to back it up?"

Ueno's eyes cut to Alex. "That's where you come in."

"Me?"

"You work at the WRA mess hall. Serving all them staffers."

Alex swings his eyes to Frank. Then back to Ueno. "So?"

"We need you to find out stuff."

Alex stares at Ueno incredulously. "You want me to ask around? They'll never give up their own boss—"

Frank steps in. "No, knucklehead. We want you to *look* around. They've got to be hiding the stolen goods somewhere. So peek into the commercial refrigerators. Check under the mess hall for any secret cellars."

"Frank, you can't expect me to snoop around—"

Frank's face hardens. "This is how you redeem yourself, Alex. This is how you show where your loyalties lie: with them, or with us."

"Redeem myself? What the hell, Frank?"

Frank sighs with hot anger. "There are things happening in this camp that you have no idea about, Alex. You've got blinders on. You think everything's just fine, that we're all singing around a campfire holding hands." He jabs a finger at Alex. "You have no idea how angry most of us are. How upset we are at being taken from our homes and unceremoniously dumped out here."

"I'm upset, too, Frank. You're not the only one who's pissed off. But some of us think it's pointless to just go around sulking and making a nuisance of ourselves. Because we're better than that. And we need to show America that we're good Americans—"

"That's bull, Alex! We need to hold America accountable for what it's done to us. And simply playing nice isn't the way to do that." Spit flies out of his mouth in disgust. "It's time to pull your head out of the ground and open your eyes. It ain't all peaches and rainbows around here."

"Yeah, well, maybe you're the one who needs to open your eyes! You see what you're doing to Mother? How she's so sick with worry over you?" His voice reaches a fevered pitch. "Have you even looked at her? She's got a limp now. She's wheezing all the time. She's not sleeping. Have you seen what you're doing to her?"

"What *I'm* doing to Mother? How about what *America's* doing to her!"

"I'll take it from here, Frank," Ueno says, stepping between the two brothers. He gives Frank a squeeze on the shoulder and turns to Alex.

"We're asking, Alex. We're not making you do this. But we hope you can come around and see our point of view. This has nothing to do with patriotism. And everything to do with infants getting sick. At some point we have to speak up against corruption, don't we?" He puts a hand on Alex's shoulder. "Just think about it, okay, Alex?"

His hand is warm and affirming, his eyes sincere.

Alex turns around, walks out.

Frank catches up with him three blocks away. "Alex!"

Alex keeps walking. A moment later, he feels Frank's firm hand on his shoulder, turning him around. "Alex, hear me out."

"I'm not doing it, Frank!" He squirms his shoulder away from Frank's hand. "I'm not snooping around for you."

"Come on, Alex!"

"If I get caught, and then branded an agitator and Jap sympathizer, you ever think what that'll do to Father?" He stuffs his hands into his pockets. "Whatever slim chance he might have of being released, *poof,* it'll be gone just like that." Alex takes a breath, tries to steady his breathing. "So we *both* need to stay out of trouble."

Frank shakes his head angrily. "You're an idiot if you think staying quiet and a model citizen will achieve anything."

Alex looks away. *Leave. Just go.* But he can't. "You ever consider something, Frank? You ever think that maybe Winchester and Campbell aren't the ones stealing the sugar? That maybe someone else is?"

Frank's eyes narrow. "Like who?"

"Oh, I don't know. Maybe any one of ten thousand people who wouldn't mind a little more meat and milk for their kids, or maybe sugar for their coffee? Or heck, maybe sugar for the bootleg sake they're distilling?"

"Who've you been talking to?" Frank's voice, harsh and accusatory.

"It's common knowledge, Frank. Everyone's cooking up some of their own sake. In hidden cellars beneath the barracks—"

"Why are you so quick to side with *them*?"

"And why are you so quick to accuse them?"

Frank suddenly reaches for Alex, unzipping Alex's jacket and flinging out his security badge. "They got to you, didn't they? Made you all sympathetic so you can't see past their blue eyes and white skin and shiny white teeth. Serving them, kowtowing to them all day and night, it's gotten to you."

"Frank, you just—"

"They took Father away, they took us from our home, they threw us into this hellhole, and you're still kissing their white ass—"

"Shut the hell up."

Frank laughs mockingly. "Oh, I like your tough-guy act. Your imaginary French girlfriend would be *so* impressed."

Alex's punch more grazes than catches Frank on the nose. But it's still enough to draw blood. A small drop that trickles out of his nostril.

"Wow," Frank says, in mock praise, wiping his nose with the back of his hand and examining the faint smear of crimson. "What do you know? Little brother's finally grown a pair."

Alex turns and walks away.

"Remember, Alex," Frank says, serious again. "We need you

to look around. We need you to find crates of milk, boxes of meat, anything hidden away."

Alex stops. Turns around. "Who's *we*, Frank?"

He doesn't answer.

"Are you a Black Dragon? Frank? Did you become one of those ultranationalist, pro-Japan fanatics?"

Frank blinks as if those words have struck him harder than the earlier punch. "What the hell you talking about, Alex? I ain't no America-hater, you got it all wrong."

"You should know something. The Dragons threw rocks at Mother when she left work the other day. Right outside the camouflage-net factory. They said no one should be working for the U.S. army. You're part of *that* group—?"

"Of course I'm not! I'm an American, full-blooded, not like one of those Kibeis."

Then act like one! Alex wants to scream. He turns to leave.

"Start looking, Alex," shouts Frank after him. "Stuff's got to be hidden somewhere."

But Alex, his hand already swelling from the delivered punch, has already made his mind up. He won't snoop. He won't do anything that's got even a hint of Black Dragon in it. He strides away without speaking another word, the distance between the two brothers stretching.

27

Over the next few days at work Alex keeps his head down, completes his tasks, waits the tables with his usual decorum. The Campbell family, despite living in one of only two barracks with its own kitchen, eats at the staff mess hall at exactly eight, noon, and six every weekday. They dine at a white-tableclothed table by the windows, reserved just for them.

Alex studies them from the corners of his eyes. They are solicitous. They seem happy. The children are mostly well behaved. Sometimes they laugh, loudly. Mr. Campbell is brusque and high-handed when dealing with the Nisei waiters but he does not seem like a baby killer.

Alex is careful not to be caught staring. He doesn't want to do anything that might get him fired. He's grateful for the job. Not only because it pays relatively well but also for the distraction it affords. When he isn't working, his mind inevitably drifts to Father in Crystal City. He recently submitted another release petition on Father's behalf. Alex doesn't feel good about his chances, though.

But most of the time, his mind drifts to Charlie . . . wherever she might be. He hasn't heard from her since the letter that ended so ominously. *We must not allow ourselves to be exterminated.* That was more than two months ago. Two *months* of worry and uncertainty and fear. There are days when he cannot eat, nights when he does not sleep.

But here in the staff mess hall, he is busy at least, he is preoccupied. He works hard, often doing double shifts when someone calls in sick. So he does not sneak around now for stolen sugar or meat. He does not do anything at all that might be perceived as snooping, that might get him fired, that might blacklist the Maki name and hurt his father's chances of being released.

One morning Mr. Campbell stops Alex with two raised fingers. "More coffee," he murmurs, never looking up from his newspaper. Alex pours. His hands tremble only a little.

"Sugar with that, Mr. Campbell?"

He dismisses Alex with a wave of his hand.

28

My dear, dear, dearest Alex,

I do not know where to begin. So much has happened. When I tell you there were times I think you will never hear from me again, I do not exaggerate. Terrible things have happened.

On the night of July 16, I waited at Papa's factory for my parents to get me. All night I stared outside to the dark streets, wanting them to come and grab my hand and say urgently "Il est temps de partir, Charlie! Nous devons nous dépêcher!"

But they never came. When morning arrived, I did not know what to do. I was so afraid. I walked back to my neighborhood. The apartment was empty. Two suitcases were half-packed, still lying open on the bed. That's when I knew my parents were taken. Right in the middle of packing, in the middle of the night.

I went out to the streets. They were empty. But once in a while I see a small Jewish child walking the streets alone. In tears. One boy was wearing a thick jacket even in the summer, and I soon realized why: he pulled out money that had been sewn into it. The child offered me money to find his parents.

Then some scouts, members of the Éclaireurs Israélites de France, came along. The group I've been wanting to join. I watched as they comforted the small child, asked for his name. Then led him away, holding his hand. I stopped one of the scouts. She was young and Jewish, like the other scouts. A teenager. Just like me.

"Where are you taking the boy?" I asked.

"To a safe house," she replied. "Then away from Paris." She looked at me carefully, glanced at my yellow star. "You should join us. Help our cause. Be useful."

I wanted to. But I needed to find out about my parents. And just then, a group of gendarmes, French police, came.

The girl told me to run.

I didn't understand. I went to the gendarmes for help.

They arrested me. It was French police who rounded us up. French police leading away French citizens, can you believe that? (Maybe you can.)

They put me on a bus. That took me to a place called Vélodrome d'Hiver. It is an indoor bicycle stadium next to the river Seine. It is famous and maybe you've heard of it? A beautiful place. But no longer. Now and forever it will be Hell to me.

Thousands of us were taken to the Vél d'Hiv. Whole families, women and children. I eventually found Maman and Papa, but oh, Alex, I think I will spend the rest of my life trying to forget inside the Vél d'Hiv. It was awful. The glass ceiling was painted a dark blue so English bombers cannot see it at night. But that made the inside of the Vél d'Hiv like an oven in the daytime. All the windows were locked. All the bathrooms were locked. Can you imagine, over 10,000 people and no bathrooms? No food. No water. Only one water tap. I smelled and saw urine and diarrhea everywhere. Even now I think I can smell the stink on me.

Seven days, Alex. We were there for seven days.

Some people tried to escape. The police—French police—shot them. Some people killed themselves.

Then a week later we were taken away. From Vél d'Hiv to a camp in Beaune-la-Rolande. Just the women and children; Papa was taken from us. We do not know where. The conditions at

Beaune-la-Rolande were not much better. The staircase became a bathroom—you had to be careful not to slip on all the urine and diarrhea. They took away all our jewelry. Some of the women decided to throw their wedding rings and necklaces and bracelets into the toilet rather than give them up. When we looked down through the toilet seat and at the sewage below, we could see their jewelry glimmering in all that muck. "Like stars," a little girl said, and I don't know why but I just started to cry. I hadn't cried even in the Vél d'Hiv, but those two words got tears falling down my cheeks.

Some days later, they took our mothers away. The guards—French—just ripped the children out of their mothers' arms. The mothers fought back, of course, but it was useless, the guards were too many and too strong. Maman tried to hold my hand but the guards smashed our hands, forcing us to let go. Oh, the screaming from all the mothers—Alex, you have never heard such horror and anguish. It is a sound that even now chills my soul. I heard that some women were so overcome they killed themselves the next day.

The French authorities did this. The French government, the French people. My country, my people. I don't know how or if I will ever forgive France for doing this.

Over the next few days I tried to be strong, Alex. There were many younger children who needed help. Many tears to wipe. I thought of the scouts, those teenagers of the Éclaireurs Israélites de France on the night of the roundup. They were younger than me, yet they were so brave, leading to safety Jewish toddlers. "You should join us . . . Be useful," that teenage girl had said to me.

And for the next few days, I tried to be just that: useful. I helped the little children as best I could. Those children who cried were fine. It was the silent ones, in a daze, their eyes empty—they were the ones I worried over.

Five days later, something strange happened. A guard called out my name, told me to follow him. I was put on a truck, then taken to another camp that had less security. And the next day,

Monsieur S (who arranged the transfer and paid off the right people) pulled me out.

He brought me to this secret place. And here I live, in this small room. There is nothing to do but write to you. And try to forget the past. And worry about my parents.

Monsieur S is gone most of the time. He still travels to Vichy and back every few weeks, trying to keep his normal schedule and avoid suspicion. He will leave for Vichy tomorrow for this very reason, with this letter. But without me. It is simply not safe for me to travel without proper travel permits. Monsieur S says authorities are everywhere now, and they check everyone more strictly than ever. The opportunity to flee south is over.

So I must stay here. At least I am not completely alone. There is also a Sinti family of three hiding in this room. The boy is too noisy, we are constantly hushing him. The father never speaks, and his face is swollen with worry. But the mother is very kind. She sees the sadness on my face and whispers stories to cheer me up. I don't understand most of what she says because her French is very bad. Yesterday, she showed me these small slips of paper. I think she said they are magic pieces of paper: if I write a person's name on the slip, I will appear to that person. Like a ghost (!), she said.

Maybe I will try this someday and write your name down. If I appear to you—like a ghost—don't scream, okay? Maybe you can try, too, no?

I am sleepy now. I will try to fall asleep on this hard floor, but how I miss my bed, my room, my desk where I wrote all my letters to you! Promise me that you will one day come and visit my room. I have much to show you there. You will see how beautiful the Eiffel Tower is right outside my window, how it shimmers with dusk light. And you will see what you mean to me. Promise me, okay, Alex?

Your friend,

C

Dearest Alex,

Last night, after writing the letter, I could not sleep. I was so filled with worry. For Maman, for Papa. I wonder where they are. How they are doing. I lie awake in bed all night, every night. I worry about all the children at Beaune-la-Rolande.

A little after midnight I went outside. It was dangerous, foolish. But I could not stand the walls. I needed air, I needed the stars above me.

I walked for a long time. The moon was bright, the temperature perfect, it was a beautiful Paris night. But my heart was torn to shreds. I walked carefully, always on the lookout for German soldiers. The streets were dead. They were once alive, full of laughter. I walked past Les Deux Magots where the outdoor tables were always filled with people drinking Pernod or Rhum Saint James, their cigarette smoke curling over plates of oysters and escargots. But it was empty, it was closed and lifeless.

Like all of Paris.

My feet took me to Sorbonne. The one place that has always lifted my moods. Whenever I am there, I always imagine myself as a student walking across its beautiful campus with arms full of English literature books. I can see this in my mind so clearly, I can feel it in my heart. I want it so bad it hurts.

Last night in the moonlit courtyard of the Sorbonne, I sat on a cold stone bench. There was a stack of papers left forgotten under it. I picked them up. Handwritten poems. Some candles were left on the ground—a puddle of wax pooled around each. I imagine the group of students gathered here earlier, perhaps a campus poetry club meeting for a nighttime reading.

I stared at the candles, the discarded poems. I stared at the empty campus. Life was passing me by, had moved on without me. And I felt suddenly stripped of substance. Like I no longer mattered. Like I was invisible, a ghost.

I picked up the candles, the sheets of poems, slid them in my bag. I walked. For hours. I did not come upon a single soul. Eventually I found myself on the banks of the Seine. The silhouette of Notre Dame cathedral stood across the river.

Do you remember you once sent me instructions on how to build a Japanese floating lantern? I took a discarded piece of wood from a closed bookstall, and removed from my bag the papers and candles. Ten minutes later, I finished making a crude floating lantern. I walked down a small staircase to the river. I lighted the candle and set the boat down on the Seine. Amazingly, it floated; I half expected it to sink quickly. It was a single lonely flickering light that became smaller and smaller as it drifted down the Seine. When it blinked out and disappeared, I imagined that it hadn't sunk but instead was floating around the bend, that it was passing the Notre Dame cathedral, the Musée de Sèvres, past, I imagined, the Palais Bourbon, the Mantes-la-Jolie, and all the way through the graceful loops to the Manche, through the Celtic Sea.

And even now, as I close my eyes, I think of it floating across the Atlantic Ocean, on the big black seas, a tiny dot of light. Defying wind and sea, defying the world. And somehow finding its way to the shores of America, to, dear Alex, you.

Charlie

29

Alex finishes reading both letters. Holds them to his side, the pages shaking. It's only then that he realizes he's kneeling on the floor, bent over his cot like a penitent in a pew. He'd somehow fallen while reading the letters. He tries to stand but lacks the strength. His legs gutted, his heart gutted.

He touches the paper. He imagines he can feel against his fingertips the dips of her handwriting, and in the most tenuous of ways, it feels like he is reaching out and touching her.

Then the Maeda family start to bicker. Their voices float over the bedsheet that is hung up as a divider for privacy, and they shatter the illusion.

There is one thing Alex must do, and do immediately. He must let Charlie know he has heard her, and that he hurts for her. Never mind it'll be weeks before she reads it; he still feels the urgency. He glances at the clock: 3:45 P.M. If he hurries, he can dash off a quick letter, and run to the post office before it closes. He will write again tomorrow, and the day after; he will send her a letter every day even if the postage bleeds him dry.

He arrives at the post office panting hard with only two minutes to spare. There's only one other patron inside, a well-groomed, well-coiffed man going through some packages. The head clerk at the counter, Miss Geraldine Wool, sees Alex approach the counter with his letter. Her face instantly falls.

"What is it?" Alex asks.

She puckers her lips. "You're not going to like this, Alex." She reaches below the counter and brings up a stack of envelopes.

At first Alex's heart leaps. The top envelope is postmarked and covered in stamps. An international letter! But then he sees. It is *his* handwriting, not Charlie's.

"I'm sorry," the clerk says. "But your letters got returned."

"No way." He's already counting the stamps on the envelope. There's more than enough to cover the postage. "Did they raise the rate again? You should've told me—"

"No—"

"What then?"

"I don't really know. It just says 'return to sender.'" She looks impatiently at the wall clock. "I'm sorry. But we're closing . . ."

He slides his just-sealed letter over the counter.

"It's just going to get returned, Alex."

"I don't care."

"You really want to waste your stamps—"

"Just do your job and take it!"

"Fine." Her lips pinched as she tosses it into a basket.

He's surprised by his sudden hatred for her. Her chubby cheeks. Her sweaty fingers, how they always stain his mail. Her lilted *hello*s and *good morning*s and *sorry, nothing for you again, Alex.* Her niceness that's as fake as her painted eyebrows. Her white skin that burns so easily in the summer months, making her look like she's always blushing.

He walks out. He's halfway down the block when he feels a tap on his shoulder. A man's voice. "Sorry, didn't mean to startle you."

It's the well-dressed man who was in the post office. Closer up, he appears younger. Behind his wiry spectacles, intelligent eyes peer at Alex. He's wearing a plaid wool jacket, and this alone sets him apart from everyone else's generic redistributed army peacoats.

"I don't mean to meddle," the man says in well-articulated English, "but I couldn't help but overhear your conversation back there in the postal office."

"Yeah?" Alex says, still angry.

"You're expecting a letter from France?"

Alex nods.

"Well, look, this is none of my business, but there's been a recent development in France."

Alex tilts his head toward the man. "What kind of development?"

The man's face softens with sympathy. "Earlier this month, German forces invaded the unoccupied Vichy zone." He pauses, seems to consider his words. "And unfortunately, all mail to France, including the Vichy zone now, has ceased. So that probably explains why your letter was returned. I'm sorry."

"But I *just* received a letter from there. Today."

The man touches the rim of his glasses. "It was probably already in transit."

Alex's heart sinks. "How do you know all this?"

"The *Manzanar Free Press*," the man says with pride.

Alex knows it. The newspaper circulated around Manzanar internment camp, four pages of mimeographed reporting on mostly camp affairs: sports results, weddings, births, deaths, important events, a reminder of rules.

"My name's Ray Takeda. I'm the editor in chief. We're not allowed to report on international news. But we hear stuff on the radio. Sometimes the staff hands us newspapers and magazines." He glances at his watch. "Well, look, I need to run."

"Hold on," Alex says. "When can I . . . you must know of some way I can send my letters to France."

He pulls his hat lower. "I'm sorry. Not until the war's over.

And that won't be for a few years yet." And with that he doffs his cap and walks away, head tucked against the wind.

Standing alone, Alex feels a sharp twinge inside. His lungs collapsing into tight knots, his supply line of oxygen suddenly cut off.

30

On Friday when the lunch shift ends and most of the staff have already left, Alex is finishing up in the kitchen. The only other people in the kitchen—two senior staffers—are shooting the breeze at the prep table. This is the one-hour dead time before the dinner crew arrives.

"Hey, Maki, do me a favor," one of them says.

Alex walks over. "Yeah?"

He points to a crate of leftover raw meat. "Put that in the refrigerator, would you? My back's killing me."

"The refrigerator? Only you guys are allowed in there."

"And I just gave you permission." The man scratches his armpit. "Put it on the third shelf with all the other meats, okay? Door's unlocked."

The inside of the refrigerator is packed, every shelf filled with prep food, tubs of butter, minced meat to be turned into meatballs for the next day's dinner. He sets down the crate on the third shelf, quickly glances about the interior. The fridge is massive, with shelves running along the walls, five high.

He realizes that an opportunity has unexpectedly presented itself. If he wants to, he can take a quick look around. Not snooping, not exactly. More like a quick look-see. Not because he expects to find any stolen milk, sugar, or meat. But simply so he can tell Frank, *Yes, I searched for you, and no, I did not find anything.*

– 174 –

It would be an olive branch that would appease Frank, help patch things up between them. Things have been very tense of late.

He moves toward the back of the refrigerator. Darker back here, light from the single bulb barely illuminating the many corners and shelves. Nothing seems out of the ordinary.

He is tiptoeing on a crate and poking around the top shelf when he hears footsteps approaching.

"Looking for something?"

He spins around, almost falling off the crate. "No. Nothing. Just, um, nothing."

The man gives him a knowing smirk. "Over here," he says, grabbing a bottle from a nearby shelf. Royal Crown Cola. Uncaps it, offers it to Alex with a wink. "We won't tell if you don't."

It's only later, as he's tying his bootlaces readying to leave, that he makes a discovery. On the floor are the square contours of a trapdoor leading to the space under the mess hall.

The two staffers are turned away, chatting by the sink on the far side.

Partly because he's emboldened by his earlier search, and partly because he can hear Frank already asking—*Well, did you look for an underground cellar like I asked you to?*—he decides to makes one last stab. Quickly, he pulls up the door, and lowers his head into the space. He pulls out a lighter from his back pocket, and peers about. On the nearest side, in the flickering light he sees bottles of beer and wine, even some bootleg sake. Cartons of Chesterfield and Camel cigarettes. Tins of foreign cigars. No big deal, just knickknacks. Nothing major, no stolen jugs of milk or bags of sugar. Job complete. Now he can go. He is about to snap off his lighter, when—

He sees something. He sweeps the lighter across the far wall. His eyes widen, his blood turns cold.

* * *

He runs past Block 13, 14, 15. It's Friday afternoon, the only time of the week he knows exactly where to find his brother.

Onlookers crowd the sidelines of the football field. Alex pushes his way to the front. Less than a minute remains in this tied game, and the field is torn up into a mucky mess, the players themselves covered in mud, their faces streaked with dirt.

Alex sees Frank standing behind the offensive line, yelling out a series of numbers. A different Frank, this one joyous, energized, a throwback to the Bainbridge Island Frank. The center thrusts the ball back into Frank's waiting hands. Bodies clash. Frank: a marvel on the field, graceful and fast as a gazelle. His legs, running and cutting so effortlessly, dodging defenders who go flying past him. He pulls his hand back like a slingshot drawn, then unleashes the football, a propulsion of force that sends the ball sailing an ungodly distance down the field. And into the arms of a wide receiver. Touchdown. Game over.

The crowd roars its approval, the players go wild in celebration. Smiles on mud-streaked faces, thumps on the back. The crowd soon disperses, and Alex is left standing alone on the sidelines that have been almost completely erased by all the mud. It's almost impossible to see where the playing field starts and ends. Frank sees him then. Reads the expression on Alex's face.

He says a few words to his teammates, then jogs over.

"Alex. What is it?"

Alex steps toward him. Opens his mouth but cannot speak.

"Did you search the WRA mess hall?"

He nods.

"What did you find?"

Alex swallows. "Everything."

The next morning the camp wakes up to posters put up during the night. They're nailed everywhere: on electric poles, the sides of mess halls, outside the laundry and ironing rooms in each block. Angry diatribes against the camp administration, accusing them of stealing meat and sugar for the black market.

The posters are quickly pulled down by MPs. Police presence is increased. Throughout the day, jeeps and trucks race recklessly up and down streets in a demonstration of power. Curfew is enforced. At night, those stationed on the guard towers consider it their patriotic duty to shine the spotlight right into the barracks, waking up the occupants.

If the intent is to quell any unrest, the heightened police presence has the opposite effect. Their presence agitates, enflames, provides a target for all the internees' pent-up anger. Roving groups of young men make their way through the blocks. Yelling their voices hoarse. Barging into mess halls, fists pumped, shouting to be heard.

Alex watches with Mother from inside the barrack. Then against her wishes, he opens the door, stands in the doorway. He watches another MP jeep tear down the road, braking to take down more posters.

"Where is your brother?" Mother asks. "Is he staying out of trouble?"

Alex doesn't answer. He is thinking of the sacks of sugar, the jars of milk he discovered yesterday under the staff mess hall. He is thinking of the babies dying.

For so long he's been a mere spectator to the growing anger. Standing behind the lines of the field, firmly on his side. But now, like the football field yesterday covered in mud, the lines are blurring. The separation between player and spectator, between Frank and himself, fading away.

"Did you hear me?" Mother asks. "Is your brother okay?"

He looks at her. "He's fine," he says, and steps out.

31

Just after midnight. The door swings open, smacking against the wall. Ice-cold wind sluices in. Then a stampede of pounding footsteps, racing across the floor.

"Wake up, Frank! Get up!" The voice gruff, urgent, angry.

"What is it?" Frank's voice, thick with grogginess.

Alex sits up. In the darkness, he sees four, five men standing over Frank's cot.

"Daisuke?" Mother alarmed, her hair a riot. "What's happening?"

One of the men says to Frank, "They got him, oh hell, they got him—"

"Slow down, everyone slow down," Frank says, raising himself on one arm.

"They got him—"

"Who's *him*?"

"Harry Ueno!"

Frank shoots up. Rises up from the huddle of bodies. "What do you mean?"

"They arrested him earlier tonight. Slapped cuffs on him and hauled him off to prison."

"Prison?"

"Yeah, took him all the way to Independence."

"When?"

"About an hour ago."

Frank swings his legs onto the floor, shoves his feet into boots. "They can't just throw him into prison for nothing."

"They're saying he was involved in a gang assault earlier tonight."

Frank shakes his head in angry disbelief. "Like hell he was. There's no way he'd get himself arrested. Not when he was just about to prove Campbell stole food rations."

"Well, they did, on trumped-up charges."

Frank throws on his jacket. "He has paperwork to prove everything. He's about to blow the whole thing wide open."

"Daisuke, where're you going?" Mother's frail voice is irrelevant in the dark.

"Go back to sleep, Mother." He slips a scarf around his neck. "And don't come out. Things are going to get dicey."

"Daisuke!"

They tromp across the floor, fling the door wide open. A sharp gust of cold wind whistles in as they slip out into the night.

News travels fast in Manzanar. The lines outside mess halls, latrines, showers become grapevines through which rumors spread like wildfire. By early morning, reports of Ueno's arrest have reached everyone.

There is anger. Ueno is popular: the outspoken man who made rice snacks for children; who labored under the hot July sun to build a rock pond for others; who is fighting for their babies, standing up to the corrupt camp administration. Finger-pointing ensues. Not only at Ned Campbell and Joseph Winchester. But also at the internees in bed with the camp administration. They are accused of being sellouts, stool pigeons, and, most derogatory of all, *inus* (dogs): informers for the camp administration who out of a misguided patriotism dished dirt

– 179 –

on other internees for their perceived loyalty to Japan. It doesn't help these informants' cause that their barrack apartments are often decorated with the best furniture, and that they almost always seem to be in possession of jars of sugar and jugs of milk.

The camp administration can douse this growing fire. They can come forward with explanations. They can apologize. They can come clean about the stolen rations, they can fire Campbell. They can release Ueno.

Instead they double down.

A convoy of buses of MPs arrives in the late morning. Each bus is a droplet of kerosene flicked into the fire, packed with newly recruited MPs, some only a little older than Alex. They are bushy-tailed and eager to protect the homeland.

For many it's their first time seeing a Nisei or an Issei, and they don't know the difference between the two, they're all only *Nips* and *Japs* to them. They see the teeming masses and project onto their faces every stereotype they know: slant-eyed, buck-toothed, bandy-legged fifth columnists all too eager to send TNT dynamite into the heartland. Most of these MPs have been rejected from what they really want to do: fight Nazis and Japs overseas. But now the war has come to them. They lick their chops. This is their shot for glory, their chance to put notches on their belt, to have a barroom story to tell.

Hours later, Alex sees another two buses pull in. A crowd has gathered to watch this arrival, and Alex sees the anger on the internees' tense faces. A tipping point is about to be reached. Everything is coming to a head quickly. When the MPs move into the camp, the first inkling that something awful might happen—perhaps even tragic—flits into his head.

A meeting is called by the de facto leaders for 1 P.M. in a mess hall in Block 22. Alex hurries over. Instead of the expected few dozen, *hundreds* show up. The meeting is moved outdoors to the firebreak.

A microphone and loudspeakers are quickly cobbled together into a public address system. A large oil tank serves as a make-shift stage. Five leaders take turns venting their outrage. "Every time Ned Campbell speaks he thinks he talks to a slave!" yells one of them, a Hawaiian-born First World War veteran who'd fought for the U.S. army in France.

The youngest of the group takes the mike. "Enough of this crap," the man cries out. The loudspeakers squeal with feedback. "We've lost everything! And now to rub salt into the wound, they're taking our food for their own profit. We're being jerked around while our children go sick, our parents topple over, and our babies die."

The crowd roars with approval and anger. Alex, standing in their very midst, feels their collective fury thrum through his bones. He pushes his way through the crowd to the very front.

"They think we're going to take this lying down. They think we're powerless. They think they can get away with anything. Because who's watching them? The locals in Lone Pine and Independence? They hate our guts, too! But enough, I say! Enough! This is America gone wrong! And we need to call them out on it!"

The applause is thundering. The crowd is electrified. At last someone is giving voice to pent-up emotions that have festered within, that have rendered them powerless and full of self-hatred.

The crowd swells. The crowd moves. Sensing a new muscu-larity in its mass, it heads down the road toward the camp entrance. Alex walks with them near the front, his voice joining theirs, his arm raised in solidarity with the crowd.

At the gate, the MPs are waiting for them, lined up in for-mation and reinforced by troops from a local military base. Mounted machine guns are revved and ready. Director Ralph Merritt scurries over. He is newly appointed—the fourth direc-tor in only nine months—and nobody ever told him that the Japs could be so unruly. They're supposed to be compliant and polite, these people who are told what to do and unquestioningly do it. So what is this? What is this uproar?

"Stay in formation," he says to the armed MPs. "This will all be over soon."

The crowd of thousands draws nearer.

32

A tense standoff ensues. Minutes pass, the two groups glaring at one another. Ralph Merritt, escorted by two MPs and second-in-command Campbell, steps forward. From the other side, a small contingent of internee representatives steps forward. They meet Merritt's group in the middle.

The conversation between the two groups is long. There is back and forth. Demands made, demands refused, insults exchanged, tempers almost lost. The crowd grows, becomes more restless. Merritt finally capitulates: Harry Ueno will be released from Inyo County Jail six miles away and brought back to a Manzanar camp jail that afternoon.

Except it is not enough.

Later in the evening, the crowd—which had mostly dispersed after Merritt's promise of returning Ueno to Manzanar—regroups. Only it is even larger now. Four thousand strong. Virtually every able-bodied young man. Even after they are told that Ueno is indeed back in a Manzanar camp jail, it is not enough.

As long as Ueno is still behind bars, it will never be enough.

Alex feels the raw visceral energy of the crowd more than ever. He hears their grumbles, their chants, the slogans they shout in unison and the pains they share quietly with the people around.

They speak of the wrongness of this imprisonment. How they

feel this wrongness every second of every minute of every hour of every day of every month. They feel it every time the wind blows and throws foreign grit and alien dust into their eyelids. They feel it every time the searchlights blind them. They feel it every time they piss and crap in the filthy latrine in full view of strangers and, worse yet, of family, their parents, their children. Their dignity stripped, their self-respect wiped away. They feel it every time they see barbed-wire fences, which is all the time, which is in every direction they look. They feel it every time they line up in the freezing winter or under the baking sun, which is all the time, only to line up again, and again, and again, and again. They feel it every time another uncle commits suicide. They feel it every time they hear someone sobbing in the middle of the night. They feel it in every damned breath they take: the utter wrongness of being confined somewhere they shouldn't be, of living a cheap cardboard imitation of life.

For the first time in almost a year, the anger is not self-directed. For the first time it propels and energizes. It has a target now.

They move toward the jail. They will free Ueno. And as they walk, they walk with focus. But not with weapons. Not with violence. No hammers or hatchets or knives are carried despite what an erroneous self-serving WRA report will later claim. They chant. They shout. They even sing. But no windows are broken. No staff vehicles are smashed. No camp stores or mess halls are looted.

Yet the tension is palpable. Again Alex searches for Frank. But he's nowhere to be seen in this massive crowd. He's not at the front or the back, or anywhere in the middle as far as Alex can see. It is a large, shifting crowd, four thousand strong, and Frank could be anywhere.

The crowd arrives at the police station. They meet very little resistance. Only a single MP in the main sentry post cowers with fear. He fires his pistol into the air three times, not so much a warning shot as a call for reinforcements. The crowd ignores the baby-faced MP. They move into the police station.

Inside, there's even less resistance. The few Internal Security officers practically hand over the keys to Ueno's cell. It doesn't take a math genius to know they're seriously outnumbered. In mere moments, Ueno is freed from his cell. Easy. Too easy. Almost anticlimactic.

But Ueno refuses to leave. "This ain't right," he says. "If I'm to be free, it's because Ralph Merritt sets me free." Ueno walks back into the cell, waits there for Merritt to arrive. His rescuers are bewildered; they look at each other, uncertain what to do next. The "rescue" has turned out to be a dud, truth be told. They're ready to walk out, tell the crowd to disperse. It's over.

But then, Director Merritt.

At that very moment he's watching the scene from afar, behind the slightly parted curtains of his staff home. He's petrified. He picks up the phone and orders 135 MPs to head to the jail immediately. He orders martial law to be declared. He pauses, pressing the phone against his whitened ear. And then he calls in the troops, too. The boys with the big guns.

The MPs and troops haul ass for the main jail, eager for action. Earlier that afternoon, when Director Merritt capitulated to the internees' demands, they'd thought that was weak. That wasn't strong leadership. *Show some backbone for God's sake,* a few had muttered while cooped up in a barrack all afternoon. *Show them Japs who's boss. Put them in their place. Remind them who they're up against, the goddam U.S. of A.*

Now the MPs have energy to burn. They sprint into position, their boots thudding the ground. Their hearts pounding, their adrenaline racing. *Booyah.*

But the jailhouse is a disappointment. The internees—the dozen or so inside the jailhouse—are a disappointment. They don't put up a fight. They leave when ordered. And Ueno, he just sits in the cell. Inexplicable. His cell door unlocked and wide open when they burst in, he could've walked away.

Outside, the MPs form a protective barricade between the jail and the crowd. The officers are armed to the teeth with rifles, shotguns, submachine guns, two heavy machine guns. The crowd sings. The crowd chants. The crowd flips birdies at the MPs. They rip their shirts, beat their chests. They mock the MPs, calling them *boy scouts*.

Alex again looks for Frank. It's nine thirty now and he hasn't seen his older brother all day. Alex is worried now. Something's about to happen. If not now, then soon. Something awful. He thinks to run back to his barrack, check on Mother.

But then two men step forward: the commanding officer of the MPs, Captain Martyn Hall, along with his lieutenant. They are tall, imposing, silver-haired white men used to getting their way. Especially with minorities, with Oriental types. They tell the crowd to disperse, it's time to go home.

"Don't tell us what to do!"

"You're breaking camp rules!" Captain Hall yells.

"Screw camp rules—"

"—and martial law has just been declared!"

"Screw martial law!"

"Anyone who violates martial law will be—"

A rock is thrown at Captain Hall. It whizzes by his head, almost hitting him. His eyes are wide with indignation. To think a *Jap* would have the temerity to throw a rock at *him*—

"TEAR GAS!" he orders the MPs. "Fire them in!"

His lieutenant starts pulling him back. "Martyn, tear gas? You sure?"

But it's too late for second-guessing. MPs are already tossing tear-gas and vomit-gas grenades into the crowd. The crowd yells, disperses as the canisters hit the ground and go rolling. White fumes hiss out. But a northerly wind blows most of it harmlessly away. The crowd returns. Pissed.

"You're teargassing us?" they shout angrily. "We were just standing here! You going to shoot us next?"

Insults are hurled, cigarette stubs, sand. That is all the crowd has to throw. Then someone finds another rock.

It is thrown at the MPs. They duck, glare back, trying to spot the culprit. Some MPs are frightened. Others are chomping at the bit: action at last.

Another rock is thrown at the MPs. The crowd getting louder, pushing forward.

"Hold the line, boys," Captain Hall shouts. "Remember Pearl Harbor! Exactly one year ago. Remember what they did to us."

The crowd edges closer. It hollers, shouts.

"Put on gas masks!" Captain Hall orders. "Fire in all the tear-gas cylinders. On my go!"

The crowd, seeing the MPs putting on the masks, becomes incensed. It edges closer. Yelling, fists raised high into the sky, hollering—

BANG!

Not the blast of gas canisters.

But a gunshot.

The crowd freezes. *It can't be, no way, not a gun, why a gun—*

BANG BANG BANG.

A different kind of blast, this the *rat-a-tat* of a submachine gun.

Panic. Pandemonium. Screams, high-pitched and unstrung.

Warning shots, Alex thinks, *these were warning shots fired over our heads.*

A young man in front falls, legs cut out from under him, arms flailing. The crowd spins, backpedaling, sidestepping—

Another person drops.

More gunfire tears into the night.

More bodies hit the dirt.

"Frank!" Alex screams. He's shoved from behind, gets spun around. Now he's facing the MPs. He sees muzzles flashing, two of them. Someone smacks into him from the side, sending him to the ground. Raw pain swims up his left side. "Frank!" His cry a wheeze.

Dust everywhere. Smoke everywhere. The ground shaking, from thousands of panicked feet. From within this pandemonium, the sound of a car, the screech of rubber, more gunfire, a crash. Screams, shouts.

Then quiet. Bodies lie scattered along the ground, some curled into fetal positions, others quivering. A few stationary. Moaning starts from all around.

He hears screams of panic, of anger, he hears MPs shouting, perhaps at one another.

"Alex!"

Frank's voice. Alex lifts his head. He can't locate his brother, it's too dark, too much swirling dust.

"Alex!"

There. Frank. Ducked low beside a barrack.

"Frank."

Their eyes meet. Frank runs over, his big brother, his head bent low. "Alex, you okay?"

Alex has no idea. "I'm fine, I'm fine."

"You're grabbing your side."

"I'm fine."

"Did you get hit, my God, did you get hit?"

Alex doesn't know. He's clutching his side. Frank pulls his hand away. Shoves up his sweater, his shirt, and Alex is already flinching. But the exposed plate of skin is pale and unbroken.

"We have to move, Alex. Get up!" Frank hoists Alex up, pulls him along. They start legging it. Searchlights cutting manically left and right, making shadows dance in macabre fashion. Shouts. Chaos. The air frizzled with the stench of smoke.

A dark pool of shadow before them. A man, crouched in it, cradling someone unconscious. "Help!" he screams louder. "Somebody help!"

Frank bends down to help. He jerks up. Stares at his own hands. They're coated with slick, thick blood. Blood from the man on the ground, so much of it pooling around him.

"Grab his legs," Frank yells at Alex and the other man. "We've got to get him inside!"

Together, the three carry the unconscious man into the nearest building. The police station. His body, slack and limp and slippery with blood, is difficult to carry. Around them, screams, shouts. Other people lying on the street.

Frank kicks open the door, settles the man down on a table. Ceiling light shines down on the victim's face.

"He's just a teenager," the other man says. "They mowed down a kid."

Frank's face is stricken white. "It's James," he whispers.

"You know him?"

"A friend from school."

The man pulls James's sweater vest up, searching for an entry wound. "I can't find anything."

"All this blood, though."

They flip James over onto his stomach. A dark, bloody hole in the center of his vest.

"They shot him in the back," Frank mutters, his face drained of blood.

"My God," Alex whispers. He backs away from the table. "I never thought they'd shoot us. I never thought America would do this to us. To their own." He stumbles backward, his head spinning. The world gone mad.

"Alex?" says Frank.

Alex pushes through the door. But outside, there's no reprieve. More bodies lying on the street, in pools of blood. Friends bent over them, trying to help. Some of the injured are groaning. Blood leaking from wounds in their backs or sides.

They were all shot while retreating, while running away.

Alex feels something breaking in him. And hardening, too.

That night searchlight beams slash through darkness like slicing scissor blades. Everyone retreats into their barracks. MPs patrol the roads, their holstered weapons bigger and darker than ever. No one comes out of the barracks, but voices grumble out, angry voices, pained and shattered.

After midnight, the mess-hall bells start to toll. From every block. Over and over, urgently, continuously, solemnly. They ring all night like cathedral bells that toll for the dead. MPs drive over and force the men to stop. But as soon as the jeep drives away, they recommence. The bells ring as night cedes to dawn; they ring through the morning hours when nobody leaves their barracks, not for work, not even to eat. They ring until noon in a seemingly deserted city of tar-paper barracks.

They are the only sound in those vast empty plains of windswept nothingness.

33

What surprises Alex most is the laughter. Five days after the riots, after he's been forced to report to work because—surprise, surprise—no one wants to work there anymore. He hears it almost as soon as he steps into the staff mess hall. A tinkling, relaxed sound, with a carefree country-club quality. Over the next half hour as he maneuvers between tables with arms piled with dishes, he hears all kinds of laughter, in all its varying permutations: cackling, chortling, giggling, sniggering. He has never thought of laughter in quite this way, but it strikes him that laughter is actually a form of violence.

He carries utensils and glasses on a tray. He can barely breathe. He nears a table of off-duty MPs, the utensils rattling on the ceramic plates, the water sloshing up and down in the glasses. These MPs are young. The same age as James Kanagawa, who died with bullet holes in his back. Who died with his stomach and pancreas ripped up, who died pleading, *I don't want to die, I don't want to die.* The same age as James Ito, also riddled with bullets in his back, who died a few days later. These white young men here are laughing and full of life and enjoying a nice dinner. James Kanagawa and James Ito are presently not far from where they sit, except they are six feet under, except they are not laughing but silent; they are cold and smelly with decomposition; they are in small, cheap coffins.

Eleven others are still in the hospital recovering from bullet wounds. All shot in their backs while retreating. The Military Board of Inquiry that came to investigate tried to get the doctor on duty at the hospital that night to change the autopsy report. But Dr. James Goto refused and stood by his report: the eleven injured and two deceased were all shot in the back and sides. Days later, Dr. Goto was unceremoniously shipped off to another camp.

"—and then I tell him, 'Yo skinny bones, time to pump some iron, why don't you?'" Laughter. Grins.

It's not what they're saying that upsets Alex. It's the silliness of it, the lightness of this banter. As if, just a stone's throw away, ten thousand people aren't grieving and fuming under a heavy cloud. Like they don't matter. Like they don't exist.

"And I want to tell him—ya know, Mr. Celery Sticks For Arms—that it doesn't matter how much you pump, gals ain't never gonna . . ."

Alex sets the glasses down, places one before every soldier. The MPs laugh, grabbing at the water. None of them thank him, none of them even look at him. They wrap their fingers around the glasses and Alex wonders if those white fingers were the ones that pulled triggers a few days ago. He wonders what they did that night after everyone had scattered, after the dust had settled, after they returned to their staff housing. Did they talk softly? Did they toss and turn, have nightmares?

Or did they laugh? Did they boast to one another?

A minute later Alex is in the kitchen, getting their entrees. From the dining hall, someone thumps the table appreciatively at a well-told joke. Alex lifts the tray of entrees. He realizes this is the last time he'll carry food in this mess hall. This will be his very last minute in this building.

A strange calm settles over him.

"Your spaghetti with meatballs," Alex says as he reaches the table. He tosses the first plate onto the table; it bounces, half the spaghetti sliding out of it.

"Yo, watch it kid."

"Oh, you want some spaghetti, do you?" He tosses the next plate even more roughly, and this time all the spaghetti slides off the plate and into the lap of the MP.

"What the hell!" The young man stands up, outraged. A large dark splotch in his groin area, spaghetti strands dangling off like pubic hair. "What the hell, kid?"

"Spaghetti for you, too, sir." Another plate flung to the far side of the table, the whole plate bouncing like a skipping stone, striking the man in the chest. Pasta sauce and spaghetti drapes across his narrow chest. He looks like a man shotgun-blasted in the chest.

All the men are rising out of their chairs now. Everyone in the dining hall has turned to look. Alex glares at their white skin, their blond and brown and ginger hair, their green and blue eyes.

"I've got spaghetti for all of you," Alex says. "And spaghetti for you, and you, and you"—each *you* punctuated with a tossed plate. The plates are crashing to the table now, smashing into broken porcelain. Spaghetti and red sauce and meatballs flying around.

A hand grabs his shoulder, upending the whole tray. A ridiculously loud clatter like a cymbal dropped. People at other tables are half standing out of their chairs.

"Who the hell do you think you are?"

Alex responds with a calm he never thought he could possess in the heat of such a moment. His unpremeditated words: "I am James Ito."

"The hell?" The seven men, glaring at him, moving toward him.

More chairs sliding back, footsteps quickly approaching.

"You have it coming, kid," one of the men says, wiping off spaghetti.

"Don't call me kid. Call me James Ito. Call me James Kanagawa."

"You're dead." The man grabs Alex by his shirt. Right at the base of his neck. "You son of a—"

"Stand down, officer!"

Everyone freezes.

It's Director Ralph Merritt. His face bright red, yelling from across the cafeteria. "I said *stand down!*"

The man lets go of Alex.

"Get out, kid," Ralph Merritt says.

Alex doesn't realize his hands are bunched into fists. He relaxes them, his fingernails leaving crescent marks in his palm. He walks through the group of men, refusing to turn his shoulders to slide through. Shoulders bump, elbows graze. Alex walks across the cafeteria, undoing his apron, letting it drop to the floor.

34

Winter arrives in earnest, baring its merciless fangs.

Everyone yearns for just one hour of warmth, one hour to bask in the blazing sun in T-shirt and shorts, to sweat, to pant, to swear never to complain about the heat again.

Old men and old women dream of hot public baths where steam rises from the water like ghosts and ciphers.

Children dream of fireplace hearths; of feet toasty in warm bunny slippers, and marshmallows held out on sticks and roasted into a perfect char, shadows and firelight flickering across their faces.

Teenagers want to stop shivering in cold empty barracks. Want to stop envisioning their alternate selves living full lives back in their hometowns, a world untouched by war and filled with parties at the beach; double features at the local drive-in; breakfasts of unlimited, unrationed bacon and butter; and nighttime drives in the Model T, the warm summer wind in their hair.

Young lovers are not anymore; not young, not lovers.

During the cold endless nights, Alex stares for hours at the rafters overhead. He wonders if his tussle with the camp staff is the reason Father's second release petition was just denied. He wonders if his rash action has doomed Father, slammed shut all doors. The guilt gnaws at him.

He worries about Charlie. All the time; it borders on obsession. He hasn't heard from her in four months, and he wants to believe she made it safely out of Paris and is now in Nice. But at night the worst thoughts—that she is in prison somewhere, languishing—keep him awake.

Some nights he simply wants to curl up and shut himself off from everyone, from the world. He feels himself becoming callous inside, his heart becoming as hard as the icy ground outside.

He is not alone. Everyone around him seems to be hardening. Their hearts hardening against the camp staff. Against the MPs. Against parents. Against each other. Against, at last, America.

35

Alex is watching a movie when a strange feeling comes over him.

He's in a converted mess-hall-turned-movie-theater with several dozen other viewers. In the warmer months when the night is balmy and stars shine overhead, movies are shown in a fire-break between blocks. Hundreds lay their blankets on the ground and watch *Road to Zanzibar* or *Here Comes Mr. Jordan* or *Sweater Girl* on a screen as large as a drive-in screen. But in the winter, movies are moved indoors.

Alex is sitting beside Sandy Soto, a girl who had unexpectedly spoken to him that morning in church just as service ended.

"Want to see a movie tonight?" She was in the pew in front of his, returning a Bible to its holder. Her large eyes were on his.

"Me?"

She straightened her back. "Come on. Alex."

"Huh? What?"

She blew the bangs out of her eyes. "This is awkward enough, a girl asking out a guy. But we're in the middle of a desert with absolutely nothing to do. What excuse could you possibly think of?"

Not a single one, apparently. Because hours later, with the sun beginning to set outside, he finds himself seated next to her. The "theater" is crowded, surprisingly so. Alex had expected the place to be half-full at best. But almost every chair is taken.

Perhaps people are simply stir-crazy from being cooped up in their barracks for weeks on end. After the riot, the city of ten thousand ground to a halt. Martial law was imposed. Schools were shut down for over a month. Children were forced to remain indoors by nervous parents. People refused to report to work, and basic services came to a screeching stop. Barracks stayed dark at night.

But maybe that is coming to an end, Alex thinks, looking around. The young can take confinement for only so long.

The opening credits of the movie, *The Hunchback of Notre Dame*, begin to roll. When Maureen O'Hara's name appears in the opening credits someone yells out, "Ohara? She's Japanese?" And there is group laughter, the first such sound in weeks.

The movie, to Alex's surprise, lures him in. He's mesmerized by the scenes of Paris even though he knows the movie was likely shot on some Hollywood soundstage. Sucked into the screen, he's transported from the dust-ghetto of Manzanar to the bell tower of the Notre Dame cathedral. Even in black-and-white, Paris is beautiful. The city of lights. The city of splendor. The city of dreams. Of love. The city of Charlie Lévy. He can almost smell its air, feel its cobblestones beneath his feet.

By the time the hunchback rages to Maureen O'Hara, "I'm not a man, I'm not a beast, I'm as shapeless as the man in the moon!" Alex has all but forgotten his immediate surroundings. He's in Paris.

It's at that moment . . . he feels an odd sensation. A tingle at the base of his spine.

Onscreen a man is laying almost atop Maureen O'Hara, their lips scandalously close, an inch from touching. She whispers, *Say again you love me.*

"Don't do it," someone shouts to laughter.

I love you.

More than anything in the world?

I can't do anything more than just love you.

"Oh please," the same person says aloud before being shushed.

The tingle grows more insistent. Spreading up his spine, warming his cartilage. But there's a prodding sensation to it. Like a beckoning. He stands, blocking the projector's beams, the image of the beast rippling on his clothes.

"Are you okay, Alex?" asks Sandy, peering at him quizzically.

He barely hears her, stumbles past her and through the exit.

Outside, an orange tinge lines the horizon. The Sierra Mountains loom in the distance, their snowcapped peaks topped with dusk light, their lower halves already darkened in the shadows of night.

The odd sensation has only grown stronger. It's now a heat coursing through him, radiating along his rib cage, directing him.

He lets it. He finds himself walking past the church in Block 15, past the elementary school in Block 16. He keeps walking, and now he is past the Guayule Lath House, where rubber is extracted to aid the war effort. He hears the faint trickle of Bairs Creek, which cuts, briefly and teasingly, across the southwest corner of the camp. In the winter it is as deserted and still as the loneliest crater on the moon.

He stops. Something is about to happen. Slowly, he turns around.

Someone is standing there. Blurred, a smear of light, right up against the fence. In a light blue dress, a large jacket thrown over it. The image quivers like the reflection on a rippling pond. It's a woman; no, younger, a teenage girl.

"Hello?" he says.

She turns. Her face is blurry, as if underwater. A white girl, that much he can see. The daughter of a camp staffer? Probably. Perhaps going out for a walk at sunset.

The wind blows and her hair dances wildly in the wind.

She begins to fade. The edges to her form blurring first, becoming translucent. Her eyes rising up to meet his, and in that short moment they hold each other's gaze. There is an intensity in her brown eyes, steely and lit up even in her wavering, vanishing form.

And suddenly his heart is breaking to pieces.

He steps toward her, a name caught in his throat.

Dust blows into his eyes. He blinks. Opens his eyes.

She is gone. If she was ever there in the first place. Nothing but the vast empty landscape, dusk's light spilling gauzily across it.

It was merely an optical illusion, he thinks. A dusk-lit reverie of dancing dust playing tricks in the windswept plains. Nothing more than a figment of his overripe, yearning, lonely mind.

He stares at that empty space where she was and then was not. And whispers:

"Charlie."

He runs home. Pulls out the suitcase from under his cot. Riffles through her letters, his fingers fluttering with excitement. He finds the envelope, pulls out the letter. Eyes swing to the sentence he'd glossed over.

. . . they are magic pieces of paper: if I write a person's name on the slip, I will appear to that person. Like a ghost . . .

At the crack of dawn the next day, he goes back to that spot by the fence. He gets as close to the fence as he dares without drawing attention from the guard tower.

Nothing. No footprints in the dust, no sign that any had ever been there.

By evening, filled with doubt and feeling foolish, he's already discounted it ever happened.

But the next morning, just before dawn, he steals out. Heads past the Guayule Lath House. Past Bairs Creek. He waits. An hour passes. The dawn sun rises into the sky, spilling its ochre light.

No one appears.

Still he waits. Casting his eyes left, right, near, far.

Charlie.

Charlie.

Charlie.

In the barrack, everyone is still sleeping. He stomps over to his cot, takes out his sketchbook, an expensive leather one Charlie sent him for his thirteenth birthday. Every page has since been filled with sketches of her, what he has imagined her to be, anyway. Except the very last page. That, he's kept empty, saving it for when she's finally sent over a photograph.

He's still waiting for it.

He turns to that page now. Takes a deep breath, puts pencil to the cream wove paper. He draws from memory: her slight form by the fence, her chin tilted defiantly upward, her hair tossed in the wind, anger and despair in her eyes.

But he's not even halfway done when he slams the pencil down. This is all wrong. It is accurate but it is clinical. There is nothing of her spirit. Her essence. He grabs his eraser, starts over.

But again it is not right. And it is never right, no matter how many times he erases and starts over. He stares down at the page covered in tiny eraser shavings. He'll give it one more go, he decides, blowing the shavings away.

Twenty minutes later, hand aching, he holds the page up. This sketch, *almost.* But not quite. He reaches for the eraser. Pauses.

This will be the closest he'll ever get. He gazes critically at the sketch:

Then closes the sketchbook.

36

LATE JANUARY 1943

Every day he looks at the drawing. Every day he visits the same spot by the fence. Every day he stops by the post office, and every day he is waved off. Sometimes with a sympathetic shake of the head, more often with an irritated sigh.

"Nothing, Alex. Nothing but your returned letters."

Everywhere he walks, he walks with searching eyes. Sometimes he catches in his periphery a blur of swirling color, and his heart leaps. But it's only a colorful shirt or blanket on a clothesline blown by the wind, or the dulled reflection of the setting sun caught in a swinging window.

She is nowhere. She is everywhere.

There are moments of lucidity. When the absurdity of all this slams home. When he accepts that her appearance was merely a trick of light. A stupid, juvenile flight of fancy, a deceit of a lonesome mind. In those moments, he laughs at his own idiocy, turtle boy with his head in the clouds.

And yet. She is on his mind all the time. He rereads her old letters over and over. He finds himself wondering what she is doing at that very moment: Is she sleeping? Eating? Reading?

Is she even alive?

This last thought surfaces only in his nightmares, where every night he roams the empty Parisian streets, searching for her in café after café filled only with Nazis who bark out in haughty

German demands for more beer, more Camembert, and he walks past them with head tucked down, walking all over Paris until his feet blister and the cobblestones rub his tender soles raw.

Sometimes he startles awake. He lies in the darkness, his only company the snores and strangled sounds of others. He wonders what is happening in Paris. In France. In Europe. He wishes there were some way to find out. Even a drop of information would connect him, however tenuously, to Charlie. But out here in the desert, cut off from the world at large, there is nowhere to get such news.

One morning, walking empty-handed out of the post office, he suddenly stops. He is realizing: *that is not entirely true.* He is suddenly thinking of the man he met here months ago. The editor of the *Manzanar Free Press*. Ray Tanaka. No, Takeda. Ray Takeda. The man who knew about the Vichy occupation. About the stoppage of international mail. Who had access to international news.

Fifteen minutes later, Alex is standing outside a barrack in Block 15. An awning hangs over the door:

OFFICE OF REPORTS, MANZANAR FREE PRESS

He knocks. No one answers.

He pounds again, harder, more insistent.

The door opens. A man stands silhouetted by light, a cigarette dangling out of one hand. Handsomely dressed with carefully coiffed hair and clothes that seem tailor-made.

"There's no need to pound the door," Ray Takeda says, clearly annoyed. He pauses, his intelligent, curious eyes studying Alex. "I remember you."

"Tell me," Alex says, panting hard, "what's happening in Europe. In France."

Takeda regards Alex with a hard stare. For a second it looks as if he's about to shut the door on him. Then he swings the door wider. "Come in."

The interior is like that of any other barrack. The same walls and wooden planks, the same tepid air inside. But there are a few differences. A metal file cabinet in the corner. An Underwood portable typewriter sitting on a desk. A blond veneer armchair, the cushions covered with a faded blue pinstripe flannel. A cheap bookshelf made of corrugated steel, its shelves stacked with newspapers. *The Los Angeles Times. The New York Times. The Santa Ana Register. The San Francisco Chronicle.* And stacks of magazines. *The New Republic. The Atlantic.*

"Would you like some tea?" Ray Takeda asks, observing Alex.

Alex swings his eyes from the bookshelf back to Ray Takeda. "Tell me what's happening in France."

"Well, there's a lot, depends on what you—"

"I have a friend who lives in Paris. She's Jewish. I think something may have happened to her." He glances at the stack of newspapers. "Do you know anything?"

Ray Takeda looks at Alex for a very long time. "Are you sure you want to know?"

"Yes."

He hesitates. Brushes off dust from his sleeve. "I've been reading things," he says after a moment, his face grim. "Disturbing stuff. I need to warn you—"

"Tell me."

"There've been rumors of roundups."

"I know that already. But you know more, don't you?"

Ray Takeda's voice is soft now. "There are other stories. Of whole families, women and children, being sent by train to undisclosed locations. To camps. And then . . ." His voice falters.

"Then what?"

"This is just a rumor. But there are rumors of . . . executions."

"Executions?" Alex feels his stomach turn. He points to the bookshelf. "Show me these articles."

Ray Takeda shakes his head. "It's just tidbits of information."

"Still. Show me."

"Like I said, it's a sentence here, a few words there scattered among different news reports." His voice turns grave. "But I suspect we'll be hearing more in months to come."

"Then I want to read everything you have. And every magazine and newspaper as they come in."

Ray Takeda snorts. "This is not a public library. It's a printing press. And the staff, we're very busy."

"So I'll work."

"We're not hiring."

"Then I'll intern. As a volunteer reporter. Whatever. I just need to be here."

Ray Takeda takes off his glasses, starts polishing them with a handkerchief. "Listen. I understand your situation, and I'm sympathetic. Truly, I am. But we don't need writers currently. We've got college students on leave from Harvard and Princeton who write better than you."

"Then I'll draw."

He shakes his head. "We're strictly a printed-word publication. No illustrations."

Alex quickly whips out the blank page from the typewriter. Grabs a nearby pencil.

"What are you doing?"

Alex ignores the question. Seconds later, he holds out the sheet. He's drawn Ray Takeda, a quick caricature. "If I had another ten seconds," he boasts, "it'd be twice as good."

Ray Takeda puts on his glasses. "You have talent. Clearly." He hands back the paper. "But like I said. We don't print illustrations."

Alex refuses to take the paper back. "Her name is Charlie Lévy," he whispers. "I haven't heard from her in months. I don't know what's happened to her. I don't know if she's even alive."

He looks at Ray Takeda. "This is my only way of . . . staying connected to her."

Ray Takeda blows out his cheeks, walks over to the window. Stares outside. "Fine. You can work here. Strictly as a volunteer. Mostly you'll sweep and mop the floor, you'll wash out our coffee mugs, you'll run errands to and from the post office. But you get in our way, you so much as sneeze too loud, and you're gone, do you understand?"

Alex is already grabbing the broom.

37

At the crack of dawn most days, Alex rises from bed, puts on his boots, and slips out. The camp is eerily quiet and deserted and beautiful at this hour. Faint figures dot the dawn-rimmed horizon: mess-hall staff working the breakfast shift; or those carrying laundry, hoping to get an early jump; or the elderly heading to the bathroom for the illusory promise of privacy. A few, even in the cold, wear getas, traditional Japanese clogs made out of wood, to keep their feet clear of mud.

Some mornings he arrives to find the office in a flurry of action. Three, maybe four staff workers hunched over desks, glue and tape and scraps of paper scattered about, the Underwood typewriter clacking out its tune. Ray Takeda, always unflappable, always immaculately dressed even after working through the night, typing away in rolled-up sleeves, a lit cigarette dangling seemingly forgotten from his lips.

But most mornings he arrives to find the office unoccupied and dark. He turns on the lights, empties ashtrays, sweeps the floor, brews a pot of coffee. All to give evidence that he has been at work in case Ray Takeda should walk in.

And only then does he read. Starting with any magazines or newspapers that have come in, then working chronologically backward through the stacks, picking up from where he left off. He pores over any news about Europe. *Time* magazine prints a war map every week, and he sees the black spill of Nazi occupation across Europe, the dense black soaking up the nations, absorbing France. Paris. Charlie.

Ray Takeda wasn't lying: news about the plight of Jews in France—or in Poland or the Netherlands or anywhere—is scant. A sentence here and there. A remark about some rumor overheard. Of prisoners in striped clothing, starving to death. Shaved heads, even numbers tattooed onto their arms. But nothing more than those throwaway pieces of information.

Charlie seems so far away.

He finds other articles. Not about the situation in Europe, but closer to home. About Japanese Americans. Like this "Survey of Opinion" published by the *Los Angeles Times*:

> Do you favor a constitutional amendment after the war for deportation of all Japanese from this country, and forbidding further immigration? **Yes:** 10,598; **No:** 732.

> Would you except American-born Japanese if such a plan as the above were adapted? **Yes:** 1,883; **No:** 9,018.

One morning he arrives to find Ray Takeda and three other staff standing over a stack of flyers. "Ah, good, you're here," he says on seeing Alex. "We need you to help post these up around the camp."

Alex picks up the top flyer. This must be a cruel joke. An April Fools' joke come two months early.

President Roosevelt announces establishment of the 442nd Combat Team, a military unit composed exclusively of Japanese-American soldiers.

"No loyal citizen of the United States should be denied the democratic right to exercise the responsibilities of

citizenship, regardless of his ancestry. The principle on which this country was founded and by which it has always been governed is that Americanism is a matter of the mind and the heart; Americanism is not, and never was, a matter of race or ancestry. A good American is one who is loyal to this country and to our creed of liberty and democracy."

"That's fresh, coming from him," Alex says. "He throws us into jail in the middle of the desert. And now he wants us to fight for him? In a segregated unit? Is he for real?"

"These flyers are for real, and that's all that matters," Ray Takeda says. "And we have our duties. Everyone to your assigned blocks and post these on the bulletin boards."

At Block 9, Alex nails up the flyer and turns around. A crowd has already gathered.

"You've got to be kidding me," someone says.

"What does this mean?" a teenager asks.

"It means we can enlist," another teen answers, peering closely at the page. "It means they finally want us. We can fight for America." The teen bounces from foot to foot. "Hey, we get to wear uniforms. Shoot weapons. Fight Nazis. We get to leave this dump!"

"You're an idiot," someone tells him.

"How old do you have to be?" the teen asks.

"Probably eighteen."

Alex steps away from the bulletin board. He'll be eighteen in two months. Not that it matters. There's no way he'll enlist. Not after this country has taken away Father, taken away their freedom, and thrown them in this prison. Not after that "Survey of Opinion" showing this country would overwhelmingly choose to deport him—a fellow citizen—to Japan, a country he's never even visited before.

Alex walks off. In the next block, he goes into the bathroom and drops the remaining flyers down into the cesspool.

38

A week later an army recruitment team pays a visit to Manzanar Internment Camp. The team is made up of a lieutenant and three sergeants. The top brass, not the low ranks, the grunts. They're here to impress.

This surprises most people.

The mess hall is packed fifteen minutes before start time. Most in attendance have ulterior motives. Memories of the December riot are still raw and fresh, and these four military uniforms standing before them draw icy stares. Alex squeezes in and elbows his way to the third row.

The lieutenant speaks first, a silver-haired, stony-faced man. He's followed by two of the sergeants. Nobody laughs at their canned jokes, their corny sense of humor meant to set the internees at ease. When they make cheesy calls to patriotism and duty and honor, a few in the audience, their arms folded, snort.

It isn't until the third and last sergeant speaks that things change. Everyone noticed this sergeant almost as soon as he'd stepped into the mess hall.

His name is Ben Kuroki. A chiseled, handsome Japanese American with broad shoulders, a barrel chest, and a steady, no-nonsense gaze. Intelligent eyes. Unlike the other three, he doesn't speak loudly. He doesn't ingratiate. His voice is soft, not with timidity but with an easy confidence. Like he doesn't have anything left to prove. He tells them he is from Hershey, a small town in Nebraska, and that he grew up on a farm. He doesn't make any cheesy jokes about being a farm boy. He tells them Pearl Harbor was the worst day of his life, that he vomited three times that day and punched a hole in his bedroom wall.

Everyone leans forward to hear more, Alex included. Arms unfold.

He tells them shortly after Pearl Harbor, he ran to the recruitment center to enlist. He was rejected. He went to another recruitment center. This time, he got in.

"How?" someone shouts from the back. "Japanese Americans weren't allowed to enlist."

Sergeant Kuroki turns his eyes slowly toward the back of the hall like he has all the time in the world. Even though there're hundreds inside, his eyes lock in on the person who spoke.

"Two reasons," he says, his voice as quiet and authoritative as before. But now with an uptick of humor. "One: I had a greedy recruiter. He got two bucks for each soldier recruited. He didn't care that I was Japanese American."

Laughter.

"Two: he wrote me down as Polish. He said 'Kuroki' sounded Polish enough. And it worked."

More laughter, louder.

"And that's how I got processed. How I got to fight in Europe. How I became an aerial gunner."

"You fought in the skies?" someone asks.

"And then some. I was a dorsal turret gunner on a B-24 Liberator. Which means I sat in a glass bubble on the underside of the plane. Completely visible, completely vulnerable. And in that confined space, in that glass eye, I saw the world. I shot down Nazis."

The audience is hushed with awe.

"That was one of the most dangerous assignments. It was no

desk job. And I flew over thirty combat missions." He grins, the first time a smile cracks his lips. "And the only reason why I'm here talking to you chumps and not flying the skies over Europe is because on my last mission I got hit by Nazi flak. Trust me on this one, I'd rather be shooting down Nazi planes than looking at your ugly mugs."

More laughter.

"It's the best job in the world, let me tell you. With the best of company. Because those soldiers in the plane with you? They're more than just soldiers. More than just friends. They're your brothers. When you fight in tight quarters, their lives in your hands, your life in theirs—you become family. You learn that sweat and blood and tears are the same color, no matter where you're from. Our left waist gunner was Irish, our bombardier German, our tunnel gunner Jewish. And I'm Japanese. But you know what? No one cared. When you're under fire, no one cares about the color of skin. You're all American. You're fighting for each other. You're fighting for your country. And you realize, man, there ain't no other place you want to be."

The room is quiet and full of beating hearts.

Kuroki scans the crowd, slowly taking in each face. "I got into the army and flew the skies and killed Nazis because of a greedy recruiter and under a Polish name. But you won't need to. You can get in as Japanese American. You can get in as *you*. You get in because America wants you. Because America needs you." He turns to look through the windows, stares at the barbed fences, the barren landscape. "You're all stuck here. Doing nothing. Waiting for your life to restart. I say: See the world. Go to the beaches of Greece, the farmlands of Italy, the cobblestone streets of France. And fight for America. Fight for your friends, fight for your family, fight for your mother, fight for your father, fight for freedom." He pauses, gazes steadily at them. "How can you not?"

He steps back. The room is silent.

The white lieutenant steps forward. "Thank you, Sergeant Karaki."

"You mean 'Kuroki,'" someone from the crowd says. "Jeez."

"Yes, *Kuraki*. That's what I said." The lieutenant turns red. "I'll now field any questions you may have."

The questions come quickly: when and where and how to enlist, where they will be fighting, fairly standard questions—

Alex suddenly finds himself raising his arm. And asking a question he didn't know, until now, has been burning inside him. "If I enlist, will that help my father?"

Every head turns to look at him.

"Tell me about your father," the lieutenant says.

"He's at Crystal City, Texas. In the prison there."

"You mean the internment camp."

"Like there's a difference!" someone yells, to cheers.

"If I fight for America," Alex shouts over the jeers, "will that get him released? Will they finally let him join us here?"

The room falls quiet. Alex isn't the only one who wants to know.

The lieutenant licks his lips, as if sensing an opening. "Of course," he says. "You fight for America, and America will reward you. You show you love America, and America will love you right on back." He steps toward Alex. "If you enlist I'll personally see to it that your father gets brought here." The sergeants behind him are silent, their eyebrows slightly pulled together. "And that goes for all of you," the lieutenant says. "Any other questions?"

"Why are we getting lumped together?"

The lieutenant swivels his head to the back corner. "Excuse me?"

"Why a segregated unit? Why can't we fight in a regular unit?"

The lieutenant has a prepared answer. "This is a favor to you people. It's great for publicity, see. The story will practically write itself, how you're all true, real Americans, giving your blood, sweat, and tears to this country. It'll play great before the cameras, all you folks together showcasing your patriotism."

"Is there a segregated German or Italian American unit?"

The lieutenant cocks his head to the side. "No."

"Then why—"

"Next question," the lieutenant says, ticked off, in full military mode now.

"I got one," someone says. Alex's breath catches short and sharp. He recognizes the voice.

Frank stands up in the middle of the crowded room. "My father's done nothing wrong, but he's in jail. My mother's done nothing wrong, and she's behind a barbed-wire fence. I've done nothing wrong, and look at me. Tell me why I should fight for a country's that treated us like common criminals when our only crime was to dream the dreams America promised. Tell me why I should—how'd you put it?—oh yeah, give my blood, sweat, and tears to a country that's screwed us over royally."

The sergeant speaks in a scolding tone. "This is your chance to prove yourself. To show that you're really an American—"

"I *am* an American! Why should I have to prove it?" His face is scarlet now. "And how do I know that after the war you won't take away my citizenship? That you won't take our family's farm, our land?"

The lieutenant looks smug. "Don't you worry about that. The Fourteenth Amendment will protect you. The Fourteenth Amendment, in case you don't know, guarantees that no law shall—"

"Abridge the privileges or immunities of citizens of the United States; nor deprive any person of life, liberty, or property, without due process of law; nor deny to any person within its jurisdiction the equal protection of the laws." Frank stares at the lieutenant. "That Fourteenth Amendment, you mean?"

The lieutenant stares back with hard, cold eyes.

Frank continues. "The same Fourteenth Amendment that did such a dandy job in protecting me from being thrown into this camp like a common criminal? That same Fourteenth Amendment? Gee, I feel so safe now."

The lieutenant sniffs with contempt. "Don't quite know what you're getting at. Why don't you sit down, son."

"I may be jumping to conclusions but I'm pretty sure I'm not your son."

"Next question."

A barrage of questions are yelled out. The lieutenant has lost control. MPs step in and escort the recruitment team away.

Alex leaves the mess hall as it explodes into bedlam. Two blocks later, a cold wind whistles into his ears but he barely hears it. The lieutenant's words are echoing in his head. *If you enlist I'll personally see to it that your father gets brought here.* Alex had gone to the meeting without the slightest intention of enlisting. But the lieutenant's promise has got him suddenly, almost reluctantly, thinking.

Walking past Block 18, Alex hears someone calling after him.

"Yo, Alex," Frank says, giving him a friendly thump on the back. "Can you believe that bull?"

Alex doesn't answer. Keeps walking.

"The gall they had, coming in like that! Making it look like they're doing us a favor." Seven strides later: "Alex, you hear me?"

Alex gives a quick nod of his head.

"And that Kuroki guy. What a patronizing piece of work. He was so full of himself."

"I thought he was all right."

Frank flings his head at Alex. "Really? Guy's a total sellout. He's lucky to get out of here alive, let me tell you. Heard some guys talking. They were thinking of beating the crap out of him. But he took off. What a coward."

Alex can hardly believe his ears. "We're talking about the same guy here? Sergeant Kuroki? The guy who shot down Nazis. Twenty-five combat missions? Him a coward?"

"If he had any self-respect at all, he wouldn't be here. Wouldn't allow himself to be paraded about like a little puppy. Would refuse to be their puppet. I get that he's military and you need to obey orders. But heck, at some point you've got to draw the line somewhere. Have a little self-respect, for God's sake."

Alex stays quiet.

They pass a barrack. From inside, the sounds of a newborn baby screaming, a couple bickering, parents yelling at children. An elderly man, despite the cold, sits outside on the steps to the door. Doesn't even look up as they walk past.

"Even so," Frank says, "there will be some idiots who'll still enlist. And that's stupid. That's foolish. They'll think it's patriotic. But it's not. It's being gullible. And they won't realize this until it's too late, until they're lying on the battlefield, their guts oozing out of them, and finally thinking, *Oh boy, I'm an idiot, America's just used me as cannon fodder, and America doesn't care, America won't even remember me.*"

He stares at Alex, eyes wet. "But real Americans won't do it. Real Americans will show their patriotism the principled way. By protesting. By calling America to account. Exactly what I've been doing here at camp. And what I'll keep on doing." He drapes his arm around Alex's shoulders. "I'm so glad you've got better sense than all them military idiots, Alex."

"I don't know, Frank."

A slight break in his stride. "What d'ya mean?"

"Did you hear that lieutenant? Enlisting might help Father get released from Crystal City."

Frank waves his arm dismissively. "Nah, that man's full of crap. He'll say anything to get us to sign up."

Alex shrugs off Frank's arm from his shoulder. "But what if he's right, Frank? What if it'll help Father get released?"

Frank is silent, his jaw set hard.

"And with Father reunited with Mother, she'll return to her normal self," Alex continues. "Everything will be back to the way it was—"

"Things will *never* be back the way they were," Frank spits out.

Alex looks at Frank. "We're his family. His sons. We've got to do whatever it takes to bring him here."

Frank turns with a suddenness and a quickness. "Is this your way of being a hero, little bro? Your way of saving Father? Because I've got news for you: it'll do squat."

Alex keeps his eyes on the ground. "Yeah, well, at least I'd be doing something! Instead of wasting away in here—"

"I *am* doing something. I'm standing up to wrong. I'm protesting—"

"Which is doing nothing for Father! Or Mother!" Alex glares at Frank. "You used to care, Frank. About Father. You wrote a release petition even though you hate writing. You went after FBI agents, slammed your fists on their car. What happened, Frank?"

"I do still care! But it's all noise, Alex, don't you get that? Stupid release petitions, hitting FBI cars, and now enlisting? None of it makes a damn difference! It's all just shaking fists at the sky. This country's too big and we're too small."

"What, and doing stupid protests, that's supposed to help Father? Shouting into the wind when no one outside cares or even sees—how the hell does that help Father?" He's furious now. "Listen. If it's me who has to enlist to help Father, then I'll do it."

Frank is silent, his face closing in on itself. When he finally speaks it is with a quiet, seething anger.

"I hate to be the one to break it to you, but you'll die out there. You're not cut out for war, plain and simple, baby brother. Get your head out of the clouds, out of your little fantasy world where you're some imaginary tough guy, okay?"

The words slide in, silent as razors, cutting deep. Because it's true. Alex won't survive war. He's a weakling afraid of violence. A bookish kid who couldn't even boil a frog, who gets light-headed at the sight of blood. He won't make it out there on a battlefield.

Frank isn't done speaking. "And you think you'll be helping Father? The opposite—news of your death will break his heart, he'll literally have a heart attack out there in Texas. Because he's got everything riding on you, his favored son."

"Don't be ridiculous, you're his—"

"No, *you* don't be ridiculous. I know what my future holds. I'm a farmer at best. But you, you're his brainy son, his future dentist son, his retirement pension. So you dying for a country that spits on us—that will kill Father. And Mother. If you enlist you've just about shot them yourself."

There are about a thousand red-hot words Alex wants to yell back. But he doesn't. He swallows them down, the words like mangled paperclips cutting bloody trails down his throat. Because deep down Alex knows Frank is right. America *has* spit on him. Why should he put his life on the line for it? Why should he do as asked? He thinks of that incident years ago in front of the hardware store. Father being mocked by kids, then told by the policeman to move along. And Father kowtowing with a stupid grin, doing as told.

Alex enlisting would be just that. Kowtowing with a stupid gullible grin, doing as told.

He says none of this to Frank. The two brothers walk the rest of the way in a tense silence.

39

In the early morning, Alex walks into the office of the *Manzanar Free Press*. The smell of printer ink and glue floats faint in the air. He turns on the lights, starts sweeping. He glances over at the in-box shelf where all the latest magazines and newspapers are stacked. It's empty. News from Europe has slowed to a trickle.

He's putting away the broom when he sees a magazine opened on Ray Takeda's desk. It's unusual for Takeda's desk to be anything but immaculate, the stationery placed in its stands, fountain pen ink containers tightly capped and wiped clean, and notebooks aligned perfectly flush against the edges of the desk. An opened magazine on Ray Takeda's desk is unusual, and Alex, curiosity piqued, glances down.

The New Republic, December 21, 1942, issue. He reads the title. "The Massacre of the Jews," by Varian Fry.

He picks it up. The pages tremble in his hands like the leaves of a shaken branch.

Two minutes later he drops the magazine. His mouth has turned to chalk.

The door opens. "Morning, Alex," Ray Takeda greets him. A pause as he observes the dropped magazine. "Alex." He takes a step toward him. "I was going to let you know."

A scrim of vomit burns his throat. *Slaughterhouse, starvation pens, extermination centers.* He cannot fathom these places. He cannot associate them with humans.

Of the 340,000 Jews of France, more than 65,000 have been deported.

That was back in December. It's now almost April. How many more have been deported since then?

"Alex? Sit down. You look like you're about to faint."

Alex swipes aside Ray Takeda's arm. He stumbles across the floor, picking up the magazine, and walks out. The cold air, it should sting away the nausea. But at the next barrack he up-chucks.

He gets off his knee. Stumbles along. Dark barracks drift by like ghost ships on a cold dark sea. He is chased by words (*purged, Judenrein*), by numbers (*nearly two million already slain*), by phrases (*there is burning alive . . . asphyxiation by carbon mon-oxide . . . starvation . . . embolism . . .*), by a horror he cannot outpace; it chases him down. *The good old-fashioned system of standing the victims up, very often naked, and machine gunning them, preferably beside the graves they themselves have been forced to dig. It saves time, labor, and transportation . . .*

He needs Frank. Frank to comfort him, put his arm around him. Or Mother. Father. But he realizes the only person he wants to talk to about Charlie Lévy is . . . Charlie Lévy herself. But she's not here. She's over there, across the globe, unreachable.

Slaughterhouse, starvation pens, extermination centers.

He walks. Through funnels of windblown dust, through mud-sloshed grounds. He never stops moving, as if to do so would allow dark thoughts to catch up and devour him.

Nearly two million already slain.

He goes without breakfast, walking past the long lines. Lunch, too. He keeps walking, welcoming the pain that shoots up his aching legs, the cold that seeps into his bones, the thirst and hunger that consumes him whole and raw. Anything to drive out the thoughts, the words.

Hours later he is still walking. Only he is hobbling now, his eyes bleary and unfocused.

Asphyxiation by carbon monoxide . . . burning alive.

The words still clinging, refusing to detach from the wet of his brain.

Still he keeps walking. The sun begins its descent. Hours later it drops behind Mount Whitney. Soft dusk light streams past that raised mountain like river water around a large boulder, the light filtering across the plains, and enduing the land with softness. The barbed-wire fence catches the last of this light, its coiled metal softly glittering.

The scenery is meaningless to him.

Soon the air turns a cold black. The stars come out in force, piercing and sharp.

He finds himself in Block 11. Standing before a packed mess hall. Music from a miked-up phonograph blares out. Through the doorway Alex can see tables and benches pushed off to the side, a few streamers strung between ceiling beams. It's Dance Night. Young couples, mostly older teenagers, crowd the dance floor, jitterbugging away. Everyone trying to shake off the gloom that settled over the camp after the riot and never quite went away. Wanting to be young and crazy and carefree, or at least remember what it was once like, and forget what it is like now.

There will be cups of water inside, he thinks, perhaps some simple snacks. It will be warm. Benches to sit on, rest his feet. He steps toward the mess hall. Stops at the doorway.

For a long time he stares at all the teens inside. They're worried about the lack of pomade in their hair, or if they should finally ask that person to slow dance, or if he's holding her hand too tightly, if his palms are sweaty, if he's going to walk her home tonight and perhaps even steal a sweet first kiss in the moonlight.

They're not worried about death in a slaughterhouse. Not worried if they'll die by asphyxiation or embolism or burning or by the "good old-fashioned system" of being gunned down naked.

"Hey, buddy, you going in or what?" someone says from behind.

He spins around, stumbles down the two steps. Nausea bubbles up his gut into his head. He starts walking again. Without direction, only wanting distance. The ground crunching beneath his boots, the wind whistling between the dark barracks. Another emotion blooms under the soil of nausea. A tingle. Beginning in the base of his spine, spreading. That same sensation he'd felt weeks ago while watching *The Hunchback of Notre Dame*.

He lets it guide him. Walks westward, toward the looming silhouette of the Sierra Mountains. Ten minutes later, the tingle has only increased into a dull throbbing that has worked its way up his spine, and through his rib cage. A tugging. A prodding. Warm, not entirely unpleasant.

He is past Block 29 when he hears shouting. People are peering out of windows and through doorways, pointing at the sky. He glances upward.

Towering over the barracks is a swirling black knot of a dust storm. A blackness bleeding into the starlit sky, snuffing out the moon, the stars, darkness itself as it churns toward him.

Everyone starts running. Someone shouts in Japanese, a curse, a cry for help, it's hard to tell. Stragglers race to nearby barracks, banging on locked doors, begging to be let in. Alex breaks into a sprint as the dust storm catches up and swallows him whole. He runs, blindly now in the swirling haze, trying to outpace it, knowing he can't. He collapses to his knees, and curls into a fetal position as his face is pelted with dust. It is the sting of a thousand wasps and hornets and bees. Sand coats his teeth, sticks against his tongue and the roof of his mouth.

A minute later the dust storm passes. Starlight filters down. Alex stands up, spits. He is surprised to find himself in Rose Park, a large, elaborate park built by volunteers, now in the final stages of construction. Decorative boulders and half-filled ponds glimmer dimly in the moonlight. A curved footbridge constructed out of wood and bamboo arches over one of the ponds, its frame silhouetted against the quivering reflection of stars. Across the way, a half-finished gazebo. Nobody is supposed to be in this park while construction continues, while rocks are erected and rose seedlings planted.

But he sees someone there. Standing on the footbridge at the top of the arched crest.

A teenage girl.

Charlie Lévy.

Alex stops breathing.

Tonight there is no color emanating from her. No orange, no pink. Only a gray hue. She is staring at him.

He walks toward the footbridge.

Her hair is all gone. Completely shaven off. But not a clean shave; ugly tufts are clumped randomly about. Her cheeks sallow, her eyes sunken. Skinny. She is a charcoal etching. A drab work dress flutters about her, blown by the wind. A dying moth.

He nears, dust falling off his shoulders. He smells ash.

"Charlie?"

She flinches at the question.

He shouldn't have. Shouldn't have said it like a question. Because who else could it be but her?

Her eyes fall. Like death, like the blades of a guillotine falling. The light in them snuffed out.

"Charlie!" He steps forward, onto the bamboo planks of the footbridge, a bridge of dust and ash. He stops near the crest. Now they are close enough to touch. He sees her face clearly for the first time. *A plain face,* she had once described herself, *unremarkable.* She is wrong.

He drinks her in. The thick eyebrows, the large eyes tapering to, on her left side, a trinity of small moles. He wonders if she has always been so thin. If her cheekbones have always so protruded.

My eyes, she also once wrote, *they have a fire in them.* She is right. Even now, an inferno burns. A sharp clear light that is not afraid to look at the world in the face, and stare it down.

But she sways now, exhausted. She grabs for the rail with her left arm, and that is when Alex sees it. A curious tattoo on the soft underside of her forearm, a number. *14873.*

The smell of ash is stronger now.

He reaches forward, slowly moves his hand to her cheek. But instead of touching skin, he feels only air.

"Charlie . . ."

Her eyes hold his, shiny and damp. And then she starts to fade.

No. Too soon. Not yet.

He reaches for her again. But his hand again only sweeps through air. Cold air, ashy and sooty.

"Don't go, Charlie!" he pleads.

She tries to offer a brave smile, her lips peeling back to reveal a dark film of disease over her upper teeth. But she falters; her eyes fill and for a moment, magnified by the tears, the light in her eyes shines brighter. But even Charlie Lévy's eyes cannot burn through this darkness.

"Charlie!"

She reaches out with her own hand to touch his face. But he feels nothing, not skin, not heat. Still he leans his face into her palm, where her hand is cupping his cheek. Tears fall from her eyes, cutting through the grime caked on her face. And as she fades away, she whispers words he cannot hear but that are clear and audible in his head.

Find me, Alex.

And then she is gone.

Even the smell of her, of ash and soot, gone.

He is all alone in Rose Park. He is all alone in the whole camp. He is all alone in the whole world.

40

Find me, Alex. Last night, staring out the black window before collapsing into sleep, he was determined to do just that. He'd enlist, go to Europe, find her. To hell with the odds.

But in the morning, in the cold bright daylight, the idea is ridiculous. Of all the reasons to enlist, of all the reasons to put himself in harm's way, it cannot be because of a vision. Even he, Turtle Boy, knows that. Even he knows the odds of finding Charlie, assuming he's even sent to Europe, are so infinitesimal as to be negligible.

Besides, he thinks, it was all a dream. A stupid dream. A figment of his overripe, guilt-ridden imagination, brought on by the *New Republic* article.

For a long time he does not get out of bed. He cannot summon the willpower. He throws his arm over his eyes, wants to block out the light, the sound of snores coming from all around.

Strange: Mother seems unusually quiet. No coughing or wheezing.

He turns, cracks open his eyes. She is still in bed, under a pile of blankets. An empty cot is pulled up next to hers. Father's. It has sat empty for over a year. *We all need something outside these fences.*

He rubs his face. Looks again at Mother. The pile of blankets does not move.

"Mother?"

He rises, walks over to her. The wood beneath his feet is cold and hard as the top of a frozen coffin. He reaches down. Gives her shoulder a gentle shake. She doesn't respond, and his throat suddenly goes dry. He pulls her around so he can see her face.

She smacks her lips, grunts in her sleep. Relief floods him; then just as quickly, concern. Mother's face is gray and scrunched up into a scowl. Wisps of hair dangle lifelessly down, unwound spools of wire. In the cold, she shivers like a soaked baby bird, deathly thin. She's aged twenty years, it seems, since leaving Bainbridge Island.

As he pulls the blanket up over her shoulder, he feels the outline of something hard beneath. He peels the blanket back, and sees it: a photo frame clasped in her cold hands. It's Mother and Father's wedding photo. He stares at her youthful face in the photo taken decades ago, then at her sleeping craggy face—somehow even more colorless than the black-and-white photo—next to it. The shock of this contrast, not between youth and age, but life and death.

Without Father, she's free-falling into the grave.

Unable to stand the inertia and staleness of this cold room anymore, he throws on his coat, pushes out. A frigid brisk wind sieves between the barracks, cuts through him. He walks quickly, trying to stomp warmth into his cold feet, get his blood circulating. But an hour later, having circled the camp several times already, his face is a frozen carcass, his feet blocks of ice.

Dark clouds gather over the Sierra Nevada. A gray settles over the camp.

At the main entrance, he notices a bus that's just pulled into the camp, its engine clanking loudly, the dust left in its wake still afloat behind it. Only a handful of people inside.

Curious, Alex watches.

The door swings open and a pair of uniforms steps off.

A moment later, an old Japanese man stumbles out. His disheveled hair white, his frame wiry and hunched.

Alex's heart seems to miss a beat.

But it's not Father. Just another Japanese man, of similar age. Actually, as Alex takes a closer look, it's someone he recognizes. Mr. Muramoto from Bainbridge Island. A strawberry farmer from the other side of the island. A man who'd also been detained by the FBI. And who, if he remembers correctly, had also been sent to Crystal City, Texas.

His family steps into view now. A mother and a young girl. They'd been waiting for his arrival by the administration building, and now, as the shriveled old man stares bewildered about him, they walk toward him. Their surprise at his withered appearance—shock, more like it—is written all over their faces. This man, their husband and father, has aged into something ancient. Erica Muramoto, the six-year-old daughter, does not run up to him, despite her mother's prodding. She pulls back, fingers in her mouth, blinking away tears. She's afraid. Scared of this shell of a man who is her father but who is also not.

Mrs. Muramoto gives up. She leaves her daughter behind and walks over to her husband. A few feet from him, she stops and bows. He bows. They do not look at each other.

An MP walks up to them. Offers them a ride. Mr. Muramoto shakes his head vigorously. He picks up his suitcase, starts to walk, lopsided against the weight. The wife catches up to him, tries to take his luggage. But he waves her off.

He doesn't last long. A minute later, only a few yards from Alex, he drops the suitcase. "Where the hell is Kenji?" he says in Japanese, wheezing. "That good-for-nothing son of mine."

The mother doesn't say anything.

"He signs up to go to war but can't be bothered to wake up early to greet his old man." He spits to the ground.

The wife takes the suitcase. He lets her now. They shuffle past him, the father bent over against the wind, rasping for air, the young girl clinging to her mother.

Alex is suddenly thinking of the white lieutenant from the recruitment meeting.

If you enlist I'll personally see to it that your father gets brought here.

That must be what has happened here. Kenji Muramoto enlisted. And then his father was released. It cannot be a coincidence.

Alex watches the family stumble past a broken window, their reflection rippling across the cracked glass. Broken. But together.

They turn a corner and disappear behind a barrack. But after they are gone, Alex does not move. He is thinking of Mother, sickly and fading away. He is thinking of Father, probably wasting away, too, in Crystal City. He is thinking he must do whatever it takes to bring him home.

If you enlist I'll personally see to it that your father gets brought here.

Yet he stands paralyzed with indecision. He cannot make up his mind. In one ear, he hears Frank telling him not to kowtow to a country that's spat on them all. In his other ear, he hears his Mother wheezing, her health failing, needing Father. He cannot decide. He cannot move the needle, one way or the other.

Black dense clouds slide quickly across the sky, drawing darkness like a blanket over the camp. Rain begins to fall, and the first drops are big and heavy, and make dark splats on the dusty ground. Within a minute, the raindrops become a downpour, drumming loudly on the barracks' rooftops and turning the ground to mush. Alex heads back, not bothering to run. He will be drenched regardless. He is already almost soaked through.

It is only as he is passing Rose Park that he stops. A voice is filling his head, and it is not the voice of the lieutenant. Or Frank, or Mother. It is the voice of another.

Find me, Alex.

He stands for a long time. Very, very still. Then he lifts his head to the sky. A small movement, but seemingly decisive. His clear eyes do not close or even blink at the raindrops falling down on him.

41

He didn't plan on telling Mother for another day or two. But that Monday afternoon he finds himself alone with her in the room. The unseasonably warm day has lured almost everyone outside, and this unexpected privacy is too good to waste. There will be no better moment.

"Mother." He sits down at the table across from her. "I need to talk to you about something."

Her shoulders pull together. She knows already. Or has at least suspected.

Still he fidgets. Still he tries to find the opening words.

She sees the misery etched on his face. "You've decided to enlist," she says matter-of-factly.

He nods slowly. "I'm sorry."

She sets down her knitting. Her chest rises and falls, rises and falls. She asks, without looking at him, "I thought you were against joining the war."

He doesn't say anything.

She looks at him. "Then why?"

"It'll help Father," he finally says in a soft voice. "If I enlist, he'll be released from Crystal City. He'll come here to Manzanar."

"How do you know this?"

"A lieutenant promised me. Said if I enlist, Father can join us here." He looks at her. "I know you want that."

Her jaw trembles. "That's not reason enough."

"Of course it is."

She blinks once—a slow blink that seems to take forever. When she looks up at him, her damp eyes seem to see right through him. "There's another reason, isn't there?"

He pauses. He thinks of what he could say: I want to see the world. I want to be a man. And of course, floating invisibly in the background, another reason he'd never admit, not to her. *I want to find Charlie.* Ridiculous, even to him. Even to Turtle Boy.

She's quiet. Still waiting for his response.

He settles on something cryptic yet true. "If I don't do this I'll regret it my whole life."

Her lips tremble; she has a hundred things to say. But when she speaks, it is but a single word. "When?"

"I've already spoken to the enlistment officer. And signed the papers. The first bus for boot camp leaves Manzanar in five days."

Her lips silently whisper *five days.* "You should have told me earlier." She shakes her head, over and over. "Please don't. Please—"

The front door swings open. Wind gusts into the apartment. Heavy thumps on the floorboard, moving toward them. The partition is roughly shoved aside as Frank strides in.

"Don't mind me," he says without a glance. "Just getting my cigs." He goes to the dresser, riffles through a drawer. Grabs a pack, is heading out. Stops. Looks at their somber faces. "What's going on?"

Alex speaks before Mother does. "I'm enlisting."

Frank's face blanches with shock.

"What?"

"I said—"

"I must be going deaf. Because I thought I just heard you say you're enlisting. Which can't be true because only idiots and stupids enlist. And we all know that Alex Maki ain't no idiot and Alex Maki ain't no stupid."

"Frank—"

"And especially after I spoke to you about this."

"I'm leaving in five days."

His pack of cigarettes is crushed in his fist. "How could you, Alex? After everything they've done to us."

"I'm not joining *them*, Frank—"

"Oh, then who exactly are you joining?" He sneers at Alex with raw contempt. "Captain America and Batman? The Justice Society of America? The Seven Soldiers of Victory?" He snorts. "They're gonna throw you out to the most dangerous missions, guaranteed. And this ain't the comics, you get that, Alex? You can actually *die.*"

Alex wills his voice not to shake. "Look. Frank. I'm not getting into this again. I've made up my mind."

Frank points at Mother. "And you're just leaving her to fend for herself."

Alex bristles. "Last I checked, she's got another son here. Or did you forget how to be a son—"

"You shut the hell up—"

"Enough, boys!" Mother says. "Both of you stop fighting."

But Alex isn't done. "And by the way, she's also doing her part to help get Father released! Breaking her back at the camouflage-net factory while her oldest son's doing nothin' but making pretty speeches—"

In two strides Frank is looming over Alex, grabbing him by the lapels of his jacket. He hoists him up. "You want to tangle, huh? You think you're suddenly a tough guy just because you're enlisting—"

"Daisuke!" shouts Mother.

Frank lets go of Alex's jacket, dropping him into the chair. He glares down with raw contempt at Alex. "You don't have what it takes to last out there on the battlefield, little kid," he mutters through gritted teeth. "You won't last an hour."

He storms out, his words echoing off the walls.

Alex doesn't know this now, but those words will haunt him terribly. This last awful scene with Frank will be replayed in his mind over and over, in countless sleepless nights for months and years to come.

42

Alex and Mother walk slowly to the bus, Alex with a duffel bag slung over his shoulders. All the other enlistees have already boarded, having said their goodbyes to mostly mothers who are now huddled together. It's a small group of enlistees. Not nearly as large as the army had hoped for, not even close.

Alex and Mother stop just outside the door. The bus engine humming, its windows steaming up.

He looks past her shoulder. Maybe he will yet see Frank sprinting over to say goodbye, swallowing the remnants of his breakfast, a *gee-whiz* look of apology on his face. But he's nowhere to be seen.

"Say bye to Frank for me," Alex says.

Mother nods. She's stooped against the wind, swaying slightly. She seems a thousand years old. "I wanted to give you a *sennin-bari*," she says, referring to thousand-stitch belts that many Japanese mothers made for their sons heading to war, six-inch-wide white sashes with a thousand ornamental French knots, each sewn in by a different woman and worn under the uniform. "But you gave me no time. So I made this instead." She reaches into her pocket, and withdraws an *omamori*, a simple amulet made of wood. "Keep it close to you always, Koji-kun."

He rubs the freshly cut wood. "I will." He looks at her. *I'm sorry I'm leaving you, Mother. I'm sorry I can't be here for you.* Those words mired in his throat, choking him.

She reaches up to place her hand over his cheek. The first time she has ever done this. "You be safe. You come home alive." Her eyes well up.

"I will, Mother."

She smiles, sadly. "All those camouflage nets I made at the factory. I hope one of them finds its way to you. I hope it hangs over you. Because then it will feel like I'm with you. That it's my hand over you, protecting you somehow."

He nods. "I have to go now."

They look at each other. So much left unsaid.

He finds an empty seat at the back as the bus pulls away. He stares out the window. She is standing by herself, removed from the group. So small. So alone. The farther the bus pulls away, the more she seems to unspool, the more she disintegrates.

He wonders what it must be like around the country when young men head for war and leave their hometowns. He imagines a joyous affair, a festive mood. Crowds of well-wishers lining small town streets, the waving flags, the ticker tapes, the signs lofted high, the children jumping up and down, mothers dabbing their eyes with tissue, the pep band playing, the final kisses between lovers. A celebration, a rally. For these soldiers, their chests burn with an uncomplicated, pure patriotism that is a lava of red, white, and blue as they leave to fight for the land of the free and the home of the brave.

But not so for Alex, not so for the other young men in the bus. This instead: a churning. A mix of sadness, guilt, inner conflict. Their patriotism convoluted. They stare somberly back at their mothers and family who are already fading into the distance, who will soon be as small and inconsequential as the dust that gathers around them and blows them away.

PART THREE

WAR

43

On April 13, 1943, just as Alex Maki and thousands of other Japanese American men arrive at Camp Shelby, Mississippi, to begin military training for the all-Nisei 442nd Regiment, Lieutenant General John L. DeWitt speaks before the Congressional Subcommittee on Naval Affairs in San Francisco.

"A Jap's a Jap," he declares. "They are a dangerous element. There is no way to determine their loyalty. It makes no difference whether he is an American citizen; theoretically, he is still a Japanese, and you can't change them. You can't change him by giving him a piece of paper."

APRIL 13, 1943
CAMP SHELBY, MISSISSIPPI

The young men exit the steam locomotive with loopy grins and stiff legs. On the station platform, two train porters, old black men in white coats, attempt to assist them. If these two porters are surprised to see this stream of Japanese Americans pouring out of the train, they don't show it. They've learned through hard decades in the deep South to mask their emotions. They only extend their arms, offering to help with luggage. But no one gives up their overstuffed duffel bags. The young men—or soldiers, as they now regard themselves—hoist their bags onto their shoulders, and, with necks crooked and backs stooped under the unwieldy load, head down the length of the platform to awaiting army trucks. Though their legs are weakened from days cooped up in the train, excitement hastens their strides.

No sergeant yells at them, no lieutenant directs them. It's self-explanatory enough: climb into the beds of the awaiting GI trucks. Hurriedly, as if the trucks might at any moment depart without them, they rush over and climb aboard.

Alex is the first to jump in. This truck is not so different from the one that transported him from his farmhouse to the ferry pier on Bainbridge Island. The same overhanging canvas, the same dark green, the same cloying stink of gasoline. But this time there are no soldiers with bayoneted rifles escorting him. This time *he* is the soldier.

The trucks lurch forward, and those sitting in the rear are almost thrown out of the opening. *Hey, we almost had our first fatality.* They chuckle, they grin. *Give that kid a Purple Heart, he survived.* The laughter, echoey under the thick canvas, is full of camaraderie. Thick smoke chuffs out of the mud-splattered trucks. There are big stars painted on the doors of the front cab, another on the rear tailgate.

Alex stares at these stars. He thinks of Charlie, of the yellow star she'd said she was forced to wear. He wonders, as he does almost every day, where she is. He wants to believe she is safe, hiding in a secret room in Paris, or perhaps already escaped south. But perhaps not. Perhaps she is somewhere horrible, the place of his visions, a prison where the cold air is filled with ash—and this is the point when Alex always turns off his mind, refuses to think any further.

The ride is bumpy. The men stare out the open back. They point at road signs, town names, anything that might give them a clue where they're headed. When signs for HATTIESBURG, MISSISSIPPI pop up, someone says, "I told you all along it was Camp Shelby."

Camp Shelby is set out on a spread of flat land: mostly boxy barracks laid out in a grid, not unlike Manzanar or the nine other Japanese American internment camps around the nation. But there the resemblance ends. These surroundings are less desolate or harsh. Thick, lush vegetation surrounds the camp, even encroaching into it in places, lending a warmer, homier feel. Tall trees stand interspersed between the smaller barracks, and break up the monotony of the layout. A water tower stands regally in the center of camp, like the church steeple of a small quaint town.

And here there is no barbed-wire fence surrounding the camp. No guard towers with machine guns pointing inward. No searchlights at night sweeping across the barracks. There are rules, yes, to be sure; and there are consequences if you break them. But here if you walk past the perimeter without permission, you will not get shot. You might be forced to do an overnight fifteen-mile march, but you will not be gunned down.

A white soldier in his forties barks at them. He has stripes and insignia on his shirt, but none of the young men have yet learned what they signify. It is the man's whiteness and his age that gives him rank and authority, and though the young men have yet to learn the proper at-attention posture, they instinctively stand with straight backs and arms pressed against their sides.

They are issued uniforms. Two pairs of winter pants, two khakis, two shirts. The winter pants are too warm to wear, but the army still issues them anyway. Everything is too big: boots two sizes too large, shirts that button down to their crotches, khakis that flow a foot past their toes.

A few complain. A few—including Zack Okutsu, who passed

the minimum height requirement by literally a hair—ask for smaller sizes. They're ignored.

In another building, they're issued equipment: a canteen cup, mess kit, aluminum knife, fork, spoon. A service belt, too large, which they will later add notches to. They're herded into the mess hall, wide-eyed and curious, hitching up their pants, clutching their mess kits. It is past mealtime, and they are served the day's leftovers: powdered eggs, cold slices of ham, slaw, and hot dogs.

"Hey, at least we didn't have to line up," someone at the table says. No one finds that funny.

After the meal, in the fading light, they're taken out to the field. All their duffel bags have been thrown into a giant heap. For a moment, Alex thinks crazily that it's all going to be lit in a huge bonfire. A white sergeant, not much older than them, steps forward. "Last ten to find their bag will be assigned latrine duty tonight."

The young men stare at one another. No one moves. A boy from Hawaii—more than half of the soldiers here are from Hawaii—is the first to spring into action. He leaps forward, sprints toward the pile of duffel bags. That snaps the collective stupor: at once, everyone else charges, hands clutching their baggy, droopy pants. They descend on the pile like a pack of wolves.

It is pandemonium. Elbows flying, bodies jostled. Hands stomped on, faces kicked inadvertently and, as the minutes pass and the number of remaining bags dwindle, not so inadvertently. A few men stop to upchuck still-intact chunks of sauerkraut and ham, wasting precious seconds. Then there are only twenty soldiers left. Including Alex. Panic sets in. They tug-of-war over the remaining bags, start throwing punches.

The sergeant observes all of this with a wry smirk on his face.

A duffel bag tumbles from out of nowhere, unnoticed. Alex grabs it. Not his. Doesn't matter. He scampers away with it and melts in with the others, the duffel bag turned away to keep the written name—SHIG HAYASHI—hidden from view. The unlucky last ten are ordered to the latrines where they will spend the night cleaning urinals and toilet bowls.

Everyone else is taken to their barracks. Or "hutments," as they are called. These are square-shaped huts with thin wooden walls that go only as high as Alex's armpits. Wire mesh screens rise from the top of these walls to the eaves. The roof is—much like the army trucks—a canvas covering.

Alex finds an empty cot beside an unused charcoal stove. He is faintly aware of others, maybe a dozen, lying on cots or playing cards, but he is too tired to care.

"You a kotonk?" someone says from across the room. A strange accent. "Where you from?"

"What?" Alex says, his arm lying across his eyes.

"You a kotonk? Wass your name? Wassamatta why you no talk to me, braddah? You a kotonk or what?"

Alex has no idea what a "kotonk" is. A minute later he is fast asleep.

That night he dreams of latrines.

"Everyone out of bed and fall out. *Now!*" And that is how Alex is introduced to Sergeant Grieves, by a cannon of a voice shattering into his sleep. Then out onto the field where he is the last to arrive, his boots untied, the laces flinging about, his shirt untucked down to his thighs. The group is already doing push-ups, and he throws his stiff body to the ground and into a push-up. His head spinning, in a dazed blur.

It is how he will spend the next few days, in a haze of half-awake, half-asleep existence of marches, drills, exercises, exhaustion, snatches of sleep.

By the third day their feet are blistering from marches through swamps and drills in ill-fitting shoes. Their bodies are ravaged by mosquitoes, leeches, and wood ticks. Their legs marked in bloody scabs and scratches from all the chigger bites. Little red bugs that burrow deep into the pores of the skin. You couldn't not scratch, it was that itchy, even as your skin inflamed into an angry red.

Teddy Ikoma, a skinny boy with a slight frame, fights tears every night. He is last in everything: last out of bed, last out of the showers, last to finish eating, last in the marches, last in every single drill. But he never once thinks about quitting.

A reprieve arrives on the fourth day. In the form of a math test. After breakfast they are taken to a different mess hall. Pencils are distributed, most worn to the nub, some without lead. A few raise their hands to complain, holding up their blunt pencil stubs. Those soldiers are ordered out into the heat to do push-ups. Other hands holding blunt pencils quickly lower. A set of test papers is distributed to each soldier. Some sets are missing pages; some have answers only partially erased; some are torn in half. Now no one complains.

"You have half an hour," the corporal says. He props his feet up, reads a magazine. The soldiers stare blankly at the math sets, at the geometry problems.

"Is this a joke?" someone in the back mutters under his breath. "Like, we're all supposed to be good at math, right, because we're Japanese?"

Some stare dumbly at their leadless pencils. Unable to write, they scratch their heads, their itchy crotches. They fall asleep. Others attack the pages with gusto, their pencils rasping across the pages. Minutes pass. Pages rustle, the sound of autumn leaves blown across asphalt sidewalks. Some discreetly copy answers from the soldier next to them, not knowing they are writing their way to a 17 percent. Shig Hayashi writes over the faint outlines of the half-erased answers, unaware that in a week he will be, based on his top score, assigned to the artillery battalion where he will become known as the stupidest person ever to make the 522nd Artillery Battalion.

On the fifth day the men of the 442nd Regimental Combat Team are assembled. Thousands of Japanese American men who will eventually be assigned into three infantry battalions, one artillery battalion, and several service companies. Some will be sent early to join the only other all-Nisei battalion, the 100th Infantry Battalion, which is already seeing heavy combat in Italy.

Colonel Charles W. Pence delivers a formal welcome to the assembly. He is a white man standing on a stage staring at an ocean of Japanese American faces before him. Alex is expecting a lecture. Or an ingratiating speech about listening to (white) authority, the need to obey in all things, about proving their patriotism. Instead, this man speaks to them man to man, American to American. Soldier to soldier.

"You men have more than an opportunity," Pence says into the mike. A hush has fallen among the assembled thousands. So quiet, even the swaying tree branches can be heard. "You have a challenge. If there is any one lesson the history of America has taught, it is this: that the rights of American citizenship must be defended before they can be fully enjoyed."

Something about this man: a no-nonsense muscularity about him, a sincerity that is pure. Not a hint of patronage. A man who—Alex senses this in his gut—would be giving the exact same speech in the exact same tone to an assembly of white soldiers. Alex closes his eyes, lets the man's words sink into his bloodstream. It is the first time he feels less like a tossed piece of rag and actually a soldier.

His next thought: *Frank should be here. Frank would love it here. Frank would be incredible here.*

* * *

The Nisei soldiers. By day, in the heat of the broiling sun, they are the same. They sweat the same, they bleed the same. In their marches, in their drills, in their roll call, there is synchrony and orderliness. When they jog with weighted backpacks pulling them down, chanting *right, right, right-left-right,* there is unity. As they pump out push-up after push-up, shouting out the ascending numbers in unison, as they salute the flag together, shout *Sir, yes, sir!* together, puke together, simmer together, groan together, suffer together, they are brothers-in-arms.

But in the late afternoon when training ends, it all dissolves away. The boys from Hawaii separate from the boys from the mainland. The Hawaiian boys take off their fatigues and go about bare-chested, even the scrawny ones. They whip off their boots, the stink almost flaming out, and either wear zori slippahs or go around barefooted. Instead of heading straight to the showers like the mainlanders, they whip out cards. Shoot dice. They go days, in fact, without washing. A cloud of underarm stink hovers around them. Only when they get yelled at by a corporal do they shower. They squat everywhere. They stay up all night to play cards in the latrine, the only area with light after midnight. They chatter all the time in pidgin, an odd combination of English, Japanese, Chinese, Hawaiian, Spanish, and Filipino. To Alex and the other mainlanders, it is a crude, almost primitive form of English. Barbaric.

From the get-go, the two groups mistrust each other. The mainlanders look down on the Hawaii boys as uncouth and coarse and call them "Buddhaheads." "Buddha" because it sounds like *puta,* the Japanese word for "pig."

For their part, the Hawaii boys hate the haughty mainlanders just as much, if not more. Hate the hoity-toity English with which they speak. The refined way they hold utensils to eat, never replying until all the food is swallowed. Hate the manner in which they dress, careful always to tuck in their shirts and button up the sleeves even when the corporal isn't around. Hate how they run too cautiously, how they scale the obstacles with fear, and with a certain daintiness, too. Hate how their pale skin burns under the sun, how the backs of their smooth hands are lined with delicate blue veins. The boys from Hawaii see these mainlanders as nothing more than brownnosing toadies, always kissing up to the *haole* superiors. They are weak, lacking heart, lacking substance—they are, in other words, *kotonks,* the hollow sound coconuts make when knocked together.

These are not terms of endearment. The two groups—the kotonks and the Buddhaheads—genuinely dislike each other. One night, a week into basic training, Alex is walking back from the mess hall. He's chatting with Teddy, the only other mainlander in his hutment.

A group of Buddhaheads is walking toward them. That's another thing about these Hawaii boys. They're always in packs. Never alone. And chatting away, loud, as usual.

The two groups pass each other. "God, the stink," Teddy mutters under his breath.

"What you say?"

Alex and Teddy turn around. The group of Buddhaheads is facing them.

"I said you all stink. Go take a shower—"

The group descends on them. In a blink Alex and Teddy are leveled, left writhing on the ground. That's another thing about these Buddhaheads. For all their laid-back and easygoing attitude, the Hawaiians have surprisingly thin skin. Even the smallest slight—a wrong look, a perceived insult—will set them off, and retaliation will come quickly in a flurry of kicks and punches. As it does now. And they don't believe in a fair fight; they have absolutely no qualms about outnumbering the foe. Maybe that's why they always travel in groups.

Alex and Teddy return to their hutment, scuffed up and

bloodied. One of their hutment mates is squatting outside the door. A guy named Mutt Suzuki. "Howzit, braddahs," Mutt says when he notices their bruised faces and disheveled hair. He laughs and follows them in. "Oy, oy brahs," he says to the other Buddhaheads inside, "these two *lolo* kotonks like got their *manini* asses whupped!"

They all laugh like heck, as if it's the funniest thing in the world.

44

A damp heat clings to them. They sit on their helmets, mosquitoes buzzing around their heads. The corporal's voice drones on. This afternoon, as with most afternoons after lunch, the corporal will lecture them about how to set the howitzer cannon, how to get the gun emplacement, how to this, how to that. In an hour he will walk them over to an actual howitzer cannon sitting not twenty yards away, and they will all snap to and pay attention. But for now, sitting on their helmets under the blazing sun, this is all theoretical nonsense, and they nod not with attention but with sleep.

Twenty minutes in, a captain—Captain Ralph Ensminger, they will later learn—interrupts the lecture. Alex has never seen the man before but he has an innate air of authority about him. He is tall, with a face that is lean and almost ascetic. A pair of dark glasses sits perfectly perched on his high-bridged beak of a nose. His voice is surprisingly high-pitched, but unapologetically so. He speaks slowly, articulating every single word.

"Everyone walk over to Field Eighteen."

They head over quickly. They are curious but quiet.

Field 18 is dotted with numerous red flags spread about, each with a different letter printed on it.

"Get into the trench." The fifteen soldiers do so. Directly in front of the trench is a single blue flag, and instinctively they bunch behind it. They are beginning to understand. This is a test. An audition. For the front-observer position. A crucial position, one of the most highly sought-after roles in the artillery battalion. The front observer, unlike the rest of the team, is on the front lines. In the thick of it. There he scouts for enemy positions: machine-gun nests, tanks, encampments, hidden snipers. He judges the exact distance to these targets, then radios in the coordinates for the artilleries to strike them. A front observer must show grace under pressure, calm in chaos. And above all, the ability to judge distances insanely well. Everyone wants to be the front observer.

Captain Ensminger speaks from behind them. He doesn't raise his voice, but his high-pitched, well-enunciated words cut through the humid air.

"I will give you a letter. Find the red flag with that letter written on it somewhere on the field. You are to write down your best guess for the distance between that red flag and the blue flag set before you."

Papers are handed out; pencils, too. They barely have time to write down their names when the sergeant says, "*W.*"

Immediately, fifteen heads, peering over the ledge of the trench, swivel left and right. Like periscopes. Eyes squinting, trying to make out tiny letters on waving flags on this sun-blazed, blindingly bright field. Zack Okutsu's head doesn't clear the top of the trench, and he can't even see the flags.

Then the captain: "*B.*"

Panic. Many haven't even located the *W* flag yet. Random guesses are penciled in. Heads turn faster now, *B, B, B,* where is *B*?

"*K.*"

Somebody curses. Somebody looks over at his neighbor's sheet. He is immediately yanked out, his paper torn up, and made to hold a push-up position for the duration of the test. No one cheats after that. They scratch in estimates. Thirty-five yards. No, thirty, twenty-five, twenty yards. The guesses are all over the map.

Alex, though. He jots his numbers down quickly but with certainty, never changing his answers. They are exact. Precise. Pretentious, some might say. 42 yards. 19 yards. 11 yards. 38 yards.

After seven more flags, the papers are collected. Three buck sergeants quickly go through the papers, scoring them. Everyone waits in the trenches, the humidity even thicker in that crowd of bodies. The sun unrelenting.

"When you hear your name, step out of the trench," one of the buck sergeants announces.

One by one, the dejected soldiers leave the trench. Until only five remain. Four Buddhaheads and one mainlander: Alex Maki.

Another round of seven flags. The answers collected, scored. Captain Ensminger returns. His face is flushed. "Who is Alex Maki?"

Alex raises his hand.

The captain takes off his dark glasses. "Maki, stay in the trench. Everyone else out." His voice even more high-pitched than usual.

Alex feels every eyeball focus on him. None sharper and hotter than the sergeant's. "You've taken this test before, Maki?"

"No, sir."

"You've seen the answer sheet? Memorized it?"

"No, sir."

"You think you're so smart?"

"No, sir."

He stares at Alex for five long seconds, his cold eyes never once blinking. "We'll see about that." He nods to a buck sergeant, who runs out to the field. He grabs the nearest red flag, sprints to the far end. Stakes it into the ground.

"Now," the sergeant says, "give me its distance."

Alex scrunches his forehead, squints at the flag.

"Be as exact as possible, Maki."

Sweat trails down into his eyes. He blinks. And in that brief blink, he is back on Bainbridge Island. In his bedroom gazing down at Frank out back throwing the football. The higharching flight of the ball landing in a trash can set at ten-yard markers. Thirty yards. Fifty yards. Sixty yards.

"Fifty-six yards," he says. He does not blurt it out, or shout with overbearing confidence. He simply says it matter-of-factly because it is, to him, a matter of fact.

"Fifty-six yards?" the captain repeats.

Alex is about to nod; then stops himself. Captain Ensminger's words—*Be as exact as possible*—echo in his head. He stares at the flag again. "Fifty-six yards and two feet."

Snorts from behind him.

The captain's eyebrows shoot up over his glasses. "And two feet, did you say?"

"Yes, sir."

The captain pauses; he has the look of a man wondering if he's being played. "Fine, Maki, you want to be cute about this, go ahead. But tell you what, because I can be cute, too: if you're more than a foot off, this whole unit does a ten-miler tonight."

Groans from behind.

"And if I'm correct, sir?"

The captain's eyes narrow. "If you're right, within one foot, your unit gets special leave to Hattiesburg tonight."

One of the buck corporals runs out to the flag, unspooling as he does a long tape measure. Everyone is quiet. Most are glaring at Alex's back, hating him, thinking about the blisters and aching feet that await them from the ten-mile hike.

The buck corporal slows down as he approaches the red flag. He pulls his face low to the tape. His head cants suddenly to the side like he's just seen a snake. Slowly he stands up. Gets back down for another look. Stands again. "Fifty-six yards," he shouts. A brief pause, everyone holding their breath. "Fifty-six yards and one foot, to be exact, sir."

A moment of stunned disbelief. Then hoots and cheers break out from his unit. He turns to face them, and they're all grinning ear to ear, and staring at him with a newfound respect. As if he's just thrown a game-winning touchdown.

"Ho, brah," Kash Kobayashi declares with a smile, "looks like this *lolo* be our front observer, braddahs. He a da kine *moke*, fo' shua."

Alex feels a grin crack his face. And as Kash and Mutt and the rest of the guys come over and pound his shoulder, Alex finds himself wishing—desperately—that Frank could be here to see this. Little Turtle Boy making front observer, proving himself in the company of tough men, in this band of *moke*s.

45

"Hey, braddahs, we make sure this kotonk's glass never goes empty tonight, yeah?" Mutt shouts in the crowded Ritz Café on Main Street. He smacks Alex on the back, with a loopy, relaxed grin, his face, even through his dark tan, flushed with alcohol.

A few of their unit mates laugh back. Kash Kobayashi refills Alex's mug, the overflowing suds spilling over his hand, soaking his sleeve.

"Ain't got money for this, Mutt," Alex says. He burned through his cash in the first hour. But somehow the beer has kept flowing.

"You don't worry about that," Mutt says. "Us boys from Hawaii, we got you covered, braddah."

Alex leans back against the bar counter. Mutt's not lying or merely boasting. These Buddhaheads, for all their faults, are tight-knit. They have each other's back all the time.

"Look at this," Mutt says, pulling out his wallet. He slides out a small black-and-white photograph, its edges frayed. A short, stocky girl, eighteen or nineteen, is standing on a beach wearing a muumuu dress, a floral headdress, and ankle bracelets made of whalebone. She has an average face, if not downright homely, a bit wide with a stubby nose. A radiant smile, though.

"The most beautiful girl, don't you think, braddah?" Mutt says.

"Your girlfriend?"

Mutt grins. "Since we were like ten."

Alex smiles back. "What's her name?"

"Belinda. Belinda Tomo. I'm gonna marry her one day."

Alex looks Mutt in the eyes. Only one way to respond. "She really is beautiful. Killer smile. You lucky bastard."

Mutt laughs proudly, claps Alex across the back. "What about you, bruh?" he says, putting the photograph carefully away. "You got a main squeeze?"

"Nah."

Mutt holds his gaze, studying him though his damp drunk eyes. "There *is* someone, isn't there?"

"No. There really isn't."

Mutt grins, nudges him gently with the elbow. "Come on. Where is she?"

Alex raises the mug to his lips, takes a long drink. "I don't know."

"Ha! So there is someone!"

"It's not like that. It's . . . complicated."

Mutt laughs. "You're not sure or she's not sure?"

Alex doesn't answer.

"You got a picture of her? Let me see how pretty she is."

Alex shakes his head. "She never gave me one."

Mutt laughs again. "Then *she's* the one not sure." He grabs a pitcher, refills Alex's mug. "Drink up. We'll make a man out of you yet. You come back from war a warrior, and she won't be able to resist you." The beer overflows, suds and foam dripping onto the floor.

Mutt turns back to the group. In seconds he has them laughing with that carefree, easygoing Hawaiian camaraderie that Alex envies. Alone again at the end of the bar, Alex sets his mug down on the counter.

It's been over six months since the last time Charlie "appeared" to him at Manzanar. Enough time has passed for him to think rationally about the appearances. And this is what he now fully accepts: it really was just his imagination. Nothing more than that. A fantasy fueled by boredom and worry and guilt and loneliness. He'd been such a sad little pathetic boy back then, so clueless and afraid of the world, clinging to fantasy.

And yet.

He still thinks of her all the time. While his comrades snore away, he gazes at the sketch of her he drew back at Manzanar, his eyes drifting over the pencil lines, her jawline, her eyes.

Even now, during a march or while doing army maneuvers in De Soto National Forest, her voice will break into his mind with a bell-like clarity that startles. Just three whispered words.

Find me, Alex.

Three words that sometimes feel like a clarion call.

It's Alex who finally hauls the group out of the bar. They stumble to the bus stop, arms slung over one another's shoulders, taking up the whole road as they drunkenly sing a Hawaiian native song. Zack Okutsu, the shortest and now drunkest, is in the middle, almost being carried between the taller Mutt and Shig, his boots barely touching the ground.

At the bus stop, a handful of soldiers from the 273rd Infantry Regiment are waiting there. The two groups stare at each other. Early on, there'd been fights between the whites and Niseis. The white boys, although they'd been told about the 442nd, were unaccustomed to seeing Japanese faces in American uniforms. Some of them had brothers fighting in the Pacific theater. Some had brothers killed by Japanese. At USO events at camp and in bars here in Hattiesburg, there'd been more than a few brawls.

But that was months ago. The 442nd has since gained the begrudging respect of most everyone at Camp Shelby. Because they're damn good soldiers. The average setup time for a heavy machine gun is sixteen seconds. The 442nd does it in five. They scale the obstacle walls and finish eight-mile marches in full gear faster than any other unit, even with feet blistered from too-large, ill-fitting boots. In challenge after challenge, they've proven themselves quicker, slicker, better than virtually every other unit.

The bus arrives. It's packed at this time of night with soldiers trying to make curfew, and local black laborers, exhausted after long shifts, returning home. Alex and his unit mates sit in the whites' section up front, while the black passengers ride in the rear. Here in Hattiesburg, Mississippi, the Nisei soldiers are considered white, not black. They can eat in the nicer restaurants, sit in the front section of buses, use whites-only restrooms and drinking fountains. In movie theaters, they sit with the whites below the balcony otherwise known as "nigger heaven."

The bus doors groan shut.

"Yo, yo, hold up, mister!" Mutt shouts to the bus driver. "We got three more coming."

The white driver is rotund and sweaty, his belly jutting into the bottom of the large steering wheel. He glances down the street. Three black soldiers are sprinting for the bus, their arms waving. He grabs the crank for the door, starts closing it.

"Hey, what you doing?" Mutt quickly rises, stepping into the way of the closing door. He holds it open with his foot. "They miss this bus, they miss curfew."

"We got no more room for them," the bus driver snaps. "Now git the hell outta my doorway."

"There's plenty of empty seats."

"In the front half only. But the nigger half is full. No more room for them three."

"You stop the bus."

The driver turns his head to Mutt. "You Japs be riding with them niggers, I had my druthers. Now you git outta my door."

– 259 –

Mutt leans out of the doorway. "Come on," he shouts to the three running soldiers, waving them on. "Hurry up!"

The bus driver curses. Steps on the accelerator pedal, lurching the bus forward. Mutt is almost thrown out of the doorway.

The Nisei soldiers stand up, rush forward, all of them, even Teddy. Alex is the first to the driver, and he grabs the driver's arm—it's like sinking fingers into a tub of lard—and kicks his foot off the pedal. The others are pulling the brake crank, causing the bus to screech to a stop.

"The hell you doing!" the driver curses. "I'm calling the police on you."

"Sit your white ass back down," Zack shouts.

But the driver is irate. He stands, jiggling his belly past the steering wheel, pushing Alex out the way. The guy is all fat and no muscle, but there is a lot of it, and he is using it to his advantage. He shoves Alex backward, reaches down for something by the seat. Pulls out a blackjack, which he swings at Alex, narrowly missing his head.

"Yo, cool it!" someone shouts from the back.

The driver rears back for another swing, down at Alex's ducked head, and this time there's nowhere for Alex to retreat.

A body, massive and graceful at the same time, slides between bodies, grabs the driver's heft arm.

"Drop it!" Mutt shouts, his hand grabbing the pasty, flabby wrist.

The driver stares back. Then tries to wrest his arm away, and swing at Mutt.

Big mistake. Mutt yanks the man's considerable body out from behind the steering wheel, and through the opened doorway. By the time Alex jumps out, Mutt is administering a beatdown on the driver. The others join in, kicking the man. It's the three black soldiers who finally pull Mutt and the others away.

46

The next morning, Captain Ralph Ensminger gathers the men. Alex, severely hungover, can barely keep his balance. Everyone else in the unit, even Zack, seems none the worse for wear. Their backs are straight, their eyes alert. Perhaps fear of punishment has sobered them. Because there's going to be hell to pay.

Captain Ensminger stares at them for a long time. He seems to be considering his words.

"Gentlemen," Ensminger begins, and this in itself is odd because he has never addressed them as such. "Lieutenant Marquis Jackson paid me a visit this morning. He told me of the incident involving a local bus and three of his men."

He walks down the row slowly, taking his time to stare at Shig Hayashi, at Snap Nakai, at Kash Kobayashi, at Alex. Then at Teddy Ikoma who can't stop shaking, who woke up this morning fearing a dishonorable discharge, or even worse, getting arrested. Ensminger walks past all these men, then stops directly in front of Mutt.

"I have to say, I'm highly disappointed. After all these hard months of training, I expected more out of you." The corners of his mouth twitch into the faintest suggestion of amusement. "Next time," he says, looking at Mutt, "have the sense to beat the driver out of sight."

"Sir?" Mutt says.

"You heard me. Next time, do it in an alleyway or behind some building, for crying out loud." A wry grin cracks his lips. "You've left me some mess to clean up."

All the men are staring at Captain Ensminger in confusion.

"Now I believe time's a-wastin'. I can smell the hangover stink even from here. And there's no better way to flush out the alcohol from your system than to sweat it out of your pores. So grab your gear, men, and let's do the obstacle course double time."

Nobody responds. Everyone's still in shock, trying to absorb his words.

"Did you hear me?"

"Sir, yes, sir!" they shout back, Mutt the first and loudest to respond.

"Well, what are you louses waiting for? Get a move on!"

The men break formation, grinning, and sprint for their gear. For the first time ever, lazy Teddy, incompetent Teddy, slow Teddy, is the first to reach them.

47

Explosions. Bright flashes followed milliseconds later by an eardrum-ripping blast. A rumble felt through the ground, throttling the bodies pressed flat atop it. Alex fights the instinct to clamp shut his eyes and tuck his face into the frozen dirt. He keeps his eyes wide open. That's his job as front observer. Be on the front line and observe. Ignore all distraction. Ignore the *rat-a-tat* of machine guns shrieking over his head.

Mutt, his radioman next to him, shouts, "Marker incoming. Five seconds to impact." This is the initial blast, just a blank position marker. Alex's job is to watch where it detonates, note how far off the target it is, then send in the adjusted distances. Then they'll launch the real bombs. Easier said than done: in this sea of enemy and friendly flashes, the trick is spotting the marker blast.

Another blast, this one closer than any other. Dirt and debris fling toward him, spraying over his face. Still he keeps his eyes peeled, maintains the running countdown in his head . . . *three . . . two . . . one . . .* Where's the marker blast?

There. A small flash among a constellation of other blasts.

He estimates the distance and degree the marker is off, then yells the corrected data to Mutt. Who transmits them to headquarters. The team stationed there with maps, protractors, and coordinate sheets calculate corrected coordinates; seconds later, they relay the updated coordinates to the team at the howitzer. A few tweaks to the aiming turntables. *They're ready,* they com Mutt.

"Fire for effect!" Alex shouts.

And six seconds later, the bomb explodes right over the marker. Shrapnel screams down, a cone of destruction. The flag is decimated. A direct hit.

After so many months of training, of being put through the paces in chigger-filled trenches of Hattiesburg, or in the soaking-wet training fields of western Louisiana, they've become renowned around Camp Shelby for their skill and precision. They've been waiting forever to get the call up.

"Whoo hoo! *Da kine* flag is *pau!*" Kash shouts, running up to him. Alex grins right back and gestures a Hawaiian *shaka*—a closed fist with thumb and pinkie finger extended, then waggled. Kash laughs, then takes the radio from Mutt. "*Mahalo* for your *kōkua,* braddahs."

The deafening blasts suddenly cease. "What's happening?" Alex says.

Kash shrugs. They look to the headquarters tent. A gunnery corporal from a different company is speaking to Captain Ensminger with urgency.

They walk over. The other squad members gather around Mutt. "What *da kine* this about?" Shig asks.

"No idea."

"Maybe they sending us to Louisiana again," Alex says. "Another training camp."

Teddy groans. "Not again." He barely made it out alive the last time.

After a minute, Captain Ensminger calls the men to gather around.

"I have some news to give you," he says. "I've just been notified that we—the whole Four Hundred Forty-Second, that is—we got the official call up."

Everyone is too stunned to speak.

"Did you hear me, men? We're finally leaving this dump to go to Europe and fight Nazis."

The men look at each other. Realization sinks in; grins and smiles spread on their faces.

"Boom *kanani,*" Kash yells out, his eyes wide with joy and disbelief. "Dat *bumboocha* news, *l'dat!*"

"Yup," Ensminger says, laughing. "Whatever that means!"

The men start hooting and slapping one another on the back. Alex is all smiles, and says to Ensminger, "How about a celebration feast tonight, Cap?"

"Great idea," Ensminger says. "But can we pull it off so quickly?"

Kash pounds his chest, smiling. "Leave it to me, boss! Somebody helps me poach a pig, and tonight we have a real Hawaiian luau! That pig be roasting over hot coals, I can grind um all or what to break your mouth, guranz!"

Everyone laughs, even those who have no idea what he just said.

On April 22, 1944, the men of the 442nd ride past the gates of Camp Shelby for the last time. Their hearts are near bursting, their smiles broad. Their enthusiasm lasts the duration of the train trip to Camp Patrick Henry in Virginia, their port of embarkation. There: final inoculations against smallpox and typhus, gas-mask training. Every piece of clothing and equipment is marked with an identifying number: belts, helmets, canteen pouches, service caps, haversacks, everything gets rubber-stamped with a number.

And of course, there's a final dance at the USO. Competition is stiff for the scarce women. Mutt Suzuki, drunk and brazen, asks a few USO hostesses to dance. The white GIs get pissed. *A Jap dancing with a white girl!* A fight breaks out. The whole dance floor turns into a drunken brawl. A hundred on each side, knuckles flying, a stalemate. Until, of course, the black soldiers get involved. Once they side with the 442nd, the fight is effectively over.

On May 1, 1944, the men finally leave America.

They walk down the dock toward their Liberty ship, the *Johns Hopkins*. Like everyone else, Alex is weighed down by his duffel, canteen, ditty bag, gas mask, helmet, and rifle. But at least his stomach is full with doughnuts and coffee handed out by the Red Cross ladies. "You da prettiest one here," Mutt says to one of the girls. He grabs a doughnut from the next girl, does an exaggerated double take. "But you—it's you I be thinking *all* the way to Europe." He winks at her with his black eye, swollen from the previous night's brawl.

They head up the gangplank. Alex's head is suddenly full of thoughts of Bainbridge Island, the last time he was on a dock walking onto a boat. An army band plays them a farewell song from the dock, "Over There," as their boots thump along the gangplank, and it undulates beneath them, strangely in time with the song. At the top of the gangplank, he is handed a form letter from President Roosevelt. *You bear with you,* it says, *the hope, the confidence, the gratitude, and the prayers of your family, your fellow-citizens, and your President.* The same president who sent them to internment camps. Who keeps their parents and brothers and sisters behind barbed-wire fences. Few bother to read the letter. Some slip it into their jacket, the blank side to later be used to tally card scores or gambling debts, or, when toilet paper runs out, other uses. Most toss the paper into the foaming waters below.

At noon the *Johns Hopkins,* bloated with men crammed into its holds, sets off for an undisclosed location in Europe. Or perhaps Algeria, though they hope not. *Italy,* many wish for. *France,* others hope. Only one person on the entire ship intones the name not of a country, but a person. *Charlie Lévy.*

48

Alex wakes up. The dark air is foul, the dank heat stifling. A raw stink of vomit overhangs everything. His quarters are deep in the bowels of the *Johns Hopkins,* and heat from the ship's engine below has turned this small room into a furnace. Most in this hold have stripped down to almost nothing. Still they sweat, still they toss and turn in their bunks, stacked five tiers high.

From within the gray ooze of darkness, Alex hears snores, snuffles, the snap of cards, someone throwing up that night's kidney stew. Teddy sleeps in the bunk over him, and his body sags into Alex's headroom mere inches from his nose. He needs something to distract him from this hell.

He reaches into his knapsack hanging off the post, his hand squeezing deep into the bag. There. His fingers grasp the bundle of letters—Charlie's—that he'd brought with him like a good-luck charm. He removes the rubber band wrapped around them and randomly withdraws an envelope. He pulls out the letter, but it's impossible to make out the words in the dim ambient light.

He's inserting the letter back into the envelope when his fingers brush against something in the envelope. He frowns. It's something he never noticed the dozens of times he's read the letter. A tiny slip of paper, perhaps the length of half a pinkie finger, not even. He turns it over. Hard to make out any details in the dim light.

He places it back into the envelope, then leans his head back into the pillow. In the darkness, someone groans. The air is fetid and hot, and Alex suddenly finds he needs light. He needs air. The deck. He slides out, causing the whole five-tier canvas bunk to sway. He throws on a shirt, placing the envelope into a pocket.

"Tell me it's over," Teddy groans from the top bunk, his face green. He's suffered seasickness from the minute he first stepped on the *Johns Hopkins*. Now, three weeks later, the ship zigzagging to evade Nazi subs, there's been no let up. "Tell me we've arrived."

"Nah."

"Throw me overboard. Please."

"I think about doing that a dozen times a day."

Teddy turns over on his side, groaning.

The deck is surprisingly empty. Even at night there are usually a dozen soldiers braving the cold, or bent over the rails, upchucking overboard the half-digested remnants of their last meal and sending nighttime fish into a feeding frenzy below.

But an earlier rainstorm has chased everyone below deck. Now only a drizzling mist sprinkles down, fine as pixie dust. Alex draws in a breath, fills his lungs with the cold air. A cleansing. Even the saltiness in the air feels medicinal, a scouring of infestations within. He exhales, pushing out the rank breath. Draws in another gulp of air. He can do this all night. He can do this all the way to Europe and still feel like he has not expelled whatever has festered within.

He stares out to sea. Large swells move like shifting plates of scuffed armor. The enormity of the vast waters—

In the distance, a strange light. A tiny glowing dot, ghostly and ephemeral. Alex is suddenly thinking the strangest thought. The floating lantern Charlie wrote about. One she had made and set afloat on the Seine. He watches this light now, his heart beating wilder. A light between their worlds of ash and dust. It draws closer, growing larger, stretching out into a glowing string.

It's not a floating lantern, of course not. It's a mass of some kind of fluorescent plant—or perhaps a colony of jellyfish—passing by. He stares, disappointed yet mesmerized by this sight. This radiant heart light. If he had not come to the deck, it would have passed unobserved. He wonders if the world is like this: so many miracles of beauty everywhere, if only you knew where to look, that go otherwise unobserved.

He imagines one day telling Charlie about this scene. He sees them sitting at an outdoor café in Paris, talking over coffee and éclairs or maybe even that pastry Charlie has raved about, the *gâteau* St. Honoré topped with a ring of *pâte à choux.* And he would describe to her this night. The passing storm, the dark, mysterious black waters. And this massive glowing pool.

She's dead.

No. She's alive.

He stares out to the black ocean as if the answer lies somewhere within its unfathomable depths. It roils before him, solemn and silent.

He remembers now why he came up to the deck. He reaches into his shirt pocket, withdraws the envelope. It's one of Charlie's last letters, he sees now. He takes out the tiny slip inside, and examines it under the moonlight. It's blank on both sides. Probably just a *whatever* scrap of paper. He's about to fling it into the sea when he freezes.

Could it be?

He'd always imagined the Sinti slips to be large and embroidered, made of cloth or some kind of parchment, and full of gypsy curlicues along the margins, a centering watermark encircled by a phrase in Sinti. Something mysterious, magical. Imbued with a mystical aura that would tingle your fingertips. Not this: a castaway fragment of paper.

In her letter, she'd written, *Maybe you can try, too, no?*

He stares down at the slip. Is this a Sinti slip? Did Charlie put one in the envelope for him?

A gentle ocean breeze blows, and the slip begins to flutter like a streamer on the handlebars of a child's bike. *No way,* he thinks to himself. *No way.*

And yet his hand moves to his pants. To the pen in his pocket. *Charlie Lévy,* he scribbles on it. And waits.

Nothing happens. A minute passes. He glances around, sees nothing out of the ordinary. Just the rain-splattered deck, the dark cartilage of metal rising over him. No sound but the blowing of the wind, whistling through the loading booms and mizzenmasts.

Another minute passes. Two. Three. He is feeling very foolish now—

It's the smell he notices first. A sootiness mixed in with the saltiness of the sea.

He tilts his head this way and that. The smell is coming from the bow. He walks past the midship house, the flying bridge, the mainmast. The wind stronger, the smell fuller—

He sees it. Just beyond the foremast, floating above the hatch cover. A kind of hole blooming open, a mouth of frayed, indistinct edges. No, not a hole, more globular, like a sphere—

He hears a strange crackling sound, like radio static.

At the edge he pauses before stepping onto what should be a

canvas stretched across the hatch cover. Initially he feels it, the soft give under his feet. Then it hardens, feels gritty. He looks down. Dirt, black snow. He glances up.

A row of barracks. Another on his left. As dark and cold and lifeless as tombstones. A guard tower in the distance, machine guns pointing inward. Everything hazy, just out of focus. Some shapes shuffle along, but they are distant and contorted, tiny wraiths floating just above the ground.

The smell. Black and sooty and acrid.

His nostrils twitch. He takes another few steps until he is swallowed whole, and now the smells are pungent and the blurred surroundings sharpen into focus.

These barracks. They are not the tar-papered ones in Manzanar. But larger, longer, made of brick. With steeped rooftops, a chimney jutting out of each. They reek of famine, of cold soot.

A sharp wind, colder than the Atlantic Ocean in May could ever be, slices into him. He shivers. Flakes of snow—somehow black—drift past his face.

He hears nothing. No door clacking shut, no truck roaring away, no human voice, no sounds of camp life. Just an eerie silence.

He waits. She will come. Previous times, he had come to her. This time, she will come to him. He waits, his heart beating, curious yet fearful, the icy ground stinging the soles of his feet.

He waits only a short time.

She comes bounding around the nearest barrack. At a mad sprint, her legs and arms a blur. She is looking in the other direction. She swings her head toward him. Freezes. Stares at him. Big, blinking eyes. Her breath, frosting out in gigantic plumes of white.

In this vision, she is not awash in glowing light. She is gray like the barracks around them, like the abraded sky, the hard ground. But sharper and clearer for it, like a pencil sketch.

She takes a step toward him. Her eyes brimming with emotion. A flickering soft light falls on her, dim waves of purple and orange. The light is radiating from him. Because it is he who is the traveler this time, the visitor, he who is glowing with light.

The colors dance over her face, over the clothes that drape over her like an oversize coat on a skinny hanger. How dangerously thin she has become. Even thinner than the last time he saw her in Manzanar.

"Charlie," he whispers. No sound. *Charlie.*

Her lips quiver—is she speaking?—he does not hear a thing. *Alex.*

He motions to the ground. "Charlie. Write down in the dirt where you are. Write. It. Down."

She shakes her head, not understanding.

He drops to his knees, and stabs at the hard ground. He wants to write *Where are you?* but his phantom fingers touch nothing. He shouts with frustration, jabbing harder. But nothing, his ghostly hand passing through the dirt and dust, touching the plastic canvas.

She kneels down before him. Her face so gaunt.

Snow drifts past their faces, black and soft. One catches on her eyelashes; he wishes he could gently blow it away.

"Where are you, Charlie?" he says.

But instead of answering, her eyes suddenly widen in panic.

He is fading. Disappearing into the night the same way she faded on him in the past.

"Charlie!" He tugs on his uniform, points to his 442nd patch. "Charlie, I'm coming. I'm on my way to Europe! Tell me where you are!"

And she is fighting back the tears; they are running down her hollowed-out cheek, cutting through her grime-caked face.

He reaches for her arm, the numbers *14873* tattooed on her arm, a triangle tattooed below those numbers—

She is gone. No gradual fade-out. Just gone. The brick barracks, the icy ground, the black snowflakes. All gone. In their place: the rumble of the *Johns Hopkins* under him, the glittering skies overhead, the endless, bottomless ocean surrounding him.

49

The *Johns Hopkins*, more than four weeks after leaving Hampton Roads, Virginia, finally arrives in the port city of Bari, Italy. The soldiers, many filthy after refusing to shower in the disgusting salt-water stalls, are elated to be on dry land again.

"*Buon pomeriggio!*" Mutt shouts to local residents on the dock. He bends over the army's *Pocket Guide to Italian Cities*. "*Mi chiamo* Mutt Suzuki, Monsieur Mutt Suzuki. *Fammi un prezzaccio!*"

"Yo, Mutt, you sure you're reading that right?" Alex asks.

He peers closer. "Oh, dog it. Wrong line. I mean, *Piacere di conoscerti!*" he shouts, arms raised high in greeting.

But the Bari residents don't wave back. They glance with idle curiosity at all these Asian faces in military uniforms, perhaps thinking they are Japanese prisoners of war.

"Heck, could these people be any colder?" Teddy says. "Crikey, we're here to liberate them. They couldn't fake being more excited?"

"Like every girl you've ever slept with?" Zack says.

"Shut up, Zack," Teddy snaps back.

Shig pipes in. "Yeah, shut up, Zack. Teddy's never even slept with a girl."

They soon learn the reason for the cold reception. Back in

December, Allied ships had docked here. One of them—the SS *John Harvey*—was secretly carrying two thousand mustard-gas bombs as part of a contingency plan in case Germans initiated chemical warfare. But when the Germans struck the port in a devastating air raid, seventeen Allied ships went down, including the *John Harvey* in a huge explosion. It released mustard gas over the defenseless city and surrounding countryside. Military and civilian casualties numbered over a thousand, with close to a hundred, likely more, dead. The German air raid was so devastating, it was dubbed Little Pearl Harbor.

"Great," Teddy says on learning this. "Pearl Harbor happens and America hates us. Now Little Pearl Harbor happens, and all Italy hates us. Man, us Japanese Americans, we can't catch a break, can we?"

They're not in Bari for long. They load up into forty-and-eight boxcar trains—so named for the forty people or eight horses that can fit in each carriage—and ride westward across the boot of Italy. Through the open doors, they see farmlands and towns passing by with names that mean nothing to them. Barletta. Tressanti. Buonalbergo. Sant'Agata Dé Goti.

The picturesque Italian countryside offers little evidence—except for the occasional overturned mule cart or car or burned-down farmhouse—that the world is actually at war, or that an evil enemy lurks. They play cards. They talk until they're sick of the same regurgitated jokes, the same stale stories of sexual conquests. They cradle their rifles, tap fingers on their helmets. They wonder if they will ever actually fight, if war is actually a real thing.

At dawn they arrive in Naples. And here, in this crowded city of slopes and narrow stone stairs, the first signs of war. Bombed-out buildings reduced to empty husks. Upturned cars, tires gone, the metal frames blackened and twisted by some explosion. Building walls pitted with bullet holes, entire sections charred black. An air of desperation everywhere.

But it's the squalor that's most telling. Only men wear shoes; the women walk around barefoot, their blackened, calloused soles looking hard as black leather. And the children, God, the children. Scrawny, desperate, dirty. Constantly flitting about, asking the soldiers for handouts. For candy, for gum, cigarettes, anything. *Joe, Joe, chocolate? Cigarette? Joe? Joe?* Their darting, gnatty hands everywhere, pulling on cartridge belts, tugging on jackets, digging into pockets. If one raggedy kid gets something, a whole crowd comes swarming.

"Buzz off, maggots!" Zack Okutsu finally shouts. He's barely taller than most of the kids.

No *Life* magazine photo op here, of beaming GIs surrounded by friendly, smiling children, arms around each other.

In the afternoon, a general stink rises above the city, of rotting fish, stray dogs, raw sewage flooding the street gutters. The locals jostle in the city plaza, selling their wares to foreign soldiers: American, British, New Zealanders, even French Algerians. A potato for fifty cents. A loaf of bread for one dollar. A pen for fifty cents, which Teddy buys after bargaining it down to twenty cents. He still writes to his mother every day. An egg for three dollars. A signorina for two dollars, a very nice girl, they are promised.

Alex walks to the outer edge of the plaza where it's less crowded. Here, tortoiseshells and cameos and other pilfered jewelry are being sold. A young boy is displaying broken crockery on a slab of fallen concrete. The items—cups, bowls, plates—have been glued together with mortar. They remind Alex of Japanese *kintsugi* pieces that his mother loved to make and collect: broken ceramic bowls sealed back together not with mortar but a gold-dusted lacquer. The result is a bowl whose delicate cracks are highlighted, not concealed, with gold. Beauty in all the broken places.

When they return from town, the GIs get doused with some kind of insecticide. Because of the lice in town, they are told, because of the disease, because of the filth of war. That night, when Alex opens his rucksack, he finds the small bowl he bought shattered into five pieces.

After Naples, Rome. Then, in a caravan of jeeps and trucks, they head to Civitavecchia. Next a little Tuscany village of Belvedere. Where, at last: war. In all its senseless, unspeakable, insatiable brutality.

50

In the hour before dawn, a few soldiers walk through the bivouacked camp, quietly waking up the battalion.

There are no grumbles this morning, no mouthing off at the assigned soldiers tasked with this thankless job. Everyone rises efficiently, quietly, lips pressed into thin white lines. Boots thrown on, bladders emptied.

Alex, like many of his fellow soldiers, is already awake. Has been for hours, his sleep fitful through the night, grabbed in brief, fractured snatches. But he is not tired. He is more alert than he has ever been. *Is this the last day of my life? Are these my final hours?*

A quick breakfast. K rations opened up. Everyone is forced to eat two packs. "You don't know when you'll eat again," Captain Ralph Ensminger says. To Alex, it sounds like: You don't know *if* you'll eat again. They eat sitting against tree trunks. Squatting on the ground. By the ridgeline, staring off into the distance, chewing somberly on gummy pork loaf and stale crackers, thinking of first kisses and last letters.

After breakfast, Captain Ensminger gathers E Company along with Alex's artillery team. Alex, as front observer, will be on the frontlines with the E Company infantry team.

"Listen up." This morning there's no need to shout to get their attention. Ensminger has their eyes, their ears, their undivided attention. "The Nazis are beating a retreat northward up Italy. And they've established a southern line of defense, starting with the town of Belvedere just over that hill. They've set up an SS battalion command post there. It's well fortified, and the Krauts will fight to the death to protect it." He taps on an *X* scrawled on the large map. "It's on an elevated position. Which puts them at a distinct advantage over us. Also in their advantage: they've got more troops, more weapons, more equipment, more vehicles, more tanks."

He pauses; everyone's heart is beating, faster, faster, faster-faster.

"They will not give in. They will fight to the death to protect it." He gazes at them, his pale blue eyes staring evenly at their brown ones. Now is the time to give the rah-rah speech, the *And we will fight them to the death, too!* speech. But he doesn't. He has never been that way, never really raised his voice even back at Camp Shelby in all their months of training together. He treats them as comrades, with respect. That's a big reason why they are so loyal to him, why many will fall on the sword for him. He only says, "Remember everything we learned together back at Camp Shelby. We do that, and we do it well, and we will prevail today, gentlemen."

The soldiers have a few minutes before they set off. They check their weapons and supplies. Some scribble hurried last letters, which they put not in their jackets but leave behind in their tents. In case they are blown apart.

Alex is staring over a ridge, into the distance. He takes out his drawing of Charlie. The paper is now smeared and in danger of crumbling away; but her face, her eyes—they seem as alive as ever.

He hears someone approaching. He slides the drawing into his pocket.

It's Mutt. He saunters up next to him.

"Hey."

"Hey."

"Doing good?"

Alex nods.

They stare at the Tuscan countryside.

"They don't ease us into war, do they?" Alex says.

Mutt cocks a grin. "Baptism by fire, baby. The only way to do it."

Alex hesitates. "Yo, Mutt, I'm afraid."

Mutt turns to look at him. "Hey, we're all scared, braddah. I puked twice already."

Alex lowers his head, speaks quieter. "All my life I've been this skinny quiet kid. Who stayed home reading comics. Even after Camp Shelby, I don't know if I've got it in me. This war stuff."

Mutt elbows him softly. "You stick with me, brah. I got your back."

They fall quiet.

"My older brother, Frank. He said that I wasn't cut out for war, that I'll die in seconds." Alex hangs the binoculars around his neck. "That's what I'm most scared of. Not the dying part, not really. But when the bullets start flying, I'm afraid I'll . . . you know, freeze up."

"That happens, I'll kick you forward." Mutt gives him a sideways glance. "Besides, your brother can shut up about you. The last I checked, there's only one Maki brother fighting in this war. You'll be fine."

"Yeah?"

"Yeah. But just in case you do die, hey, can I have your cigs?"

Alex smiles. "You're an idiot, you know that, Mutt?"

He laughs.

* * *

E Company heads out at 6:30 A.M. No more talking. At a half crouch, their steps slower, their bodies tensing as they near Belvedere.

They hunker down before a short hill, weapons laid flat before them. On the other side, a dip leads down to a flatland that rises up to the final hill upon which Belvedere sits. They'll be fully exposed in that flatland, target practice for the blind.

Captain Ensminger looks at Alex, points two fingers forward. Alex nods. Crawling forward, he eases up the hill, Mutt, carrying the SCR-300 field radio, right next to him. He pokes his head over the top. Never has his forehead seemed so massive, his helmet like a shining lighthouse. After a few minutes, he crawls back down.

"Nothing," he tells Ensminger. "No Kraut in sight."

Captain Ensminger doesn't show any emotion. "Call in again," he says to Mutt.

"C Battery, report in," Mutt says into the radio.

Garbled static comes back. Then Teddy on the line with bad news: *All artillery units still on the move. Howitzers stuck in mud because of heavy rain. The order is for E Company to move in on Belvedere ASAP. F and G companies already on the move. Coordinated timing is crucial. Do not delay, move in ASAP.*

Captain Ensminger curses. Moving in without artillery cover is sheer lunacy. But he's a military man through and through; obeying orders is his knee jerk. And plus there are F and G companies to consider. Can't leave them out to dry. "On my order, we go. Half speed." The order is whispered down the line on either side of him to the ends. Every head turns toward Captain Ensminger, who raises his hand. Then drops it.

Everyone rises. They move down the exposed side of the hill. Boots quietly thumping down, pants swishing, too loud, too loud. Weapons half raised, fingers near triggers, bodies half bent. All eyes nervously scanning the Belvedere hill, the surrounding high elevation hiding spots. Skin prickling now, arm hairs standing tall. Alex feels a burning sensation on his chest—a phantom target mark, the false feeling that a sniper has just put a target on you.

They reach the middle of the open field. If the Krauts have their number, now's the time they'll strike. Everyone knows this. An electric charge runs through them, tension like they've never felt before. But nothing happens. Maybe the intel is bad. Maybe the Krauts aren't in Belvedere—

Gunshots crack the air. Right on cue. Coming from the Belvedere hill. German nine-millimeter MP 40 submachines. *Burp. Burp-burp.* The sound almost comical, the impact anything but. Bullets striking everywhere, kicking up spouts of dust and dirt, like fat raindrops falling on a pond.

It does not register. Not at first. At Camp Shelby the simulated gunfire was harmless white noise. Every bullet blank, every grenade a dummy. The *rat-a-tat* meant only to scare, to distract. Not to cut down, not to kill.

But now. The soldiers are paralyzed, in a daze. The *burp-burp-burp* coming in faster, puffs of dirt lining in toward them.

On Alex's left, a soldier falls to the ground. No cry or shout. Simply collapses, arms splayed, with a muted thud. Death, so routine and anticlimactic in the end, all the more horrific because of it.

Then the soldier in front of Alex. A *dink* as bullet strikes helmet, whipping it off. The next second, the soldier's bared head explodes, and pieces of skull go flying amidst flung viscera. Blood sprays across Alex's face. He blinks, gasping, feels the nauseating slick warmth—

"Take cover!" Captain Ensminger shouts.

But there is no cover, no trees, no ditches. They've fallen right into the Germans' trap. Walked in stupidly. The Krauts must be laughing.

They drop to the ground. All except Alex, who is still standing. His mind going blank, his worst fears being realized, that he is a coward, that he is a child in the end. Hands grab him from behind, Mutt's, throwing him to the ground.

Gunfire echoing off other hills. And now the screaming starts. Alex thinks, *So this is war.*

Then right next to him. A different kind of gunfire, a crackling spitfire. Mutt half kneeling, firing off return fire with his machine gun. The sound glorious, an announcement, a declaration.

It sets off a chain reaction. Other soldiers let loose from the ground, squeezing triggers. Not controlled; everyone is panicking. A year of training lost in the fog of war, in the panic of adrenaline.

"Retreat!" a solider shouts, "back to the woods—" A bullet into his cheek, through his tongue, neck, carotid artery, and cleanly out. He goes spinning, his arms a whirling dervish, a geyser of blood ribboning out.

Alex whips his head side to side. They need to retreat. But they're cut off, the woods too distant.

"Follow me!" Captain Ensminger shouts. "This way!" He's hoisting a fallen soldier on his shoulders, beckoning his troops to follow. Not back to the woods, but forward. Into a nearby wheat field.

"Keep moving in!" Captain Ensminger shouts even as they plow into the tall wheat stalks. "Deeper!" The wheat stalks snap against their faces as they run through them, shifting and swaying like corrugated ripples, and giving their positions away. Captain Ensminger orders his men to freeze.

They do. No one moves.

Gunfire ceases. An eerie quiet settles over the land.

Through stalks smeared with blood, they gaze back at the open field. Dozens of bodies on the ground. Some are screaming, some moving slightly, groaning lowly. Others completely stock-still.

"We go get them, Captain? That's Stan out there, and Magnet—"

"We get 'em later," Ensminger answers through clenched teeth. "Right now we need to spread out, we're too clumped together. Disperse on the next wind, men."

They wait. Then comes a wind, blowing the sun-washed stalks this way and that, waves of buttery yellow. Using that as cover for their own movement, the men fan out, spreading deeper into the field until the wind dies. Gunfire comes again, but this time more sporadic.

Crouched low, the men wait.

So do the Germans. A stalk of wheat so much as flinches, and it's met with a hail of bullets.

Mutt speaks into the radio in a low voice. "Teddy, we're pinned here. We try to make a break for it, they'll pick us off one at a time. We need the howitzers. Like, now."

"Working on it, Mutt. Will have it set up in a half hour, tops."

"Make it fifteen minutes. Serious, Teddy."

No response. Just the sound of Teddy yelling at someone. Then static. Mutt shuts off the com. They wait. Try to block out the sound of their fallen comrades' pained moans.

Then, out of nowhere, a different sound. A high-pitched whistling. Up above, coming from the skies, getting louder.

Alex doesn't need to look up to know what it is. Artillery shells. German. A far-off artillery makes a whistling sound, an almost gleeful *whoom-whee!* Hear that whistling sound and you're fine. For now. The deadly rounds are the ones you don't hear, not until a second before they strike, when they make a *swish* sound. And the next second, you're dead.

Whoom-whee!

The earth shudders beneath them. Wheat stalks and dirt are

sent up into the air. More shells fall, over and over with bone-rattling force. Casualties mount in the wheat field, no telling how many exactly.

Captain Ensminger crawls over to Alex and Mutt. Sweat pours down his face, mixing in with blood and dirt. He grabs Alex's shoulder, squeezing so hard Alex will find bruise marks there the next day. "We stay here any longer, and they're going to shell us out. But soon as we leave, those machine guns will cut us down. We need our artillery to take out their machine-gun nests, and we need to do it now!" His voice hoarse, barely audible through the shelling. "So get eyes on them, Maki. Give us coordinates for those machine-gun nests *now*!"

"Teddy said the howitzers aren't ready—"

"You worry about getting the cords, and let me worry about the howzies. Now go!" Those are the last words Alex will hear him say. Captain Ensminger will die later that day fighting alongside the young men he trained.

Alex pushes out with Mutt by his side, the two crawling side by side, back the way they came. At the edge of the wheat field, they hunker low and scan the Belvedere hill. They wait for the next flare of muzzles flashing.

Minutes pass. An almost—

There. Bursts of light in quick succession halfway up the hill. Alex ignores the *pfft-pfft-pfft* of bullets striking ground near him. And now he is back at Camp Shelby staring at fields dotted with small flags; now he is back at Bainbridge Island watching Frank playing football. The high arch of the thrown pigskin, the plunk down into open trash cans. Twenty yards. Thirty-seven yards. Seventy-nine yards. In his head, measurements and yards and grids now interpose upon the terrain. Numbers run in his head. He grabs the map out of his pocket, distills the distances cleanly into coordinates certain. "One fifty-three. Five twenty-three. Two thirty-four," he shouts to Mutt.

Mutt yells into the mike. "Don't tell me you're not ready, Teddy, tell me you're dug in and ready to go!"

"We're ready, we're ready!" Teddy screams back.

Mutt smacks the ground in relief, yells out the coordinates.

Teddy repeats them. Mutt confirms. "Sending out a marking round in three, two, one," Teddy says.

Seconds later. Splash. A flash of light where the blank marker shell detonates. Twenty-two yards east of the target. "Three degrees to the west, same range," Alex says.

Mutt repeats the adjustments into the radio.

"Now fire for effect," Alex says.

"Fire for effect," Teddy confirms over the radiophone.

The artillery shell, when it detonates fifteen seconds later, explodes right over the machine-gun nest. A perfect strike. Shrapnel rains down on the German soldiers, a shotgun blast of death right to the tops of their skulls.

For Alex there is no celebration. No shout of victory. There is no time for that. German artillery shells are still falling. Right into the wheat field behind them.

He gives out the next coordinates. "Two forty-seven. Two eighty-two. Three twenty-four," he says, his face dotted with blood.

"Two forty-seven. Two eighty-two. Three twenty-four," Mutt repeats into the mike.

"Sending out a marker," Teddy says.

"No need," Alex says. "Fire for effect."

Mutt looks at Alex for a second. "Fire for effect, Teddy."

"No marker?"

"No. Fire for effect. All you've got. The coordinates are good."

They are. Fourteen seconds later the other nest is blown to smithereens.

51

And like that, the tide turns. The first crack in the Germans' defense, wedged open by Alex's artillery team. The smallest gap. But it is enough. The 100th Battalion, who've been in reserve all morning, are ordered to move in. They do, pouring through the gap, and they penetrate with ruthless, skilled, devastating force. It's a battle that's supposed to take days. But by midafternoon, the 442nd has already reached the top of the hill and breached the town.

They flank, surround, storm. Go house to house, flush out with grenades the German soldiers who come running out, only to be picked off. They are left dead or writhing on the ground cursing out in German, or sobbing for their *mutti*. Some escape on amphibious jeeps; the 442nd chase them into olive groves and gun them down in a bloody barrage, stopping all seventeen jeeps. Those who survive flee on foot. Sharpshooting American riflemen cut them down. Sometimes in the head. Sometimes in the back. Sometimes even when the German soldiers have their arms raised in surrender. Because, war.

By the end of the day, the 442nd will have suffered devastating losses. But they will have accomplished what they set out to do. Which is to take the SS battalion command post. Which is to be soldiers of war. They kill 178 Germans and capture 86 others. For their efforts, they will later be awarded the Distinguished Unit Citation.

Baptism by fire, indeed.

52

September 2, 1944

Dear Frank,

Hope you're getting these V-mails.

Haven't heard from you but I'll keep writing, okay? Or are my letters getting all blacked out by censors and there's nothing left for you to read?

Listen, I hate to keep asking, but any news about Father? Have they released him yet? I wrote to Lieutenant ▓▓▓▓▓▓ *(remember the guy who came recruiting at Manzanar?) and reminded him of his promise to get Father released if I enlisted. That was some time ago. Yet to hear back.*

God, these have been brutal months. I'm exhausted. Death, everywhere, Frank. Death in ▓▓▓▓▓ *and* ▓▓▓▓▓, *death in the streets. Death in my platoon.*

Just don't tell Mother, right? How is she doing? Are you taking care of her?

We have them on the run, them Jerries. Chasing them northward out of Italy all the way to ▓▓▓▓▓▓▓▓. *Giving them the boot, we like to say (get it?). It's slow going, though. They've built their defensive positions on hilltops, and it's hell trying to dislodge them from their higher ground. But we do it. Cap said we've killed over a thousand Nazis over the past two months. We're good soldiers, the guys in* ▓▓▓▓▓▓ *Company.*

Frank, you'd like them. The guys in my platoon. You really would. They're tough as nails. Fight hard. And their love for America is incredible. Really infectious. I'll be the first to admit that my motives for enlisting were mixed. I didn't do it for love of country, not really, but mostly to help Father.

But these guys: they bleed red, white, and blue. Most of them are from Hawaii and they were never put into camps. Too many of them, and locking them away would've wrecked the local economy. So these Hawaii boys have no reason to distrust America. They love this country with a patriotism that is pure.

They're great soldiers, great Americans. It's downright impossible to be around them, to fight alongside them, and not have their love for country sink in, become your own.

Let me know if you hear anything about Father.

Alex

V-mail collected at Bruyères, France, and later sent out from the army post office in Marseilles, France.

October 19, 1944

Dear Frank,

You'll never guess where I'm writing this V-mail from.

France! A town called ▮▮▮▮▮▮▮▮▮▮ *, to be exact.*

In late September, we left Naples by boat and three days later arrived in Marseilles. After traveling a gazillion miles by train and on deuce-and-a-half trucks, we reached the ▮▮▮▮▮▮▮▮▮▮ *Mountains. There in its black forests was a German-held town called* ▮▮▮▮▮▮▮▮ *.*

Or was it called Hell? Because for four days the Germans defended that stronghold like it was Berlin itself. So many of us died in ▮▮▮▮▮▮▮▮ *. Including Kash. And Leo.*

There's so much hatred in me now. For the Krauts—they've killed so many of my brothers. We've trained together, eaten together, played cards, laughed, crossed seas, bled together. And when one of us dies, it feels like family dying. So all I want to do is kill more Krauts. When I call out coordinates and rain down on them shells from our 105mm guns, my heart does a little jitterbug when I see the explosions. It's easy to hate people who hate you.

After four days of intense fighting, we finally drove the Krauts out of ▮▮▮▮▮▮▮▮▮. We had to shell that beautiful town good, unfortunately, thousands of artillery rounds. Afterward, all the local town folks came out from their underground cellars where they'd been hiding the whole time. Blinking at their pulverized town that's been reduced to smoking rubble. Even stone buildings were opened to the sky, their roofs caved in, the walls charred black by artillery strikes. The people gawked at us, at our uniforms, at our faces. They were confused. They couldn't believe we were Americans.

"Hey, don't feel bad, you're not the only ones," Teddy said. "Folks back home in America can't believe we're Americans, either."

But once they got over their shock, they were mostly nice, these ▮▮▮▮▮▮▮▮ folks. Because we'd liberated them from their invaders.

But they were also angry. At each other. I was walking with Shig and Snap when we passed a mob. They were surrounding two local women whose heads were freshly shaven. People were spitting on them, throwing rocks. The two women cried for mercy. One was pregnant, her bulging stomach dotted with people's spit. I stepped in, trying to calm the people down. But the townsfolk ignored me, and only seemed to get angrier at the women. Shig and Snap pulled me away, saying it didn't concern me, it was a local affair. I tried to break out of their grip, but couldn't, and they dragged me away. Even now I can still hear the sounds of the women as they pled for mercy.

That night, while everyone else was sheltering indoors from the cold rain, I walked alone around ▮▮▮▮▮▮▮. This next part is a bit stupid. But I was looking for . . . Charlie Lévy. I was thinking, *like an idiot, hey this is France, this is the closest I've ever been to Charlie. Maybe, just maybe . . . Charlie might be here? I knew it wasn't likely. Not even needle-in-a-haystack likely. But still. I walked with my eyes open, praying for a miracle: that somewhere in* ████████████, *or on the cobblestoned rue* ████████████, *or in the rain-soaked town square surrounded by smoking rubble, I would chance upon a girl with fire in her eyes.*

But she wasn't there. Of course not.

Alex

P.S. Any news about Father?

V-mail collected at Biffontaine, France, and later sent out from the army post office in Marseilles, France.

October 23, 1944

Dear Frank,

Another bruising battle in the ████████████. *This time to liberate the town of* ████████████. *Gut awful. The Nazis really dug in their heels, showed more teeth than ever. We lost good men driving them out. Archie. Yogi, not dead, not yet, but soon.*

And, yeah, don't tell Mother any of this.

But we did it. Climbed through the dense ████████████ *forests, up the slick, muddy slopes, and into* ████████████. *Moved house to house, flushing out the Jerries. But we're all so exhausted. Just feel a deadness inside. And the rain: cold and unrelenting, continues to beat down on us. Winter's come early, and the boys from Hawaii have experienced nothing like it. Doesn't help that we're still in our summer uniforms. It's like wearing paper in a winter downpour. Can't talk without teeth chattering, can't sleep without body constantly shivering. Skin's always wrinkled and white and sloughing off.*

But at least we get a break. Just yesterday, the powers that be pulled us out of line for some rest and recupe. We were taken to a nearby town called ███████████, and I'm almost crying with joy. First, we got hot showers. We peeled off our stinking wet clothes and boots, and stepped into hot showers. It was only one minute—30 seconds to lather up, 30 seconds to rinse off. But bliss. All the grime and mud and caked blood from the past ten days washed away. Then we put on new, dry clothes. You have no idea how that felt. We were human again. Then we got put up in somebody's home. Some hot chow, and we were all out. I slept in an actual room with actual walls, ceiling, and floor for the first time in forever. Dry. Warm. Safe. We slept like babies. No, we slept like the dead.

But all good things come to an end, right? And this time all too soon. Even though we were supposed to be here at least a week . . . something's happened. We got called back on line again after less than a day. Much cursing from the guys. We leave in just a few hours. Everyone's trying to get as much sleep as possible.

But me, I'm here still awake. Can't sleep. I've never felt this way before a mission but something's bothering me about this one. I feel . . . it's hard to put into words. Like something terrible is about to happen. Like death awaits us.

Alex

P.S. I've asked you to write to me but you never have. Not a single letter. It'd mean a lot if you did.

53

Alex is right. Death awaits them.

At three in the morning, the 442nd walks out of the town of Belmont and marches eastward toward the Forêt domaniale de Champ. The night is soaked with a freezing rain that in the darkness feels like shavings of drifting ice. None of the men speak. Their footsteps, muted by the damp soil, are sullen thuds. Many are simply bone-tired. Others are silent because they feel it, too. The same disquiet, the same sense of foreboding Alex feels. Something is wrong about this mission. Something off. Something worse than Bruyères. Worse than Biffontaine. A cold wet film lines their stomachs.

They've been told little by their platoon sergeants. What they know: three days ago a regiment from Texas—the 141st, and one of the finest—advanced too far ahead of the other battalions, unaware they were moving right into a German trap. Too late, they found themselves stranded deep inside the Forêt domaniale de Champ. Before they could retreat, the Germans swiftly surrounded this isolated regiment like a noose around the neck.

And for the past three days, the Lost Battalion—as they are now known—have been cut off behind enemy lines, all supply and rescue lines severed. Over two hundred white boys from Alamo, Texas, hunkered down in foxholes, desperate and terrified. Their supply of food, water, medicine, and ammo virtually gone, if not already depleted. Their own numbers dwindling with every passing hour as they die from festering wounds and trench foot and exhaustion and German attacks. Every attempt to break out of the German stranglehold has proven to be both costly and futile. Another few days, and this stranded unit will be completely annihilated.

That is all the 442nd know. What they don't know is that the 2nd and 3rd battalions have already attempted to rescue the Lost Battalion. But the Germans easily thwarted their rescue attempts, and inflicted heavy casualties in the process, mercilessly pounding each battalion with heavy mortar and machine-gun fire. Fact: the Germans have the higher ground. Fact: they have spent weeks preparing for this, building dug-in and concealed trenches in the woods. Fact: six hundred fresh German soldiers have just arrived to augment those already there, along with tanks and Granatwerfer 34 mortars. They are ready. They are licking their chops. For a bloodbath. For a massacre. Fact.

Now it's the 442nd's turn. They move in under cover of night, their rest in Belmont cruelly cut short before it's even really begun. On the map, the distance to the Lost Battalion is not far. Only five miles. But the Forêt domaniale de Champ stands between them, and it is a dense, unending forest of sixty-foot pine trees set on steep hills and narrow defiles and ravines that drop precipitously, cliff-like, to the valley floor hundreds of feet below. As hellish a terrain as they come, made worse by the unceasing rains that have turned the steep forty-five-degree hills into rivulets of slick, boot-sucking mudslides. Five miles might as well be five hundred.

At the edge of the Forêt domaniale de Champ, the men pause. The towering wall of pine trees looms over them, a black fortress. The leaders consult a map, radio in a few questions. This will be the last time they will speak by radio. Not only to maintain stealth but because radio communication will be compromised in the dense Forêt domaniale de Champ.

As they wait for final orders, someone sidles up next to Alex. Too dark to see who it is until he speaks.

"Something off about this one," Teddy says. "Feels like a trap."

"Yeah?" Alex waits for Teddy to continue.

"Them Krauts, they could have mortared the Lost Battalion to a crisp already. But ask yourself: why not, why are they keeping them alive like a squirming worm on the hook." He takes off his helmet, tilts the excess rainwater off. "'Cause they're baiting us in. It's all a trap."

Alex doesn't respond. It makes sense. A cold, discomforting sense.

Lieutenant Dreyer puts the radio down. "Ready up, men. It's dark in there. And muddy. And steep. We go slow. But we keep going. Maintain visual on the man in front, don't stray."

They move into the forest of darkness and death.

The German forces attack ten hours later.

By then the 442nd, after a whole night and morning trudging through the steep slopes and ravines of the mud-drenched jungle, are exhausted. And freezing. In the driven rain, their summer uniforms—issued to them in Italy during the hot summer—have become soaked through. It'll be another week before the shipment of winter overcoats, gloves, wool socks, and hats arrive, and by then it will be too late for most of them.

They are cold. They are shivering. They are exhausted.

They are targets.

The first mortar shell strikes about fifty yards from Alex. Out of nowhere, after hours of the gloomy monotony of mud and trees and darkness. A whining screech cutting through the air. Everyone drops to the ground. The explosion pulverizes two trees, sends out their shattered trunks in shotgun blasts of exploded bark that are as sharp and deadly as shards of glass and steel.

One man is cut down, dead, sudden. Three others lie groaning, clutching their bleeding wounds.

Mortars rain down. A cataclysm of violence. Then the *brrrp* of German automatic weapons fired from concealed machine-gun emplacements built weeks ago on higher ground. Men screaming, yelling. And then the snipers. Concealed in trees farther up the rain-drenched slopes, drawing a bead on the men. Their bullets slicing silently through air, striking targets who quietly slump forward as if suddenly falling asleep.

"They're up the hill!" Mutt shouts, pointing with his rifle. "Take cover!"

They scurry around the backside of trees, or lie squeezed up next to fallen trunks. What they should do: retreat slowly, from tree to tree, back down the hill to safety. Because fighting a well-fortified, well-armed enemy positioned on higher ground is a losing proposition. They must retreat.

But they don't.

They hunker down. Then slowly, inch by inch, foot by foot, tree by tree, like men possessed, they press forward. Up the slippery slopes, cold mud sliding under their uniforms, sludging along their skin.

Until the Germans, even those on higher ground and better armed, find themselves staring at the wild, obsessed eyes of a mud-covered soldier throwing himself over the rim of their machine-gun nest and spraying bullets with a manic cry. Or watching a live grenade land into their artillery station, and rolling casually against one of their German boots. Or peering through the scope of the Walther G43 sniper rifle only to land on another sniper with his rifle pointed right back; a curious *Kaugummifresser,* this one, in an American uniform but why is there a Japanese face on—

Until the Germans find themselves overrun and overmatched. By dusk, the 442nd has captured that hill.

But there are many more hills between them and the Lost Battalion. They covered only two miles today. Still three more to go. Three more miles into the heart of wet dark cold hell.

The next day, even worse. Hails of bullets gush down the hillsides in a waterfall of death from concealed positions with clear lines of fire. Mortar shells rain down on them, the explosions hellacious thunderclaps that rattle their skulls, shake the ground. German snipers take down those cowering on the backsides of trees.

All day the ground shudders, trees explode, sending out rocks, bark, hot metal shrapnel; all day men die.

But like yesterday, the 442nd push forward. Toward the Lost Battalion. Retreat not an option.

Night descends in the dense forest, cold, inky, heavy, black. Alex is alive. He did not expect to be. Others have died, their dying screams still echoing in his ears. But here he is, heart still beating, digging out a slit trench as best he can with his helmet. Mutt and Teddy beside him, Teddy digging with a trenching knife, Mutt with an empty mess kit.

They dig until exhaustion claims their wrecked arms. Alex, the skinniest of them, squeezes in and scrapes out space at the bottom for their legs, giving the trench an *L* shape. Without that, they'd be sitting cramped all night with kneecaps pressed up against their chins. They sit on their helmets, the bottom of the trench already filled with freezing water.

They break out their K rations. They eat the cold beans and stale bread grimly, dutifully. A long, savage day; they covered only one mile. Tomorrow, they'll have to cover two miles to reach the Lost Battalion. They try not to think about this.

The shelling begins an hour later. The ground rocked, tree trunks exploding and spraying out blades of white-hot metal and wood shrapnel. A soldier, on his way to a pond to refill empty canteens, leaps into their trench for shelter. The canteens rattling behind him like shaken bones.

At least the darkness conceals them. The Krauts are only guessing. The hours pass slowly with nothing to do but sit in their slit trenches, eyes heavy, backs screaming, while explosions rip the forest apart, hoping that the shells don't come any nearer, that the tree bursts stay on the other side of camp, or better yet, move farther afield.

Alex opens his eyes, not sure if he's actually slept. His left foot is a cauldron of heat. The pain like scalding hot water being poured on his foot.

"Braddah," Mutt says sleepily in the dark, eyes half opened. "You okay?"

Alex is not. He has trench foot, a condition caused by the constant exposure to cold and moisture. He knows without even having to look that the skin on his foot is wrinkled and gooey-soft, the tissue beneath infected.

"I'm fine," he says, wincing.

"Want me to take a look?"

"Nah. Probably can't even yank it out of my boot, it's that swollen. Besides, don't wanna be caught barefoot if they surprise-attack."

Mutt lights a Camel and takes a long drag. He holds it out to Alex. "I got lots more, brah."

Alex takes it, nodding his thanks.

Mutt rubs the ball of his hand into his eye. "So damn tired

but can't sleep. Keep hearing them sounds, you know? The screams." He takes out another cigarette, lights it up, careful to keep the flame below the rim, out of sight from German scopes. Around his ankles, floating in the puddle of rainwater, five or six butts float like sickly water lilies.

A faint drizzle, fine as mist, sprinkles down.

At the end of the trench, someone shifts. The soldier with all the empty canteens. He's from the 100th Battalion, he'd told them. Fighting since Salerno, over a year ago. He grunts; a moment later comes the hollow sound of water trickling into metal. He's pissing into his helmet. Finished, he tosses it out, then scoops muddy water from the trench bottom into the helmet. Swishes an expert swirl before flinging that out. Slaps the helmet back on, and is asleep almost immediately, lines of dirty water trailing down his face and neck.

"That'll be us someday," Mutt whispers, staring at the soldier. "Seen everything, feel nothing no more. Nothing on your conscience. Can see death all day and then sleep like a baby all night."

Alex closes his eyelids. Sticks his tongue out to catch raindrops.

"I'm glad Belinda dumped me," Mutt says unexpectedly, his voice low and soft.

Alex opens his eyes. "What?"

"Belinda. I'm glad she said no."

"What are you talking about?"

"I proposed. She said no. Got her Dear John letter a few days ago."

"No way."

Mutt pulls his rifle against his chest. A condom is wrapped around the muzzle end with a rubber band to keep dry the ammunition inside. "I'm glad. No, really. Because when I get back to Hawaii I'll be, you know, this different guy. A brute. An animal. Like that *lolo* chump"—he points to the snoring soldier at the end of their trench—"and nothing like the decent young man she remembers me as."

Alex shifts his position in the tight quarters. "You're still the same, Mutt. I mean, you stink right now. And you look horrendous. But you're the same guy."

Mutt takes a long drag on his cigarette, flicks the short butt to the bottom of the trench. "We've all changed, brah." He pulls out another smoke. "How're things with your girl?"

"What girl?"

A small taut smile crosses Mutt's lips. "Right." He lights his cigarette, looks at Alex. "The girl you talked about once. In that bar in Hattiesburg."

Alex shrugs.

"Come on, brah," Mutt says. "I see you take out that ragged piece of paper every day. The drawing of that girl. I see the way you look at it."

Alex leans his head back. "Her name's Charlie."

"Charlie?"

"Yeah. She's French. From Paris."

A moment passes.

"Why you never talk about her?"

Alex stays quiet. Rain falls harder now, filling the air with a static hiss. After a minute, he speaks quietly, his voice barely audible. "We wrote to each other all the time. For years. Shared everything about our lives. But it's been two years since I last heard from her." He shuts his eyes. His eyelids feel impossibly heavy, and he can feel a wetness gathering behind them. A minute passes, and another, and he finds himself speaking again.

"On my worst days, I think she's gone. As in, dead." He shakes his head. "Or maybe she's still alive. I don't know." He touches the breast pocket of his shirt, feels the slight bulge of folded paper in a waterproof pouch. "Maybe that's why I keep looking at this drawing. It's my way of keeping her alive. That make sense? It's like, the day I don't look at her is the day she finally . . ."

In the distance, a mortar strikes. But it is far away, the sound muted.

Alex takes off his helmet, tilts his head up at the pouring rain. "She seems so far away. Not just her. But my whole life back on Bainbridge Island. The strawberry farm. My school. My dog. Everything that once made me happy. They feel a million miles away and a billion years ago. Like none of it was real." Raindrops pellet his face, cold and hard, mixing with his tears and making rivulets that flow down his cheeks, his neck. "Even my parents. And my brother, he's never written back to me, not a single letter. Honest, some days it feels like . . . none of them ever existed." He looks at Mutt. "I'm a terrible person, aren't I, Mutt?"

Mutt gazes at him with red-rimmed eyes. "Nah," he says softly. "You're not, brah. You're not."

Sometime after midnight the artillery shells start up in earnest again. A macabre display of rumbling lights that strobe over the cratered, befouled forest. Rain falls heavy in this eternal night.

54

The gray dawn vomits its light over the ravaged forest. Those who are alive stumble out of the trenches. Their drenched clothes and skin are the color of sewage, and where soldier ends and forest begins, there is no telling; sometime during the night they have become congealed into a wet sop.

Some cannot even walk. They crawl out, hoping to stamp some life into their trench feet. Others don't bother. They begin the long crawl back, two miles over mud and tree roots and fallen trunks through ribbons of fog and down the mountain to the aid station.

Alex stares at his left boot for a long time. Gritting his teeth, he wrenches the boot off. His foot balloons out, a bloated mess. He tenderly peels off the wet sock. The skin is a dark blue, almost black, with a waterline on his shin matching the level of water in his boot. Dotted around his ankle, like eyes, are red blotches of open weeping.

"Damn," Mutt whispers, looking down. He sticks his hand under his uniform, removes a balled-up pair of socks from his armpit. "Here. Dry and warm, right out of the oven."

"The fresh scent of BO come free?" Alex says, putting it on gratefully. He balls up his wet socks, stuffs them into the pit of his underarm. His swollen foot is near impossible to cram back into his boot. "There," he says finally, his eyes damp with pain. "Out of sight, out of mind."

Minutes later, K Company pushes forward. Reluctantly. What they want is to retreat. Or at least hunker down for the day, wait for reinforcements and supplies to arrive. But they have been ordered to advance. By General John E. Dahlquist himself. Because if they don't reach the Lost Battalion today, those boys from Texas will perish.

And so K Company pushes forward. Through the grater of German minefields, artillery and mortar strikes, tanks, machine-gun emplacements, six hundred enemy soldiers. They push forward even though they're armed with only nine-and-a-half-pound rifles, bayonets. Push forward even though as a unit they've already suffered massive casualties, been cut down to half their size, even though they are at the end of their physical strength. Yet still they push forward with rifle to shoulder, head tilted to aimer, with fingers pressed against triggers, even though they sense—correctly—that they are cannon fodder. That many will perish today.

By afternoon, there's good news and bad news.

The good: they're only one mile from the Lost Battalion.

The bad: they can't advance. Before them is a narrow uphill ridge with drop-offs so steep on either side, it might as well be a suspension bridge. The Lost Battalion is on the other side of that razorback ridge.

And the worst news: General Dahlquist has ordered K Company to advance. Across the ridge.

"No way," Alex shouts back to their squad leader, Sergeant Snap Nakai. They're flat on their bellies, spread on the cold muddy earth. "That's a funnel of death. It's booby-trapped with mines, full of concealed machine-gun nests and snipers behind every tree. We won't survive a direct frontal assault."

"We've got orders!" Snap yells back. "There's only one way to reach the Lost Battalion. Through that ridge!"

Mutt grabs Snap by the shoulder. "There's no way—"

As if overhearing and now mocking them, a spray of German machine-gun fire rips into the ground before them. They press against the bark of the large tree.

Zack tightens his helmet straps. "It's sure death—"

"It's a direct order from General Dahlquist! We push through at all costs."

"Screw Dahlquist!"

Snap Nakai glances at the men of K Company to the right and left of him, sheltering behind trees. "This whole battle comes down to us, men. The dozen of us. Right here. Because we're the tip of the spear. We decide if the Lost Battalion gets saved or not. Just us."

A mortar shell strikes nearby. The men duck, their ears ringing.

"We're not cowards, sir," Teddy shouts over the bedlam. "But we're not stupid, either. That ridge is suicide."

"Listen to me!" Snap Nakai shouts. "Everyone who's died fighting, died to get us to this point." He grips and regrips his machine gun. Looks to his men. "Now shut up and be soldiers. On my go." He stares ahead, swallows hard. "Now!"

They rise as one, sprinting out from the protection of the trees.

They get about ten yards. A barrage of machine-gun fire mows them down. They fall, all of them, most ducking behind trees for shelter, a few facedown in the mud, dead. Zack's fallen, but he's not dead. He's on his back, twenty yards away, clutching the side of his stomach. Blood pouring out of an open wound, blackening the mud. Writhing in pain out there in the open, trying, vainly, to lie still. To not catch the attention of snipers.

Mutt leaps out from behind the tree.

"No, Mutt!" Alex grabs his shoulder. But he's too late.

Before Mutt can even get into the open, German guns open up on him. He retreats behind the tree, cursing.

A sniper shoots, striking Zack's thigh. He curls in agony, drawing up his leg. A moment later, another shot. This time the other leg. In the ankle, shattering it. The boot—always too large for Zack—goes flying off. Zack howls even louder, a lonely, pain-filled sound. They're toying with him, a cat with a maimed mouse.

"Gotta get him, gotta get him," Mutt says, his face flushed with anger, his body tense and ready to spring. But even he knows there's nothing that can be done.

Another sniper shot. Into Zack's shoulder.

Silence. They think Zack is dead now, mercifully. But then he starts wailing, a terrible pain-drenched howl, "*Okaasan. Okaasan.*" He's crying for his mother.

Then a single crack of the sniper.

Zack's head explodes.

And with that, the mortar shells once again fall from the skies, and the fusillade of bullets rip the ground and trees apart. There's no choice now. Under such a barrage, they need to retreat.

Except.

A soldier in the next tree over. Teddy. Lazy Teddy. Incompetent Teddy. Homesick Teddy who was always last in the drills, last in the forced marches, who always just wanted to be with his family, even if it was back in a tar-papered barrack in an internment camp. He's unsheathing his M1 bayonet, attaching it to his rifle. An obsessed, almost manic fire burning through the prism of tears in his eyes. He doesn't say anything, doesn't even look at the other soldiers. But something is coming over the others as they watch him; and in the next moment they, too, are unsheathing their M1 bayonets, attaching them to their rifles.

Teddy rises and, with a scream, charges. He is yelling, in Japanese, in English, it doesn't matter, not now. With tears in his eyes, with blood pouring down his face, with lice in his hair, venereal disease in his groin, fatigue in his bones, grief and anger in his heart, this boy who always sang "The Star-Spangled Banner" the loudest, who loved nothing more than fishing rainbow trout in the Fryingpan River of Colorado with his pals on a hot summer day, who dreamed of one day marrying the pretty Jenny Anderson, now charges up the ridge, shooting a Tommy from the hip, spraying bullets.

"GO FOR BROKE!" he yells. "GO FOR BROKE!"

And with that cry, the others rise as one behind him, and charge up the ridge as the earth explodes around them. Alex's painful trench foot forgotten in this hot mix of adrenaline and fear and violence.

Teddy goes down in a hail of bullets. But he rises in the next moment like a miracle, his legs wobblier, his eyes more fanatical even as life gushes out of him. He throws a grenade, and this boy who couldn't hit the ocean from a yard above it somehow lands it right in the machine-gun nest. It explodes, sending up German soldiers and metal fragments. And still he charges up, his company right behind him, still he is yelling and screaming, his expended Tommy tossed away, firing his bayoneted rifle.

"Banzai!" he shouts. "Banz—"

The bullet catches him in the neck. This time, he stays down. Blood spurting out from his neck, the artery severed. By the time Alex and Mutt reach him, he's dead. Alex grabs Teddy's rifle, charges up the hill, only he is faster now, and more accurate. Anger sharpens focus.

Next to him, Mutt. Armed now with a BAR weapon that he picked up from one of the dead. Aiming at a machine-gun nest, he unleashes a torrent of gunfire. As he does, Alex runs around the side of the nest, certain that at any moment he's going to be seen and shot.

But he isn't. He leaps over the lip of the nest, spraying his machine gun into the backs of the four Germans until the clip is expended.

"Maki!" Mutt shouts, reaching the nest. "Okay?"

"Okay," Alex shouts back, throwing away the machine gun and grabbing a German one. "Cover my back!"

Mutt finishes reloading his BAR. "You cover *my* back." And he is leaping over the edge of the nest, charging uphill for the next.

Behind them, their brothers are a strong force that follows. I Company. Many are cut down, but many also are pushing through. Throwing caution to the winds, charging up through the ridge that will later be called Suicide Hill.

Something has taken hold among the men. Something savage. Some are felled by the barrage of German bullets, but no matter; the others race up the ridge, like wave after wave crashing upon the shore. Until they are at the next nest, screaming with wild maniacal eyes and leaping in to engage in hand-to-hand combat. It is so elemental and raw, this face-off. A schoolyard scrap, a tussle. A tangle of arms, sudden grunts, leveraging for position, gasps for air. Only here it ends in death, when they find themselves pushing bayonets into soft German stomachs, necks, temples, eyeballs. Or find themselves impaled, killed with air hissing out of punctured lungs, or with blood filling the chambers of their pounding hearts.

Then there is only one last nest. Mutt, Alex, and two other soldiers they've never seen before but who are now brothers for life. Screaming with blood-streaked faces, flinging their last grenades into the pit, they leap in just as the smoke clears. Helmets get knocked off, German and American, revealing photos taped on the inside of girlfriends and wives and children and babies and mothers, German and American both.

They thrust their blades over and over into the enemy's chest, stomach, face, neck, as curses are thrown out in German and English and pidgin in a bloody tangle of arms and hands. One German spits out what must be a curse over and over as Mutt sinks his blade slowly into his throat, *Ich habe zwei Töchter, Ich habe zwei Töchter, Ich habe zwei . . .*

And then there are no more nests. No more snipers. No more Germans.

K Company and I Company have taken the ridge.

Alex and Mutt collapse to the ground. Not sure if the blood on them is German or American. Or even their own. Not sure if they are alive or dead or dying.

55

They find the Lost Battalion the next day.

Alex, Mutt, and a couple of others are out on patrol. They walk slowly, partly because of Alex's trench foot, partly because they're on the lookout for lurking Germans. It's Mutt who discovers the cable wire. He's scanning the ground for possible mines when he sees a tar-covered cable line. Thin, the width of a spaghetti strand. They bend, pick it up cautiously. It's an American communication wire. Probably laid down by the Lost Battalion a week ago.

Excited now, they move faster, following the wire. At the bottom of the hill, just as the mist begins to clear before them, Alex stops. He's seen something.

"What is it?" Mutt whispers.

Alex points to a tree. "Over there. I saw someone."

"Where?"

"Swear I did. Peeked out from behind that tr—"

A solider steps out. Blond, blue-eyed, Aryan.

Immediately, Alex and Mutt raise their rifles.

"Hey!" the soldier yells. Even in that short syllable, a Southern drawl. "Hey, there!"

Still cautious but lowering their rifles, Alex and Mutt walk over to the man. The soldier is staring at them with confusion, eyes going from their faces to their uniforms.

"You guys American?" he asks.

Alex nods. Just past the tree behind the soldier, movement. A foxhole, well hidden, the logs covering it packed with mud and brush. Eyes peering out.

"You guys the Four Forty-Second?" the soldier asks, more animated now. "Good God." He spins around. "Y'all, they're here! The Four Forty-Second are here!"

And with that, soldiers pour out of the foxhole. Filthy, emaciated, stinking of piss and worse, eyes blinking at Alex and Mutt. They are gaunt, staggering with dizziness and fatigue, phantoms recalled from hell. But smiles are breaking out across their mud-smeared faces.

"You guys want a cigarette?" Mutt says, holding out his pack of Camels.

"Sure do. Oh, man, I can't believe you guys are really here. We thought we were goners for sure."

Mutt cups the match with his hands, leans over to light the cigarette dangling from the soldier's lips.

"So happy to see you, man," says another soldier, patting Alex on the back. "How the hell did you break through? We tried. Never could." More soldiers come out of the foxhole. They surround him, patting him on the shoulder with relief and happiness beaming from their tired faces.

Alex thinks of Frank. How his teammates would huddle around him and look to him to lead them. How they would thump him on the back or shoulder pads after he called out a winning play. It's what Frank lived for, Alex thinks. He understands why now. The feeling is intoxicating. To be a hero to them. Or better yet: to simply be one of them, accepted completely.

The soldiers move aside to let their leader through. The tall man steps up to Alex and Mutt. Despite a scruffy beard he has a youthful face. "I'm Second Lieutenant Marty Higgins." He pauses. His eyes tear up. "Thank you, gentlemen. Thank you for breaking through. For saving us. You look like giants to us."

Alex looks down to the ground, not sure how to respond. It's Mutt who speaks up.

"I thought *I* stink." He grins. "But holy cow, you guys *stink* like you wouldn't believe."

"Oh, *I* believe it, trust me," Higgins says with a smile. "I've been cooped up with these knuckleheads for a week."

They all laugh, tears in their eyes.

56

*Transmission at 16:00. From Lost Battalion to CO
Dahlquist at Headquarters:*

Patrol from 442nd is here. Tell them we love them.

57

The 211 men of the Lost Battalion are evacuated back down the mountain, many of them carried by litter bearers on stretchers. But the 442nd is ordered to press on. To continue up the mountain. Cross the next ravine. No rest for the weary. Chase the Krauts back into Germany.

Not Alex, though. He can't. His left trench foot. No longer can he ignore the acidic pain flaming out from it. When he pries off his boot—it takes him ten gruesome minutes—the medic takes one look at the swollen monstrosity otherwise known as his left foot and orders him to the aid station.

"How you've been able to walk on that is beyond me," the medic mutters, shaking his head. "We're out of stretchers so you'll need to crawl. Or get someone to carry you down."

"I'll do it," Mutt volunteers.

He piggybacks Alex the way they came. Slow going, the slippery mud slopes treacherous. They walk through the bloody carnage on Suicide Hill. German soldiers lie atop one another in machine-gun nests, jaws slack, eyes glassy, arms and legs sprawled like a stack of dropped mannequins. American soldiers lie unmoving behind tree stumps, or in slit trenches, eyeballs as hard as ice, hair festooned in icicles. One soldier is facedown in the mud, his exposed hands partially devoured. Paw prints of some animal—a wolf?—dot the mud and snow around him.

"How can we just leave our men lying out here?" Mutt says. He hoists Alex higher up his back. "I'm coming back for them, Alex, I swear. After I drop you off."

"You need to rest. They'll have recovery teams out soon enough."

But Mutt shakes his head adamantly. "This is wrong. This is wrong."

The bivouacked aid station is packed. Men waiting outside on fallen tree logs, their heads wrapped in dirty bandages, or nursing arms snapped in two, jutting bones exposed. Gamely gritting down on cigarette stubs, waiting their turn. Everyone shivering. Alex and Mutt fall asleep against a charred tree trunk. In the late afternoon, they're brought inside the open tent.

"Another day longer, and the infection would have spread," the medic tells Alex. "And you'd be dead."

"Patch it up and I'll be on my way."

The medic shakes his head, starts scribbling on a medical transfer form. "You're done. At least for a few days. Sending you to a clearing station in the rear. You leave tomorrow morning. For tonight, you sleep here. Can't have you in a trench, your foot getting all wet again."

They get up to leave, Mutt walking past the medic. The medic crinkles his nose, turns to Mutt. "Hold on."

"What is it?"

The medic bends toward Mutt's feet. "I can smell it from here."

"Smell what?"

"The infection. Show me your feet."

"It's nothing."

"Show me your feet," the medic says forcefully.

They are barely recognizable, Mutt's feet. The size of watermelons, the texture of leprous skin. Blisters and open lesions, the color of rotting eggplants, the skin completely sloughed off. A horrendous stink rises from them.

Alex's mouth falls agape. "Mutt. You never said a thing. What the hell, man."

"You leave tomorrow, too," the medic says, signing off on another transfer form. "A clearing station. Then probably an evac hospital."

"Hospital? No, I—"

"Infection has spread. Amputation of both feet possible. At least you get to go home now."

Mutt falls silent.

"This whole time, Mutt?" Alex says incredulously. "You had trench feet this whole time and you didn't say a thing?"

"Didn't bother me."

"Like hell it didn't. You gave me your socks. You shouldn't have. You had it worse than me."

The medic leads them out back. Shelter halves are spread out on the ground, weighed down by a dozen soldiers lying on top. Each soldier has at least one foot wrapped in fresh bandages. The smell of infection is ripe in the air. "You two stay here tonight," the medic says, already heading back. "There should be a bottle of talcum powder somewhere. Or packets of sulfa powder. And absolutely no walking."

The tarp stinks; the ground beneath is cold. Tree roots jut into their backs. A brisk wind whistles through the trees, flaps the corners and edges of the tarp. But after four nights sleeping in soggy slit trenches while being bombarded by mortar and artillery strikes, it is the softest mattress in the quietest, safest bedroom they've ever slept on. Despite the early hour and pain in their feet, Alex and Mutt fall asleep almost immediately.

58

Alex wakes up in a bewilderment of confusion. The quiet, the sense of safety—none of it is familiar to him. He sits up. Around him, in the open air, a dozen bodies snooze away. Three men sit at the corner of the tarp, playing cards by moonlight.

Alex gazes up. The clouds are finally breaking apart, and stars glimmer through, the first time he has seen them in what seems like a year. The miracle of them, light from a million burning suns a billion light-years away in a vacuum of eternity.

Mutt is gone. Probably went to piss in the woods.

Words float over to Alex. The men, shuffling the cards, talking softly. About their fallen friends, the awful ways they died. The random, arbitrary way death chose them.

". . . can't touch the bodies," one of the murmurs. He shuffles the deck one more time. "Gotta leave them out in the field. The Germans rigged some of them with mines."

The men suck on cigarettes at the same time. Three dots of orange glow in the dark.

"Sarge said engineering teams coming tomorrow to make sure the bodies ain't booby-trapped. Then we can move them."

"Damn Krauts. They did the same thing at Anzio beach." They slap cards down in the space between them.

Alex closes his eyes. Lies back down. The men's voices murmur low and strangely soothing, the names of friends they've lost—Robert Hajiro, Kaz Fukunaga, Gerry Akamine—in the towns they died: Livorno, Lanuvio, Monte Cassino. Alex drifts back to sleep.

. . . wakes up suddenly. Snaps into a sitting position. His heart hammering away for some reason. How much time has passed? The three men have stopped playing—two have fallen asleep. The third man sits staring into the dark woods, smoking.

Mutt is still gone.

"Hey," Alex croaks.

The soldier turns to him. "Yeah?"

"The guy who was sleeping next to me. Did you see him walk off?"

The solider shrugs.

"Did he say where he was going?"

The soldier snorts, turns his back to Alex.

Alex stares into the woods. Then at the tarp. Five cigarette butts lie discarded where Mutt slept. He'd been up a while, then, before heading off. Thinking something over. Stewing.

Where would he go?

The answer comes at Alex like a cold wind. He stands up immediately, hopping as he squeezes his left foot into the boot. Tears of pain fill his eyes. He hobbles off the tarp, past the aid station. Past a few jeeps. Heads up the slope toward Suicide Hill.

How can they just leave our men lying out here? I'm coming back for them, Alex.

Alex's feet move faster, despite the pain shooting up from his left foot. His breath expels faster, hotter, the cold air sawing through his lungs. The landscape before him, caught in a silvery X-ray film of moonlight, stark and cruel.

"Mutt!" he shouts. "Mutt!"

The trees, those still standing, stare blankly back at him like uninterested, tired sentries.

. . . can't touch the bodies. Gotta leave them out in the field. The Germans rigged some of them.

He walks faster, his breath gusting white out of him. Past a nest of dead Germans. Wind blows, sending a thin sheet of snow sliding down the slope. He shivers. Keeps moving, the hill so steep, he's almost on all fours.

There.

A small dot moving against the white, moon-bleached landscape. Farther up the hill, about a hundred yards away.

"Mutt!" But the wind muffles and carries his voice away. "Mutt!" he shouts louder. He sees Mutt limping toward a black form on the ground. A dead soldier. "Mutt! Stop! Don't touch the body!"

But Mutt still doesn't hear. He keeps moving toward the figure, his arms extending toward the body. Slowly, so slowly.

Alex is sprinting now, pain shooting up his left leg with every step, his feet fumbling over roots and rocks and branches. Dangles of saliva fluttering out of his mouth. "Mutt! MUTT!"

At last Mutt hears. He stops, turns toward Alex. Alex sprints faster, shouting, flapping his arms, trying to warn Mutt. But the wind picks up, carving up his words, their tone, their urgency.

Mutt lifts an arm, waves back. Alex can almost imagine the smile on his face. *What's up braddah, you come to give me a hand?*

He sees Mutt reach down toward the body.

"MUTT!"

The explosion is no more than a little pop. Not loud at all. A misfire, it must have been a misfire. He almost expects to see Mutt picking himself up, dusting off the ice and dirt, laughing.

59

Alex clutches the blanket. For a moment he thinks he's back at Manzanar. Everything is weirdly familiar: the same cot, the same army-issued blanket, the room itself airy and cold and full of the sounds of others snoring, wheezing, murmuring in feverish nightmares.

But he's only in the clearing station. His third day here. Tomorrow he'll be released to make room for the more seriously wounded. His foot hasn't quite healed, but he's deemed well enough. His whole time here, he's barely eaten, barely spoken. His immediate neighbors have tried conversing with him. He hasn't said a word back. He doesn't know their names, doesn't want to hear their stories, or how many Fritzes they've killed. In the daytime, he curls up and sleeps, pretends to, anyway.

His cot lies before a large window in the coldest section of the room. A draft whistles through the imperfect seal all night and day. He doesn't mind, doesn't care. He feels nothing these days, not even the cold. Not even the needles when they inject him in his foot, his arm. They could inject him in the eyeball, and he'd feel nothing.

The only time he felt anything was yesterday morning. He'd gotten his hands on a newspaper. The rescue of the Lost Battalion had made the news. A photo splashed on the front page, of Marty Higgins, leader of the Lost Battalion, shaking hands with a Lieutenant C.O. Barry of "the relief unit." Lots of smiling teeth and faces in this photo, but not a single Japanese American face in sight. He read the article. *Doughboys Break German Ring to Free 270 Trapped Eight Days.* In it, no mention that the doughboys were in fact Japanese Americans, or that they suffered more than 450 casualties in the rescue.

60

They stand shoulder to shoulder in the bracing wind, drifts of snow lightly powdering their new boots and helmets. The sky is overcast this afternoon, swirls of black clouds darkening the French farmland beneath. The men of the 442nd, finally able to shuck their lightweight uniforms for heavy field jackets and shoepacs, stand in formation, stoic and expressionless.

Before them stands Major General Dahlquist. Two white stars on the front of his helmet stare unblinkingly like his own eyes as they scrutinize the assembled regiment before him. This is the man who ordered the 442nd to rescue the Lost Battalion "at all costs." The man who, many say, used the 442nd as cannon fodder. Who ordered troops to charge up Suicide Hill even against his lieutenants' objections. Who threatened those same lieutenants with court-martial unless they obeyed.

He has now ordered the 442nd to assemble here on this farmland in Bruyères. Pulled them out of Fays and Lépanges-sur-Vologne where they were resting, after finally being taken off the line after weeks of brutal fighting. Even after two days of rest, though, the men are still exhausted. None of them wants to be here. Not here before the small retinue of army photographers with Dahlquist, chest puffed out, preening for the cameras.

Dahlquist is irate as he stares at the assembled soldiers, his hound-dog cheeks twisting into a scowl. He turns to his adjutant and points at two companies where only a few soldiers stand.

"What companies are those two?"

"I and K companies, sir."

"And how many soldiers are there in I and K companies?"

"Four hundred men went into battle, sir."

Dahlquist bristles. "Then why do I count only twenty-six soldiers here? I told you I wanted *everyone* to attend. Where are the others? Why aren't they here?"

His adjutant pauses. "That's all that remains. Sir."

Dahlquist flinches. A stunned expression washes over his gray face. *Twenty-six?* he seems to whisper, his lips moving silently, his eyes blinking. The expression of a man who for the first time sees the blood on his hands.

Later he makes a speech, his voice droning on. He makes no effort to be heard, and the soldiers make no effort to hear. His useless words about courage, about bravery, about patriotism, about America, about freedom, his patronizing words. Everyone wants him to shut up.

Afterward he approaches selected soldiers standing in the front row. One by one he pins medals on their lapels for their acts of bravery. Some stare him in the eye, giving away nothing in their vacant faces. Others look down to the furrowed ground, refusing to look him in the eye.

When he stands in front of Alex, Alex does neither. He only continues to stare straight ahead, looking neither up nor down, but straight through Dahlquist's chest. As if Dahlquist isn't even there, as if he is insubstantial and Alex can see through him to the very edge of the dark forest.

"Well, done," says Dahlquist, extending his hand.

Alex doesn't say anything. Keeps staring dead ahead, and for a long moment doesn't extend his hand in return. Finally, and only because he is a soldier, only because he has obedience stamped into his bones, does he dutifully extend his own hand. Dahlquist's hand envelops his, swallowing it whole with bone-crushing force. As if trying to force Alex to look up, pay some respect, for God's sake. Alex doesn't blink, stares straight ahead.

Later, the names of the dead are read. The soldiers, still standing in formation, are rock still. From the edge of the field, a gloved bugler plays the twenty-four notes of "Taps." Snow drifts down, slowly, mournfully from the gray skies. Everyone thinking of brothers lost. Zack Okutsu. Teddy Ikoma. Mutt Suzuki. Their faces. Their voices. Their laughter. The bugler goes quiet; a wind picks up. Eyes well up in the silence. A few cry, but with silent, solitary tears. Most stare vacantly at the ground, or across the farmland at the dark line of trees.

Three volleys of rifle fire into the air.

PART FOUR

CHARLIE LÉVY

61

January 19, 1945

Dear Frank,

It's been forever and I still haven't heard from you. But I'll keep writing.

My artillery battalion was separated from the 442nd, and we've become a detached unit. We were on the move for weeks, trudging along on a slow motor march, cooped up in the transport trucks for days on end. We stopped only briefly in towns and villages, sleeping mostly in tents, but sometimes we lucked out and got to sleep overnight in abandoned houses. The names of the towns and villages are a blur now, and would be forgotten if I didn't jot them down: Mâcon, Cheniménil, Dijon, Valence, Menton. Someday Charlie might be curious, and I want to tell her exactly where I'd been.

I'm currently stationed way up in the French Alps at an observation post near Sospel, where the air is thin and razor cold. An empty world with snow-peaked mountains everywhere. Snow flurries never seem to let up this high in the mountains, but the flakes are light and soft.

It was hell getting up here to the observation post, though. We had to hike on trails that were ice-packed and steep. Mules carried the heavy equipment, but these mules, man they were stupid. Stooooopeeed. And stubborn as heck. Always trying to shake off the pack saddle, rubbing the attached pots and pans and armory against *the rocks, the rattling they'd make. Always biting and kicking at us before trying to scamper off.*

Then we got to the switchbacks: narrow, stacked up on top of one another like a messy pile of pancakes. We couldn't trust the mules with the howitzers on the tight turns. So we had to push the howzies ourselves. That was no fun. Them stupid mules kept grinning at us the whole time, God, I wanted to smack them right in their noggin. Or push them over the edge.

But now that we're up here, the view is pretty darn amazing. There's time and space to think and reflect. I'm looking forward to coming back. Never thought I'd say this, but those hot barracks in the Manzanar summer seem like heaven to me. Saunas to thaw out the cold that's so deep in my bones. I've been shivering for months.

But of course, there's still the war to be won, right? Hitler's not backing down. We heard the Nazis were putting up a fight in Belgium and Luxembourg not so long ago. But we daydream about coming home. My Hawaii brothers, all they do is talk about hot Waikiki beaches and hot pig roasts and hot Hawaii girls. Cap tells us to keep our mind focused on the war.

And he's right. Just yesterday I was on guard duty when I noticed something suddenly poke out of the mountains, on the Italian side of the border. Grabbed my binoculars. It was a German railway gun brought out of a concealed tunnel. Aimed right at us. Like staring down the barrel of a gun.

I never worked faster. Grabbed a grid map, worked out the coordinates, radioed it in. Took only two markers, then three salvoes. BOOM. BOOM. BOOM. That explosive ball of orange and red fury, it was a thing of beauty, raw and pure, against the white snow and blue sky. It swallowed up that German gun, brought down that tunnel. We felt the boom concuss across the mountain range.

Cap was pleased. He gave me a day pass to this place called Nice. I get to go in several weeks with a few other guys. They're already talking about hitting up some bars and a brothel. Me? I got other plans. Nice is where Charlie vacationed one summer long ago, staying with a family friend. I remember she wrote me a few letters from there.

Do me a favor, Frank? Go through Charlie's old letters—they're in a suitcase under my cot—and see if you can dig up those letters from Nice. This was the summer of '36 or maybe '37. There should be a return address on the envelopes. Let me know what that address is, will ya?

Your brother,
Alex

Alex rereads the letter, sighs. He shouldn't have mentioned the observation post. Or named all those towns, for that matter. The army censors will have a field day blotting them out. He picks up an eraser. Then a moment later, puts it down. Never mind. Who cares.

Because censored or not, it'll make no difference in the end. Frank still hasn't written to him. Not a single letter. Not even a postcard all these years. It can't be because Frank is still angry at him. At least, Alex doesn't think so. It's not like Frank to hold grudges this long. Something else is keeping him silent.

Screw it, Alex thinks. He's not going to erase anything. The censors can do what they want with this letter. Block out the whole damn page if they want to.

62

February 22, 1945

Hey Alex!

It's your brother here! Remember me? Sorry for taking so long to write back. Yes, I'm a schmuck. But you know me—writing's not really my thing.

Hey, good news. No, <u>great</u> news! Father's back! Yup, he arrived here a couple of weeks ago. He's a skeleton now, feeble, we barely recognized him when he first got off the bus. Clive, one of the MPs I've become friendly with, gave us a ride on his jeep back to the barrack.

Mother's taking care of Father now. Sneaking food back from the mess hall, tending to him day and night. It must be tiring work but it's like she's got this new lease on life. She's all energy now, bustling around, restoring Father back to health. When I hear them quietly talking and even chuckling together, I'm glad for them.

You did right, enlisting. I'm sure it's only because of you that Father was released. But you know what? It should've been me who volunteered. I'm the oldest son, after all. Instead all I did was protest here. Which was the right thing to do, I guess, but many nights I lie awake wondering what waving placards and screaming into the wind really achieved.

You're the hero, Alex. The leader, the real quarterback of this family, while all I've done is warmed the bench. And it's been really tough for me to accept that. And I guess that's the true reason why I never wrote back to you. Because, yeah, I'm pretty ashamed of myself. There, I said it. Ashamed. I feel like I let you all down these last two years. Some days, I can barely look Father in the eye.

But I'm over that now. I'm just so proud, man. At who you've become. At what you've done. We've all heard about the heroics of the 442nd. I've cut out and stuck to the wall newspaper articles about you guys. And I must've read your letters about a hundred times each. You don't know how many nights I dreamed I was there, fighting alongside you in Italy, France, Germany.

I look up to you, you little goober. We all do. You've done us proud.

Your bro,
Frank

P.S. Almost forgot. But I went through Charlie's letters like you asked. And yes, I found the letters sent from Nice. The written return address is 11 Quai des Deux Emmanuels, appt. 3, Nice, France.

P.P.S. Something else I found in that suitcase: your sketchbook. Well, I took a quick peep. On every page, there's a drawing of someone. That's Charlie, right? You're clearly in love with her, you little dolt. You kind of always have been, haven't you?

As I was flipping through the pages, a magazine article slipped out. From <u>The New Republic</u>. It was about Jews being sent to extermination camps.

I always had a hunch there might be another reason why you enlisted. And now I know.

Yes, my weird, strange little brother, you've always had your head in the clouds. But that ain't so bad a place to be when your heart's in the right place. And crazy as this sounds, I hope you find what you're looking for.

63

Nice is nothing like Alex imagined it.

He envisioned a provincial little beach town. But instead it's a bustling city: alive, vibrant, with a mind of its own. The other three soldiers in the jeep perk up as they speed down boulevard Victor Hugo, their heads swiveling back and forth at the passing buildings and people. And at the women, so many of them. As soon as they reach the town center, they leap off the jeep and race across the street, hooting and laughing, for a brothel around the corner.

Not Alex, though. He has other plans.

Thanks to Frank—whose letter Alex must have read a dozen times, each time with tears—he now knows the address of Monsieur Schäfer's summer apartment. 11 quai des Deux Emmanuels, appt. 3. Alex doesn't really expect to find Charlie—or even Monsieur Schäfer, for that matter—in that apartment. This is nothing but a stab in the dark. A fool's errand.

But Alex has no other way of finding Charlie. He has to try *something*.

He asks locals for directions. But they are tired of foreign soldiers, and rude. For three years, foreign troops—first the Italians, then the Germans, now the Americans—have invaded their city. The locals wave Alex off, or stare at him in confusion, this Japanese man in an American uniform speaking passable

French. Only an older man in an open square stops his bowling game to point Alex the way.

But it is the wrong way. For hours he walks past stores, restaurants, cafés, helplessly lost. One hotel, the Excelsior, inexplicably gives him the chills as he walks past. He asks a storekeeper for directions, is sent down to the shoreline. There he walks on a wide promenade alongside a rocky beach. Less than a year ago the beach was littered with mines and antiaircraft weapons and barbed wire against an Allied invasion. Now it's been scraped barren and ugly.

He keeps walking, certain he's heading in the wrong direction. A dilapidated pier extends out from the promenade, and he sees, at the end the Palais de la Jetée, a massive building modeled after London's Crystal Palace. It's been razed down to a husk, its metal stripped by the Nazis for building warplanes. A metaphor, Alex thinks, of what war does to places. And to people.

Few strollers walk the promenade, and those who do ignore his request for help. By five o'clock he's cold and miserable. He begins to wonder if such an address even exists. Or even why it would matter. Charlie stayed there many years ago, after all. His plan is absurd and naive, full of childish optimism. Why did he bother coming?

Almost ready to give up, he turns a bend in the promenade. He sees a pier. Sailboats and rowboats docked along its length, the sound of anchor ropes creaking. *I can see a pier from my window,* she'd written long ago. *The sea so blue!* He walks on, faster now. A few minutes later he is standing in front of 11 quai des Deux Emmanuels.

Apartment 3 is on the second floor. He takes the stairs two at a time, then hurries down the length of the hallway. In front of the apartment, he pauses, his heart thumping wildly. His throat has gone raw and dry. Then he raps the door with his knuckles.

Footsteps. The door opens, only partway. Through the slim

gap, Alex sees a man with a full head of sheer white hair and sharp intelligent eyes. He frowns at Alex, stares confused at the uniform.

"*Excusez-moi,*" Alex says. "*Êtes-vous Monsieur Schäfer—*"

The man narrows his eyes. He answers back in a torrent of French, too fast for Alex to understand. He starts to shut the door.

Alex rams his boot into the gap. The man's eyes widen angrily at Alex.

"Stop!" the man shouts. He leans against the door, pushing hard. "Take your foot out!"

Alex ignores the pain. "You can speak English, then."

The man stops pushing. "Go away," he growls.

"Please. I don't wish to cause trouble. I'm looking for someone. His name is Monsieur Wolfgang Schäfer. This is his summer apartment."

"Who? Go away."

"You don't know him? Monsieur Schäfer?"

"You have wrong place. Go away."

"Please. He's a businessman from Paris." Alex tilts his head, staring keenly back at the man. "Are you Monsieur Schäfer?"

"I do not know this man. Perhaps he live here before. But I cannot help you."

"Please, can you—"

"I already tell you. I cannot help you." He leans against the door again.

But Alex only wedges his boot deeper into the gap. That's when he notices through the narrow opening the shoe the man is wearing. A two-toned oxford. With fancy wing tips, pattern swirls, a distinctive monk strap. Identical to the pair Charlie once sent him.

"Your shoes," Alex says. "They're very distinctive."

The man stops pushing. He looks down, then back up at Alex.

"A friend once sent me a pair just like those," Alex says. "A girl from Paris. Her father owned a shoe factory with Monsieur Schäfer."

The man blinks. He examines Alex carefully as if reading tiny words on his face.

"You are Monsieur Schäfer, I know you are." Then the question comes out like a breath too long held. "Where is Charlie?"

The man stares back, then shakes his head. "I cannot help you."

"Did she ever make it here? Is she still alive?"

"I said I cannot help you, Monsieur Maki."

"Please tell me," Alex whispers, and there is a deep dull aching in his lungs. He puts his hand into the gap, wraps his fingers around the edges of the door. "Anything you know."

Monsieur Schäfer stares at Alex. Finally, with a sigh, he opens the door wide. "Come inside."

In the small kitchen Monsieur Schäfer motions to the table while he busies himself, putting the kettle on and lighting a few candles. His movement is efficient and decisive, and even in these simple actions, an intelligence percolates.

Alex pulls out a chair, sits. A lifetime's worth of fears and hopes tumble inside his head. But he knows better than to pepper the man with questions. Not now. Not yet. He listens for sounds of another in the house. But hears nothing in this quiet, immaculate apartment. Even the kitchen is tidy, not a utensil out of place. Only a bookshelf set off against the far wall is in disarray, stuffed with books every which way. Books in French, German, English.

The far window overlooks the pier, and in the deepening dusk, Alex sees the gentle bobbing of boats. On the windowsill stands a framed black-and-white photo of two young soldiers, grinning. One of them is clearly a young Monsieur Schäfer. The brashness of youth in both men's eyes, their arms draped comfortably around each other.

"That's Charlie's father?" Alex asks.

He nods without looking up. "It was many years ago. A lifetime ago." He brings out two empty teacups, sets them on the kitchen counter. Then, reluctantly it seems, he moves to the table and sits down across from Alex. In the candlelight he seems softer, less stern.

"How do you know I am here?" asks Monsieur Schäfer. "I have tried to be very careful. I don't even use my real name anymore in Nice."

"Charlie spent a summer here. Many years ago. She wrote a few letters to me. That's how I got your address."

"And how you found me." He nods to himself. "Of course, it makes sense now." He blinks slowly, then stares grimly at the trembling candlelight. "You asked about Charlie. She never come here."

"Then where is she now?"

"I do not know." He takes a long breath. "You asked me if Charlie is alive. I also do not know this. But I think maybe she is not alive."

Alex feels the air in the room drain away.

The kettle starts to whistle. Monsieur Schäfer gets up, returns with two cups of tea. He sets one down before Alex, adds a few drops of honey.

"How much do you know?" Monsieur Schäfer asks. "Do you know about Vel d'Hiv?"

Alex nods. "And Beaune-la-Rolande. I know you rescued her. And that you hid her in your factory. With a Sinti family. But after that—I have no idea." He leans forward. "What happened?"

Monsieur Schäfer drops his eyes to the flickering flame. "Someone at the factory informed the French police. The gendarmes came when I was out, and took Charlie. The gypsy family, too."

"Where to?"

He stirs his tea with taut circular turns of the spoon. "At first I do not know. But then a few months later I received a letter. From her."

Alex sits up. "From Charlie? Where is she?"

"She wrote from a camp. A camp in Auschwitz."

"Auschwitz? What's there?"

He pauses. "It's a . . . a very bad camp. In Poland. Terrible things happen there. People die."

For the first time Alex can hear the faint ticktocking of a clock from an adjacent room. Five seconds pass. Ten.

"The letter was written in her bad German," Monsieur Schäfer says quietly. "And very censored. But now I knew where she is." He picks up his teacup, brings it to his mouth. But barely sips anything.

"I traveled there. Immediately. It was dangerous for me, yes, but I went. I have a friend in a high position at that Auschwitz camp. I thought maybe I could use that connection."

"To get her out?"

"But it was impossible. Because she was in some trouble."

"What kind of trouble?"

"There was a . . . how to say? I do not know English word. A révolte."

"A revolt."

"Yes, of course. A revolt. At the camp. Four women prisoners were arrested for trying to steal gunpowder. They were trying to use the gunpowder to make big explosion. To destroy . . . the fireplace."

"Fireplace?"

"Where they burn bodies."

The kitchen seems darker now, the candle flame flickering, weakening.

"These four women. Charlie was one of them?"

"No. But she was involved. She was helping them somehow. To start a revolt."

Oh, Charlie, thinks Alex.

"The four women were . . . attacked. No, the word is . . . *tortured.* They were tortured. But they refused to give up any names. Including Charlie's."

He puts down his teacup, pulls out his packet of smokes. Lights it with a slightly trembling hand.

"The four women were then hanged. But the camp guards didn't stop there. They killed hundreds more."

"Hundreds?" Alex finds it impossible to breathe. "What about Charlie?"

"When I got to Auschwitz, my friend would not release Charlie to me. He said she was a suspect. She was part of the revolt. She was about to be executed."

"They killed her?"

Monsieur Schäfer shakes his head. "I was able to get her out."

Alex's heart skips a beat. Then begins to race. "What?"

"I spoke to my friend, the one in high position. I asked him to give her to me. He said, impossible. But then I insist. I say this girl's father cheated me in a business deal. And now I want revenge. I have come all this way because I must have revenge. My friend said don't worry, they will kill her for me. But I said I want more than just death. I said this girl is pretty, I always had my eye on her, such a pretty girl. Just give her to me only a few hours, and then I will give her back to be killed. It will make my revenge better."

He stops, catching the expression on Alex's face. "I had to make it real. You must speak ugly to ugly men if you want to seem real." He takes a long, quivering pull on the cigarette.

"He brought her to me. Said do what I want, but bring her back in half an hour." His voice, trembling now. "She was so thin. Her hair gone. A skeleton. I did not recognize her."

"But you got her out? You—"

"Only past the front guards. And then there was nowhere to hide her. No car, nothing. If I took her back into the camp, she dies. For certain. So I put her in the only place I can find. On a train."

"A train?" Hope leaps up in Alex. "To where?"

"It was just leaving. But at least it gets her away from Auschwitz. From certain death."

"To where?"

"I didn't know it at the time. But now I know. The train went to Dachau."

"Dachau?"

"A camp in Germany. A bad camp. It is like Auschwitz."

"But you can get her out of there? You got her out of Beaune-la-Rolande before, you got her out of Auschwitz, surely you can get her out of this Dachau camp—"

"*Oh, taisez-vous, vous êtes stupide!*" he shouts, his hand slamming the tabletop, rattling the teacups sharply. The candles wobble, throwing flickering light across their faces.

Monsieur Schäfer clutches his fist, takes a few drawn-out breaths. "I am sorry. I apologize." He rubs his face, hand calluses scratching against his scruff.

"A week later," he continues after a moment, in a quieter voice. "I tried to find her in Dachau. But there is no record of her. No, of course not. Now it is impossible." Ashes fall off the end of his cigarette. "You asked me if she is still alive. I do not know. Maybe she died in camp. Maybe she died on train even." He stubs out the cigarette into the ashtray. "Or maybe she is alive still. I do not know."

He stands up suddenly, the chair tipping over backward, the crash of it jarring. He stumbles to the sink. Leans over it, then lifts his head to the framed photo. Stares at that moment captured in time: his arm around Charlie's father, invincible in their youth. "Back in Paris, I should insist more. I should have yelled more, Jacob, escape with me *now* to Nice. And then maybe we all flee to Switzerland. Then he is alive today. And Naomi. And Charlie, too. But I did nothing."

"You didn't do nothing. You did a lot for this family. Everything you could."

"It wasn't enough." He turns and looks at Alex, his eyes half lidded, as if ashamed of their deep blue. "Nothing is enough now."

"You believe Charlie is dead?"

"Yes." He looks at his hands. "But sometimes no. What do you believe?"

"I think she's a fighter. I think she loves life too much. I think she'll do anything to stay alive."

Monsieur Schäfer stares at Alex with a hard-to-read expression. Perhaps pity. "It is good to be young, to have such hope."

"She's alive. In my gut, I know she is. And I will find her."

From the room next door, the clock starts to chime. Six times.

"I know, I know," Monsieur Schäfer says, observing Alex turn to the clock. "I see this happen every day at six. The American jeep come to town to pick up American soldiers. And so you must go now. If you hurry you will catch it."

Alex shakes his head. "I want to know more. I don't care about the pickup."

"There is nothing more to say. And I don't want to talk about this anymore. So please leave me now."

At the door he hands Alex a folded letter.

"She was writing this when the police came for her in my factory. They broke down the door and took her and the gypsy family away. I found this letter later on the floor where it fell."

Alex stares at the letter in disbelief. A letter from Charlie.

"I kept it all this time," Monsieur Schäfer says. "Because I always think maybe this will happen."

"What will happen?"

"That you will come. Looking for her. Because you have such strong friendship." He holds out his hand. "And now you must go. Read the letter later. Or you will miss the jeep."

The two men shake hands.

And there is something else that still must be said.

"Thank you for carrying our letters all these years," Alex says. He grips the man's hand for a moment longer. "Whenever I received a letter from Charlie—it felt like the best thing in my life."

For the first time the man smiles. "And Charlie, too. She always talked about you. Always said how funny you were, your jokes, your wonderful drawings. You were a joy to her. Especially toward the end, you meant so much to her."

"I did?"

"Of course, but you know this already." He swings open the door, and as Alex steps out, Monsieur Schäfer holds up his hand, remembering something. "On the day I pulled her out of Auschwitz. She said something to me. Something so curious."

"What?"

"It was the last thing she said. I put her on the train, and she turned around. And she said, 'If you see Alex, tell him this. Tell him I said, *I am still the leaping frog.*'"

"I am still the leaping frog?"

Monsieur Schäfer nods. "What does it mean?"

Alex closes his eyes, feels them wet and shimmering behind his eyelids.

64

Dearest Alex,

Day 93. Here I am, still hiding in this small room in the factory. Speaking in whispers. Constantly shushing Djangela, the little Sinti boy. Walking with soft careful feet. I have lost track of the date. I have lost track of who I am. I am a ghost.

It is unbearable.

There is only one thing I can do to keep sane: I think of the future. I imagine myself in that world. When this war is finally finished. When I no longer have to hide in this tiny room. When I will be free, when I can walk the streets without fear, without shame, without the star, with my face tilted upward to take in the full sunshine. When my life is restored.

Oh, Alex, promise me one thing: when this war is over, come to Paris. Join the Cité Internationale Universitaire program in the 14th arrondissement. They offer excellent fine arts classes for talented artists. Many American exchange students studied there before the war, and they all lived in a beautiful residence called the Fondation des États-Unis. Sorbonne is not far from there.

I will show you Paris. I will take you everywhere. Because even now, even after all Paris has done to me, all the ways she has failed me, hurt me, even arrested me and let me be taken away, all the ways she has betrayed me—I still love her. Maybe Alex, maybe loving a city, a country, is like loving a person: you love her despite her faults, you forgive her constantly, you always believe in her, fight for her, you never give up on her.

And in my beloved Paris I will take you to the bookstalls along the Seine and we will bargain fiercely with the bouquinistes. I'll take you to the Ile Saint Louis in the summer and we'll sit on a bench and share ice cream. We will go to the Île aux Cygnes and stare at the replica Statute of Liberty and pretend we have gone to Manhattan together. I will take you under all the bridges where I painted the leaping frog as resistance graffiti, the Pont Alexandre III, the Pont des Arts, and you will laugh at my horrible painting skills, how my leaping frog looks more like a squashed escargot.

In the autumn we will go to the Jardin des Tuileries and drink hot chocolate and eat crêpes. When the cold of winter arrives, we will go to one jazz club after another in the Latin Quarter, and drink in the music until sunrise. We will sit on the grass of the Square du Vert-Galant on beautiful spring afternoons and there I will look at your latest drawings, and you will read my latest stories. We will talk about your classmates, and gossip about my Sorbonne classmates, about our professors, those we admire and those we hate. Sometimes I will force you to speak to me in French to help you improve. Or we won't talk at all; we'll sit side by side in an intimate silence and drift in and out of lazy naps. I will take you to the theater, to the exact seat where I once whistled in the dark at a Nazi newsreel.

All these places in the city I love, Alex. I can almost feel myself already there with you, the sun warm on my face, the gentle breeze in my hair, the smells of a boulangerie surrounding us, the sound of a street musician in the background, and your presence next to me, your hand in mine. It will be so good to be warmed under the same sunlight as you, to later lie under the same moonlight.

Oh, Alex, forgive me for this. For letting my imagination get ahead of me. But it is the only way I can escape my lonely existence, and this awful small room, and my

And there the letter ends: the very moment when the French police must have barged into the room and snatched her and the Sinti family away. He stares at the blank rest of the page, the sheer shock of white, the violent, vulgar emptiness of it. A decisive snip, a string cut, Charlie vanished.

65

Defeat hangs in the air.

It is everywhere in Germany, this sense of closure, permeating every city and town and village. In the countryside, the German army is teetering, barely putting up any resistance.

Alex is on the side of the victors, but in his heart he feels as defeated as the Germans. He is as joyless and dejected as this miserable cold spring. The barren land is as hard as ice, and instead of the fragrance of blossoming *Palmkätzchen* and crocuses in the air, there is the stink of rot and wet ash. Alex feels a bleakness in his bones he cannot rid himself of. He is tired all the time. He has not smiled in weeks, in months.

In late April, Alex and a second lieutenant named Clay Ohtani—who's been in Europe so long he claims to be conversant in French, Italian, and now German—come upon a farmhouse. Smoke tendrils rise from the chimney. A German soldier is sitting outside in a lounge chair, dozing in the sun.

"We've got the building surrounded," Clay announces, awakening the soldier in crude German. "Tell your mates to come out with arms raised."

The German soldier rubs his eyes, then rises and saunters inside with all the casualness of a man going to take a long piss. A minute later, a dozen haggard German soldiers file out with arms raised. They surrender without fuss, only wanting to know how far the prison is, and does Clay have any chocolate to spare?

In late April, C Company from the 522nd Artillery Battalion peels off from the 442nd Regiment, and crosses the Danube River into Bavaria. There are rumors that they're headed to the Eagle's Nest, Hitler's private alpine retreat in the mountains of Berchtesgaden.

"There's one reason, and one reason alone why we've been ordered there," Clay says, one hand on the steering wheel, the other holding down the mess kit bouncing in his lap. "Hitler's up there, I'm telling you."

"Hope so," Chuck Yamazaki says from the front passenger seat, chewing loudly. "God, I'd love to wring his little neck."

"Listen," Clay says with seriousness. "If Hitler's really up there, I'm calling dibs. I'm the one who's gonna put a bullet in his head, understood? No one else touch him."

Stanley Sakamoto laughs from the back seat. "Tell you what we should do. Before we slit his throat, we tie him up. Then shave off that silly moustache. Then we say, *Die, Führer!*" He smacks his thigh, laughing. "That'll really put us in the history books."

"You're such an idiot, you know that?"

Clay turns to Alex in the back seat. "What about you? Any ideas how we should do in Hitler?"

Alex taps the map spread out on his lap. "Let's just focus on the assignment. Reconnoiter the area for possible howitzer targets."

"Always the killjoy, Maki, I swear." He opens his mess kit, stuffs a piece of bread into his mouth, chews loudly. "And whatever the hell does 'reconnoiter' mean?"

Over the next hour, they drive quickly through the German countryside. Snow covers the fields even this late in April beneath a drab, overhanging gray sky.

Clay says, "What's that?"

"What?"

"Over there." He points at a mound of snow by the road.

"Probably just a dead horse under there."

Less than a minute later, Clay points again. "Look. Another one." He slows the jeep.

"Don't stop," Stanley says. "Just keep going."

But at the next mound, Clay slows to a stop. This mound the largest of the three. The four soldiers disembark the jeep, approach the mound carefully.

"What do you think? Two horses?"

Clay pokes the mound with the butt of his rifle. Chunks of snow fall away.

A human face stares out.

"Oh!" he flinches, jumping back.

Cautiously, they brush off the top layer of snow. Beneath it, bodies clothed in striped outfits. Others are naked, their clothes ripped off, their arms and legs entangled like broken-off bare tree branches.

"Let's go."

"God, there must be a dozen bodies in here."

"Let's go."

They hop on the jeep, drive away.

But they come across more mounds, with growing frequency. Some are large, others small, the size of a single person. Or a child, perhaps. *A dog,* they tell themselves. *Just a dog.*

"What the hell happened here?" Clay turns to Alex. "Where are we exactly?"

Alex bends over the map. "Near this town called Hurlach."

"Hurlach. Never heard of it."

"It's just south of a place called 'Da-chow.'"

Clay shakes his head. "Never heard of 'Da-chow,' either."

Ten minutes later. "What's that over there?" Alex says.

Clay slows the jeep.

None of the men says anything. It's a camp. Enclosed by barbed-wire fences, and filled with rows of black barracks. Something is just wrong about this camp. They all feel it instantly.

"It's off our route," Clay says. "What do we do?"

"Drive to it," Alex says.

"Germans, though."

Alex peers through his binoculars. "I don't see any. The camp looks unguarded."

They drive slowly to the gate. Stanley radios in to headquarters for instructions. A dead horse lies in a roadside ditch.

Alex gets off.

"Hey, Maki, we should wait."

He ignores them, walks to the gate. There are people on the other side of the fence. Standing in bare feet in the mud and snow. Staring back at him listlessly. He looks past them deeper into the campgrounds. More people standing or lying in the snow. Everything so still, like a black-and-white photograph.

"Hello," he says to the people at the fence. They stare back mournfully. "American. I am American." He jabs a finger at his chest over and over.

They don't answer, these skeletons, these misplaced scarecrows. Gaunt eyes, sallow cheeks, heads shaven, barely able to hold themselves up. Many wearing striped pajamas.

What Charlie was wearing in his visions.

Footsteps next to him. "My God," Clay whispers. He doesn't speak another word, can't. This man who never stops talking, speechless.

The people behind the fence stare back. Some shuffle away.

They all have a patch on their striped outfits. Triangular in shape, on their chests, with different colors: yellow, brown, red.

Alex walks over to the gate. Tries to open it but it's padlocked shut.

From the jeep, Stanley shouts, "HQ's telling us to leave."

Clay: "What?"

"They said we're not to engage the camp residents. We're not to enter the premises. We're to leave immediately."

Clay shakes his head. "Why the hell should we leave?"

Stanley stands up in the jeep. "Guys. We should leave. Head-quarters will send med teams."

Alex shakes his head. "We can't just leave them." He pulls the strapped carbine from around his back. "Stand aside."

"Maki!" Stanley says. "We have our orders. They don't want us opening these gates."

"Of course they don't," Clay says. "Jap boys liberating a camp? Doesn't play well in the newspapers."

"Screw HQ," Alex says, already aiming his carbine at the lock. He shoots it off, the gunshot echoing across the camp. At once, every head inside turns toward the gate.

Alex kicks it open. Steps inside the camp. And it's as if he's crossed some invisible barrier. A nauseating stench of death, ripe and raw, fills his nostrils. Even the temperature seems to drop a few degrees.

Alex and Clay, with Chuck right behind, walk deeper into camp. Past people lying on the ground. Not all of them are dead. Not yet. Some breathe even as they lay there, their chests rising slowly, shallow, their lips puckering like beached fish slowly dying.

"God," Clay whispers. "Oh, God."

More inmates stumble out of barracks, triangular structures that resemble thatched roofs. The inmates, barefoot and hardly clothed, blink at the overcast skies, barely able to stay upright. The smallest breeze will topple the rickety structure of their bare bones.

"Germans!" Clay shouts, as they walk past the triangular-shaped barracks. "*Wo sind die* Nazis?" No one answers. Clay switches over to his broken French. "*Où sont les* Nazis?" He turns to a tall thin man with a red triangular patch on his breast who might once have been regal and proud, not this broken twig. "*Wo sind die* Nazis? *Où sont les* Nazis?"

"Speak English?" the man croaks, a speck of saliva dotting the corner of his chapped lips.

Clay nods, taps his chest repeatedly. "American. We are American."

The man walks up, gestures to his mouth. "Food? Yes? You food?"

Chuck, his face pale as the gray snow lying around, reaches into his pocket, takes out a chocolate bar. Hands it to the man.

Who stares dumbly at it, eyes blinking in amazement, like he's just been offered the greatest miracle on Earth. Others see this, and they come toward the three American soldiers. Swarming them. Extended arms, grasping hands, eyes wide with hunger and yearning. Making the same gesture, hand to mouth, hand to mouth.

Alex opens his mess kit, starts breaking up the K rations into smaller pieces, distributing them as he walks. As do Clay and Chuck. In seconds, all the food is gone, and Alex tosses the empty mess kit. A stick-thin man picks it up, licks it clean. Someone tugs at Alex's water bottle. Alex undoes the strap, hands the bottle over. But the man—or is it a woman?—doesn't have the strength to twist the cap open. He does it for her. Her lips wobbling, her mouth pathetic, water falling everywhere but in. He helps her. More people surround them.

"No more, sorry, we have nothing else for you," Chuck says. The three push past the crowd. They walk to the other side of camp, past rows of barracks. Past three smoking heaps of barracks recently burned down. The foul stink of ash and charred flesh rising from them.

They come to an open space. They stop. Before them, a huge pile of naked bodies, a tangled web of what must be a hundred bodies. Heaped on top of each other.

Charlie, Alex thinks. *Charlie . . .*

Alex reaches for his helmet, takes it off. Chuck, too. They cannot process this obscenity.

They walk back to the jeep. The crowd still milling about, gawking at them. Alex takes off his gloves, gives them away to a man. The gloves dangle off the man's arms like kitchen mitts on a stick. An almost-naked woman, shaking with cold, approaches. Alex starts unbuttoning his jacket. "If you want to help them over the long haul," Clay says, "you'll need to stay warm, Alex."

At the opened gates, a pastel-pale man speaks in a thick French accent. "France? Where?"

"What?"

"To France. Where?"

Stanley points westward. "That way. But France is very, very far away."

The man pulls up his collars and starts hobbling down the road in his striped pajamas and ratty shoes.

Outside the camp, he limps past a small group of people who've just walked out. They've set upon the dead horse by the roadside. Cut it wide open using sharp rocks, right at the soft belly, and their hands are digging into its flesh. Eating it raw, its blood smearing onto their hands, their faces, down the front of their clothes.

Alex stumbles over to the jeep. With a trembling hand, he picks up the transmitter and speaks into it, his voice shaking. "Send help. Send lots of food. Send lots of clothes. Send med teams. Good God. Send everything."

66

Army trucks arrive six hours later. Loaded with bottles of water, blankets, American Red Cross food packages: raisins, liver pâté, corned beef, biscuits. Alex, Clay, and a dozen other soldiers distribute the food. More inmates limp out of the barracks, in even worse shape than the others, and stream toward the trucks. They swarm the soldiers handing out the food but are so slight and frail, the soldiers easily move them back and restore order. Then, as quickly as the food arrived, a call comes in.

"Take the food away?" Alex says. "Why?"

The sergeant touches his moustache. "We're getting reports from other camps. If we feed them too much, they'll die."

"Other camps?"

The sergeant shrugs.

"They got to eat, Sarge. If they don't, they'll die for sure."

"Look at them, Maki. They're skeletons. We overload their systems too quickly, they'll die."

"Sarge—"

"Look, you think I like this? But I've got my orders. As do you now. Stop distributing the food." He reads the concern on Alex's face. "You want to help them, Maki? Go distribute some blankets. Not to the people outside. They're the healthier ones.

But go into the barracks, to those too sick to even stand. Take Clay with you."

Charlie Lévy. She is all he can think about. Every time he goes into another barrack, her name is on the tip of his tongue, her face looms large in his mind. His greatest hope but also his greatest fear is that he will find her in one of these barracks.

But inside every one, it is the same. The same foul, diseased stench wafting out, the long rows of shelves, three high, packed with prisoners lying down. Their eyes, blinking against the light streaming in through the doorway, rolling in sunken sockets, their wispy necks barely able to lift up their skulls off the wood platforms.

Clay stays at the entrance, his shirt held over his nose. Alex walks down the aisle between the rows of prisoners. His knuckles sometimes graze their shaven heads; their skulls feel as light as papier-mâché.

In every barrack as he distributes the blankets, he whispers, *Connaissez-vous Mademoiselle Charlie Lévy? Connaissez-vous Mademoiselle Charlie Lévy?*

No one ever answers.

Nighttime. Light snow falls from the black sky, an endless winter. Alex climbs into the back of the truck, collapses with fatigue. He leans back against the tarp, closes his eyes. Around him, the other GIs are asleep, or softly talking. Outside the truck he can hear prisoners rummaging through the trash pit, going through the soldiers' dinner mess kits.

"More blankets will arrive tomorrow morning," a soldier says. The tip of his cigarette glows as he takes a long pull. They've all been smoking like chimneys in an effort to cover the stench. "Heard they're bringing a medic team, too."

"It's too late," the other murmurs. "Hate to say that, but it is. These prisoners still here—they're the sick ones, the dying ones left behind. The healthier ones, they were forced out on a death march. Two days ago, I heard." The cigarette tips glows. "Thousands of them walking on these frozen roads to God knows where. We should focus on saving them."

A long silence. The tip of the cigarette glows. The other soldier speaks.

"They're probably dead, too."

Exhausted as he is, he can't sleep. Images keep dripping into his mind, everything he has seen through the day. He pulls himself into a sitting position. A few other soldiers are up, a motorcyclist runner, two others he can't remember even seeing before. They're hunched over a candle, snapping cards.

Alex is in no mood to play. Or talk. He reaches into his jacket pocket, takes out the drawing.

Charlie Lévy stares up at him. The edges of the page are tattered, the penciling faded. A large water stain has claimed the bottom half. But her eyes seem as alive as the first day he drew her. He stares for many minutes, until his eyes grow heavy.

A warm sensation suddenly presses the base of his spine. His eyes fly open.

This sensation. He's felt it before, back in Manzanar. While watching *The Hunchback of Notre Dame.* Then later, in Rose Park.

It can't be. He waits. Nothing. He was just being foolish, he should just close his eyes—

Again. But even warmer now.

He throws off his blanket, stands up. Folds up the sketch, puts it into his pocket.

The three soldiers, snapping cards, turn to him. "Eat something bad?" Laughing.

He ignores them, leaps off the back of the truck. Stops after a few steps, turns back to the soldiers. "Give me the key."

"Key?"

"For the motorbike. Now."

"Yeah, I don't think so. Besides, it's out of gas. You know that, that's why I'm stuck here—"

"Shut up, give it to me," Alex says. "Direct order."

The soldier snorts. "We're the same rank."

"Give it to me."

He stands up. "Come and get it, asshole."

Two minutes later, Alex is tearing down the road on the bike, the icy wind slicing into his newly bruised and bleeding face. He hardly feels the pain, though. The only thing he feels is the hot sensation clamping on his rib cage like a vise. He doesn't understand what's going on, not really, but all he can think is—

She's alive. She's alive. Charlie's alive and *she's nearby.*

He pulls back on the throttle, ignoring the gas needle on E, willing the motorbike to travel another mile, and another, faster, faster. He sees a small cottage just off the road. Smoke curls out of a chimney, thick and black, even against the night sky. He thinks briefly about stopping to siphon gas—

The sensation surges. Urgent. Hotter. He's getting closer.

But then a minute later, the bike, already running on fumes, coughs, sputters.

He lets it coast to a stop. He gets off, not bothering with the kickstand, simply lets the bike fall to its side. The headlight fades out, plunging Alex into darkness.

He spins around, searching. Nothing moves in the snow-covered fields.

"Charlie!"

The cold landscape stares indifferently back.

This is the moment. He feels it in his bones. The moment his heart has ached for, only he hasn't realized how much until now. This is the hope that carried him through the hell of Bruyères and Biffontaine and the Vosges Forest.

"Charlie!" he shouts, louder now. He spins, certain he will see her standing. In the moonlight, a sparkle in her eyes. *You came,* he can almost hear her, *you found me, Alex.*

But the road is empty. Nothing moves.

He stays where he is for two minutes. Five.

A silence pervades the land. No sound of traffic or insects or birds, just a hush, like the universe is holding its breath. Or has stopped breathing altogether.

Overhead, clouds slowly tear apart. Sickly moonlight filters through, creeps forward on the land. Past the road, into the woods. He sees other things now. Along the road, the mounds of snow. He shudders. This whole time, he's been standing so close to dead bodies.

He walks to the other side of the road. And that's when he sees the person.

It is by a tree at the edge of the forest, sitting slumped against the trunk, its shape in the shadows vague and lackluster.

"Charlie?"

He takes a cautious step toward it, then another, faster, his boots crunching on the packed snow.

He stops. His breath frosting out before him, curling like a question mark.

It is a young boy. In a fetal position, arms clasped around bent legs, dressed in striped pajamas. Eyes half-open, blue lips parted. A face ravaged by hunger, by sorrow, his sunken cheeks evidence of a drawn-out, unspeakable suffering. Only nine, maybe ten years old. The age when Alex first started to draw. When he first started to write to Charlie.

The boy is dead. Of course. A Jewish boy in a German countryside in the middle of a winter night during wartime must be dead. Still, Alex reaches forward, touches the boy's face.

Cold and hard and lifeless as flint.

Expected. Yet Alex jerks his hand back, still he gasps.

It is the youth of this boy. Death incongruent with it. The suffering etched into the innocence.

He thinks: I cannot leave him like this. He deserves a proper burial.

But the ground, even at the edge of the forest, is icy and hard. Alex does what he can. He uses the butt of his carbine to loosen the earth. He gets on his knees and uses his helmet to dig. The grating sound of metal against rock, a gritty, ugly sound that seems to travel for miles. His arms, numb with exhaustion and cold, become cement blocks of fatigue. His fingers shred to bloody ribbons.

After fifteen minutes, he has done little but scrape the ice-hardened topsoil.

He needs a shovel. A pickaxe. Three other soldiers. He needs a heart, a will, a resolve. But he has none of these.

He stands up, exhausted. He stares at the open eyes, the parted lips, the expression of despair frozen in time. He takes off his jacket and gently lays it over the boy. Never mind that the boy is dead and this jacket won't make a damn difference. Somehow it matters.

Alex turns, starts walking away. The wind already cutting through his thin shirt. A few strides later, he stops. He's forgotten to remove something from the jacket. His sketch of Charlie.

He pauses. For a long moment, he does not move. He does not breathe. Then he takes a step, and another. Not toward the boy, but back to the camp. His jacket untouched, the sketch left behind. Ice crunches and snaps under his boots. The wind is brutal, a butcher's knife clawing all the way to his skeleton. But even with this wind and dropping temperature, he does not get any colder. What is already frozen cannot get colder.

67

Dear Frank,

I'm coming home. Just got my papers. Will leave France and be back on Bainbridge Island in only a few weeks. Can't believe it. Doesn't feel real.

I have a one-week leave before my departure. My first real leave where I get to go anywhere I want. So I've decided to head up to Paris. Not to see Charlie. I think she . . . I think she passed, judging from all I've read and heard. Don't really want to talk about it.

But I'm still going to Paris. To fulfill a promise I made to her a long time ago.

Alex

68

No. 4 rue de Buenos-Aires, 7th arrondissement. How often he has scrawled that address down on the front of stamped envelopes, hundreds of times before the war. So strange to be standing here finally. To see that white *4,* painted so nonchalantly in a square block of blue like an afterthought.

Over the years, Charlie had described her apartment building in bits and pieces, leaving it to Alex to fill in the gaps. Standing before the building now, Alex marvels at how close reality matches his imagination. The elegant façades, the intricate cut stonework of carved-head statues and clusters of grapes, the curled balconies around the curved corners of the building. The only aspect of this upscale neighborhood Charlie never really described is its affluence. Its wealth is evident in its wide, tree-lined streets, its proximity to the Eiffel Tower, the Seine River, the Champ de Mars, the attire of its residents sitting outdoors in ritzy cafés.

He walks over to the door marked CONCIERGE by the main entrance. From what Charlie wrote before, the concierge manages the general affairs of the apartment building: cleans the stairways, delivers the mail, possesses keys to the apartments, takes note of the comings and goings of the residents. She's the one he needs to see.

But there is no answer. So he pushes open the metal-grilled

main entrance and walks into the lobby. It is dark inside, and empty. He waits for the elevator, his heart beginning to thump faster. When it arrives an elderly woman with a cane steps out. *The concierge?* No, she is too old, far too well dressed. She barely glances at Alex as she passes.

Inside, he presses the top button (so strange to think that Charlie's fingers have pressed this very button many times before). The elevator heaves upward with a groan. Charlie has been in here thousands of times. Are there molecules of her breath still lingering? He closes his eyes, inhales deeply.

The elevator doors open.

There are only two apartments on this floor, each on either end of the long hallway. He walks to the nearer door. The family nameplate has been scrubbed off and in its place a brass covering with German words.

He presses the doorbell. He is expecting a chime. Instead an ungainly buzzing sound comes from inside. No response. He presses the doorbell again, holding it down. No one comes.

He is about to turn away when he notices something. Tucked in the upper right corner, discreet, is a small mezuzah. Exactly how Charlie described it in her letters.

He feels his heart beat faster. With a trembling finger he presses the doorbell again. Then he starts pounding on the door, heavy thumps over and over. Approaching footsteps.

He cannot breathe. Charlie? *Charlie?*

The door swings open.

A large rotund woman with a broom in one hand and a garbage bag in the other scowls at him. "*Qui êtes-vous?*" she demands. "*Que voulez-vous, monsieur?*" Her breath hot and full of garlic.

He doesn't understand. The words are coming too quickly. He tries to look over her shoulder into the apartment, but she steps forward, not afraid to use her ample bosom to push him backward.

– 364 –

He retreats two steps. He's drawing a blank, can barely recall even a single French word. "Madame Lévy? Are you . . . *êtes-vous Madame Lévy?*"

"*Non. Je suis la concierge.*" The woman blinks at him. As if for the first time taking in his American military uniform, his Asian face. Her eyes suddenly widen with realization. "*Monsieur Maki?*" she stammers. "*Êtes-vous Monsieur Alex Maki?*"

She brings him into the apartment. It is stuffy inside, even with many windows opened. Furniture has been pushed off to the side, bookshelves emptied, the walls stripped bare of any paintings. All the smaller household items—plants, vases, lamps, anything remotely decorative—are missing. Perhaps stored away. Or stolen.

The apartment does not look lived in. Not for at least a few months.

He looks around for evidence of Charlie. A woman's jacket or scarf draped over the sofa, her favorite books, a well-thumbed copy of *Jane Eyre* lying around. But there is nothing.

The concierge is trying to explain something to him. Rapidly in French, something about coming up here to air out the place once a week, and clean it up a little—

He ignores her, looks around. On a bureau against the wall he sees a small photo frame, lying facedown and apparently forgotten. He walks over, picks it up. He is momentarily confused. It is not the portrait of Charlie's family he was expecting, but a photo showing a family of four sitting before a church, the two boys grinning. In the background, street awnings hang with German words.

He turns the frame over. Undoes the small metal latches on the back. When he pulls away the backing, he finds another photograph tucked behind the displayed one. This portrait is of a dignified-looking man with his wife. Both in their forties, perhaps. And standing between them, their teenage daughter.

Charlie.

He gasps.

His first time seeing her. And she is as he imagined her. She is the Charlie of his visions. The trinity of moles at the corner of her eyes. Except here she is radiant with life, her hair long, her eyes burning with a ferocity undimmed even in this black-and-white photograph. A small smile threatening to leak out of her lips. A sparkling, healthier Charlie than the one in his visions. But the same one.

He doesn't understand how this can be. He doesn't understand anything anymore. He flips the photo over. On the back, cursive handwriting he recognizes as Charlie's: *L'amour d'une famille est quelque chose de merveilleux.* He turns to the concierge. *"La famille Lévy. Où sont-ils?"*

She sets down the bag of trash, the broom. When she speaks it is with simple words, with gesturing hands. Even then Alex understands perhaps only a quarter of what she says. But it is enough. It is too much. The concierge does not know the whereabouts of Monsieur and Madame Lévy. She has heard little since that night of the Vel' d'Hiv roundup, she tells him. They simply vanished into thin air. She says that this apartment was afterward requisitioned by the Germans. High-ranking soldiers lived in this apartment, drank in here, slept in here, spoke their filthy German in here.

Alex stares at the concierge. She has spoken only of the parents. *"Et Charlie Lévy. Savez-vous où elle est?"*

She shakes her head. Lowers her eyes. *"Je ne sais pas."* She is lying. She knows something. He can see it in her tightened grip on her meaty forearm. The white imprints it leaves there.

I have been looking for her for a long time, he wants to tell her but can't. *I have thought about her every day during this war. In the Vosges Forest. In every slit trench at night, shaking with cold. In the French Alps staring at snowcapped mountains. I have worried over her. I have ached for her. I have been looking for her for a very long time and now you are my last hope.*

But he does not know how to say this. "*S'il vous plaît,*" he simply whispers, his voice the rasp of sandpaper. "*S'il vous plaît.*"

She hesitates; her eyes avert down to the floor.

"*Je suis désolée,*" she finally says. She looks up at him and her eyes are big and soft. She has heard things from the other tenants in this building, she tells him. And from the other concierges in the neighborhood. Rumors about Charlie—no, more than just rumors, these were eyewitness accounts that Charlie . . . Her words drift away. She will not look at him.

He feels himself pitching forward, the floor canting left and right. He grips the top of a dining chair. "She did not survive?" he says. "Charlie didn't make it?"

The concierge frowns, not understanding. So he has to ask it in French, and these three simple words are like razors on his tongue. "*Est-elle morte?*"

The concierge pauses; she laces her fingers across her apron. And then she nods. Just once. The shortest, and most decisive and most obscene motion humanly possible.

He pulls back the dining chair, sits down. On the table are large scrolls of paper, some tubed, some simply rubber-banded. Maps and diagrams, all written in German. His heart turning to chalk, crumbling.

"*Vous êtiez de si bons amis,*" she says quietly as if to comfort him. "*Chaque fois que je lui donnais une de vos lettres, elle rayonnait de bonheur.*"

He isn't really listening. It's all noise to him now. Nothing matters anymore.

She falls silent. Outside, the faint hum of Paris traffic.

He gets up to leave. His legs unsteady, his face numb. There is nothing more to see or say or do. He starts walking to the door. Then stops, remembering the reason why he came. *Promise me, Alex,* Charlie had written, *that you will one day come and visit my room. I have much to show you there.*

He turns to the concierge. "*Puis-je voir la chambre de Charlie, s'il vous plaît,*" he says. "*Où est-elle?*"

"*Sa chambre?*"

"*Oui.*"

She leads him down the hallway. Outside the closed door she tells him Charlie's room has been unused for years now. Paris suffered three harsh winters, colder than any in recent memory; and with coal shortages, it was difficult to keep large, airy apartments warm. So the German soldiers did what most wealthy Parisians did in these apartments: they permanently closed off entire rooms, never opening them. Including Charlie's.

The door is unlocked, she tells him, walking away.

It takes him a minute to finally put his hand on the knob. He turns it, pushes open the door.

It swings open with a loud screech, the hinges creaky with winters-long hibernation. He steps into the room. Charlie's room.

It is dark inside, and musty. He sees very little apart from the rims of light from drawn curtains across the room. He treads carefully over to the window, slowly getting used to the darkness. His fingers touch the thick heavy cloth of the curtains, and he flings them wide open.

A rush of light, blinding, floods his eyes. He blinks. Outside her window, Paris in all her glory. The Eiffel Tower looming over him, the gardens spread below. Charlie had spoken of this view often in her letters, but he never imagined the tower to be this close. He brushes away a spider's web wrapped around the window handle. The window opens with a rusty protest. A flue of fresh air whistles in, the first air in years.

Sounds of traffic drift in. Children playing in the nearby park, sounds of a popping cap pistol, laughter. He opens the window wider. More air gusts in.

And now a different sound, from within the room, comes from all sides: the whisper-rustle of fluttering papers.

He turns.

There are sheets of paper taped all over the room. On every wall, from floor to ceiling. Dozens of them, some small, some larger, all flapping like the wings of baby birds taking flight for the very first time.

They are his drawings. All the illustrations, portraits, cartoons he sent her over the years. Aglow now in the sunlight, fluttering softly in the breeze. From his very first hesitant drawings when he was only nine to later, more accomplished portraits and drawings and illustrations and cartoons he never dared show anyone else. He always thought she tossed them away, maybe not immediately but eventually.

But now he knows. She kept them all.

He sees cartoons of odd turtles with elongated heads; portraits of his brother, Frank, throwing a football. Of their strawberry farm. Of himself, punching a French Métro conductor.

One sheet, taped onto the bed headboard, glows whiter than the others. A more recent drawing. He goes to it now. He'd drawn it on the train to Manzanar: of Charlie and him standing worlds apart on separate shores but with a string strung between them, connecting them. *I have a strange feeling with regard to you. As if I had a string somewhere under my left ribs, tightly knotted to a similar string in you.*

He feels his legs giving way. He pulls out the desk chair, sits down. A film of dust covers the desk, over the ridges and grooves of wood, over the worn-down smoothness in its center. This is the desk, then, where she had written all her letters to him. During the dusk hours, her favorite time to write. He can see her here, madly scribbling away, occasionally lifting her head to stare at the Eiffel Tower aglow in the sunset.

He thinks of all those hundreds of letters over the years, for almost a decade. Thousands upon thousands of words scratched into existence. Her stories, her jokes, her thoughts, her hopes and fears. Written for him. Just for him. No one else read them; they were meant just for him. For a lonesome skinny American boy halfway across the world on a place called Bainbridge Island. Lonely Turtle Boy.

His eyes fill with tears.

He places his hand on the desk. Feels the soft silt of dust. He stares down at the uneven wood, the knots and whorls like the scutes of a shell. Charlie will never sit here again. She will never write again. She will never have another thought again. He thinks of her lips, how they will never curl into a smile, or spread with laughter. Her eyes, how they will never sparkle with life. Her feet, how they will never walk the pathways of the Sorbonne campus. He thinks of that café in Paris where they will never drink coffee together, that empty table set for two, those two empty chairs, the conversations they will never share, the moments together they will never remember for the rest of their lives.

"Charlie," he whispers, "God, Charlie," and he bends over until his forehead touches the desk, and he feels the ridges press into his skin, and the tears, they flow out now, sinking past the dust and into wood.

69

Everything seems smaller than he remembers. The ferry, Puget Sound, even Bainbridge Island as it slowly appears on the horizon.

One thing that remains the same, though, thank God. Its beauty: the smell of salt in the air, the sun dancing off the million little platelets in the rippled waters, the sight of bald eagles in the sky, a sea otter basking in the sun as they approach the pier. He's glad to have come out onto the deck even on this cold October morning, to take in the sights unimpeded by the ferry's dirty glass windows. He stands alone at the bow, duffel bag at his feet, the wind loudly flapping the American flag, his army hat held in hand lest it blow away.

Charlie's words come to him now: *Maybe, Alex, maybe loving a city, a country, is like loving a person: you love her despite her faults, you forgive her constantly, you always believe in her, fight for her, you never give up on her.*

As the ferry pulls into Eagledale Pier, he scans the dock. A group of commuters stands waiting, clustered together against the cold. A few glance curiously up at him, at this Japanese American man in military uniform. If anyone recognizes him, they don't smile or wave. Alex stares past them, scans the pier. Frank is nowhere in sight.

Several weeks ago, Alex received a postcard from him. Frank

had written but a brief message: they'd all recently been released from Manzanar, and were now back on Bainbridge Island. They were waiting for Alex to return.

He has that postcard in his pocket now, his ticket home. He'd put it in a small plastic bag to protect it from the elements. In that bag he also carries a photograph. Of the Lévy family, of Charlie, taken from the Paris apartment. *L'amour d'une famille est quelque chose de merveilleux.*

Alex walks down the gangplank, the last to disembark. The commuters heading into Seattle get on the ferry, none giving him a second look.

The ferry pulls away and now Alex is left standing alone on the pier. This quiet, empty pier. So different from that day when they all left, and the white community had come out to bid them farewell and good luck. He's returned as something he never imagined he'd become: a bona fide war hero, a member of the 442nd. A unit, he has recently learned, that suffered staggering numbers of casualties, whose blood is spread all over Europe. A unit awarded eight Presidential Unit Citations, twenty-one Medals of Honor, and over nine thousand Purple Hearts. It has become the most decorated unit for its size in United States history. Only you wouldn't know it from the empty pier welcoming him back now, or from the diner he was thrown out of two days ago in Orange County.

The sound of barking. From behind. Familiar—

It's Hero. Older, thinner, but undoubtedly him.

"Hero! Come 'ere, boy!"

The dog, stiff with age, bounds even faster, his tail working furiously. Alex gets down on a knee, and Hero bulldozes into him, almost knocking him over.

"Good boy, Hero!" Alex laughs. "Good boy!"

The dog circles around, claws clattering against the dock,

his tail whipping against Alex's face, whining with joy, his dog breath sour and warm and wonderful.

Alex sees him then. A lonely figure standing by the lamppost, one hand holding a leash. Frank.

They walk up to each other. Frank, so much thinner than Alex remembers. But he seems well rested, the bags under his eyes gone. His skin a healthy bronze, the kneecaps of his pants browned with soil; he's been working the fields.

Two yards from each other they stop.

Frank looks at Alex for a long time. "We weren't sure exactly when you were returning."

"But here you are. How'd you know I'd be on this ferry?"

"I didn't." Frank hesitates. "I've been coming down here every morning for two weeks." He smiles shyly. The first smile Alex has seen in years, and it looks like a miracle, feels like magic. "What took you so long, kiddo?"

Alex grins back. The brothers step toward each other, arms extended to handshake. But in the last second Alex brushes aside Frank's hand and they embrace. Tightly, with white knuckles and clenched, damp eyes. Frank's sweater, recently pulled from boxes Mother had stored in the basement years ago, smells of mothballs. But also of open fields, of sunlight, of strawberries, of the raw musky earth.

And of America, always America.

EPILOGUE

The beach is calm tonight, the tide mere whispers. Overhead a few stars are beginning to peek out. Darkness presses in, making the world smaller, cozier. At the tide's edge Alex kneels down on the soft sand. He opens the bag, removes the square planks of wood, the candle, the pages of his latest, wildly popular comic book. Slowly, carefully, he constructs the floating paper lantern. When he is finished, he removes his shoes and socks, hikes up his trousers as high as they'll go, and heads down to the water. The cold sand turns wet and squelchy under his feet, makes sucking sounds.

Then he steps into the sea. It stings with cold. When the water reaches his kneecaps, he stops. He places the floating lantern onto the water. It bobs lightly but securely on the small waves. He pulls out his lighter, carefully lowers the flame to the centered candle until it catches. That moment always beautiful, when the four walls of the lantern are set aglow, softly and palely, the illumined cartoon characters brought to brief, flickering life.

For a moment—just a little longer—he holds onto the lantern. Then with a gentle push, he releases it into the wide open sea.

He stares after it. A gentle riptide carries it slowly out to sea, the glowing light bobbing but never sinking, never disappearing. He watches as it gets smaller and smaller against the infinite horizon. When the cold of the sea begins to numb his ankles and toes, he sets back for the beach. On the shore, his feet caked in the fine fuzz of sand, he turns to look.

There. That pulsing light between two worlds, still beating out to sea.

He imagines the lantern journeying across the ocean. Past cargo ships and cruise ships, past glowing colonies of jellyfish, past vast pockets of emptiness and darkness and desolation. He sees it entering the English Channel, then slipping into the small gateway of the Seine River. Floating down its length, under the Pont Neuf, past the Sainte-Chapelle, past the Notre Dame Cathedral.

And there on the banks of the Seine, even now, even after so many years, he imagines a woman strolling along. Her head turning with curiosity as she notices this floating lantern. Bending down to grab it before it floats past. A smile slowly lighting upon her lips.

Alex, she whispers, a glow in her face, a fire in her eyes.

ACKNOWLEDGMENTS

My deepest thanks to Susan Chang, editor par excellence, who has believed in this story from the start and guided it with wisdom and generosity. Thanks also to my agent, Catherine Drayton, for her continued support through the years.

I am grateful to those who helped shape the manuscript in myriad ways: Matthew Bird, Elizabeth Vaziri, Perri Lin, Mary-Ann Johanson, and Augustin J. Farrugia.

My friends in Japan have impacted this book in ways large and small, and I am grateful for their lasting influence on me: John Blocksom, ChaCha Goss, Pat and Betty Kwan, Paul Miller, Chris Momose, Takashi and Kayoko Sano, Debby Sukita. Psalm 16:3 (ESV).

And as always, John, Chris, and Ching-Lee. *L'amour d'une famille est quelque chose merveilleux.*

AUTHOR'S NOTE

Whenever I'm asked where I get my book ideas from, the question usually leaves me stumped. But with *This Light Between Us,* there's a simple answer. The book was born when I learned, within days of each other, two independent historical facts.

The first: Anne Frank had an American pen pal.

The second: A subcamp of the Dachau concentration camp was liberated on April 29, 1945, by a segregated all–Japanese American military unit.

These two facts bumped about in my head for quite some time. I researched historical time lines and pondered creative possibilities. Ideas began to churn and spin. Gradually, two characters emerged from the thicket of my thinking, and I realized I had a story to tell.

This Light Between Us is primarily a work of fiction, but I've tried to stay true to historical actualities as much as possible. While the main characters are fictional, others, such as Major General John E. Dahlquist, Ned Campbell, Harry Ueno, James Kanagawa, James Ito, Sergeant Ben Kuroki, and Second Lieutenant Marty Higgins, are historical. Most of the key events—the Bainbridge Island evacuation, the Manzanar riot, the Vel' d'Hiv roundup, the Sonderkommando revolt at Auschwitz-Birkenau, the rescue of the Lost Battalion, to name a few—are drawn from the pages of history, and depicted here with restrained artistic license. In other minor instances I've exercised less restraint in order to maintain narrative flow. A high school football game being played in March is one such example.

Many thanks to my college professor, Dr. Gary Y. Okihiro, who in a classroom many years ago first introduced me to the history of the internment camps. His tempered anguish about their injustice resonated in me and left a mark that never went away. It is a history always threatening to repeat itself.

BIBLIOGRAPHY

RECOMMENDED READING

In my research for this novel, I drew upon a number of reference works. Those listed below were especially helpful.

Asahina, Robert. *Just Americans: How Japanese Americans Won a War at Home and Abroad.* New York: Gotham Books, 2007.

Berr, Hélène. *The Journal of Hélène Berr.* New York: Weinstein Books, 2008.

Duus, Masayo Umezawa. *Unlikely Liberators: The Men of the 100th and 442nd.* Honolulu: University of Hawaii Press, 1987.

Gordon, Linda, and Okihiro, Gary Y. *Impounded: Dorothea Lange and the Censored Images of Japanese American Internment.* New York: W.W. Norton, 2006.

Houston, Jeanne Wakatsuki, and Houston, James D. *Farewell to Manzanar.* New York: Houghton Mifflin Harcourt, 1973.

McCaffrey, James M. *Going for Broke: Japanese American Soldiers in the War Against Nazi Germany.* Norman: University of Oklahoma Press, 2013.

Rees, Laurence. *The Holocaust: A New History.* New York: Public-Affairs, 2017.

Reeves, Richard. *Infamy: The Shocking Story of the Japanese American Internment in World War II.* New York: Picador, 2015.

Rosbottom, Ronald C. *When Paris Went Dark: The City of Light*

Under German Occupation, 1940–1944. New York: Back Bay Books, 2014.

Williams, Arthur L. *Reflecting on WWII, Manzanar, and the WRA.* Victoria, BC: FriesenPress, 2014.

I am especially grateful for Densho: The Japanese American Legacy Project, whose extensive digital collections online (https://ddr.densho.org/) proved to be invaluable. The thousands of photographs, journalistic articles, and letters available on their website enabled me to gain a fleshed-out feel for this time period. The many detailed personal interviews with former internees and 442nd veterans were essential to my research. I hope their collective voices are always heard.